Collected Stories

For Kitty

Collected Stories
Leslie Norris

seren
is the book imprint of
Poetry Wales Press Ltd
Wyndham Street, Bridgend, Wales

© Leslie Norris, 1996

First published in 1996
Reprinted 1997

ISBN 1-85411-133-7

A CIP record for this title is available from
the British Library

*The publisher works with the financial assistance of the
Arts Council of Wales*

Cover Illustration: 'Suliau Mebyd/Sundays of my Youth'
by John Elwyn

Printed in Plantin by The Cromwell Press, Melksham

Contents

New Stories

The Waxwings

Alwyn would have gone a fortnight ago, on his birthday, if he could have got away. All that day, despite the presents and the birthday cards and the afternoon party, he had been conscious of an enormous weightlessness behind his ribs, an almost irresistible awareness of freedom. On any other Saturday he would have gone, full pelt up the street, across the wide road where you had to be careful, then fast over the river bridge. He would have gone past Mr Rampling's sawmills, past Mr Rampling's house, which was the last house in town, past the laundry. Then the hills began. But that Saturday he was seven years old, and the petty responsibilities of his celebrations, the excitement of his little brothers, his friends visiting with parcels of toy boats and model aircraft, all had kept him firmly at home, locked in the centre of the five short streets grown suddenly so irksome.

Then last Saturday his Uncle Ernie had come to see him. Uncle Ernie was so amusing, so inventive in his jokes, so daring in the games he improvised that the boy had no time to think of his escape. All afternoon he had played football in the garden, furiously and full of laughing, admiring his uncle's outrageous skill. After tea Uncle Ernie had drawn two dogs on a piece of cardboard and cut them out. One was Fred and one was Bert. He had been Bert, a black dog, and they had gone for a walk together all around the dining table. Fred, who was really Uncle Ernie, had said such mad and funny things that the game had to stop from time to time for Alwyn to get his breath back. He wouldn't have wanted to get away last Saturday.

Once he had gone alone to the High Street, where he wasn't allowed on his own. This was because of the traffic and some other reason he couldn't remember. His mother had suddenly discovered that she had no milk in the house, and she had sent him to the Italian shop in the High Street. It had been a Saturday and everything was unnaturally still and quiet, the tall shops sleeping fast behind the fawn blinds that covered their windows. It had been a generous man in the Italian shop. He had dipped his gleaming scoop twice into an urn of milk, and then added an extra splash to the boy's white jug.

'That's a pint,' he had said, 'and a little drop more for you.'

Every day the milk came to the house in pint bottles, early in the morning, and he had never carried it in a jug for such a long way before. It lurched and slopped up to the rim of the jug as if it had some malevolent life of its own, often leaping clear of the lip to spray itself in tiny, blue-white showers on the stones. The boy carried the jug very carefully in both hands, walking with small gliding steps so that the milk didn't have to jump up and down. George Evans saw him and jeered at him, so he put the jug down gingerly in a doorway and chased George Evans up the road, but he didn't catch him. The milk was quite safe when he got back to it, and he carried it home safely too. That was the farthest he had been on his own.

But today was different. He was walking calmly and deliberately up his street, and he was going to make it. He walked as quickly as he could without anybody noticing he was hurrying, and he was listening meticulously in case his mother should call him. Once he got as far as Mrs Morgan's door he would not turn back whatever happened. His senses were screwed so tightly that his mother's voice, thin and distant, but unmistakably clear, sounded suddenly in the deepest coils of his ears. 'Alwyn,' it called; but it was only inside his head that made the sound. He looked back for a second. The front door of his house was blandly shut and his mother busy somewhere inside. Relieved, he lost his caution and ran.

He didn't stop until he was over the bridge and half-way down the fairground. It wasn't a proper fairground except for two weeks in the summer and at Christmas, and now it was quite empty except for some huge logs waiting to go to the sawmills. As he looked, the front gate of Mr Rampling's garden opened, and a boy on a delivery bike wobbled out, kicking the gate shut behind him. It was Archie Baverstock, a big boy from school and a butcher's boy on Saturdays. Archie's face was round and serious, and he wore a striped apron. He looked down from his bike at Alwyn.

'Hello, young 'un,' he said tolerantly. 'You're out of bounds, aren't you?'

The boy felt an immense gratitude to Archie. He had never heard anything so precise and evocative in his life before, and he grinned his delight at the older boy. 'Yes, I am, Archie,' he called, 'I'm out of bounds.'

But Archie did not turn his head. Moving with slow, unthinking circles of his legs, his heels on the pedals, his toes turned out, he entered cautiously into the stream of traffic on the road at the end of the fairground.

Alwyn hurried on toward the sawmills. He could hear already the petulant rasp of the saw as it ate into the wood, he could smell the moist, absorbent scent of the sawdust as it whirled in smoky falls from the whining teeth. There would be sawdust everywhere, on the ledges, whitening the forearms and eyebrows of the sawyers, in drifts on the ground, with wet brown patches underneath leaking places in the roof. It was fine in the sawmills, but he wasn't going there. He stopped only to drink from the brass tap that stood on a long pipe coming straight out of the ground. On a journey as long as his might be, you never knew where the next drink was coming from.

Once past the laundry he was on the narrow road, just wide enough for one vehicle, that led up into the hills. He looked at it speculatively. Up to now it had been remembered ground, but from here on it would be all exploration. He took a deep breath and went for the hills.

For perhaps a mile it was gentle gradient, cutting into the side of the mountain and running south, climbing so imperceptibly that the boy was astonished to see the roofs of the town unfold themselves below him. He saw Mr Rampling's house as finely detailed as a doll's, he saw the long grey roof of the laundry with little jets of steam pulsing out of its pipes, and far away he could see, he thought, the roofs of his own street. But he wasn't sure. The town lay flat and strange under his eyes.

Then he turned into the steep of the track, leading to a thin mist of wood high up, and beyond that, the bare ridge of the summit at which he was aimed. He climbed now with a steady certainty, feeling his legs push away at the gravel, his lungs labouring a little. Here and there paths led off to the the small hill farms, their houses painted white, their suspicious collies barking as he passed the gates.

A stream was running alongside the road now, a narrow stream with occasional music only, too swift and shallow for fish. But as he met the small shrubs at the entrance to the wood, the water had filled enough of a depression to make a pool. A young man squatted near the pool, on his hunkers, as colliers sat. His suit was blue and shiny, and his cap lay on the grass at his side. Standing up to its hocks in the water was a brindle greyhound, so still that its reflection shivered only in the moving water. Alwyn was as unmoving as the dog, but the young man knew he was there.

'This stream, now,' he said. 'Did you know it has some remarkable qualities?'

Alwyn walked over and sat near the young man.

'No,' he said. 'What do you mean, remarkable qualities?'

The young man looked at him thoughtfully.

'It heals,' he said. 'If, for example, you had sprained your ankle

— although that would be unlikely for someone as young and limber as you are — but if you had, all you would need to do is to hold your feet in the curative waters of this pool.'

'Is that what your dog is doing?' asked Alwyn.

The young man nodded.

'Goliath,' he said, 'is suffering from a slight muscular strain, or perhaps he has injured a fetlock. Whatever it is, you may be sure that he is cured now. You might care to put that to the test. Here is Goliath's lead — we'll fasten it to his collar, thus, and you will take him at a fast trot up the road until you hear me whistle. Observe the perfection of his action, and only half an hour ago I had almost to carry him here.'

Alwyn arose at once. An opportunity to take this marvellous silent dog for a walk was not one to throw away. He took the leather strip and trotted up the lane. Docile and graceful, the long dog went with him. He was not a bit lame, and when they were whistled back Alwyn wheeled around in his tracks and Goliath paced elegantly with him.

The young man was stretched comfortably, about to light a cigarette. He told Alwyn that his name was Terence O'Neil, and that Goliath was his father's dog.

'If it were my dog,' he said, waving his cigarette expansively, 'I should give him at once to you, because I have never seen so immediate an affinity between boy and dog. And Goliath is not a dog who gives his affection lightly, no, anything but.'

Alwyn looked at Goliath. To own this dog would be an unthinkable honour. He sighed.

'In any case,' he said, 'I shouldn't think my parents would let me keep him.'

Terence nodded with understanding.

'I'll tell you what,' he said, 'I'll let you take him again, exactly as you did last time. I wouldn't let anyone else do this, since exercising a greyhound is a very exacting business. Go more slowly this time.'

And he took out a newspaper from his pocket, a pencil from another, and began to underline certain names of horses on the racing page. He was generous enough to allow Alwyn to take Goliath for several more walks, but at last, after a quick glance at his watch, he thanked Alwyn with ceremony, took the lead, and walked rapidly away. The boy watched him go, and then he turned uphill.

Now he was in the thin cover of the hawthorn wood, the dark red berries shining like beads on the short, leafless trees. It was much steeper too, and occasionally he pushed with his hands on his thighs, to help him climb. He couldn't see the top of the mountain any longer, but he knew that once clear of the trees, the bare line of the summit would not be far away.

Then the birds came. Ripping in hundreds through the dry twigs of the hawthorns, they tore and devoured the scarlet berries with ferocious, brittle energy. They were so brilliant that the boy cried his delight aloud, holding out his arms to them. Their voices were weak and high, whispering and trilling unceasingly as they flew, but their colours, oh, the colours. Their heads held crests of chestnut, a black stripe ran dramatically through each eye, their bodies were tinged with pink, the incredible tails, short and thick, were tipped with a band of yellow as bright as summer. But it was their wings, carrying them boldly through the trees as they ate like locusts, that the boy saw most clearly. Strongly barred with black and white, the secondary feathers looked dipped in vermilion sealing wax, as hard and shining as sealing wax. He thought they were like hundreds of candles sparkling through the trees. First there were a few birds, then a flying cloud of them going through for as long as a minute, then the stragglers, at last only the echo of their thin, persistent voices. Alwyn turned to watch them vanish through the wood, his eye led down the path and on to the town lying still and far under him.

He knew it was time to return. Nothing left on the mountain could equal that visitation of the waxwings, the glittering birds that had flown from Scandinavia, from the cold hunger of Russia. They had flown in their packs over the snow-pocked rollers of the North Sea almost into his fingers, and they blazed in his illuminated mind as he jogged downhill through the dying afternoon.

He saw the chimneys of the town begin to push the heavy smoke into the sky as people warmed their houses for the evening. It was late. He wondered if there had been a search party out for him. He was very hungry.

Turning into his own street, he slowed to an aching walk. His mother was outside the house, waiting for him. She was angry, and her voice was high and shrill. He stayed some distance away, watching her, measuring the extent of her anger.

'Where have you been?' she called. 'What have you been doing?'

Already a quick relief was replacing her temper. She had watched for some time his growing independence and had half expected something like this, some exploration into his own identity. Now she saw with compassion the small boy standing before her, his face bewildered and frustrated by his inability to express the significance of his journey, the marvellous vision of the waxwings. She saw the puzzled tears form in his eyes.

'Oh, Mam,' he said, 'my boots is hurting.'

She put her arm around his shoulders, and smiling, led him indoors.

Sliding

The cold had begun very suddenly on Tuesday night, when Bernard had gone out to play. The boys were playing kick-the-tin in the lamplight at the top of the street, and nobody realised how cold it was until Randall Jenkins went home for his cap and scarf. Then they all felt the bitter weather — at their knees, their wrists, the tips of their ears. Bernard went indoors and borrowed his father's knitted scarf and found his own old gloves from last winter. Pretty soon, the game was on again and they forgot about the weather.

That night in bed, the sheets were hard and slippery, unfriendly as ice. Carefully, by an act of will, Bernard made warm a place in bed exactly the same shape as his body, thin and hunched under the covers. He extended it gradually, inch by inch, sending his toes gently into the cold until at last he was straight and comfortable. Everything was fine then, except that he had to pull the blankets firmly about his ears and shoulders. In the morning, the window was covered with frost flowers, and the kitchen fire blazed ferociously against the Welsh winter. He called for Danny Kenyon, as usual, on the way to school. Danny was his best friend, and they ran all the way, although Danny was short and plump.

Bernard was used now to the ice. Out in the yard, the tap had been frozen for days and a tongue of glass poked out of its mouth. Every morning was grey and spiteful, churlish light making the whole world dingy. Patches of hard grit gathered in the gutters and at the corners of streets, whipping against the boy's face and into his eyes. All day long, the shops kept their lights on, but there was nothing cheerful about them; only Mr Toomey's shop was strong with colour, because of the brilliant globes of his pyramids of oranges.

In school on Friday morning, Albert Evans began to cry. The teacher asked him why, but Albert wouldn't answer. It was Randall Jenkins who told about Albert's legs. The inside of his thighs was chafed raw — red all the way from his groin to his knees. The skin was hard and angry, and there were weeping cracks in it. The teacher let Albert sit in front, near the stove, and he didn't have to do any arithmetic. When Bernard told his mother about Albert's legs, she narrowed her mouth and said that Annie Evans had no more sense than the day she was born, and then she took a pot of ointment over to Albert's house. While she was out, Bernard's father told him it had been the coldest day in more than twenty years. It was funny about skin and cold weather. Some boys turned red because of the cold, and some rather blue, and Danny Kenyon's knees went a kind of mottled colour — but he only laughed. When Bernard's mother came back, she was vexed. 'Poor little scamp,' she said. 'It's agony for him to walk at all.'

After breakfast on Saturday morning, Bernard climbed into his den, which was the room above the stable in the yard. His father had whitewashed the walls for him, and together they'd carried up some old chairs from the house. Two large kitchen tables, covered with paints and bits of models and old newspapers, stood side by side under the windows. His record-player was there, too, and it was warm because of the oilstove. It was a fine room, with an enormous spider in the corner of the roof and a web thick and black against the white wall. Bernard sat in a chair near the stove and began to think of the things he would do when the summer came and he would be nine, going on ten. He and Danny Kenyon would go camping, they would find a field that nobody else knew about, and every day would be cloudless. He made the field in his head — the perfect green of its grass, its great protective tree in one corner, and its stream so pure that you could see every fragmentary pebble, every waving strand of weed in its bed. They were too young to go camping. He knew that.

And then Randall Jenkins climbed the stairs. He was grinning. He carried about his neck a pair of heavy boots, tied by their laces. He took them off and dropped them proudly on the floor, where they stood bluntly on their uncouth soles, exactly as if they still had someone's feet in them and invisible legs climbing up from them. Randall held out his hands to the stove and danced slowly round it, revolving so that he warmed himself all over.

'Coming sliding?' he said. 'This afternoon? We're all going — on the big pond; it's holding.'

'I'll ask,' said Bernard. 'I expect it will be all right.'

He thought of the big pond under the hills, its heavy acres hundreds of yards wide, the water cold and thick. It held in its silence fabulous pike, more than a yard long and twenty pounds in weight, although Bernard had never seen one. He didn't like the big pond.

'You'll need special boots,' said Randall. 'I've borrowed my brother's — take a look at them.'

He lifted the great boots and held them for Bernard's inspection. The soles were an inch thick and covered with a symmetrical pattern of bold nails — flat squares shining like silver. Crescents of smooth metal were screwed at heel and toe into the leather, the edges worn thin as a razor.

Randall rubbed his sleeve over the scarred toe caps, breathing on them as he burnished.

'These are the ones,' he said. 'My brother's old working boots. They might have been made for sliding.'

'They're too big for you,' said Bernard.

'Size 7,' said Randall with satisfaction. 'My brother's grown out of them. Three or four pairs of socks and they'll fit me — you watch, I'll scream right across the pond.'

He moved the boots through the air as if they were fighter planes.

'You'll need a pair like this,' he said. 'Otherwise you'll never go any distance.'

Randall was lucky to have big brothers. Bernard thought dismally of his own boots — light, gentlemanly, with rubber soles and heels. His grandfather didn't like rubber soles and heels, either. Only thieves and policemen, he had said, two classes of society with much in common, wear rubber on their feet. Bernard didn't understand that.

'Is Danny Kenyon coming?' Bernard asked.

'Sure,' Randall said. 'We're all going. I told you.'

After lunch, they all went to the pond, protected by layers of clothing against the wind's knives, their woollen hats pulled over their ears. Some of the boys had managed to borrow heavy boots, just to be like Randall Jenkins, and they clumped awkwardly up the hill as they learned to manage their erratic feet. Randall Jenkins turned out his toes, shuffling around corners like Charlie Chaplin, and they all laughed.

Bernard began to feel very happy. He began to imagine the long quietness of his gliding over the ice. He thought of thick ice, clear as glass, beneath which the cold fish swam, staring up with their goggle eyes at the sliding boys. He thought of ice like a dazzling mirror set in the hills, on which they could skim above their own images, each brilliant slider like two perfect boys — one upside down — joined at the feet. In his happiness he jostled and bumped against Danny Kenyon, and Danny charged right back at him, until they were both laughing and the wind blew away their white breath in clouds from their mouths.

But the pond was a disappointment. Winter had taken all the life from the hills, and the face of the ice was grey and blind — the colour of the flat sky above it. There were no reeds at the lake's edge. Featureless, the ice stretched on, swept by an unhindered wind. The boys bent their heads down against the brutal cold. Their voices were feeble; they felt small and helpless. Only Randall Jenkins was unaffected. Whooping and waving at the ice, he began to run, lifting his enormous boots in slow, high-stepping strides. He ran on, planting his laughable feet one after the other so heavily that Bernard imagined he could hear the whole bowl ringing; and then, his legs rigid, both arms raised for balance, he slid with comic dignity. They all rushed after him, sliding and calling. The afternoon was suddenly warm and vigorous.

Bernard was a good runner, and he hurled himself along so that the momentum of his first slide would be memorable. He raced past two or three of the boys and then stopped, his legs braced wide, head up, arms raised. He was expecting something birdlike, something approaching flight, but nothing happened. His rubber soles clung wickedly to the surface of the ice and he slid no more than a few yards. He was inconsolable.

He shuffled cautiously along the margins of the ice, tentative and humble. Far out, in the wide middle of the pond, he could see the dark figures of his friends, freely sliding, gyrating, crouching, skating on one leg. Their voices came bouncing to him high and clear like the calling of seagulls. But he ran alone at the edge of the lake, unable to slide. Then, unexpectedly, without warning, he found himself free of the binding friction that had held him. He had begun to glide. He sat on the bank, lifted one foot, and inspected the sole of his boot. A thin layer of polished ice, thinner than a postage stamp, had built itself onto the black rubber. He saw that the other boot was also transformed, and he ran jubilantly into the heart of the pond, far out-stripping the loud boys, sliding far and fast, hearing their admiration and surprise. The pond was his.

Late in the afternoon came two young men, tall, with deep voices, all of seventeen years old. They strapped on their sharp and proper skates, and skated expertly. Briefly the boys watched them, but soon Randall Jenkins had organised a game of follow-my-leader. Randall was a superb leader, his invention and audacity encouraging them to a skill and daring they had not known they possessed. The last dare was to run as fast as they could toward the ice from the shore itself, leaping from the bank at full speed. Randall raced forward, his long slow legs gathering pace as he ran, and then he leaped high outward from the bank, landing yards out. Rigid as a scarecrow, he sped on, stopping at last a prodigious way out, and standing absolutely still in the attitude of his sliding. One by one they followed him, although nobody was as brave as Randall, nobody would hurl himself as uninhibitedly from the steep bank. At last, only three boys were left. Bernard thought he had never seen anything as lovely as the dark ice, hardly lit at all as the light faded, and the still figures of his friends dotted about on it, not moving, their arms in a variety of postures, their bodies bent or upright. He took a great breath, and ran. He had never felt so light, he was full of fiery energy. He reached the bank and thrust himself so urgently, so powerfully, that the exhilaration of his leap made him gasp. He hit the ice beautifully, and felt at once the speed of his sliding, and he knew that nobody had ever slid so far. Stopping at last, he looked around. He was yards farther than Randall Jenkins, miles farther than the other boys. Jackie Phelps was slowing miserably a long way off, and only Danny was left to jump.

He could see Danny up on the bank, preparing to run, swaying from one foot to the other, bent forward at the waist. Cupping his hands, Bernard shouted, 'You'll never reach me!'

Danny waved furiously. You could see that he was going to give it all he had by the way he set his shoulders. He ran forward and leaped wildly from the bank. Bernard could see him so clearly that everything seemed to happen in slow motion. He saw Danny hit the ice and knew that it was wrong. Danny landed on his heels, not on the flat of his feet, and his body was already tilting gently backward. He sped along, the slope of his body already irrevocably past the point of recovery. They saw his heels leave the ice, and for a perceptible moment he sailed through the unsupporting air before the back of his head cracked frighteningly against the surface. He lay broken and huddled. Bernard could not move. He could see Danny in a black heap, but he couldn't move toward him. It was Randall Jenkins who reached him first, and they all ran in behind him.

They crowded around Danny, looking down at him. His face was still and white, his eyes closed. As they looked a little worm of blood appeared at one nostril and curled onto Danny's lip. What if he should die? Bernard bent, and in an urgency of terror lifted his friend. Randall helped him, and together they hauled Danny to the bank. Some of the boys were crying, and Randall set them to collect twigs, pieces of paper — anything that would burn. Bernard took off Danny's gloves and rubbed his hands in his own. Danny's fingers were very cold, but in a while he began to move and groan. Twice he opened his eyes, without recognising them and without saying anything. Randall lit a fire, and it burned with a dull light, sullenly. He sent all the boys except Bernard to find more fuel, told them to

rip branches from small trees. Bernard wiped the blood from
Danny's nose, and after a while the bleeding stopped. It hadn't been
very much, he comforted himself. His knees hurt from bending
down so long. Behind him, Randall had whipped the fire into a huge
blaze that pushed away the darkness, and the boys sat near it, not
speaking. Danny moved heavily, sat up, and looked at Bernard.

'Oh, my God,' said Danny Kenyon. 'What happened?'

He was all right; everything was all right. The boys cheered,
slapped each other on the back, put Danny to sit even nearer the
fire. They danced and sang, released from fright, and they were pert
and arrogant when one of the young men suddenly appeared.

'What's the matter with him?' he asked, bending over Danny.

'Nothing,' said Randall airily. 'Nothing at all.'

'None of your business,' said Jackie Phelps, out of the darkness.

'How old are you?' said the young man to Bernard.

'Ten,' lied Bernard. He pointed to Randall. 'And he's eleven,' he
said.

'Get that boy home,' said the young man. 'How do you feel, son?'

'Great,' said Danny. 'I feel great.'

'Get home,' said the young man. 'And the rest of you see that this
fire is out.'

He skated into the darkness. Bernard could feel the iron shearing
of his blades.

The fire was very hot. Bernard could imagine it warming a thin
crust of frozen soil, then maybe deeper, a half inch deep. Already
he could hear the ice hiss in the released ground. He sat with his
back up against Danny's back, so they were both comfortable. All
the boys sat around. They were very quiet.

Bit by bit, the dark and the cold crept into the interstices of the
flames, winning the night back for winter. Randall got up and
stamped about. His feet had gone to sleep.

'Time to go, lads,' he said. 'Time to go.'

They stood up and followed obediently behind Randall. Bernard
was so tired that his legs were slow and stiff, and his mind was always
about two steps in front of them, but in a little while they got better.
The boys went down the lane past the old rectory and started down
the hill toward the town. A night wind flew at them as if it cared
nothing for people and meant to blow straight through them.
Bernard began to shiver. What if Danny had died? He saw again
Danny's face as he lay on the ice, as white and stiff as a candle. As
he looked, an imaginary worm of blood crawled from Danny's nose

and covered the side of his cheek. He closed his mind from the terror of it and put his arm over Danny's shoulder.

'How do you feel?' he whispered, but Randall heard him.

'He feels great,' Randall Jenkins roared, his voice red as fire. 'What's the matter with you? He feels fine!'

'I'm OK,' said Danny. 'Honest, I'm OK.'

A few small flakes of snow fell out of the sky. The boys felt them hit their faces, light as cobwebs, and then vanish. It was intolerably dark and cold. As they entered the first streets of the town, the boys moved together for solace and started to run. They trotted close together, moving home as one boy through the darkness, united against whatever terror might threaten them.

Cocksfoot, Crested Dog's-Tail, Sweet Vernal Grass

The year I was thirteen, my father died. He died in the middle of July, and he was buried on a Wednesday, in the cemetery at the edge of town, on a hot day. Up there on the low hill, a trace of breeze was welcome. I was in my mourning suit, buttoned to attention, and the lightness of moving air was scarcely perceptible on my face. We stood unmoving at the side of the raw grave, the preacher's voice as dry as a rasp of grasshoppers. My uncle, down from Northampton, stood next to me. I had been named for him: Frederick. We were both Frederick Galloway. That morning, he had put his hand on my shoulder, but I had moved away. I'd done my crying. Now I watched the heads of seeding grasses on the neighbouring boundaries of the cemetery as if they alone were real. They moved delicately and aimlessly in the tiny wind, obeying rules of an excellent sort. When the service ended and the men of the family and their friends began to talk again, breathing vigorously in an attempt to become immediately normal, I let them go. I watched them move down the hot paths toward the gate where the cars were waiting for them, and then I stepped among the tall grasses, looking at them, staying with them. I was there a long time.

Boys of that age are the world's experts. Driven, perhaps, by a new need to understand at least something of an increasingly perplexing world, they choose some part of it — pigeons, motorcycles, the activities of pop stars or footballers — and this they study with an absorbed energy, knowing everything. With me, it became grasses. When I got to bed that night, I still saw clearly the dipping heads of grass, heard the harsh stalks rustling together in the heat.

That summer, I read all I could find about grasses. Even now, I can remember their names: perennial rye grass, timothy, meadow foxtail, quaking grass, erect brome (with beautiful purple heads), sheep's fescue and red fescue, cocksfoot, crested dog's-tail, sweet vernal grass.

We lived in a South Coast town, small, tightly knit, very provincial. A slow river ran past the edge of the town and through an untidy marsh into the sea. In the spring of the year, I had been walking on the salt flats, through muddy rivulets, looking for ducks' nests. Few people ever went there, but I was there often. In winter, it was marvellously wild and solitary, although it couldn't have been more than a dozen acres altogether.

That spring day, before my father died, I met Edgar Martin down on the marsh. He was a big, awkward boy, a class above me at school, but we'd never spoken before. He had three eels in his hand, and he held them up in quiet triumph. Grey and shining, they hung easily in his grip, as if they were relaxed, as if they were going along with him willingly, trustingly. One of them was the biggest eel I'd ever seen. We became friends, Edgar Martin and I.

I used to spend a lot of time that year up at the Martins' farm, north of the town, and as the year grew warmer we swam most afternoons in the river pool at the bottom of the big meadow. It was a perfect pool. The river had cut deeply into the mild soil until it reached stone, and now it rested, four or five feet deep, on a long slab of rock. If you dived underwater, you could see the stone, layered and flat, tilted slightly, and carved by the melodious filing of water. It looked dark green in colour, but if you brought out a loose, flat stone, it dried grey, with darker streaks running through. I didn't like that. I threw every dry stone lying about the pool back into the water. I used to do this after I'd had my swim, marching up and down, reclaiming stone after stone for the river. Edgar Martin used to laugh at me.

One hot afternoon, I walked down to the pool. Edgar was already in, floating on his back and churning the water with his feet into a small foam. I'd been to the hospital to see my father, and it hadn't been interesting. He was asleep, and I sat there, close to the white metal bed, for thirty minutes. We never spoke much, my father and I, but it was better when he was awake. He would say some quite funny things then, clearing his throat first so that his quiet voice would have a better chance of being heard. That afternoon the nurse told me that I could leave, since it seemed unlikely that he would wake up, and I walked up the hill through the streets until I came to Edgar's farm.

I was glad of the sweet water. I let myself loll through it as if I were as boneless as waterweed, drifting from the head of the pool along its slow-moving currents, then swimming back and floating again, over and over. The whole afternoon slept in the heat.

It was a sharp call from Edgar that aroused me. I turned to see a snake swimming toward me, its head two or three inches out of the water, like a periscope. I couldn't see its body, but some movement of the surface, or perhaps a minute swaying of its head and neck, suggested its wriggling length. I saw all this with perfect clarity, and the next second I was out of the water and crouched on the riverbank. I don't know how I did this; it was a kind of effort I had never made before. Edgar began to laugh, but I could see he'd been impressed.

'Boy,' he said, 'you can go like a bloody fish when you've a mind to!'

We dressed slowly and lay on the grass to wait for the cool evening.

'That's the cemetery up there,' said Edgar, 'that's the back of it. The council wants to buy the next field so they can make the cemetery bigger, but the man who owns it won't sell.'

'I know,' I said.

I turned on my side to look, spitting out a sweet white stalk of grass as I did so. The cemetery stood on its little hill, and the heat wavered all the outlines between, so that the hill danced on shifting air and nothing was real.

'It was only a grass snake,' Edgar said when we got up to go. 'Quite harmless.'

'I know,' I said.

We walked through the farmyard, and Edgar's mother asked me to stay to supper, so I did.

The next day, my father died. It was a Sunday.

My mother and father were both north country people, she from Hull, and he from the North Riding of Yorkshire. They had travelled south immediately after their marriage, knowing there was little chance of work in the north. At first, they had thought themselves fortunate, but as time went by they realised that their successes would be small and ordinary. My father found work almost at once as a booking clerk on the railway. He was a small, dapper man, quiet and droll in his speech. He seemed amused by everything he saw; he wore his mouth always in a gentle smile.

They worked long hours in those days before the war. When I was small, I used to lie awake in the little room above the front hall until I heard the sound of my father's cane tapping against the pavement as he walked toward the house. He would open the door so quietly that often I wouldn't hear him enter. I wouldn't know he was home until I heard his light cough. I'd go to sleep then. He always carried a cane. It was an affectation that annoyed my mother. She thought he was making himself old before his time, but when she said this he would only smile.

When I was older, I sometimes spent a winter evening sitting with my father down at the railway station, in the booking office. He had a large fire there, always, but it was still unbearably cold. I'd sit by the fire until I saw my father begin to fidget. He was afraid that the stationmaster, silly, self-important Billy Fletcher, would come in and catch me sitting there. I was not afraid of Billy Fletcher. His two sons, Sam and Edwin, were in school with me — round, timid boys who turned their heads away when I looked at them. I used to threaten them and beat them up sometimes, because my father was afraid of the stationmaster.

Some time after my father died, I went down to the station. It was in the early winter, in November. There were only two platforms. From one the trains moved eastward along the coast before turning inland for London, and from the other the slow files of carriages moved once an hour down into Hampshire and Dorset. In those days, I knew the times of all the trains. The platforms were lit by gas lamps overhead, each light formed of three frail gas mantles like buds of stiff lace set in a triangle under a glass dome. They threw irregular circles of weak, yellow light on the wooden planks. Bleak, unexpected winds searched the corners of the station buildings, and if you stood under one of those gas lamps, the night seemed to hiss and pop as small flames puffed in the gusts. It was as desolate and sad a place as I've ever stood in.

My father was never promoted. He just moved slowly through his life, a thin, slow booking clerk, getting thinner and slower.

I'd always been pretty good at school — not marvellous, but good. That year, somehow, everything went wrong, and I began to let things slide a little. I used to stay away two or three afternoons every week, and I'd walk through the fields, not thinking very much about anything. That was the time I learned about grasses. I watched them grow heavy-headed with seed, I watched them yellow and die, I saw them become spent bents and tussocks flattening under winter.

My Christmas report from school was bad, and my mother was more angry than I'd seen her before. She had a thin Northern face, and her voice had got into the habit of complaining. From then on, we seemed to be enemies, and I spent very little time in the house. One day at school, old Hughes, who taught English, spoke to me.

'Your work,' he said, 'your work is so bad now. What are you going to do?'

'I don't know, sir,' I said.

'You can't go on like this,' he said, very kindly. I could see he was worried.

'No, sir,' I said. At that moment, I was determined to work

immensely hard, to astonish everyone by my industry and progress.

'Now, look,' said old Hughes, 'it seems to me that you have very little interest at all in your work here. You're fourteen now — it might be better if you were to leave school and get yourself a job. What does your father want you to do?'

I looked up at him savagely.

'I haven't got a father,' I said roughly.

He was bewildered and dismayed, and I was merciless. He had no right to live in a comfortable world where the death of my father was unknown.

'He's dead,' I said. 'He died last July.'

Old Hughes' face was red and stupid.

'All the more reason, then, for you to work hard, either in school or out of school, wherever you decide,' he said.

That night I had another fierce row with my mother. I remember that the skin of her thin neck was blotched with anger and that she was shaking with temper. And I remember what she said as I left the house: 'You're like your father. He never fought and you'll never fight. You'll go down as he went down.'

My little sister, six years old, began to cry.

The next day, I looked for old Hughes at school, and told him I would be leaving at the end of term.

'Fine,' he said. 'Come and see me before you go.'

I nodded, but we both knew it would never happen. We'd said our piece.

It was time to leave. I knew that. I wasn't really like my father. My hands and feet were much bigger than his. I walked differently, more heavily; my features were larger and coarser. I looked older than fourteen.

I was an embarrassment to my mother, who hoped, I knew, to marry again. One day I found that she had cleared out everything that had been my father's, giving things away, burning things in the garden. I rescued his razor and brushes from the bonfire and kept them in the garden shed. They were in a small leather case — a safety razor and two Bakelite tubes for the brushes. She didn't know I had them. After the bonfire, she looked a lot happier and began to sing about the house. I think she was seeing one or two men. She was only thirty-five.

One Saturday morning before the end of term, I walked down to the station to see old Billy Fletcher. He was standing outside his office, encased in officialdom, his uniform tight, his peaked hat brave with braid. I asked him if I could speak to him. I was taller than Billy Fletcher, despite his proud hat.

'Of course, my boy,' he said. 'Any time, any time. Come in, come in.'

We went into his office. From his windows you could see a long way down the track. A mile along the narrowing line, I could see the signal box, and I wondered which of my father's friends was on duty there. I sat on the edge of a chair and let Billy Fletcher talk.

'We miss your father here,' he said, 'yes, we miss him. A real gentleman, and there aren't too many of them about. A sad loss, and so young, too. Well, there it is.'

He blew sadly and complacently down the swell of his plump vest and asked what he could do to help me.

'I'm leaving school in just over two weeks, and I'll need a job,' I said. 'I was wondering . . . .'

He shook his head and let his eyes look importantly at nothing.

'There's nothing,' he said at last. 'No, nothing at all. The company would like to help, but we're full staffed. It would be different now if you were prepared to leave home.'

'I can leave home,' I said quickly. 'I'd prefer to leave home.'

Mr Fletcher opened his eyes in surprise and smiled with baffled content.

'You boys,' he said. 'You youngsters! You'll try anything. My two are just the same. Try anything!'

I thought of Sam and Edwin Fletcher, those soft, cowering boys, and sneered in my head.

'Come in next week,' said Billy Fletcher. 'I'll be in touch with Head Office on Monday, and we'll hope to have good news for you.'

He was as good as his word. On the following Tuesday, I had a letter offering me a post as parcels clerk in Swindon, to start immediately I left school.

I left home on a Sunday evening in April. As I carried my case down the street, I saw my sister playing with five or six other little girls. They were skipping, using a long rope, two of them turning the ends while the rest hopped seriously inside the whirling rope, each with her hands on the shoulders of the child in front, and they sang in time as they skipped:

> The big ship sailed on the Alley-alley-O
>   The Alley-alley-O
>   The Alley-alley-O
> The big ship sailed on the Alley-alley-O
> On the fifth day of September.

The rope slapped the road at every beat of the song. My sister left her friends when she saw me, and stood apart. She didn't smile or anything like that. She held her own skipping rope in her hand — one she'd had as a present for her birthday. It had bright wooden handles and a glittering weight halfway along the cord to help it turn. My sister put her finger in her mouth and looked at me very carefully for a long time, and then she ran up the road, her dark hair flying and bouncing as she ran. I never saw her again.

I think of Swindon as a Victorian town. The office in which I worked was enormous, its ceiling so high that it sent back an echo of everything we said, so that we worked almost without speaking. Even then the air seemed curiously hollow and trembling, as if we sat in a tiled cave. But that might well have been because of the darkness. I remember that we had fishtails of gaslight flaring on the walls, although this may not be true and I am inventing where memory is empty. Certainly there was dust everywhere — on the spiked files of our invoices, settling on the white pages of our ledgers, dust filming the polished black of our shoes as each morning we entered the building. I stayed five weeks in Swindon.

I lodged with Mr and Mrs Guthrie — it was all arranged before I arrived. Arthur Guthrie was a clerk in the same office, a stolid man, pale, unemotional, deep-voiced. He had the most beautiful hand-writing I've ever seen, and I used to copy it on odd bits of paper whenever I had the chance. We walked to work together in the mornings and home together in the evenings, through the used streets of the town. I liked him, and I liked Mrs Guthrie, too.

Arthur Guthrie kept canaries in his garden, in a lean-to aviary built against the back wall of his house. On sunny evenings, the tiny yellow birds sang so stridently that the house seemed to throb. When they sang like this, Arthur Guthrie would lift his head and listen intently, but he never said anything. I got into the habit of going into the aviary after supper. I'd clean out the cages and give the birds fresh seed and water. It was something to do.

One evening, returning indoors from the aviary, I heard them quarrelling, Arthur and Mrs Guthrie. They weren't shouting, and for a time I thought they were speaking ordinarily, but when I heard my name I listened more carefully. It was a nice little house, the Guthries', and late in the day the kitchen was filled with light. It faced west, I expect. I looked through the open door and saw Arthur sitting stiffly on a wooden chair, his elbows on the table, his wife opposite him. They didn't know I was there. There was a yellow-and-white checked cloth on the table, and dishes from the evening meal were stacked neatly in the middle.

'He's only a boy,' said Mrs Guthrie.

'He may be,' Arthur said, 'but he's a nuisance. I can't stand him. I can't stand his chattering, nor the way he copies my handwriting. I can't go into the aviary without him following behind. I didn't want him here to start with. It was your idea from the first.'

'There's nothing we can do now,' said Mrs Guthrie. 'Give him a few weeks. Perhaps he'll find friends of his own.'

'If he was my own boy,' Arthur said, 'I wouldn't mind, I can see that. But he isn't. I don't want a son. A lodger is what I thought he was. He'll have to go.'

'You'll have to tell him,' Mrs Guthrie said. 'I won't tell him. That's a man's job.'

I went outside quietly and walked about the garden until I felt better. Then I went in the house.

'Hullo, boy,' said Arthur. 'Do you want a cup of tea?'

I could see him struggling to be fair to me.

'No, thanks,' I said, 'I think I'll take a walk down the road.'

I could feel my face pretending to smile.

'That's right,' said Mrs Guthrie. 'Enjoy yourself.'

For the life of me, I can't remember her first name, but it was something quite ordinary, like Ethel or Margaret.

I collected my wages that Friday night, and the next morning I told Mrs Guthrie I was going home for the weekend. I didn't see Arthur. It didn't take long to pack my bag and I was at the station in less than ten minutes, but I didn't go home. Instead, I caught a train to London. When I got there, somebody told me where the YMCA was. I took a room there, and in a week I was working in a stockbroker's office in the City.

Three years I was in London, loving every minute of it. In those days, there was a spaciousness about the place, and a good-humoured assumption by its inhabitants that they were better in every way than people anywhere else. I believed this. People lived in the heart of London then, not, as now, on the outskirts, the centre a lit emptiness after business is over. I began a new life in London, forgetting almost completely what had happened to me before. I moved from job to job, urgently and expertly. I did my growing in London, became tall and elegant, a fashionable young man as far as money would allow. At last, when it was time for me to leave the place, I even had a new name.

The summer of 1939 was brilliant, cloudless. In the city squares, the plane trees had put out their leaves early, always a good sign, and after lunch I would saunter back to the office through gaudy sunlight filtering green and gold among the trees. I worked then for a firm of lawyers whose main function was the management of several large estates of houses — old properties most of them, divided into flats. Three days a week, I went out collecting rents, and on Thursdays and Fridays I did the paperwork connected with my houses. There were three of us at this, and we operated a sweet little fraud that brought us several illegal pounds every month.

One Thursday, a little late from lunch, I reached the office and realised that we had been caught. The place was silent and miserable, my friend Edwards white-faced and despairing at his desk. He looked as though he'd been crying.

'So there you are, there you are,' said the chief clerk. 'Mr Fawcett will want your ledgers in a few minutes.'

The old fool was so excited that he almost skipped as he spoke. We'd not been too kind to him, Edwards and I. I smiled at him cheerfully.

'They're all ready,' I said, 'except the final balance, and that can wait. I'll take them in now.'

I picked up my ledgers, put them under my arm, walked out of the room. I went calmly along the corridor, down two flights of stairs, and away. I'd had to leave an almost new raincoat behind, but that was no worry. The ledgers went into a wastebasket in Oxford Street, just before I walked into a recruiting office and joined the Army. Although the recruiting officer wanted me to be more ambitious, I joined the infantry. I knew exactly what I wanted. In a conveniently short time I was Private Sutton, GA, at a training camp in Wiltshire. I was seventeen years old.

The war began before we were trained: I hadn't thought of war. Early in winter, we were sent north to Blackpool, living in huts at the edge of that holiday town. I had enjoyed my first weeks in the Army. What I liked best was the intricate ritual of the barrack square, the perfection of rhythmical movement as line after line marched and counter-marched, the precise order firm and unbroken, despite the increasing complexity of our tramping patterns. It was almost better when we got to Blackpool, for we arose there in the winter mornings, formed our long columns in the breathing dark, and moved out into the streets. The town was asleep and half dead; only the hibernating proprietors lived in the small hotels and boarding houses, waiting for the war to end and for plentiful summer to come. We swung into the town, not a light showing, and marched along the miles of sea-front, the waves on one hand and the summer shops, their windows boarded against the wind that blew in from the Atlantic, on the other. As we marched, our heels would hammer the scatterings of little pebbles thrown over the road by the sea, and they'd rattle away in step with us, like the ghosts of kettledrums. In that hypnotic rhythm, we stepped away our days, perfectly, mindlessly.

Most of the boys in my company were badly educated, some quite illiterate. In my hut, I alone wrote and read fluently, and my Sundays were taken up with writing letters to mothers and girls. It wasn't long before my proficiency was noted and I was transferred to the company office. My marching days were over.

There was not enough work to keep me busy, and most afternoons I went to the zoo in the Winter Gardens. I used to visit a tawny brown puma, kept in a pen with other big cats. He sat alert at the back of the cage, missing nothing, tense for the chance that he knew must one day come. Or he walked with fluid beauty, up and down, up and down, always at the back of the cage, as far away from us as he could get. He was a great cat, and I think of him still from time to time.

In the spring, when we left for Scotland, I was a full corporal. The routine of the company office was at my fingertips. In small ways, I already had some power.

We lived under canvas. I had a tent of my own, near a stream at the edge of camp. So smooth was the run of water that it seemed not to move, but at night, in the poor light of the moon or in the near-darkness of the reflected sky, the ripples of its steady flowing could be recognised. I sat there every night, near the water.

I read a lot in Scotland. The town had a superb library, and I went through it like a plague. Had we stayed there a few more months, I should have read every book they had.

By this time, most of the work in the office was left to me. I made decisions, I acted, the strokes of the pen were mine. I was a sergeant long before we went to Africa.

What I most admired about the Army was the way in which the system was simplified and made effective. Life at first was difficult and ritualistic, the day filled with tiny ceremonies which existed only in order that men should have something to do, or because they were thoughtlessly continued long after the reasons for their performance had been eroded. But as the war became more fierce and desperate, so, too, did life become simpler and more pragmatic. I learned that from the Army. I learned to profit from all opportunities, and there were many, and I walked very much alone.

I was a warrant officer when I left in 1946. I could have stayed on. Three times I was offered a commission. But I had outgrown the Army. This way and that, I had made some money. I put my money to work. It grew, it multiplied, it worked for me.

My secretary is a sensible woman, not young. She's competent, tactful, doesn't try to run things herself. She has come back to a career because time was hanging a little heavily, I think. Her husband is a doctor, and she has two sons at Cambridge. She's in her early forties.

Last week, I said to her, 'Mrs Braithwaite, forty-two years are long enough for a man to live'.

I can't think why I said such a thing. It certainly wasn't in my mind to say it. She was amused, knowing that I'm past fifty.

'You'll be saying that when you're eighty,' she said, 'and I've no doubt you'll still be sharper than anyone else in sight.'

She gets a good salary, that woman. I'm a rich man.

My father was forty-two when he died.

Perhaps I should go back there, to the place where I was a child. I never have, although once or twice I've been fairly near. My sister, if she's alive, would be forty-three now. She might have children — my nephews and nieces.

About ten years ago, when I was buying a lot of land for invest-ment, I had a sudden urge to get hold of Edgar Martin's farm. Farmland was comparatively cheap then, although I knew its value was increasing and I'd already got hold of three or four very large places — two estates in Scotland and one in Sussex among them. They made a lot of money later on, when I sold them. Edgar Martin's place would have been useless to me. It was only about thirty acres, not worth troubling with. But I thought seriously about it until I realised that I was influenced by forgotten things, the river pool, the memory of Edgar holding aloft those shining eels on the salt marsh, old, intangible summers.

I'll never go back; I know that.

Lately though, at night, on the edge of sleep, when the mind is undefended, I have seen again those grasses at the cemetery's verge more vividly fresh and green than they were long ago. Luminous, possessing the obsessive clarity of things seen in dreams, they let me trace at will their characteristic outlines, to recognise with the faultless certainty of my youthful knowledge each typical specimen. They hold themselves quietly for my recognition, and I make a ceremony of their names.

And this morning, as I shaved, I could hear those names clearly under the hum of the razor: couch, perennial rye grass, false oat, timothy, meadow foxtail, quaking grass, sheep's fescue and red fescue, erect brome, cocksfoot, crested dog's-tail, sweet vernal grass.

The Highland Boy

The first greyhound I ever owned was a blackbrindled dog called Highland Boy. He was a small dog, weighing perhaps fifty-three pounds, and his coat was a dull black with sparse streaks of rust-coloured hair running through it. He was not attractive at first glance, and his expression was at once conciliatory and untrustworthy. I had known him for a year before I became his owner, because he belonged to my Uncle Cedric.

My Uncle Cedric owned a tobacconist's and confectionery shop in Victoria Road, very near to our house, and it was my habit to visit the shop on Saturday evenings to buy a quarter of a pound of chocolate caramels. Cedric would take a paper bag as big as a pillowcase, and thrusting his hand into all the glass jars around him, would fill it with a sweet assortment of flavours enough to last a week. This situation was not as perfect as it seems, for Bertie Christopher soon discovered my Saturday evening fortune, and he and his gang would perch like a row of twelve-year-old vultures on the railings opposite my uncle's shop, waiting for me to emerge. Fighting was out of the question since the very weight of the sweets was an embarrassment. I used to hover patiently behind the door of the shop until something broke momentarily their brooding concentration, and then I'd run for it. Sprinting and jinking like a startled buck, I'd break past three or four fairly easily. After that it was head down and knock my way through. Most Saturdays at that time I could be found fingering a swollen eye or some other temporary and violent blemish, gloomily eating a chocolate-covered almond or a marzipan whirl, wondering if it was worth it.

Highland Boy was often in the shop with my Uncle Cedric on Saturday evenings. They would both have been to the unlicensed track at the top of the town, and my uncle would usually be staring in a bewildered fashion at Highland Boy. All the dog ever did was to whisk his thin tail once or twice and then look shyly and resignedly at the floor. I often thought my uncle took a kind of defiant pride in the dog.

Uncle Cedric was a tall, thin man, almost completely bald although he was only twenty-eight. He had the most ferocious eyebrows I have ever seen, and my grandmother said that if he were to comb them back over his bare skull, they would offer more than adequate compensation. She never said this in Cedric's hearing because he was sensitive. Cedric wore checked suits, and he would stand with his hands, his fingertips anyway, in the little pockets of his waistcoat, which made his elbows stick out like the stubby wings of a sparrow and his shoulders lift almost up to his ears. He was mild and slow-moving enough normally, but phenomenally strong and brisk when angry. Nobody cared to argue with Cedric. I once saw him argue with three Irishmen who had decided to contest, as a matter of entertainment, a debt of honour. Cedric stood against a shop-window in case they should attempt to attack him from behind and set about dealing with them.

'B'Jasus, he's a daisy,' cried the admiring Irishmen as they reeled and staggered away. 'Didja ever see the dint he gave Paddy, now?'

They all four went into a public house, and I was left to mind Cedric's van.

On a golden Saturday in late August, at eight-thirty in the evening, I went as usual for my trove of sugar. Bertie Christopher and his gang watched my every step with cold, unblinking eyes. The shop door was open, and Cedric and Highland Boy stood inside. I knew at once that there was some serious trouble. The dog was absolutely still, head and tail hanging low, and he did not give me even a hint of a greeting. I looked up at Cedric. Great, silent tears were rolling down his face.

'What's wrong?' I asked. 'Uncle Cedric, what's the matter?'

He was shaking with anger, but his voice was remote and controlled.

'This bloody dog,' he said, 'has kept the bookmakers in affluence, with my money, since the day I bought him. I have been involved in many a disgraceful and undignified scene because of the deceitful manner in which he races, people believing that I, in some devilish way, have control over his actions. All this I have put up with because of my love of animals. But he has killed my cat, and that is the end.'

Cedric loved his cat, a large, somnolent, ginger creature. This was gasping tragedy. I looked at Highland Boy. His eye was mild and distant, and there were flecks of ginger fur about his mouth.

A small, nervous man came in for cigarettes, and Cedric wept unashamed as he served him with a packet of the wrong brand.

'What are you going to do?' I asked.

'Take him out of my sight, boy,' said Cedric. 'I make him over to you as a present. Tomorrow I'll give you his pedigree and registration papers, but take him out of my sight.'

I hooked my fingers behind Highland Boy's collar and went. Bertie Christopher was surprised enough to let me pass without a struggle, and then Highland Boy and I trotted down the garden and into the house.

My father was sitting in his armchair reading Dickens, which is what he always did when he wasn't busy.

'What's this?' he said.

'A dog,' I said, 'Highland Boy.'

'He needs feeding. You can keep him in the wash-house,' said my father. The dog looked at him, and he looked at the dog. They liked each other.

So began my career as a greyhound owner.

I used to get up very early each morning and exercise that dog over the moors. I became hard and stringy, able to run for prodigious distances without distress, but Highland Boy seemed completely unaffected. When I had enough money — the fee was five shillings — I would enter him for a race on one of the unlicensed tracks either in our town or in one of the neighbouring towns. Neither he nor I was popular on these tracks.

I have thought since that the dog was an imaginative genius. There may be ways of reducing a race to chaos that he didn't invent, but I doubt it. Sometimes he would shoot away with every appearance of running an orthodox and blameless five hundred and twenty-five yards, which was the usual length of a race, only to feel lonely up there in front. He would wait for the second dog and gambol along beside him, smiling and twisting in an ecstasy of friendship. This commonly so upset the other dog that he ran wide, turned round, or lost ground so rapidly that he was effectively out of the running; I'd have to avoid the owner of such a dog for months. He won a solitary race, in Aberdare, in so strange a fashion that I was almost ashamed to collect the prize money. Running with a controlled abandon which left the honest journeymen who were his competitors far behind, he got to within a foot of the winning post and stopped dead. The second dog, labouring along twenty lengths behind, ran heavily into him and knocked Highland Boy over the line. Four Chinamen, heavy and regular gamblers, leaped and capered as they ran for the bookmakers. They were the most scrutable men I ever saw, and the only men who ever made a killing on my dog. After this race, Benny Evans, who was the handicapper at the track, suggested it might be sensible if I kept my dog away until people's memories grew dim. I could see his point.

Every September, as if to give an added splendour to the death of summer, a great open competition was held at the Tredegar track, twelve miles away over the hills. The prize was twenty-five pounds and a silver cup. My Uncle Cedric now possessed a marvellous dog, the beautiful Special Request, and he would certainly enter him. He spoke to my father and me of his well-founded hopes.

'When I went over to Ireland,' he said, 'to buy this dog from Father Seamus Riordan, I was assured there wasn't a dog to touch him. And they were right. That silver cup is as good as in my hands, barring accidents, and the twenty-five pounds too.'

He beamed at the glorious tan-and-white greyhound, silken-coated and sided like a bream.

'He's a beauty,' I said.

'You ought to take your dog. I'll pay for his entry,' my father said.

'Why not?' said Cedric, with the large generosity of a man who knows he is not to be affected by the decisions of lesser men.

I went over to Tredegar on the bus, on the Thursday night of the qualifying races. Highland Boy behaved admirably, running second to a very good dog which had been specially imported from Bristol. This meant that he went into the semi-finals the next evening. Cedric's dog won his heat very easily and broke the track record. Almost everybody from our town was on him to win the final, and our hopes were high.

When we got to the track on the Friday evening, we found that the two semi-finals were to be held last on the programme. Cedric was amused to find that our dogs were in the same race, Special Request in Box 6, which was lucky since he was a superbly fast starter, and Highland Boy in Box 3. The first three dogs in each race would go on to the final, to be held a week later. I knew I had no chance. Highland Boy was too small to stand the buffeting that would certainly go on in the middle of the track.

'Never mind,' said Cedric, 'he's done very well to get as far as this.'

The lights were shining on the track by the time our race was announced. I went down to the paddock and put the racing coat with the large number three on it around Highland Boy, taking care not to fasten it too tightly under his stomach. He seemed only half the size of the other dogs. I felt like crying. I put his racing muzzle on. He was unperturbed, perfectly at ease among the eager whining of the other dogs. The stewards made me wear a long white coat to walk him down to the boxes. It was too long and I had to hold it up with one hand and everybody laughed.

'It's ridiculous to allow a boy to put his dog in an important race like this,' said Paul Davies, a thin lame man, as we walked down the track. 'Particularly a dog like that thing; he can ruin any race.'

My uncle gave him a red look.

'The cure for your lameness, Paul, is to break the good leg,' he said.

Paul, whose disability had given him guile and cunning, thought of the three Irishmen and gulped.

'I hope you don't think I was talking of your nephew here,' he said. 'Why, this boy is a credit. He has a real sense of vocation and will be just like you, Ced, in a couple of years.'

We walked silently down to the line of six boxes, put our dogs in one by one, and ran across the field over to the finish, so that we would be ready to collect them after the race.

They flew out of the traps, and Special Request was well in front by the second bend. I couldn't even see my dog. On the back straight he was last and not moving very freely, but as they hit the last bend he began to run, weaving through the field with breathtaking speed. I was proud of him. He finished third, well behind the first two, but he was in the final.

Now I had a week before the great day. I gave Highland Boy two raw eggs a day, fed him on minced beef before putting him in his straw, walked him until my feet were raw. He didn't seem an ounce different.

On the night of the final we went in a hired bus. We carried with us all the loose money in the town, and we were thick with strategies for getting good odds from the bookmakers. I sat in a front seat, behind the driver where I could get a good view of the road, and Highland Boy sat between my feet. I wore my best suit, the one with a grey stripe, and I wasn't going to wear a long white coat whatever happened.

We got to the track, and I waited about through the dragging tedium of the earlier races. I could see my uncle's friends, jovial with expectation, their eyes full of money. Highland Boy was drawn in Box 1, a good position if he got away quickly enough, right on the rail. Cedric's dog was in Box 5, which was perfectly all right for him. He was a big dog and could barge his way through.

I went down to the paddock in a dream, my fingers shaking so that I couldn't fasten the racing coat, and Cedric did it for me.

'Good luck, Uncle,' I said.

'He'll dawdle it,' said Cedric. 'My Special Request will dawdle it. The only interesting question is, who's going to be second?'

I put Highland Boy into the first box and he went in like a gentleman. When I popped around the front to have a look at him, he gave me a serious and apologetic glance, and I knew how he felt.

'It doesn't matter, you've done well,' I said.

The bell went, and the hare began its run from behind the starting line. I could have sworn that Highland Boy's box opened seconds before the others, but I know that's impossible. He was fifteen yards clear at the end of the first straight and fled around the bend, tracking so closely to the inner fence that I thought he would leave the colour of his skin on every inch of it. He coiled and stretched with brilliant suppleness and vigour, throwing his length into a stride like a flying dive, balling himself tight, his back arched high, then unleashing again. I knew, everybody in the stadium knew, that the race was over before it was halfway run. My dog won by fifteen easy lengths, and I had collected him, put on his lead, and begun to walk away when the second dog reached us, panting and exhausted. I was spring-heeled with elation, but I held my face stiff because I knew it was wrong of me to feel even remotely happy. I thought of Uncle Cedric, his pockets full of red and white ribbon he'd bought especially to decorate the cup. I looked down at Highland Boy. The muscles on his quarters were shivering, but he seemed all right otherwise. He was a heartless dog.

They made me walk him around the track, and he danced on his toes every inch of it. He knew he'd won. They gave me a cheque for twenty-five pounds and a dented cup, said to be silver. Everybody cheered derisively, except the relieved bookmakers and the silent, ominous party of my uncle's friends. People jeered Uncle Cedric, and he had no reply. We filed into our cheerless coach. Nobody congratulated me. I held the unwanted cup on my knee until it began to get heavy, and then I put it under the seat.

We sat together, Uncle Cedric and I, on the seat nearest the door, and Highland Boy coiled himself into a tactful ball at our feet. My uncle put Special Request on the seat between us and then hunched into his overcoat, dark with gloom, unmoving except for the fingers of his left hand, which absent-mindedly fondled the folded ear of his defeated champion. Behind us, from the back seat where he sat with four of his friends, I could hear the bitter voice of big Carl Jenkins. He spoke quietly at first, but now his voice grew heavy and bold.

He was very nasty. He said that although he had known my uncle to be the biggest crook in four valleys, he had not thought Cedric would swindle his own friends of their hard-earned money. This, said Carl Jenkins, was the lowest of my uncle's many abominable tricks. He reasoned that my uncle was bald only because nothing as honest and natural as hair would live on him. 'And,' added Carl

Jenkins, 'like master, like dog. We all know that Highland Boy could never be trusted.'

There was a lot of muttered support for this opinion, and one or two bolder spirits began to threaten my uncle with violence. He sat unmoved, as if deaf.

'Oh, he's a fly one,' said Carl Jenkins. 'You won't find many as fly as Cedric. Have you ever known him to do an honest day's work? Never. All he does is sit in his shop, growing rich and planning the schemes and tricks by which he robs his friends of their money. He pretends,' continued Carl Jenkins with a sour irony, 'that the dog belongs to the boy there, but we all know the boy will do whatever Cedric tells him.'

The bus swung slowly round the corner at the end of Bennett Street and hung above the hill into High Street. My uncle tapped the driver on the shoulder as a signal that he should stop. The bus sidled in to the curb.

'How much money did he take over to Tredegar,' trumpeted Carl Jenkins, swollen with eloquence and sorrow, 'money which his trusting friends had asked him to put on that fine dog Special Request, which would have won if he hadn't been up to his criminal tricks? How much money did you steal from us, Cedric?'

The bus stopped, and my uncle stood up. His smile was genial and terrible. He looked slowly about him, nodding his head here and there, as if thoughtfully recognising certain people in front of him. His hands were deep in the pockets of his overcoat.

'Jump off, boy,' he said, 'and trot home all the way. The dog could do with a loosener.'

He didn't look at me at all. I scuffled under the seat for the rolling trophy, grabbed Highland Boy's lead, and prepared to jump.

'Two hundred and forty-one pounds,' my uncle said, very mildly. 'I took two hundred and forty-one pounds to Tredegar with me tonight, and a hundred of them were my own.'

He sighed deeply.

'Has anybody on this bus lost as much as I have?' he asked. 'A hundred pounds? Because I left the whole of that money, the whole two hundred and forty-one pounds, in the hands of the bookmakers. I've cheated nobody, and I've lost more money than anybody else. If there is a villain, then it's Highland Boy. But he ran a good race, he ran a fine race, and he beat us all. Hurry up, boy. And now, Carl Jenkins, I'll push your nose through the back of your neck and tie your lying mouth in a knot.'

As I jumped from the bus, already moving slowly, I saw my uncle advancing majestically upon his enemy, but although I pounded downhill after the bus, I saw no more.

I went home and told my father. He was sitting by the fire reading P.G. Wodehouse, which is what he did when he was very happy, usually on Saturday evenings and at Christmas, but when I told him that Uncle Cedric was fighting Carl Jenkins in the bus, he got up, put on his hat and coat, and left. I could not remember my father ever having left the house at night before.

Later, after perhaps an hour, he returned.

'Did you see Uncle Cedric?' I asked.

My father nodded.

'Was the fight over?'

My father thought about that one; he was a very precise man.

'It was all over as far as Carl Jenkins was concerned,' he answered, 'but there were one or two others your uncle felt aggrieved with. However, the police were about to arrive, and I persuaded Cedric that he ought to catch the late train to Cardiff, to stay with his cousins, just for a while. Now you'd better go to bed.'

For some weeks my grandmother kept behind the counter in my uncle's shop. When I went on Saturdays for my quarter of a pound of chocolate caramels, she would weigh them out with hairbreadth accuracy, five to the ounce, as if I were any casual customer. Life seemed to have lost much of its savour, and I was too dispirited to avoid Bertie Christopher wholeheartedly. I took to fighting him so often that I soon knew every move he was likely to make, although his right swing was always risky. In the end we knocked each other into a grudging friendship, and when Uncle Cedric came back from Cardiff after a month, I rather liked sharing my Saturday candy with Bertie and the other boys.

By that time my father had taken Highland Boy to live in the house. Without anybody saying anything, it was somehow agreed that his racing career was over. He had a basket down by the fire, but most of the time he'd be leaning against my father's knees, fawning on my old man in the most shameless manner. It used to be sickening to see them together, watching them walk down the garden with leisurely dignity, or stand silently together while they contemplated some gentle problem. It was annoying to see Highland Boy a reformed scoundrel, wearing his drab colour with the proud humility and decency of a deacon.

He lived with us for another twelve years, dying the month after Bertie Christopher went to work in London, but it was longer than that before I owned another greyhound.

The Mallard

This village is rich in ponds. I don't mean the enormous gravel pits, some of them many acres in area, which lie some miles to the west, although these are very remarkable. Once or twice during the war I flew above them at night and they were clearly visible, great sheets of calm, much lighter than the dark farmland and the little town they encircled. I like the gravel pits. A lot of wild ducks live on them — garganey, teal, the little black-and-white tufted duck, and of course the ubiquitous mallard.

But the ponds we have in the village are small and hidden. Driving through, I doubt if you'd notice one of them. Fed by the narrow streams that drain water off the downs, they stand at the corners of fields, hidden by clusters of unimportant trees. They are rarely more than twenty feet or so across, or more than three feet deep. I have one at the end of my paddock, where my two acres join Rasbridge's land. I suppose it's his pond rather than mine, since his house is very near it.

Come to that, this house of mine is built on what used to be a pond. When I bought the site I had the pond filled in, felled the enormous elms that fringed it, and dug a new channel for the stream. Where my front lawn is now, that was the pond.

There were mallard on it then, quite a number. Old Normanton, who lives up the lane in a converted barn, was out cutting the grass in one of the fields, Rasbridge's fields now but they weren't then, when he saw over his shoulder the whirling blades cut straight through a mallard duck. He stopped and jumped off. She was dead of course. She had sat tight on a nest of twelve eggs and the blades had sliced her. Oddly, the eggs were unharmed, and old Normanton put them in the hedge in his cap. When he went home for lunch he put them under a broody hen and they all hatched out in two or three days. Later, he clipped their wings and they all seemed to live fairly happily on the pond where my house is. By the time I filled the pond in, only one old drake was left from that original settlement. He could fly, but in a curious lopsided way, sideways to the face of the pond. Then, as he landed, he flicked his body somehow, so that he hit the water face down, or stomach down anyway.

They didn't move, these mallard, all through the time we were building the house. I think they were the descendants of some of Normanton's ducks and of an old Khaki Campbell duck which was still around. She was absolutely tame, of course, and so much the leader of the flock that they all followed her example. Some of the young duck were very much bigger than ordinary mallard, and a lot of them were paler too, and these were her children and grand-children. When we moved in eventually I had a lot of fun with these birds. They are pretty intelligent, are ducks. At night they used to lie around on the new banks of the stream and as I walked past them they'd gossip to me. I knew them individually. They were extraordinarily different. Every day the baker used to deliver a couple of stale loaves, just to feed them. There were two young drakes able to catch pieces of bread in their beaks while they were swimming, as if they were performing seals. We had some trouble occasionally. Youngsters would stone the ducks, particularly the baby ducks in May and June, and this used to make me mad, but in a way I could understand it too. After about three years the old boy who farmed most of the land around here retired, and Rasbridge moved in.

The first time I met Rasbridge was over the affair of the poplar trees. I saw old Normanton, who stayed on to work for Rasbridge, planting half a dozen young silver poplars at the edge of my paddock and went over to have a word with him. It isn't that I don't like the trees, but it was thoughtless to plant them there without asking how I felt about them. I have a marvellous view from the end of my little field, right over the flat, rich arable of Rasbridge's acres, on to Slindon Woods at the edge of the downs, and then the bare curve of the hills themselves. In May, as it is now, the downs gleam like chromium in the sun where the plough has laid the white chalk open. In two years, or less even, the quick-growing poplars would have taken most of this from me. I said as much to Normanton. He's a nice old man, real Sussex. I've known him for years.

'You're right,' he said. 'I never thought of that.'

'Do you think I could have a word with your boss about them?' I asked.

''Tisn't worth it,' he said. 'No, you leave that to me, look, and 'twill be all right.'

I left it to him. I saw him in the pub a few days later and he came over to me, shamefaced. I let him take his time over things because he's not a man you can hurry, and in the end he told me all about it.

'No luck about them poplars,' he said.

I didn't say anything. The technique is to let him assume you know all about everything and then he doesn't have the embarrass-ment of explaining.

'No,' he said, 'no luck.'

He took a long pull at his beer.

''Tis his wife,' he said, 'but she shouldn't have said what she did. I told Mr Rasbridge straight. That house of Mr Simmonds, I said, is a pretty little house and Mrs Rasbridge hasn't got any call to say what she did. A terrible little modern house she called it. She can only see it from two of her upstairs windows anyway.'

I laughed. I didn't think I cared what she thought, but I must have.

'Have another pint,' I said to old Normanton.

'Thank you, Mr Simmonds,' he said. 'That'll be lovely.'

We both looked out of the window at the dusty Sunday cars racing to the sea.

'Beans he's got in that field,' said old Normanton, 'dwarf beans. We're growing them for the frozen-food people. Very particular they are, make us use some very strong sprays to keep the weeds down. I shouldn't be surprised, then, if those trees, young like that, was to take permanent harm from a strong dose of spray.'

He looked at me guilelessly before he smiled. I could see suddenly what he'd been like as a boy.

Rasbridge introduced himself to me a week or so later. He was a tall, thin man with a bony and rather refined face. He spoke quickly, with real energy. His teeth were large and yellow and he wore a grey moustache.

'Sorry about those trees,' he said. 'Didn't think you'd object. Make a very necessary windbreak, you know. That's a damnably draughty house we have.'

The house had been there for five hundred years and had its old trees all around it.

'Oh, that's all right,' I said, and I smiled as falsely as he did.

One night in the summer I took out my thin pruning saw and cut a neat circle around the base of every one of those poplars. I felt like a murderer when I did it, because the sap was strong and under the bark the flesh was wet and living. I painted the soft, white wood with some stuff I bought for the purpose and walked home whistling. All the trees died except one, and that's so maimed and runt I can scarcely bear to look at it. They rotted at the bottom and the young leaves shrivelled and died. In November a strong wind blew all five poisoned trees to the ground and they were never replaced.

But by that time my ducks were gone.

We had a lot of young mallard that year and it was the habit of people in the village to bring up their small children to see them.

There's nothing quite as engaging as ducklings and when I saw two strange youngsters in my garden, a boy of about ten and a girl some years younger, looking at the ducks, I wasn't surprised. They were pleasant children, confident and polite, and I liked them. I showed them all my parlour tricks, how I called the birds down to feed them, how I soaked the bread for them in a large bowl. They were charming children.

That evening I heard young voices calling from Rasbridge's garden.

'Bill bill bill bill bill!' they called, exactly as I did, and a group of young, unattached drakes cocked their glossy heads and took off for Rasbridge's pond. I saw them feather over the tall horse chestnut that shades his water and imagined them dropping down with a flutter of their braking wings. My ducklings grew up and, in the natural way of things, dispersed. A number of older birds went too. By summer's end I had less than half a dozen mallard on my stream and soon they went too. In the colder mornings I could hear them call from Rasbridge's yard. They were probably being fed grain there. My stream is too small to support many birds anyway. I was left with the old Khaki Campbell. Her domesticity kept her with me. She died about the time the poplars were blown down. I found her in the stream. She was very old and had been lame for weeks. Perhaps she hadn't enjoyed life without her flock around her.

I've never had birds permanently on my water since, although I always get a pair or two come over in March, bring up their two broods, and go back again to Rasbridge's. One of the ducks I've grown to know well. She's a small, dark bird with the loudest and most demanding voice I've ever heard. When she's sitting, and I've never been able to find her nest, she flies in about six-thirty in the morning and demands to be fed. I have it all ready for her and get up in my dressing gown, go down to the garden, and feed her. She talks to me all the time she eats, chuckling and muttering confidentially. A duck can't look at you directly, since their eyes are set at the sides of their heads, so they turn to look at you with one beady eye. This gives them a comically knowing expression. When she'd see there was no more food she'd race over the lawn and plunge into the water, throwing it ecstatically over her back and head as she rocked vigorously backward and forward. Then she'd squawk once or twice, swim up the stream, and take off. I'd see her circle the house, her neck outstretched, her hammerhead set at an angle.

'Bill bill bill!' I'd call, and she'd give one raucous answer before flying swiftly off, her stubby wings flashing.

In the warm afternoons the young drakes come over and sit on
the lawn or indulge in loud splashing horseplay in the water. They
are incredibly handsome in their breeding plumage, reminding me
of groups of very young men dressed in their finery, parading for no
other purpose than the gallant manipulation of their fashionable
clothes. My friends and I were rather like this, when we were sixteen
or seventeen.

When I was sixteen I thought I would be a great athlete. I didn't
know whether to be a footballer or a boxer, but I trained assiduously
every day. I belonged to a good amateur boxing club in those days
and often represented it at tournaments. I was a slender boy, nearly
always taller than my opponents, and I had been taught to box in
the orthodox way, upright, elegant, left hand out. I was quite good
at it. Sometimes, however, something startling happened to me. If
I were very confident, or if I were hurt, my style changed suddenly,
and without my being able to do anything about it. I seemed to drop
into a crouching, urgent stance, my feet close together, and my left
hand swinging low across my body. It would hook to the body and
head of the boy I was fighting with an accuracy and ferocity that had
nothing to do with me. It was like being taken over; perhaps it was
a sort of inspiration. Anyway, it frightened me. At last I spoke to my
father about it. It was no good going to him for pleasant conversation
— you had to have something serious to say before you dared bother
him — but he was marvellous when you were in trouble. He listened
very carefully, nodding now and then in encouragement and understanding. When I had finished he looked at me quietly and said, 'If
I were you, I'd give it up now'.

So I did. It was very easy and direct. I often think of things like
this when I look at the young drakes.

Last Tuesday my dark mallard duck didn't come to be fed as
usual. I got up early just the same. There had been some shooting
the night before in the fields behind the house, but I hadn't taken
much notice of it. Rasbridge's boy after pigeons I thought. I got the
car out when it became obvious my duck wasn't hungry, and drove
through the early lanes on the downs.

Just before lunch, about eleven o'clock I suppose, I went down to
the end of my paddock and found the duck. She was dead. She had
been shot through the breast and she was dead and stiff. I picked
her up. She was unbelievably light and her poor feathers were dry
and harsh. Her eye was a blob of excrement. That morning I had
seen in one of the lanes the body of a hare which had been knocked
by a car. A crow was standing on it, tearing at the soft belly. I had

accepted this as one of the things that happened, but I was shaking
angry as I brought the duck home. I buried her in the garden,
knowing how useless it was.

I had a bad night that night, unusual for me, and I didn't sleep
much until morning. When I got up I didn't want breakfast, so I
went into the garden. The baker's van was down the road a little
way. He was probably delivering to Mrs Rogers. I walked down the
drive and leaned on the gate. Rasbridge drove up in his green estate
car. When he saw me, he pulled up and leapt out.

'A pleasant day, Simmonds,' he said.

I opened the gate and walked toward him.

'Things are beginning to move,' he said. 'I've just been over to
see my wheat and it looks good, really good.'

He looked over the gate at my roses.

'By Jove,' he said, 'your garden is looking very well too.'

He smiled at me as if the sun shone for him alone.

'By the way,' he said, 'I've had to cull some of the mallard. Far
too many of them, you know — they're keeping me poor.'

I don't know what I said, but he stopped laughing and swung at
me. It was pitiable really. I'd hit him twice before his fist had finished
its backswing, and a slow trickle of blood came from his nose. Then
suddenly I was crouching and weaving, my left hooking him to head
and body so hard I thought he'd snap. Whatever it was I had thought
buried in me was not dead. There was no need for the right hand I
gave him as he went down. I would have stamped on him, I think,
if the baker hadn't grabbed me. Strangely enough I wasn't upset. I
looked down at Rasbridge, at his yellow face with the quick swelling
on the temple above his right eyebrow, the bruise on the cheekbone
and the right side of his jaw. I suppose I must have hit him seventeen
or eighteen times.

The baker, kneeling near him, looked up at me, his eyes round
and staring.

'You'd better bring him into my terrible little modern house,'
I said.

'No sir,' said the man, 'I'll take him home.'

When he could stand, we helped Rasbridge into his car and the
baker drove him home. I've heard nothing about him since then and
that was two days ago.

My wife came home from town and I told her all about it. She's
a good girl and didn't say very much, but this afternoon she asked
me if I thought the life of a duck was worth such a disaster.

'Too damn right it is,' I said, but I knew what she meant. We've been over to Rasbridge's several times for a meal or drinks, and they've been here too. I like those two kids of his very much. I suppose he was entitled to think I was his friend. Sometimes I think it must have looked very comic, Rasbridge and I brawling outside the front gate. After all, I'm fifty-two and he must be at least three years older. But the way I hit him wasn't funny at all. I saw myself unawares in the hall mirror this morning and for the first time in my life I look older than my years.

I haven't been outside the house for two days. I don't know what to do.

A Big Night

I used to train at the Ex-Servicemen's Club three nights a week,
Tuesdays, Wednesdays, and Fridays. Training began at six, but
I was always late on Tuesdays and Wednesdays because of homework. I used to like getting there a bit late. As I hurried through the
long passage that ran beside the room where the old, dry miners —
hardly any of them ex-servicemen — were drinking away their age
and disappointment, I would hear above me the slithering feet of
the other boys as they moved around the ring or the punch-bags and
the pungent smell of the liniment would come greenly down the
stairs to meet me. I would watch them working out a bit first, looking
particularly for my friends Bobby Ecclestone and Charlie Nolan,
before going into the dressing room to change into my shoes and
shorts. I used to wear black shorts with a yellow band round the
waist and a yellow stripe at the side of each leg. In Warrilow's Sports
Emporium they had satin boxing shorts, immaculate and colourful.
Mine were home-made. Most of the time I used to skip. I loved that
rope and I could do some very fancy skipping, very fast and for a
very long time. Tiredness was something I'd only heard about. Then
I'd box a few rounds with Charlie and Bobby, and sometimes with
one of the older and more skilful boys. They were always very kind,
showing me how to slip a left lead, or how to move on the ropes. I
hardly ever used the heavy, shapeless punching bags; when you're
thirteen years old and weigh eighty pounds it doesn't seem very
necessary. Then I'd do some exercises on the mat and finish off with
another burst of skipping.

Boxing with Charlie Nolan was best of all. Charlie had been in
school with me, in the next desk, until he'd moved to another
district. He was almost the same age and size as I was and his
footwork was a miracle of economy and precision. His feet brushed
the floor like a whisper as he moved perfectly about me, in a kind
of smooth ritual. I, on the other hand, would jig up and down in a
flashy and wasteful way, careering around the ring at top speed and
not caring very much where I got to. But Charlie's hands were slow.
They would sit calmly in front of him, now and again mildly
exploring the space between us, and I would hit him with a variety
of harmless punches that left him blinking and smiling. As he passed
us, Ephraim Hamer, our trainer, would say, 'Well done, Charlie!'.
He rarely said anything to me. After we'd showered we'd sit about

listening to the bigger boys, or boasting quietly between us. Bobby
Ecclestone would tell us about his work in a grocer's shop; he was
errand boy in the shop where we bought our groceries and I often
saw him sweeping the sawdust boards, or staggering out with huge
loads to the delivery van. It was Bobby who had first brought me to
the Ex-Servicemen's Club. He was fifteen and the best boxer among
the boys.

One Friday evening after we had finished working out and we were
sitting warm and slumped on the benches, Bobby asked me if I was
going to the weigh-in the next day. I didn't even know what it was.
I was always finding that there were whole areas of experience,
important areas too, about which I knew nothing and other boys
everything.

'Where is it?' I said carefully.

'Down at the Stadium. One o'clock,' said Charlie. 'I'm going.'

Everything fell into place. Next day at the Stadium our local hero,
Cuthbert Fletcher, who everyone said would have been feather-
weight champion of Wales except that he was coloured, was to fight
Ginger Thomas, the official champion.

'Are you going?' I asked Bobby.

'Of course,' he said. 'It's my dinner-time. See you outside at
ten to.'

All Saturday morning I hung about in a fever of anxiety in case
my lunch wouldn't be ready for me in time to meet Bobby and
Charlie at one o'clock outside the Stadium. But it was, and I was
the first there, although Charlie was not long behind me. He hadn't
had his lunch and was eating a huge round of bread and jam which
he'd cut for himself from a new loaf. Bobby wouldn't let us go inside
the Stadium until Charlie had finished eating. A few men hung
about in a corner of the empty hall, their hands deep in their overcoat
pockets. They whispered softly and tunelessly and they all carried
an air of vast unconcern, but when Cuthbert and Ginger Thomas
appeared, they hurried forward to greet the boxers, talking excitedly
to them. It was exciting too. I don't know why it should have been
so, but we all felt a curious tightening of the air as the boxers smiled
formally at each other. Cuthbert stepped on the scales first, and a
great fat man adjusted the weights, flicking them up and down the
bar with finicky little movements of his enormous fingers before he
called out, in a high voice, 'Eight stone and twelve pounds, gentlemen'.

Cuthbert smiled, ducked his round, crinkly head at his friends,
and moved away. Ginger Thomas was a lean, pale man, elegant and

graceful, his mahogany hair brushed smooth and close to his head. He, too, stood on the scales and his weight was called in the fat man's brittle tenor. Everybody shook hands and at once the place was deserted.

'That's all right then,' said Bobby.

'Nothing in it for weight,' said Charlie.

We stood together silently, for a long time.

'Are you going to the fight?' asked Bobby.

'No,' said Charlie, 'my father won't let me.'

Bobby looked at his shoes as they scuffed the ground in front of him, first the right shoe, then the left one.

'I can't go,' he said. 'Don't finish in time on Saturdays.'

'I expect I'll go,' I said, 'if I want to.'

'Will you?' said Charlie, his eyes big.

'I expect so,' I said, although I knew I couldn't.

At eight that evening I was in Court Street, one of the crowd milling around the Stadium, knowing I could not get in. Slow, comfortable groups of men with money and tickets moved confidently through towards the entrance, talking with assurance about the fights they had seen in the past. On the steps near the door Trevor Bunce danced up and down, his wide, cheeky face smiling as he asked the men to take him in with them. An arrogant boy and leader of his gang, Trevor Bunce was bigger than I was. You could see him everywhere. Incredibly active, his string-coloured hair hanging over his eyes, he bounced with energy through a series of escapades wherever you went. The street lights came on suddenly, and we all cheered. I knew with certainty that Trevor Bunce would get in somehow.

Now the whole road was thick with people and the few cars prodding through to outlying districts honked and revved with impatience and frustration. I moved cautiously to the pavement. I saw that, prudently, they had built a temporary barrier of corrugated sheets of metal above the low wall which separated a little yard, belonging to the Stadium, from the road. On lesser occasions many daring boys had climbed this wall — an easy feat — and run through a nest of little rooms into the hall itself. There was even a large door, always locked, which led directly into the raucous noise where even now the first of the bouts was being decided.

As I looked at the new metal sheets, Trevor Bunce threw himself past me, leapt on the wall, and, with unbelievable strength, forced back the long edge of the barrier. For a moment only, it was wide enough for a boy to wriggle though and Trevor Bunce did just that.

But before he was half clear, the inexorable metal wall snapped back, pinning him at the waist, his legs kicking wildly; and even as we looked, we heard clearly and without mistake, a sound as of a dry stick breaking. Then Trevor Bunce began to scream.

In seconds, it seems to me now, we had ripped away the corrugated wall and its wooden framework, and men's gentle arms carried Trevor away. I saw him as he went, his face white and wet, but his eyes were open. He cradled his right forearm carefully, because it was broken.

By this time many of us were in the yard itself, aimlessly stacking the six-foot sheets of tin in an untidy heap near the wall. There must have been forty or fifty of us; boys, young workless men, and a few older men who were there by chance, it seemed. Yet, haphazard and leaderless as we were, we suddenly lifted our restive heads and, like some swollen river, streamed for the door that led to the Stadium's lesser rooms.

I didn't want to go with them. Some shred of caution tried hard to hold me back, but my treacherous legs hurried me on, gasping. We met nobody, except in a corridor an old man wiping saucers with a wet cloth. He pressed himself against the wall, his mouth wide open, and we were past him before he got a word out. And then we were in the great hall itself, our force broken against the huge weight of the legal customers. We lost ourselves among them at once.

The noise, the heat, the immense, expectant good humour made the whole place intoxicating, but I could see nothing except, high overhead, a blue, unshifting cloud of cigarette smoke. Agile though I was, I could not push or wriggle another inch nearer the ring. It was Freddie Benders who came to my help. Freddie didn't fight much, because he was nearly thirty years old. His ears were rubbery and he had few teeth, but he often came down to the club and sometimes he'd let us spar with him. You could hit him with everything you had, right on the chin, even, and he'd only laugh.

When he saw me he shouted out, 'Make room for the boy there, let the boy get down to the front'.

Grumbling and laughing, the men inched more closely together and I squeezed my way almost to the ringside.

'That's right,' shouted Freddie. 'That boy is going to make a good 'un. Keep your eyes on Cuthbert tonight, boy!'

I saw the fight. I saw every moment of the fifteen rounds, and it was a great fight, I know it was. Yet all the time it was on, all the time incisive Ginger Thomas moved forward with a speed and viciousness I had not imagined, what I really saw was Trevor Bunce's white face, what I heard was the stark snapping of his bones. When the fighters moved around the ring, the crowd was silent and absorbed and at the end of each round there was a great sigh before they clapped and shouted. I think Ginger Thomas won, but at the end the referee held Cuthbert's arm up and we all cheered, with relief and pride rather than with certainty. Ginger Thomas stood in the centre of the ring, aloof and unmoved; his pale eyes glittered in the arc-lights, and then he turned and swaggered easily away. His lack of emotion disturbed me more than the terrible, precise fury and venom of his attacks.

When I got home my parents had nothing to say to me. I was so late, my crime was so enormous, that all they could do was to point to the stairs; I hurried up to my room to shiver gratefully under the icy sheets. I knew I should never sleep again and, even as I realised this, fell at once to sleep. When I awoke all was dark and confusing, and my right forearm was throbbing with pain. Struggling with darkness, I found the fingers of my left hand tight in a cramping grip around my right arm. The pain made me think of poor Trevor Bunce, in hospital surely, and I felt with quick relief the whole, frail bones in my own arms.

The following Tuesday I was late getting to the Club, but only because I had found my French homework particularly difficult. I waved to the boys, changed eagerly, and soon had the old skipping-rope humming away. Everything began to feel fine. It wasn't until I put the gloves on to spar with Charlie Nolan that I realised that something was wrong. I kept on seeing Ginger Thomas, destructive and graceful, his hands cocked, moving into Cuthbert, as he had on the Saturday night. I could see his face, relaxed and faintly curious, the sudden blur as he released three or four short punches before sliding away. I knew too that I was doing this to Charlie, but I couldn't stop. Charlie was bleeding from the mouth and nose and he was pawing away with his gloves open. I could tell he was frightened. Yet I kept on ripping punches at him, my hands suddenly hard and urgent and the huge, muffling gloves we used no longer clumsy. I could hear Mr Hamer shouting as Charlie hid in a corner and then somebody had me around the waist, throwing me almost across the ring. Charlie was crying, but in a little while Bobby Ecclestone put an arm round Charlie's shoulders, talking to him softly. Nobody said anything to me and I sat on the bench. I thought I was quivering all over, but when I looked at my legs they were all right. I felt as if I were going to be sick. Nothing seemed to matter very much. I walked to the dressing room and began to change. I was so tired that it was an effort to take off my ring clothes, and when I pulled my vest over my head I could feel my face wet with my own tears. I took a good look at the room before I went out, then I shut the door behind me, very quietly. It sounded just as it always had, the slithering of the shoes around the ball or the heavy bag, the rhythmical slapping of the rope on the boards as somebody did some lively skipping.

Nobody saw me go. As I went down the stairs I could see through the window little groups of quiet drinkers in the room below, but they could not see me in the dark passage.

I never went back there. Sometimes when I went for groceries, some cheese maybe, or some canned stuff, I would see Bobby Ecclestone in the shop. He didn't say anything to me and I didn't say anything to him. It was as if we had never been friends.

A House Divided

I'm glad I had my boyhood before the war, before the '39 war, that is. I'm glad I knew the world when it was innocent and golden and that I grew up in a tiny country whose borders had been trampled over so often that they had been meaningless for centuries. My home was in a mining town fast growing derelict, in Wales, and the invincible scrawny grass and scrubby birch trees were beginning to cover the industrial rubbish that lay in heaps about us.

It all seemed very beautiful to me, the small, tottering cottages in peeling rows on the hillside, the pyramids of black spoil that lay untidily above them, the rivers thick as velvet where the brown trout were beginning to appear again. But I read in a book that the last great silver fish had been caught there in 1880, and I knew there had been a more complete perfection, a greener Eden.

Further west was such a green county, Carmarthenshire. When I was eleven years old, I was put on a bus for Carmarthen town, there to meet my aunt with whom I was to stay for a whole summer month, and it was then that I entered into my kingdom. My aunt met me at the coach station and we got into a smaller bus, full to its racks with people, parcels, chickens, bundles of newspapers, two sheep dogs. I had never seen grass so ablaze with emerald, nor a river so wide and jocund as the Towy. The bus was full of the quick Welsh language of which I didn't know a word, so I sat warily on the hard edge of my seat, observing from the rims and corners of my eyes. My aunt said nothing to me.

Groaning brokenly, the bus hauled up the hills north of the town, lurching to an occasional amiable halt in the centres of the villages, outside the doors of simple inns, at deserted cross-roads high on the moors. Through its hot, moving windows I saw small white farmhouses appear, one after the other, each at the heart of an aimless cluster of irregular fields. I knew I would sleep that night in such a house. I had never been away before, not even for one night. I looked at my silent and terrible aunt. She grinned suddenly, dug me ferociously in the ribs, and gave me a round, white peppermint. Comforted, I worked my tongue around the hot sweet. It was going to be all right.

We had reached the flat top of the mountain and the little bus throbbed doggedly along an uncompromisingly straight road. Then we began to drop, running through sweeping shallow bends that took us lower and lower into a valley of unbelievable lushness. As the nose of the bus turned this way and that, I caught glimpses of a superb river, rich and wide, its brilliant surface paler than the sky it reflected. My aunt and I got off at the river bridge. The stone parapets were built in little triangular bays. You could wait in them while traffic passed. My aunt and I did this, and I looked down into the water, relishing its music, its cold clarity dappled over stones.

We had perhaps half a mile to walk, the road turning from the river as it swung south, and then we took a farm track back in the direction of the water. We passed but one house all the time we walked and that was a small, one-storied cottage with a low door and three windows set in its front. An old woman sat straight-backed on a wooden settle outside the door. She was shelling peas, placing the pale green ovals as if they were pearls into a china basin held in her lap, letting the empty pods fall into a bucket. She didn't stop doing this all the time she was talking to my aunt. Her long dress, made of some hard material, had been worn and washed to a faded blue. At her throat was a gold broach which said 'Mother'.

'That's Mrs Lewis,' said my aunt. 'A tough old bird, she is.'

I looked back at Mrs Lewis, upright and purposeful outside her front door in the evening sunlight.

'Is she very old then?' I asked.

'Not so old,' my aunt said. 'Over sixty though, I expect. She used to work the farm next to us until last year. Worked it on her own, she did. Now she lets it to her nephew, Emrys. You'll see him about — his farm is on the river side of this lane and ours down here, on the right.'

My case began to get heavy, so I hoisted it on to my shoulder.

Not long afterward we turned off the lane and followed a little stream which took us to the house, where my uncle was waiting.

I can't remember what else happened that day, but the pattern of following days is clear in my mind. Every morning I'd get up reasonably early, wash, and go downstairs to the kitchen. My uncle, a plump, voluble man, would begin talking as soon as he heard my foot on the stairs, and was already launched into some wild tale when I got into the room. He would be stretching up, on the tips of his small feet, to cut rashers from the side of bacon which hung from the beamed ceiling. The knife he used was large, black-handled, and sharp as fright. The bacon, pallid with fat, had two streaks of lean meat running meanly through it, and it swung about as he cut, but years of practice allowed my uncle to carve a slice as uniformly thin

as if it had been done by machine. The frying pan, and the kettle
too for that matter, hung from hooks above the enormous fire. My
uncle always cooked my breakfast. He would take three of the yellow
rashers and place them gently in the iron pan, adding, when the fat
had begun to run, a thick slice of bread. Then he'd crack an egg and
put that in. It was delicious. The bacon, crisp and dry, broke
beneath my knife; the bread, fried brown on the outside, was
succulent and full as a sponge with warm fat. Every morning my
uncle would put my plate before me with a mild pride. He never
stopped talking to me. He stood in front of his fire, his thumbs in
his pockets, rocking gently forward and backward on his tiny feet,
his eyes opening wide when he reached the climax of some innocent
tale. When I'd finished my food he would go off to the fields, there
to work with furious, haphazard energy. He had always finished,
apart from the evening milking, by early afternoon.

Sometimes I worked with him and he liked this. But more often
I would wander away on some inconclusive ploy of my own. Once
I tracked the source of the little stream which supplied all our water
at the farm, and which had never run dry, they said, even in the
hottest summers. It started less than a mile away, in the foothills, a
small, round pool filled by three bubbling heads of water. I stayed
almost a whole morning, lying on the grass, watching the water burst
through a fine white sand, grains of which were carried up and away
in an erratic dance. After a time I began to see that there was a kind
of regularity in the way the springs gushed up, a kind of pattern. I
told my uncle about the springs. He had never been there, but my
aunt said she went once a year to clear it of leaves. There were no
trees near it. I think she used to go there just to see the sand dancing.

By this time I'd met Emrys Hughes, Mrs Lewis' nephew and our
neighbour, so I thought I was entitled to walk over his land, too. The
first time I did this I saw Emrys standing beside his dairy. I waved
to him, but he didn't wave back. He stood there a moment as if
confused, then he turned and dived out of sight. I told my aunt and
uncle about this.

'Oh, he's very shy, is Emrys,' my uncle said. 'You needn't worry
about that. He don't mind you being on his land, not at all. He'd
like you to go over.'

My aunt sniffed gently.

'Emrys is very nice,' she said, 'very helpful.'

She thought deeply and then gave her judgement.

'Yes, very nice,' she said delicately, 'but not quite the round
penny, if you know what I mean.'

I thought of Emrys, of his long awkward body and innocent, gentle face, of his habit of ducking his head at meaningless moments. I could see what she meant.

'Oh, he's all right,' said my uncle stoutly. 'He's his father all over again, and old Dafydd Hughes never did a mite of harm to anybody.'

So I continued to walk through Emrys's fields and after a while he waved back at me and even spoke to me. He had very little English and our conversation was simple and limited. Mostly we'd stand and beam at each other. His wife was more talkative altogether, and I got into the habit of calling at their house about mid-morning. We used to drink tea, the three of us, out of large Victorian cups, and eat a great many of the round flat cakes full of currants that were baked on a thick iron plate directly above the open fire. I used to read the local paper to Emrys and his wife. It didn't occur to me until much later that they couldn't read. They were both about twenty-three when first I went to stay with my aunt.

Emrys's farm had one great advantage over ours; it was bordered on the west by the miraculous river. What I liked to do was to have my breakfast, do a few jobs about the farm, and then go over to Emrys's. I'd read to them, or we'd hold one of our slow, repetitive conversations, and then, very gently and by a roundabout route so that I would enjoy the going, I'd go down to the river. But one morning I awoke particularly early, startling my uncle, who was alone in the kitchen, singing and cooking his own breakfast.

'Good God, boy!' he said. 'What's the matter? Can't you sleep?'

We had our food together and I went straight out into the early world. I had never known that such pure light existed and I was suddenly and overwhelmingly filled with a wish to see the river. I ran through Emrys's fields toward the water, and even some distance off I could see the man on the far bank, staggering slightly and hauling away at his fishing rod. When I arrived at the bank, gasping, I could see he'd got into something big, his rod bent in a deep arc from the butt, held in his gripping hands, to the tip which was only inches above the water. I couldn't see the line, even when he heaved sturdily back before winding in. He was not a young man and he wore a clergyman's collar.

'I wish you were over here,' he called. 'I've been half an hour with this one, and I could do with some help.'

I ran for the bridge, over it, and down the other bank, splashing through stony shallows most of the way. But it took me seven or eight minutes and by the time I'd got down to the old boy he'd landed his fish. I'd never seen anything so enormous, nor so beautiful. I spoke for some time to the old man, but apart from the fact that he was on a fishing holiday and that he lived in the Midlands, I can remember nothing of him. I can remember everything about the salmon. I could take you now, at this moment, to the place where I first saw him lying hugely in the grass, his great head up against a clump of dock. I know the gradations of his colour, the position of his every scale. A trickle of blood came over his lower jaw.

'A fresh-run fish,' the old man said.

I didn't know what he meant, but I knew that I soon would. I went home in a daze. I was caught, all right.

It was easier than I had imagined. Both my uncle and aunt thought it entirely natural that I should want to catch salmon.

'Where's that old rod of mine, Marged?' asked my uncle. 'The boy can begin with that. I'll get him a licence when I call into town. Don't forget, boy, the river is dangerous, you'll have to learn it like a book. And have a word with Emrys — he's a marvel with fish, is Emrys.'

He was, too. Boys learn a great deal by imitation, and I learned by imitating Emrys. He knew where every salmon in the river was to be found; he could point out places where legendary fish of the past had been caught by his father or his uncle. I was killing biggish fish right from the beginning, most of them with an old two-piece greenheart that Emrys had used when he was a boy. He had a box full of tied flies, lures of an entirely local pattern that I've never seen anywhere else, although I've caught fish all over the world since. I still have them, the old greenheart and Emrys's box of flies. I've not used either of them since 1948, when I bought the first of my split-cane rods. When my month was up I didn't want to go home.

My uncle jollied me along.

'Time you went,' he said. 'The boys in the Cerys Arms are complaining that there won't be a fish in the river unless we send you home soon.'

He loaded me with gifts, shook hands as if we had been friends for fifty years, and told me to come back at Easter.

'March,' he said. 'That's when the season begins. We'll be waiting for you.'

So year after year I spent my springs and summers in that fertile and timeless place. I'd go to into town the day after my arrival. I'd go into Mr Protheroe's shop and buy my river licence. Mr Protheroe would tell me what fish had been caught already and I'd inspect his new stock of tackle. Then it was off to the water. Although Emrys came with me less often than on my early visits, we always had at least five or six long days together. We did some night-fishing, too, after sea trout. The river was unbelievably busy then, its noises louder and more mysterious than in secure daylight, its cool air hawked by bats and soft-flying owls.

The summer of '39 was long and hot, and the river had fallen sadly below fishing level. One Sunday morning Emrys and I were out on the water, fishing for memories mostly. We sat on the bank, throwing a line now and then over runs where we'd caught good fish in other years. The water was warm and stale, and we knew it was no good hoping for anything. The little salmon parr, little fingerlings, sidled lazily in the shallows. We saw my uncle come slowly through the fields, head bowed under the sun.

'Daro!' said Emrys. 'It must be hot to make your uncle walk slow like that.'

But it wasn't the heat. He had come to tell us that war had been declared. We didn't say much about it. We walked back to the house and I packed my case and tackle, mounted the old Rudge Whitworth motor-cycle I owned at the time, and rode home. I knew that the world of summer fishing had come to an end. It was time for me to go elsewhere. Within a year I was in the Army.

My uncle wrote to me once a fortnight, on Sundays. His careful letters, the narrow, upright script, kept me informed of all his artless news. I learned that old Mrs Lewis had suffered a stroke and was bedridden, that Emrys and his wife had left the farm to live with her. The local lawyer, Lemuel Evans, had found a tenant for the farm until such time as Emrys could return.

Later, Emrys was called up. I couldn't imagine him in the Army. He was thirty years old then, and more naïve than most children. In the intervals of keeping myself out of the more senseless military activities, I sometimes thought of Emrys. I needn't have worried. Unable to read, his English an almost unintelligible dialect, he was of little value to the Army. He was sent home after serving for three months.

In the spring of 1944 I had some embarkation leave and I spent a week of it at the farm. There was nobody at home when I arrived — it was market day at Cardigan — but the door was never locked in that house. I went inside, dumped my case, got my rod out, and tackled up. I thought I could get half an hour in before my aunt and uncle returned, and I walked through the familiar fields of what had been Emrys's farm, savouring every moment. When I got to the

water I unhooked my fly from the cork butt and got some line out
ready to cast. The water looked right, a lot of it and a beautiful clear
brown, the colour of the peat bogs it came from. I gave my rod a
flick or two, just to clear my wrist, then threw a long cast across the
pool. Someone shouted behind me, but I took my time, keeping the
line nice and tight until I was ready to reel in. Then I looked around.

He was a thickset man, dark and hard, in his late thirties. I smiled
at him.

'What do you think you're doing?' he said.

I told him who I was.

'I know who you are,' he said, 'You have no more right to fish my
water than anyone else.'

I explained that both Emrys and Mrs Lewis had always allowed
me to fish there, but I could see it was useless. I didn't want trouble
and he looked strong enough for caution. Holding my rod above my
head, I walked out of his farmyard and up the lane. I thought of
calling at Mrs Lewis's cottage to complain to her or to Emrys, but
there was a little car outside the door when I reached the house, so
I walked on. I crossed the bridge over the river, climbed the stile,
and moved down the opposite bank. I could see my uncle's surly
neighbour standing where I'd left him. I stood with the width of the
river between us, and cast in. I've never been a stylish angler;
effective perhaps, but never stylish. But that cast was perfect. I put
the fly down as effortlessly as it could be done, the line unrolling
smoothly forward on the unblemished surface, the lure falling
naturally as thistledown. It was taken at once, as I knew it would
be, and I landed the fish after fifteen minutes. It was the biggest fish
I'd ever caught and I still haven't equalled it. Just over eighteen
pounds it went, and I cast for it, hooked it, and landed it under the
furious, silent gaze of the man on the other side of the river. It was
very satisfying. After I'd pulled it out I went lower down and caught
two more, both over twelve pounds. I wasn't out more than a couple
of hours altogether, and then I waded across downstream, just above
an old woollen mill where Emrys and I sometimes fished, and
walked back across the fields to my uncle's house. After supper I
told my people about their neighbour's boorish behaviour.

'We don't have much to do with him,' said my uncle.

He looked uncomfortable and ashamed.

'He's not a nice man, do you see,' my aunt said, 'not like poor
Emrys.'

I could see they didn't want to talk about him, so I said no more.
Emrys and his wife came in shortly after. They were pleased and

excited. We had a merry evening, but Emrys would say nothing about his three months in the Army, however closely I pressed him.

'I didn't like it there,' he said. 'It was terrible in the Army.'

'Lemuel Evans came to see the aunt today,' said Mrs Hughes. 'She signed the will. Left everything to Emrys she has, the cottage, the farm, everything. Mr Evans read it out to us, then the aunt signed the will, two copies, then Emrys and me.'

'Why should you sign it?' asked my uncle.

'We are the witnesses,' said Mrs Hughes. 'Emrys has always been able to sign his name, although he's no scholar, of course.'

'Stands to reason I'd have to sign it,' said Emrys. 'All the money comes to me, doesn't it?'

'I'm very glad,' my aunt said. 'Let's hope that Mrs Lewis has many years of happy life in front of her and that when her time comes nothing goes wrong to spoil what is to come to you. You've been very good to her, the two of you.'

When they'd gone I spoke to my uncle about the will. I thought it unlikely that beneficiaries could witness a will they would eventually gain from.

'Say nothing,' said my uncle cautiously. 'Don't get involved in it. We are no match for the lawyers.'

I looked at him and saw with compassion that he had grown old. His talk, that bubbling mixture of innocent wild tales, chuckles, exclamations of surprise and delight, now held long silences also. Sometimes I caught him with a strange look in his eyes, as if he were measuring long distances. He died when I was abroad and my aunt lived only a few years after him.

After the war I didn't go back there. There seemed no reason for it, although I often went down into Pembrokeshire. Last month, though, I took the mid-Wales route and found myself again on that old river bridge. I left the car at the head of the lane and walked down. It seemed unchanged, but Mrs Lewis's cottage was empty and unkempt, its windows covered by an untidy lace of cobwebs and fine dirt. I started to go on to the farm, but couldn't face it now that my people were dead and strangers lived there. I pushed my way through hawthorn and nettle into Mrs Lewis's garden. The apple trees, mossed to the twigs, were covered with the hard red apples I remembered so well. There were greenfinches in the hedge, marvellous birds. I walked around the cottage, remembering. The roof looked sound and dry, the walls sturdy. You can often buy such a cottage for surprisingly little. I could use it for weekends and fish these waters again.

I drove back into town and went into Mr Protheroe's shop, walking into the back room as I'd always done. He was sitting there, white-haired and frail, but quite recognisably the man who had sold me so many bits and pieces of my youth. He had a box of flies in front of him. Mallard and claret they were, beautiful flies. I bought a dozen and then I told him who I was. It was heartwarming to be remembered.

'Come down for some fishing?' he asked.

I told him that my interest was rather different, that I had seen old Mrs Lewis's cottage and thought of buying it. He was pleased.

'You ought to come back,' he said. 'There have always been members of your family hereabouts. I went to school with your uncles.'

'We haven't been here for twenty-five years,' I said.

'That's not long when we're talking of families,' he said. 'Old Mrs Lewis's cottage now. It could look very nice with a bit of paint here and there and a good cleanup. Nobody's lived there since she died, or a few months after. Lemuel Evans is the man for you to see. His office is just up the street, next to the Post Office.'

'I expect Emrys Hughes went back to the farm,' I said.

'Well, no,' said old Protheroe. 'There was a big shock over that. When Mrs Lewis died and the will was proved, it turned out that she'd left every mortal thing to Lemuel Evans. The farm, the cottage, every mortal thing. There was a lot of talk, of course.'

He looked out of his window at the orderly garden.

'Nobody could prove anything,' he said.

'What happened to Emrys?' I asked.

'He took it hard,' said Mr Protheroe. 'He let it get on top of him, and he never was, as you know, a man quick to understanding. I see him from time to time, but he's not good for much now. No, not for much. Talks to himself and so on.'

'Not a very nice story,' I said.

'Nothing in this world is perfect,' said the old man. 'Don't let it bother you. Go up now and have a word with Lemuel Evans. Tell him I sent you and let him know who you are.'

I went up to Lemuel Evans's office and was shown into a dirty room, the lower half of its windows covered by screens of rusty gauze the colour of liver. There was dust everywhere. A few box files, sagging and empty, stood on a shelf. Evans was there, a tall old man so dry and sapless he seemed made of tinder. A great plume of white hair swept off his forehead. I asked him about the cottage.

He nodded slowly.

'It's a nice little property,' he said. His voice was astonishingly vigorous. 'A pleasant situation, and very sound. How much would you be thinking of paying for it?'

I told him that there was a lot to be done to the house before any one could think of living in it and I offered him a silly amount, really silly.

His answer surprised me.

'It will certainly need some renovation,' he said, 'and it will only deteriorate if left empty. I think we can do business at the figure you mention.'

I said I'd think about it and let him know. I couldn't get poor Emrys out of my mind. I thought I might buy the cottage and give it back to Emrys; I thought I ought to ask Evans outright why he had cheated my old friend. I realised I was shaking with anger. I walked out, Lemuel Evans following me to the door.

I went back down the hill toward Protheroe's shop. He was standing outside, waiting for me.

'You won't be buying the house,' he said.

'No,' I said.

'You aren't the first,' he said. 'No, not the first, by a long way.'

I didn't say anything. I was suddenly indifferent to everything.

'Come inside and have some tea,' old Protheroe said.

'I haven't time now,' I said.

I got in the car and drove away. It began to rain as I crossed the river bridge and by the time I'd climbed the hill a persistent soft rain drove in at me. I stopped the car and looked back. The town was hidden by falling rain, its roofs, its bridge, the little outlying cottages, but to the south, the way I was going, the river shone in its valley like an enormous snail track.

Three Shots for Charlie Betson

We moved into this village fifteen years ago, a week before Christmas. Our furniture was taken away in the early morning and we had followed by leisurely train after lunch. It was already dark when we reached Brighton and it was bitterly cold. We got on the bus which was to take us to our new house and we were the only passengers. A wind off the bleak sea came unchecked through the body of the coach and we sat huddled against fatigue and numbing cold in the faulty havens of our greatcoats. It took an hour and a half to reach the village, a distance of only twelve miles.

I couldn't find the key when we arrived at the house, but the back door was open and we tumbled in, regretting that we'd ever heard of the place. But a huge fire was burning in the grate, a loaf of bread and two bottles of milk stood on the kitchen table, and soon we began to recognise our nomadic furniture in its strange corners. I found the key in a briefcase I'd carried with me. I opened the front door and there on the step was a cabbage, a bag of potatoes and a bunch of mimosa. I couldn't see anyone about and there wasn't a sound. In those days the village street had no lighting and we had no very near neighbours. The school building opposite was merely a dark bulk against a dark sky.

I picked up the vegetables and mimosa and carried them into my wife. She was enchanted, warmed by anonymous generosity. We reinforced our hot milk with big slugs of whisky, made toast by the lovely fire, and went happy to bed. We talked before sleep of the people who had so tactfully welcomed us, because we knew nobody in the village.

Old Bill Francis had done it all himself, trudging sturdily over the three fields between our house and his, but I didn't know that until three months later.

The next morning was full of rain and we worked away indoors, eating a sketchy meal about midday. Afterwards, in a break in the rain, I dressed against the weather and went out. I found a cinder path running between two high thorn hedges. It led to a lane very little wider than itself, but properly surfaced and serving a scatter of small houses along its length. A sign called it Crook Lane.

I still hadn't seen anyone since our arrival in the place and it was a relief to find a man trying to prop open a field gate with a fallen branch.

'Here,' said the man. 'You've come just in time. Hold the gate open while I drive these cows across the lane and into this other field of mine.'

He was a huge old man, his large red face carrying an ample nose. I held the gate and he drove his three amicable heifers across the road and into his other field. The old man was lame, one leg deformed, stiff at the bent knee joint. He came up to me as I closed the gate, looking at me for a long time. He was inspecting me, his expression cheerful and sardonic, his little blue eyes alight and curious.

'Them cows,' he said, 'they can be real cantankerous, so you came in very handy. Just come to live here, have you?'

I said I had. I pointed across the fields to the roof of my house. It was the first house we'd ever owned.

'Saw your lights come on,' said the old man, 'last night. You won't stay long, you won't like it here. We're a close lot in this village, keep ourselves to ourselves. No, you won't find it easy in this village, I can tell you. We don't take to strangers.'

He was Bill Francis, and he smiled at me with enormous friendship and satisfaction.

'Come down the house,' he said, 'and have a cup of tea.'

He jerked his head towards our house.

'My father used to live in that one,' he said, 'that house of yours. Pretty as a picture it used to be.'

'You'll have hard work of it,' he said sternly, 'if you want that house to look as it did in my father's day.'

We walked together down Crook Lane towards his house. He told me that his brother was a retired sergeant of police, that he himself had over three thousand pounds in the bank, that he had been very fond of boxing when he was young.

'I loved it, I did,' he said. His great wide laughter rang in the empty lane. 'I liked nothing better of a Sunday morning than to get the gloves on with a good boy and to belt ourselves tired. Many's the time I've come home with my face swollen up twice its size.'

He shook his large head sadly.

'My wife didn't like it though,' he said. 'She didn't like it, and in the end I gave it up. She's been dead now these five years, a lovely woman she was.'

Bill Francis's garden was a delight. Although it was winter, there was about it an air of plenty: it seemed merely awaiting some signal to blossom into miraculous fecundity. It was an artist's garden, not only immaculately neat, but its proportions were immediately satisfying, the branches of his apple trees pruned so that they made clear and perfect shapes in the air, the patterns of his flower beds coherent and full of interest. Bill's house was the same, the furniture good and glowingly cared for. The cups we drank from were old, fragile, very beautiful.

It became a habit for me to walk across the cinder path in the afternoons, unless I was into something very important, to hold open old Bill's gate and walk on down to have a cup of tea with him. Years later, when he was in his eighties and grown frail, I used to go over and see to his heifers myself. He always had two or three running on, to sell when they were down-calving. I liked him.

It was inevitable that I should have come across the Betsons sooner or later, for they were so large a family that everyone in the village was in some way or another connected with them. Physically, too, they were so positive and vigorous that it would have been impossible to ignore them. I'd seen the children, without knowing who they were, on their way to school. They walked up the road as far as my garden wall, silent, tall boys, very fair and upright, and crossed over the road there. There must have been half a dozen of them — in fact, there were seven, and now that I put my mind to it I can give a name to every one of them. They never laughed or played and they ranged between six years old and fifteen.

A busy main road ran the straggling length of the village and I was often anxious about the safety of children as they went to and from the school, but not the Betsons. Casually and with dignity they walked, crossing the road when it was absolutely clear. The youngest boys were the children of the two Betson sisters, but I didn't know that. None of them spoke to me, nor did they show they were aware of me as I began, in the drier afternoons, to set my garden to rights. Lord, how they must have laughed in the village as I cut, tore, and burned. I killed a long bank of Albertine roses, the pride of the garden, through pure ignorance.

Occasionally, if it were too cold for digging, or if I were thinking of something, I'd cut through the school playground and over a couple of fields. A small river ran through a shallow valley there, and the light was so clear it gave the heart a lift even on intransigent days. Often, wild duck flew honking over the water, or landed noisily, feathering the surface with their braced feet. It's all built over now. Everything changes.

One afternoon I walked through the school fields as the older boys were playing football. I'd not long given up playing myself, had played for good clubs. I walked through the intent boys as a high

ball came upfield in an inviting parabola, made entirely for me. I
was rising to it in an instinct of joy, neck and shoulders taut, knowing
my forehead would meet the ball perfectly. Out of the corner of my
eye I saw someone come up with me, and I turned slightly so that
my shoulder would smother our impact. Even so he almost got to
the ball before me. Amused and ashamed, I challenged more fiercely
than was at all necessary. Hell, I wasn't even supposed to be playing.
But the boy dropped cleverly away, landing easily and breaking at
once into his stride. He was the biggest of the fair Betson boys I'd
seen; he was Charlie Betson.

Hodges, the schoolmaster, came over, a round, gentle, smiling
man, the most comfortable-looking man I've ever known. When I
think of him now I see his dark, smooth face and imagine him with
a pipe in his mouth. In reality, he didn't smoke at all. I got to know
him well before he moved away to a bigger school in Lancashire.
He's dead now, died unnecessarily in a stupid car smash, in fog,
about three years back.

'That was nicely done,' he said. 'I wish I were able to get up like
that, but I was never a games player.'

I grinned at him. He was about my own age, couldn't have been
much more.

'I hope you didn't mind,' I said. 'I'm just passing through to the
river.'

'No trouble,' he said. 'It's a public footpath anyway.'

I walked on and was climbing the stile when he called me.

It turned out that he was the only man on the staff of that small
school, his colleagues being two elderly ladies who taught the
younger children, and he felt the boys were not getting the games
coaching he would have liked. In the end I said I'd go across once
a week and take the bigger boys for football. I did it for almost ten
years. It helped to keep me fit and I used to enjoy showing off. Old
Bill Francis, who was on the school committee, was delighted with
me.

I've never seen another boy with such quick and accurate reflexes
as Charlie Betson. He was already taller than I am, but very thin, as
some adolescent boys are. He could kick a ball with either foot
without thinking, he could catch marvellously well. I thought I had
found a great player in the making, but it was all physical. He hadn't
an idea in his head. It took me some time to realise this, since Charlie
was so shy he didn't speak to me. I talked to Hodges about him.

'The Betsons are all the same,' he said. 'I've had dozens of them
in the school, and Charlie is the archetypal Betson. Beautiful to look

at, quiet, and hard-working, but stupid. Charlie, for example, can't read at all. He's had special tuition for years, but he gets nowhere.'

Not long after this I was in my garden when Charlie looked over the wall. I asked him in. In about two minutes it became obvious that Charlie knew more about gardening than I ever would. He came to work for me Saturday mornings and I taught him to read out of seed catalogues.

Spring comes early to this part of the country and it was particularly lovely that year, the first year we lived in the village. Towards the end of April, the sun already warm, cuckoos shouting, I was in Crook Lane talking to Bill Francis. It was Sunday, and the church bells were floating their traditional messages over the fields. My wife's birthday was that day, and I'd mentioned this to Bill some days earlier.

'Why, that'll be Primrose Sunday, look,' he'd said, 'a good day for a birthday.'

I had only laughed, but that morning we had found a small bunch of primroses on the doorstep, in an exquisite tiny jug. Afterwards he never forgot her birthday, never failed to leave her such a gift. We have the jugs still. We used to find it very moving, imagining his enormous hands plucking with such delicacy among the threadlike stalks of the flowers, placing them artfully with a few of their puckered leaves in the little jugs. I'd gone over to tell Bill of her delight and we carried on talking in the renewing warmth.

But something drew Bill's attention as we spoke. He looked down the lane, an expression at once stern, surprised and disapproving on his face. I turned to see what could have caused this. A strange little procession was moving towards us, ceremonious, quiet, celebrating ritually, it seemed, the spring of the year.

A group of young Betsons, tall and silent, were walking up the lane towards us, the smaller boys forming the erratic edges of the party. The older fellows, those who were at work and whom I had not seen before, were carrying on their shoulders a simple throne, adapted from a wooden armchair. Chestnut poles were fastened to clamps on each side of the chair, and the young men held the poles on their strong shoulders, their identical golden heads tilted away. They walked in unison, easily, unconcernedly. There was something noble in the way they walked; theirs was a willing submission.

Seated up in the chair, a plaid blanket neatly over his knees, was an old man. Up high there, his head above the uncut hedges, he had accepted his elevation as entirely natural. He wore an old hat, and a thick scarf, its ends tucked into his coat, was crossed over his chest.

As he passed us, the old man lifted a hand in greeting. He was completely at ease, relaxed as if he were sitting at his own fireside. He smiled directly at Bill Francis and his smile was full and subtle, as amused and meaningful as an hour of speech.

'Bill,' he said.

His voice was deep, gentle, and mocking. Bill Francis stood unmoving at my side, the corners of his mouth pulled down and his face stony. He nodded once, a brisk, hard butt of the head, in response to the old man's greeting. The old man was very ill. Long grey hair hung below his hat and lay on his pale cheeks. The skin of his face was thick and coarse, pitted and lumped like the skin of an orange. He was obviously the father of the tribe, the patriarchal Betson. Nobody else said a word, not even Charlie. As they passed us, Charlie took his place among the bearers, moving in to relieve one of his brothers. I could feel his eyes slide remotely away from me. Behind the men two or three little girls quarrelled and scrambled along. These were the old man's granddaughters. I only knew one of his daughters and that was Sarah Betson, a great slashing creature tall as an Amazon, two or three years older than Charlie. She moved away to London when she was nineteen, came home at Christmas for a few years, and walked through the village in her vivid clothes before disappearing from our lives forever. Facially she was very like Charlie, but bolder and more confident.

We watched Mr Betson and his splendid phalanx around the bend in the lane. He turned once and waved a hand from his dipping throne as he went, and old Bill Francis breathed deeply through his nose.

'Them owdacious Betsons,' he said, his disapproval palpable. 'There always have been Betsons in this village, and by the look of it there always will be.'

I thought it admirable that his sons should take the sick old man out in his carried chair in the first good sun of the year, and I said so. I was shocked at Bill Francis's anger. He turned on me, fairly hissing, white spittle on his lower lip, two hectic lights on his cheekbones.

'You ain't been here long enough to know anything,' he said, 'and you ain't got enough sense to look about you. While the Betsons increase and flourish, what's happening to the decent people, eh? What's to happen to the decent people, just think of that!'

He wheeled like a great ship of state and marched solemnly away. He didn't ask me down to his house. That was the only time we ever approached a disagreement.

In the summer Mr Betson died, in great agony. Charlie left school and went to work on one of the farms. I didn't see him often, and when I did it would be on a Saturday, or on some holiday, when he'd be dressed in his finery. He grew rapidly. Tall when I first knew him, he was well over six feet by the time he was seventeen, and he walked like a guardsman. Colonel Fletcher gave Charlie one of his labradors. Sometimes I'd see him at a distance, walking one of the hedges with his dog, a gun under his arm. He was great on rabbits, was Charlie, fast, cool, invariably accurate.

One Friday afternoon I heard a frightening scream of brakes outside the house. I was in the kitchen. I put down a cup so slowly and carefully that I was driven to anger by my cautious body, and then I ran outside. Two little girls were clinging together against the wall, their voices inhumanly high as they shrieked. A truck, heavily loaded with timber, was stopped halfway across the road, its front wheels wrenched at a despairing angle, and a little brown dog lay near the off-side wheel. It was pitifully broken, blood and fragments of bone everywhere, but it was still alive. I knew the little girls. They were sisters who lived higher up the village, and they owned the dog. I ran towards them, not knowing what to do, and held them in my arms. The young driver was getting out of his cab. He was white and shaking, his mouth opening and shutting without words. Everything seemed to be happening slowly and with a dreadful clarity. I could see Charlie Betson leaping over the gate on the other side of the road, landing lightly, his face expressionless and remote.

'Take the little girls away,' he said to me. 'Take them into your house. I'll see to this.'

As we went inside I heard the crack of Charlie's gun, but I don't think the girls did. Children are remarkable, so resilient. Those little girls were shocked and genuinely heartbroken and they sobbed for an hour, but they ate a good meal with us and afterwards we played a riotous game of cards before we took them home. The road was clean, all evidence of the small tragedy washed and swept away. The kids' parents were out, I remember, and we had to leave them with a neighbour. I've not thought of it for years. It happened the year Bill Francis took to his bed and I became a member of the Parish Council in his place.

Charlie moved from the village when he got married. His wife came from a little place about ten miles away and they found a house there. I saw them together once or twice, Charlie and his wife, and they looked marvellous. She was a tall girl, athletic and fair, with an open, smiling face, a generous face. They had two children quite quickly. I was amused to think of Charlie suddenly so mature and responsible. Time goes, of course; I had not seen the sudden quickening of the years.

Last year, in June, I awoke very early one morning. I sleep less and less these days and most mornings I'm alert by seven o'clock. But that day I was up and padding about before five. About six-thirty I walked up the village looking for something to do. We've a new recreation ground and I turned in there. The place has grown a lot during the last few years, new houses, new young people, and somehow it was decided that we ought to have a recreation field; tennis courts, football fields, swings and roundabouts for the little ones, the lot. I'm on the committee for the provision of this field and I thought I might look at what progress was being made.

The place lies behind houses and there's a drive of about a hundred and fifty yards to reach it. The work had been nicely done and I walked along admiring the rolled surface, the neat fencing. A little car park stands at the end of the drive, next to the hard courts, and a car was already there. I assumed that it belonged to someone living nearby, that it had been left there overnight. I began to walk along the field's boundary, near the hedge. The light dew was almost off the grass and cuttings from the mower were dry and flaky on the surface, although you could still see where a bird had disturbed the direction of the grass earlier. I hadn't gone far when I heard a shout. Someone climbed out of the parked car and waved to me. It was Charlie Betson. He came up to me, grinning.

At first I thought there was something wrong with him, but he was all right. He was very thin and he walked loosely, arms dangling and feet planting themselves aimlessly at the end of irregular strides. He held his head far back, as if to compensate for the loss of his old, controlled, straight-backed dignity. This worried me for a while, but he spoke well and naturally, telling me of his job. He was felling a stand of beech on an estate some miles away; I knew the trees well. We walked along the mixed hedge at the end of the field, blackthorn mainly, with a bit of scrub oak and some maple, and we heard something rustling on the other side.

'Heron,' said Charlie. 'That's a heron in the wet ditch. There's always one there, between the old gravel pond and the mill. Good picking in the ditch for herons, plenty of frogs and that.'

He smiled.

'My old dad,' he said, 'told me about him when I was small. Finest poacher in the country was my dad, and he told me about the heron. There was one in the ditch when he was a boy, and I reckon there always will be one. After my day, I expect.'

We poked a branch through the hedge and the long heron rose slowly, his legs trailing, and flew towards the mill. We watched him go.

'What was between your father,' I asked carefully, 'and Bill Francis?'

'Well,' said Charlie, 'much of an age, weren't they? Went to school together, grew up together, young men together. Bill Francis could beat my dad all along the line. He was stronger, he could fight better, people liked him more. And even with a gun, why, Bill could always beat my dad. Best shot I ever see was Bill Francis. My dad always gave him credit. Rivals, they were.'

He cocked an amused eye down at me.

'Of course,' he said, 'in the end my father won.'

'How's that?' I said.

'We've always been here,' said Charlie, 'Betson and Francis. Those are the true names in this village. My father had nine boys, counting Archie who got killed in the war; Bill Francis never had any. There ain't no Francises left.'

We walked quietly back down the field.

'Old Bill liked you, didn't he?' asked Charlie.

'He did,' I said. 'He wanted to leave me his fields.'

'Yeah, well.' Charlie picked up a stone and flung it away. 'Understandable, that is. You should have let him. You're about the same age as my oldest brother.'

We reached his car and I looked inside. It was perfectly neat and clean, Charlie's racing paper open on the seat the one untidy object.

'It's the wife,' said Charlie. 'She cleans everything, car, house, kids, me . . . there's no rest.'

'Charlie,' I said, 'why are you down here so early? It's not seven o'clock.'

He lowered his head, suddenly heavy and obstinate. The skin of his face was thickening and coarsening as his father's had, and deep folds were appearing at the sides of his nose under his cheekbones. When he looked up, I saw that his teeth were lined and spotted.

He got into the car and picked up his paper, folding it uneasily. I could see in him so clearly the graceless, shy boy he had been.

'It's quieter,' he said. 'It's much quieter. I get up most mornings and go on down to my mother's for breakfast. Then I bring the paper up here and pick a few winners.'

He sat there uncomfortably, as if he didn't care, his face sad and heavy, looking at something far away.

'You don't know what it's like,' he said, 'living somewhere else.

Do you know who lives next door to me? Gypsies, that's who. And it's the same everywhere, all strangers. Down here, it's quieter and I know everybody. My family, and that. It's nicer.'

I didn't say anything.

'It's lovely here,' said Charlie, 'in the morning, in the early morning.'

'What are your runners today?' I said loudly. 'What do you fancy?'

He began to read some names out of his paper.

'Is there a grey in the big race?' I said.

I was wasting time. I would have been glad to leave; I wanted some neat conclusion to our meeting.

'You like greys?' Charlie asked.

'Yes,' I said. 'A couple of years ago I went to a breeding stables in Yorkshire where they had a grey stallion. Abernant was his name — he had a lot of grey offspring, you couldn't miss them. Beautiful size, wonderful clean, round bone, and such neat, intelligent heads. Good stuff, they were.'

Charlie laughed. The life was back in his eyes.

'You don't want to bother about colour,' he said. 'A good horse is never a bad colour. I'll be better off picking my own winners.'

I went away down the road. The morning was beautiful, the afternoon cloudless and very hot. About eight that evening, as a small, cool wind began, Charlie came into the garden. He was waving a thin bundle of notes.

'Here you are,' he called. 'Two pounds at eight to one, that's sixteen pounds!'

He was delighted with himself.

'What's all this?' I said.

I was astonished at the change in Charlie. He was inches taller than he had been that morning, he moved with all his remembered certainty and assurance.

'I put two pounds on the grey for you,' he said, 'and five for myself. We've had a good day.'

'What grey?' I said, bewildered.

'Ah, you're a sly one,' he said. 'You're as cunning as a cartload. You knew all the time a grey by Abernant was going in that race. Well, you've done us both a bit of good.'

He pushed the notes at me.

'I can't take these, Charlie,' I said. 'Give them to the children.'

'They're yours,' he said, roughly. 'The kids get plenty. Take the money — if the horse had lost I'd have been around for the two pounds' stake, don't worry.'

'If you're sure,' I said.

I took the money from him and at once he moved away, waving as he went. He was full of bounce. I wondered how, that morning, I had thought him changed in any way, how anything could have so filled me with false foreboding.

That was the last time I spoke to Charlie.

Last week I heard that Charlie was missing, hadn't been seen for two days. I can't remember how I learned this; by the sort of osmosis that happens in a village, I expect. I was neither surprised nor had I expected this news. I was just filled with an unthinking certainty. As soon as I heard I took the car out and went to the recreation field. I drove through the car park and across the field itself, right to the far end. When I got out I was moving very stiffly, as if my body were a new and intricate mechanism come newly to me. I remember my eyes so tight and stiff that it would have been impossible to blink without single-minded and deliberate effort. I broke through the hedge and the heron got up about fifty yards away. A single flap of his wings turned him into the wind and he vanished over the elms.

Charlie was there, almost at my feet. He was lying there quite peacefully, untouched almost, if you didn't look too closely. His gun was at his side, the muzzle under his chest. I slid it out and walked down the ditch. One barrel was still loaded. A pigeon flew up from the noise of my walking and I shot it casually, brought it back, and put it obviously in the field about ten yards from Charlie. Then I placed the gun near his fallen hand. We're a close lot in this village, look after our own. Almost the first thing old Bill Francis said to me, that was.

When I got home, I thought about it, hard. I wasn't shocked or stunned; I was just completely sad. I'd recognised something in Charlie that last day, without knowing it, some intuition had prepared me. I got it all clear in my mind and walked over to the police house. Sergeant Watson is a sensible man, made no fuss, and the official business began.

Yesterday I went to the funeral, simple enough. Charlie's mother asked me. She came up to the house early this week, sat on the edge of a chair, and said that she expected to see me there. The church was full of young men, Charlie's friends, and in front sat a row of Betsons, tall and hard-faced. Afterwards, Charlie's wife asked me back to his mother's house to have a meal. I thought of refusing, but at her side was Charlie's oldest sister, fair-haired and implacable. The enormous Betson men were already there when I arrived, talking in their quiet, heavy voices. One by one they came up to me, shook my hand, told me that Charlie had spoken of me often, always boasted of how I had taught him to read.

'He liked you,' they said. 'Charlie liked you. He always gave you credit.'

I sat there, my plate on my knee, drinking the strong, hot tea. After a while Charlie's mother came over. She was a very old lady and she sat silent and upright opposite me. I tried to tell her that it had been a good occasion, that Charlie would have been glad to know that so many of his friends had come to wish him goodbye. Her face was calm and without expression, but there was that in her eyes which would not be comforted.

'He was a good boy,' she said, 'but he was lost. He needed safety. All my boys need safety, like their father before them. People think when they see my lovely boys, strong and proud, that nothing could ever worry them. But it's not true.'

One of the daughters stood by the table, warily, listening carefully.

'When Archie went to the war,' said Mrs Betson, 'when he was eighteen, the oldest of them, I watched him going nearly mad away from us. My boys need to be in the fields about us, nearby, where their father walked before them, where they feel safe. They need a house where their brothers are only a shout away and there's food and drink without fuss, any time of the day or night.'

The room was very still. Charlie's brothers, listening uncomfortably to their mother's unlikely eloquence, stared blankly about.

'I knew he was going lost,' said Mrs Betson. 'I knew Charlie was going lost when he started coming over here every morning, six o'clock, five o'clock. He never went to Brighton, did you know that? In all his life Charlie never went as far away as Brighton.'

The sisters began to move about, making things orderly. They gave tea and food to brothers and nephews, they arranged them in little groups, they sent them into the garden to walk between the rows of beans and potatoes. The world began to look safe and normal.

'We won't forget what you've done,' said Mrs Betson. 'We've guessed what you've done, and we shan't forget it.'

I stood up and said goodbye. The whole house was suddenly more cheerful and brisk, the day brighter. One or two of the men lifted a hand to me as I left, but most of them smoked and talked together, ignoring me.

And all day I've sat here in the garden thinking of the handsome Betson men, golden as Vikings, walking safe in the little world of our one street and its handful of fields. I thought of Charlie, who might be dead because he had left that simple and limited world for one where he had been forced to make decisions and live in a frightening freedom. But most of all I've been thinking of old Bill Francis, who had spent his life watching over the village and who hadn't any sons at all.

Snowdrops

Today Miss Webster was going to show them the snowdrops growing in the little three-cornered garden outside the school-keeper's house, where they weren't allowed to go. All through the winter, Miss Webster said, the snowdrops had been asleep under the ground, but now they were up, growing in the garden. He tried to think what they would look like, but all he could imagine was one flake of the falling snow, bitterly frail and white, and nothing like a flower.

It was a very cold morning. He leaned against the kitchen table, feeling the hard edge against his chest, eating his breakfast slowly. His brother, Geraint, who was only three, sat in an armchair close to the fire. He could see the shape of Geraint's head outlined against the flames and saw with wonder that the fire had given to his brother's legs a glow of red only slightly less bright than the leaping flames. Geraint was eating a bowl of porridge and what he did was this. He would make a crater in the porridge with his spoon, and then he'd watch the milk run in and fill the hole up. Then he would dip his spoon in the milk and drink it. The boy watched his brother.

'Hurry up,' said the boy's mother, 'or you'll never get to school!'

'Miss Webster is going to show us the snowdrops today,' he said.

'That's nice,' said his mother, looking out of the window at the grey morning. 'I wonder where your father is.'

His father came in and filled the room with bigness. He stood in front of the fire, because it was cold in the yard, and all the boy could see was a faint light each side of his father's wide body.

'It's a cold wind,' said his father. 'I can't remember a colder March.'

The man turned around and faced them, smiling because he was much warmer and the cold March wind was safely locked outside the house.

'You're a big boy for six,' he said to the boy, 'and it's all because you eat your breakfast up.'

This was a joke his father always said, and the boy smiled, thinking all the time of the snowdrops. Would it be too cold to go and see them? Perhaps Miss Webster would take only the boys, he comforted himself, because they were stronger, and the girls could stay in school out of the cold.

'The Meredith boy is being buried this afternoon,' his father was saying to his mother. 'I'm sorry I shan't be able to go. I worked with his father for two and a half years, up at the rolling mill. A nice man, Charlie Meredith, very quiet. I hear he's very cut up, and his wife too. This was their only boy.'

'How old was he?' asked his mother.

'Twenty,' his father said. 'Twenty last January. Silly little fool. That bike was too powerful for him — well, to go at that speed on a wet, dark night. Over seventy, the police said, straight into the back of a stationary truck. A terrible mess.'

'He was a nice-looking boy, too,' said his mother.

'All the Merediths are,' said his father. 'This one was very friendly with the young teacher up at the school, Webber, is it? Something like that.'

But his mother coughed and looked sharply at the boy.

'Oh?' said his father. 'Of course. I should have remembered. Come on, son, or you'll be late.'

It seemed much warmer when he got to school and he took off his overcoat next to Edmund Jenkins. Edmund had a long blue scarf which his big sister had knitted for him. They each held an end of the scarf and raced up the corridor, seeing how many children they could catch, but Miss Lewis stopped them. Then Edmund told him a joke.

'What's the biggest rope in the world?' Edmund asked.

The boy didn't know.

'Europe,' said Edmund, and they both laughed.

They were still laughing as they went into the classroom, although Miss Webster wasn't there. After a time Miss Lewis came in and sent the children into other classrooms. Miss Lewis took the top class and she was very stern and strict. He and Edmund had to go to Miss Lewis's class.

'Europe,' said Edmund Jenkins to him, very quietly, as they went into the top class. Edmund was very brave.

It wasn't too bad in Miss Lewis's class, because they had some interesting books there and the arithmetic was not difficult. When you looked out of the window, too, you saw a different part of the playground. The boy could almost see a corner of the school-keeper's house, so he wasn't very far away from the snowdrops.

Just before playtime Miss Lewis told all the children from Miss Webster's class that they could go back to their own room after play. The boy grinned in delight. Everything would be all right, he told himself. After play they would surely go to see the flowers.

Out in the playground they all began to run about, except Gerald

Davis, who seemed to fall over whatever he did. He was quite unable
to make even the tiniest step without tumbling down, and his face
was red from laughing and because he didn't know what was
happening to him. Edmund Jenkins was standing close by and the
boy could see that Edmund had been up to his tricks again.

'What's happening to Gerald?' he asked.

But Edmund only pointed to Gerald's boots, and then the boy
saw that his laces had been tied together, the left boot to the right
boot and the right boot to the left boot, so that Gerald was hobbled.
Some boys were beginning to imitate Gerald, falling about although
their boots weren't tied together. After a while he and Edmund
untied the laces and Gerald went whooping up the gravel yard like
a released pigeon.

He walked with Edmund towards the last corner of the playground, away from the wind, and they took their small packets of
sandwiches from their pockets. Edmund had three sandwiches, with
marmalade in them, and he had two sandwiches, but he didn't know
what they were filled with. He bit one of them to find out.

The taste was incredibly new and marvellous, filling the whole of
his mouth with delight and pleasure. He shook his head to show
Edmund how wonderful the taste was, and then let Edmund have
a bite.

'What's in it, Edmund?' he asked. 'What's in my sandwich?'

'Bacon,' said Edmund. 'It's only bacon.'

The boy was incredulous. He opened the second sandwich to
inspect the filling. It didn't look like bacon.

'It can't be,' he said. 'I have bacon for my breakfast every morning.
I had some *this* morning.'

'I know,' said Edmund 'but it tastes different when it's cold.'

Together they walked as far as the shed in which the coal was
stored. This was as far as they were allowed to go. Not very far away,
but tantalisingly around the corner and down the little path that led
to the garden, the snowdrops were growing.

'Do you wish,' said the boy, 'that Miss Webster will take us to see
the flowers when play is over?'

'I don't care,' said Edmund, 'because I've seen some already,
growing in my aunt's garden.'

The boy looked at his best friend, deciding carefully whether he
would ask him to describe a snowdrop. But he would wait, he
thought, to see them for himself, and then the bell was ringing to
call them in.

The children cheered and clapped when they saw Miss Webster.

She was dressed in a black frock, without any jewellery, but she smiled at them, holding her finger to her lips for them to be quiet. The bandage she had on one finger, where she had trapped it in the cupboard door and hadn't cried, looked very white and clean. She gave them some crayons and a big sheet of paper for each child and they could draw whatever they liked.

The boy drew a robin. He hadn't drawn a robin since Christmas, but just recently he had been watching one that came to his garden every day, and now he knew just how the bird's head fitted on to his round little body, and he had seen the way the legs, as thin as pieces of wire, splayed out underneath. Sometimes the robin looked like a hunchback, but he would draw this robin standing up bravely, throwing out his red chest before he sang. And the robin's song was odd. It wasn't very long, and it dropped and fell like threads of falling water. The boy closed his eyes a little while so that he could hear the robin, but he couldn't get it quite right. Soon he was engrossed in watching his robin grow on the paper. With infinite care he set its delicate feet on a brown twig, not just a flat stick as he had drawn at Christmas, but a real twig, with little knobs on it where the buds would be. At last it was finished and he leaned back in his chair, looking around as he did so. Nearly all the other children had completed their drawings some time before and they were reading their books. Miss Webster was sitting at her desk, her head in her hands. Everything was still. The boy took out his book and began to read, but most of the time he looked at the robin he had drawn.

This is what he was doing when the bell ended morning school and they were dismissed for home. Miss Webster looked at his robin and she liked it. She took it from his desk and pinned it in a good place on the wall, where everybody could see it. The boy was pleased and surprised, because he had never before had a drawing pinned up in this way, although he knew he could draw at least as well as Edmund, who had a drawing selected nearly every week.

'Shall we be going to see the snowdrops this afternoon?' he asked Miss Webster before he went home.

'Yes,' she said, 'if Miss Lewis will allow us, we'll go to see them this afternoon.'

He ate his lunch quietly, thinking in his head of a story about a wizard who could change himself into anything at all. It was a good story, but something always seemed to happen before he got to the end of it. Sometimes he began it at night in bed, only to fall asleep long before the really exciting part. Now his mother was talking to him.

'Was Miss Webster in school this morning?' she asked. His mother was knitting a pullover. The needles went over and under each other, with the same little slide and click, and a row of knitting grew magically behind them.

'Yes,' he said, 'but she came late. She didn't arrive until playtime.'

'Poor girl,' said his mother.

He thought about this for a long time.

'She's got a bad hand,' he said. 'She caught her finger in the cupboard door and her hand was bleeding. She's got a bandage on it today. She'll never be able to bend her finger again, that's what Edmund Jenkins said.'

'Oh, you and Edmund Jenkins,' said his mother.

He raced back to school, his boots ringing on the pavement as they always seemed to in cold weather. Every day he went a special way, over the river bridge, being very careful of the traffic, up Penry Street as far as the fruiterer's, then across the road by the fire station in case the doors were open; now he could balance along a low wall outside Jack Williams's garden, and at last he was in the small road where the school was. He never knew what would happen here, because he would meet many boys going to school and almost any adventure could happen. Once in this road Bernard Spencer had given him a glass marble, and once he and Edmund had found a silver medal which somebody had won for running. Edmund's father had taken it to the police, but they didn't have a reward.

But there was nobody about, except some girls skipping and giggling just inside the school yard, and he made his way inside the building. Everybody was sitting very quietly inside the classroom. They were allowed to go in early because it was very cold. Normally they would have stayed outside until Miss Lewis rang the bell, and some boys stayed outside however wet and cold it was, but today it seemed that they all wanted to sit quietly with Miss Webster, close to the cast-iron stove that had the figure of a tortoise on the top.

At two o'clock Miss Webster marked her register and then began to tell them a story. It was a good story, about a dragon who guarded a hoard of treasure in his den underground, where the snowdrops slept all through the winter. From time to time Miss Webster turned her head to look at the big clock in the hall. She could see it through the top half of the classroom door, which had four panes of glass in it. Her voice seemed to be harsher than usual, which was fine when she read the dragon's bits, but not good for the knight nor the princess. She shut her book with a snap and stood up. She hadn't completed the story.

'Now we'll go to see the snowdrops,' she said. 'I want the girls to go quietly to the cloakroom and put on their coats. When they are ready, I'll come along with the boys. Everybody must wear a coat. If you have difficulty with buttons, please stand in front and I'll fasten them for you.'

He stood up with a sudden lightening of the heart. He had known all the time that Miss Webster would not forget, and at last she was taking him to see the miraculous flowers, pale and fragile as the falling snow. He looked at Miss Webster with gratitude. Her eyes were bright as frost, and she was making sure that the girls walked nicely through the door. Edmund Jenkins waved at him and that was funny, because Edmund had his black gloves on, with a hole in a place he could push his finger through. Edmund waved his finger like a fat white worm in the middle of his dark hand.

They all walked beautifully through the playground, in two rows holding hands, and he held Edmund's hand and they gave a little skip together every three steps. It didn't take long to get to the garden. The children bent down, four at a time, to look at the little clump of snowdrops and Miss Webster told them what to look at. He and Edmund would be the last to look. When they had finished, the other children went down to the garden gate which opened onto the road. It was a big gate with iron bars and your head could almost poke through. Somewhere a long way off the boy could hear men singing. They sang softly, mournfully, the words carried gently on the air over the school wall, but the boy could not hear what they said.

'It's a funeral,' said Edmund. 'My father's there and my Uncle Jim. It's a boy who was killed on a motor-bike.'

The boy nodded. Funerals often passed the school on their way to the cemetery at the top of the valley. All the men wore black suits and they walked slowly. Sometimes they sang.

He squatted down to look at the snowdrops. He felt a slow, sad disappointment. He looked around for Miss Webster to explain these simple flowers to him, but she had gone down to the gate and was staring through, looking up the road. Her back was as hard as a stone. He turned again to the snowdrops, concentrating, willing them to turn marvellous in front of his eyes. They hung down their four petalled heads in front of him, the white tinged with minute green, the little green ball sturdily holding the petals, the greyish leaves standing up like miniature spears. The boy began to see their fragility. He saw them blow in a sudden gust of the cold March wind, shake, and straighten gallantly. He imagined them standing all night in the dark garden, holding bravely to their specks of whiteness. He put out a finger to touch the nearest flower, knowing now what snowdrops were. He lifted his face to tell Miss Webster, but she was standing right at the gate, holding the iron bars with her hands. Her shoulders were shaking.

> Mor ddedwydd yw y rhai trwy ffydd
>   Sy'n mynd o blith y byw ...

sang the men as they filed solemnly past the school. The boy knew it was Welsh because of his grandmother, and it was sad and beautiful.

After a while they couldn't hear the singing any more, but Miss Webster continued to cry aloud in the midst of the frightened children.

Prey

When the cold weather came, the sky was suddenly full of hawks. Not great flocks of them, as with communal birds, but hawks were suddenly more plentiful; wherever I went, when I looked up, somewhere, at the corner of eyesight, there would be a still point in the moving sky. A hawk, a kestrel, hovering.

In the spring a motorway was completed north of the village, two straight wide roads cut parallel through the brown dirt. For months huge earth-shifters and diggers churned through the land, but in spring all was done. The soft banks of little severed hills made easy burrowing, and in moved colonies of rats and voles and rabbits. Hawks hang on a rope of high air above the scurrying traffic, stationed at intervals along the road. I understand this. I know just where the favoured vantage points are on that highway. Often the birds, still as porcelain, keep unceasing watch above a crossroads or an intersection, or hammer into the grass for a prey invisible to me as I drive past. They claim, too, the small bodies of creatures freshly killed on the roads. I know why the hawks watch there.

But with the frost, the hawks, the autumn-coloured birds, seemed to be more numerous. I saw a kestrel high over Ernie Foster's big field where I'd never seen one before, not in twenty years. I saw it there, intent, hanging, a machine for looking and killing. I put the glasses on him so that I could watch him make his sudden little shifts as he changed his wing-tip hold on the wind, the swift flutter of tail and finger-ends as he adjusted his view of the upturned world. That morning I counted ten of them, hawks, high and solitary, as I drove the dozen miles to town. Then, in the evening, one was mercilessly beating the hedge at the side of the house.

Years ago, one swooped almost into my windscreen as I drove under the downs. He came late out of his dive, wings and legs braced in front of the glass. I saw the open hook of his beak, his furious yellow eye.

Now that winter is complete and the sky uninterrupted between the stripped bones of trees, I can see the sentinel hawks.

All my life I have been on the side of the small birds against the hawks. Two weeks ago I went down to the beach in the teeth of the wind. I left the car at the top of the sea lane and walked down past the six old cottages. They were shut fast, huddled shut as the blunt wind bundled around them. It was bitterly cold on the unsheltered beach and my eyes wept. I wrapped my coat more tightly about me, knowing the gesture useless, as I walked the path above the sand. Spray and fragmentary sand spat and stung in the working storm. On the rim of the beach grows a straggle of blackthorns, bent almost to the ground after constant struggle with salty gales. Their bare stems shone red and mulberry in the sun. Above them stood a hawk, a yard or two above them, balancing in the wild gusts. As I looked, he cut through the wind like a winged blade, sweeping along the thicket, raking it, driving the little birds out before him. He failed to make his kill.

Then the desperate small finches burst out in a cloud at him, into his jaws and talons, with such pugnacity, such unanimous bravery, that the big hawk sheered off, discomfited. I could have cheered those charging ounces; but at once the hawk resumed his iron station, holding himself a yard above the bushes, hanging and ready. I began to run toward him. Stumbling and clumsy in gumboots I ran, clapping my hands, shouting into the wind. But the scared birds flew out in puffs in front of me, like sparks struck from the iron they dived into the light, and the killing hawk was among them. In my fury I had done the hawk's work. He turned with magnificent leisure above the ploughland and flopped heavily out of sight. I should have pitied those torn birds, but I was elated, elated. I left the harried flock in turmoil behind me, under their flimsy twigs.

Goshawk, sparrow hawk, buzzard, kite, harrier, falcon, arrogant killing birds. And peregrine and merlin.

It was the last Monday in October, after the first frosts and when I was newly aware of the watching hawks of the cold weather, that I went to London. My appointment was at noon, so I went by train at mid-morning. I stood on the platform, and the weather was the clear calm often normal for that time of the year, still and clear, not so much cold as lacking in heat, like early morning in Spain. All the colour was golden, the deep gold of the turned furrows, yellow gold of the stubble, the sun turning pale gold the white of road and stone. One hawk, a kestrel, burned in the sky.

But all along the journey the birds held their watching posts on clifftops of air. High above the Arun River, they held the water meadows in the wholeness of their gaze, over widening Surrey they positioned themselves at their perfect heights or beat the thinning woods for rodent or frail bird. At the end of their eyes' range they handed over to other hanging hawks. The train was not for a moment unobserved, nor was any corner of a field, nor twitch of grass, nor lift of smoke. In London itself, only those under the safety of roofs went privately about their business. Kestrels and sparrow hawks hovered over the great parks at the heart of London. England lay under the hawk's eye.

And hawks invisible to us circle tightly the high supporting air, set high in their appointed places. At first light I walk into my garden and I am aware of them. I find on my lawn each day the evidence of hawks; a ring of thrush's feathers, skin still on the quills, where the kill has been fastidiously plucked, and sometimes a delicate claw. When I walk in the beech woods I see beheaded shrews limp-tailed in the grass.

How they bleat in harmless flocks, the weak birds. Dove, thrush, bunting, plover, warbler, pipit, those vulnerable names.

On Sunday Dennis came to see me. He comes seldom to my house, for he is a busy man, active in public causes, forever attending committees and meetings. He talks incessantly, the soft words grow about him. I cannot imagine that he is ever alone. He was in bountiful form, expansive, telling me of a jungle of small injustices, urging me to support this or that community action.

'All together,' he said. 'That's the answer. We should all pull together.'

I rarely answer Dennis. For all his kindness and endless patience, I am indifferent to him. Leaning back in my chair, away from his optimistic voice, I saw the kestrel, a female, hovering outside my window. She was so near I felt I could almost touch her. I saw the clear outline of her every feather. Rust brown, bracken brown, red where the light got to her, her back and her long slim tail were barred with strips of darker colour. Her head turned down and her yellow eye blazed with her one purpose. I stood at the centre of the room and watched her, watched her, while Dennis, on his feet at the window, waved and squeaked. The sight of the hawk there, within feet of him, was for him a miracle; but I stood still, seeing her scaled legs and her unblinking eye, and said nothing. When she released herself into her swoop she moved more slowly than I had expected, and on the ground, in the coarse grass at the garden's edge, she was ungainly and fumbling. But she arose powerfully, holding in her talons a plump rat, dead in the closed grip. I told Dennis I had work to do, and he left. After that intent and ominous bird, his gossiping voice annoyed me.

In Spain I saw the great eagles; the golden eagle, the imperial eagle, once only the tawny eagle, strayed by chance from middle Europe. How they flew, the great birds, majestically gliding and soaring, an occasional flap of great vanes holding them far above the tiny world. They held aloft their arrogant, drifting flight, crucified against the moving sky.

But I liked best the smaller birds, Bonelli's eagle and particularly the common booted eagle, smaller than a buzzard. I would watch them, never far from trees, wheel and cry in the hot morning air, those graceful birds. I saw them often when they perched on high posts or in the branches of single trees. I would stand nearby or walk beneath them, looking up at their mottled bodies. They did not see me, I was not an essential part of the world in which they lived. Hunched and contemptuous, they ignored me. But when they saw what they wanted, a small bird or animal, they became sleek and intent and I knew their yellow eyes had sharpened and focused on that one life, that the yellow concentration of their eyes was turned like a searchlight and that all outside it was dark to the hunting bird. The birds of prey have created a simple world for themselves, sifting and rejecting through their superbly organised senses all that is not necessary. All morning I would watch them, the booted eagles, until with a lift or two of the wings they took themselves into a rising current.

I've twice dreamed about hawks, vividly, memorably. In the first dream I saw a hawk on the ground, on a rock, standing among foliage of brilliant emerald colour. He was quite magnificent. All about him, on the ground and in the air, were the soft birds and animals on which he preyed, wood pigeons, mice, fat moles, voles, rats. Yet he cried petulantly, his voice harsh and wailing, and when he moved I saw that he was a crippled hawk, that one leg stuck out awkwardly from him, thin and withered, the vice of his crushing foot impotent. The second dream was darker and less detailed, and all I remember clearly is the image of a hooded falcon on an ebony perch. He was quite still. His jesses were loose about his legs, and I could see them in the light of a candle or an oil lamp which stood nearby. But his hood was extraordinary. It was stitched and embossed with so meticulous an artistry that it seemed, extravagant though it was, almost a part of the natural bird. Its polished leather, stained purple and scarlet, held all the light. Blunt and eyeless, the decorated head on the unmoving bird gave to the falcon a heraldic power. I pitied both those birds and think often of them.

All week I have been muttering to myself Yeats's line, 'Being high and solitary and most stern,' which is not about a hawk at all. The hawk is his own man, makes his own decisions, which are of death. He does not kill wantonly, but to fulfil his simple, orderly purpose. There is no chaos in his world, nor reason. He will kill or die.

As I drove home this evening I did not see the kestrel over Ernie Foster's big field, although I stopped the car and waited for ten minutes. It was very cold and a thick frost already furred the bars of the field gate, and the ground was iron. But you can't deny a hawk's nature. He'll be there tomorrow, spread wing, eye, hook, and ripping claw.

A Moonlight Gallop

Most weekends when the weather was good enough I used to go cycling in the mountains, usually the Brecon Beacons or the Black Mountains near the Herefordshire border. At that time, when I was about fifteen, I used to belong to the Youth Hostel Association, and so did Del Wellington and Charlie Bond, my friends. We used to pay a membership fee of five shillings a year and in return we got an enamel badge and a card to show we belonged to the Association; we were also sent a map which showed the location of all the Youth Hostels, most of them remote farmhouses, where we could stay for a night or two. Occasionally during the winter we'd plan, with the help of such a map, an immense journey through the dales of Yorkshire, unimaginably distant and foreign, knowing we'd never get there.

We knew all the hostels within possible cycling distance of our homes, although we rarely used them. Del's father had given us a heavy tent, already old, and we preferred to lug this about with us. We must have looked very odd on our three decrepit cycles — mine was rescued from the scrapyard and restored with loving care and some curious home-made fittings — all our strange equipment tied about us. Del always carried the tent on his bike, its bulk of canvas folded in an awkward sausage and slung beneath his cross-bar. It was so big that he had to ride bowlegged.

We had great times. Once we camped on a high moor in mid-Wales and I awoke in the middle of the night. I poked my head out of the tent into a moonlight whiter than frost, and all around us, still as wool, the sheep stood, hundreds of them, staring at the tent. I got back into my blankets and went to sleep and when the morning came there were no sheep to be seen anywhere. I didn't say a word about them to Del and Charlie.

I remember, too, camping near the foot of a waterfall. We hadn't meant to stay overnight, but we'd been attracted by the voice of the water, had pushed our bikes over a wet meadow towards the stream, and followed it up about four hundred yards until we reached the waterfall. It wasn't very high, perhaps sixty feet, but it was perfect. The white fall, never more than a foot wide, bent slowly over a ledge of rock and dropped without check into the pool beneath. We bathed in this pool. It was deep, cold enough to make us gasp, and the cleanest water I have ever used. It made our skins unrecognisable to us, as if a slippery layer of something had been stripped off us for the first time in our lives.

It took us quite a while to drag our gear up to the pool, and it wasn't easy to pitch our tent there, but we did it at last and went to sleep listening to the water's muted thunder. In the morning the green sun filtered down to us through the over-hanging branches of the trees overhead, and through the nodding ferns on the wet rocks. I could have stayed there forever.

That year we got away as often as we could. Perhaps it was a natural restlessness, the wish to see over the next hill, and the next; perhaps we realised that time was already beginning to run out for us, that there were responsibilities we would have to recognise, as well as the attractions of more sophisticated and less perfect pleasures. Whatever it was, hardly a week went by without us moving north into the deep mountains, slowly through the little villages climbing the one road out, merrily over the bare uplands guarded by buzzards. After a while we ventured farther afield; leaving our tent behind and using the Youth Hostels.

Towards the end of July the weather turned unseasonably bad. There was heavy rain, and a brutal wind sprang up in the evenings. The last Friday was depressing and we decided at school that we could go nowhere that weekend. I got home about five and began to read, eating some food aimlessly and without savour. The door-bell rang and my mother answered it. After a little while Charlie Bond came in. He had his cycle cape over his shoulders. It was black, with a hood.

'What do you think?' said Charlie.

I looked out of the window. The rain had stopped and a faint, watery sun showed tentatively behind the clouds.

'I don't know,' I said.

'It'll be good,' said Charlie. 'The wind's dropped and it's cool enough for a fast ride. Del's coming.'

'Mrs Wellington is never going to let Del go out in this weather!' said my mother. 'There must be something wrong with her! Well, you're not going, my boy, so don't ask it.'

The way she spoke I knew it was all right, so I grinned at her and got ready. I pushed my bike outside — Charlie's was leaning against the kerb.

'Where's Del?' I said.

'I haven't been over yet,' said Charlie. 'I only said he was coming so it would be easier to persuade your mother.'

Together we called for Del and I suppose we were on our way

before six o'clock. Everything went right for us. Before we were out
of town the sun was shining and the evening had miraculously
cleared. Without our tent we went at a fast clip and there seemed
about us all a surplus of energy which we controlled and directed
into the expert handling of our cycles. We were over the crest of the
mountain and dropping down into Abergavenny by seven. I can't
remember that we ever had a better ride, the roads clear and kind,
and we knowing each other so well that there was no need for talking.

Del had the maps, and he led us out on the Hereford road for a
few miles before turning left onto a narrow lane. The light was still
good and the sky unclouded above the valley along which we rode.
I've never been in so still a place. Although we passed a few cottages
at the side of the road, we saw nobody. It was as if the whole valley
were deserted, its windows blind to our passing.

We began to climb, very gently at first, and the hollow valley
opened out a little. The hedges were smaller and scrubbier and we
could see over them into the fields they protected. As we climbed
we could see, a long way off, the ruins of an abbey, its solid wall so
pierced by the procession of great arched windows through which
we saw the lit hills behind that it appeared insubstantial, a tracery
of stone. The long evening sun shone fully upon it, on the tall decay
of its towers, on its useless pillars. When at last we reached it, we
found it standing back off the road, about two hundred yards back.
We went in and wandered about for a bit, leaving our bikes leaning
against the hedge. Charlie Bond, his hands hidden in his cycle cape,
the black hood on his head, stepped mournfully through the cloisters, intoning as he went. He was a brilliant mimic, was Charlie. He
could sing so exactly like Bing Crosby that Eustace Berry, a boy in
our class, used to come miles out of his way just to walk to school
with Charlie, listening to him sing. Now Charlie trod softly on the
grass between the fallen walls, his face hidden under his cowl, his
echoing, faulty Latin moving and ominous. It was amusing too, but
I was glad when Del said, 'Stow it, Charlie. We've still got a fair way
to go.'

And at once I became aware of the fading light. Back down the
valley there was a hint of twilight about the farms and the tall trees,
and a soft mist was beginning to fill the fields near the river.

'That's for heat,' said Charlie. 'Positively it will be very hot
tomorrow.'

'I worry about tonight,' Del said: 'We have to be in the hostel by
nine, and then we have our supper to cook. I'm starving.'

We had a look at the large-scale map. We had at least five miles to go and up hills so steep that the contour lines pressed hard against each other.

'Look at those lines,' said Charlie. 'They'd depress an active goat.'

We swung our legs over our saddles and rode on. Pretty soon, so steep had the climb become, we were forced to dismount and push the bikes. The fields had given way to harsh moorland, cropped by ponies. Here and there the heather and poor grass were broken by stony outcrops. Nothing moved at all. The long shadows merged imperceptibly into a continuous darkness.

'We'll be late,' Del said.

'If we find it,' said Charlie.

Del only grunted. This was a hostel we had never visited, but we had seen it often enough on the map. We knew exactly where it was. We pushed on, searching the moor for a light. The moon came up, brilliantly lucid, and we felt more cheerful, singing gently together.

It was Del who saw the light, high on our left hand, and he led us without a falter along the rough path which led to the house. We were all glad to get there and laughed and joked as we knocked on the door. It was nearly ten o'clock.

Mrs Devereux let us in. She was the warden's wife, a tall, unfriendly woman. When she spoke, her voice was slow and surprisingly soft and she spoke with a Midlands accent. I thought she might have come from Birmingham. Her husband stood silently in the kitchen. They were not welcoming.

'You boys are late,' he said.

'I know,' I answered. 'We're sorry. We didn't know the climb would be so steep — we thought we had plenty of time.'

'You know the rules,' he said. 'I'd be within my rights to turn you away.'

We stood there, not answering.

'They might as well stay, Jack,' said Mrs Devereux, timidly. 'There's nobody else here. They look tired.'

He didn't answer so I took his silence for agreement.

'We'll bring the bikes in,' I said.

He looked at me for the first time, leaning, his hands flat on the kitchen table. He was a stocky man, his broad shoulders filling the flannel shirt he wore, but his face was worn tight down almost to the bone and his eyes were set deep. There was no expression at all on his face, unless it was a kind of impersonal weariness.

We went outside to bring in the cycles.

'Leave them in the passage,' said Mr Devereux as we went.

Outside in the light of the one electric bulb set high in the wall, I

looked at Del and Charlie. They looked quiet and withdrawn and
they did not meet my gaze.

'Cheer up, boys,' I said.

'You must be mad,' said Del, 'but speak to me after supper.'

When we got back in I asked Mr Devereux where we could cook
our supper.

'There'll be no cooking here,' he said.

'But we've had nothing to eat for hours,' I protested, indignation
making my voice sharp. 'You can let us heat a can of beans, at least!'

Del and Charlie stood behind me, saying nothing, leaving it to
me. Mr Devereux looked from one to the other of us, his dead face
empty. He waved a hand briefly.

'The wife will give you a mug of cocoa,' he said, 'and if you have
bread and cheese you can eat that.'

We settled for that, sitting around the scrubbed table. The cocoa
was scaldingly hot and sweet and we drank it without a word.
Devereux and his wife sat each side of the fireplace, on long settles.
There was an unbelievably tense air about them and they never
stopped watching us. The second that Charlie finished his food,
Devereux stood up.

'Come on,' he said, 'I'll show you the dormitory.'

We collected our sleeping bags and our rucksacks and followed
him out of the back door. We were in a courtyard perhaps fifty yards
square, cobbled and empty. The house itself formed one side of the
square, and long farm buildings the other three sides. At the far end
was the stable-block, two-storied like the house, and this is where
he took us. We climbed up the open wooden stairs and into the long
room. It was immaculately swept and clean, its short walls whitewashed with lime, the windows uncurtained. There was no light,
but the clear moon streamed in and we could see easily.

'Here you are,' said Mr Devereux, his whole manner suddenly
more relaxed and friendly. 'You'll be comfortable here. Get off to
sleep as soon as you can.'

We heard him go down the stairs and pull the door behind him.
The latch fell with a smooth click. Charlie Bond began to giggle.

'You certainly told him,' he said to me. 'You should have seen
your face when you thought you weren't going to have any supper!'

'Why not?' said Del. 'You'd have grumbled most if we had come
to bed with empty stomachs.'

There were hand basins at the far end of the room and we washed
in the cold water, unrolled our sleeping bags and threw them on
three beds near one of the windows. We turned in fairly soon.

Normally we would have talked together for an hour, but we didn't
say much that night and everything grew still. I don't know whether
Charlie and Del slept, but I certainly didn't. I was happy and warm
there, and I began to think of Charlie walking down the darkening
cloisters of the abbey, his voice echoing along the roofless walls. I
saw once again the regular turning of Del's legs and feet as he
pedalled along in front of me on the road to Abergavenny, mono-
tonously around and around. I expect I was going to sleep.

What brought me to my feet was startling enough. A door opened
in the courtyard, then there was a confused clatter of feet. That was
all right. It was the scream that stretched me. Not a scream of fright,
but a high-pitched, whinnying scream, rather like that of a horse.
And then there was a regular, light, galloping sound on the cobbles
below. I was at the window at once, Del and Charlie looking over
my shoulders.

The moonlight had divided the courtyard into almost exact
halves, the area near us being brilliantly lit, that against the house
in deep shadow. Mr and Mrs Devereux stood in the full moonlight,
close together, almost in the centre of the yard. Mr Devereux had
a rope in his hands. It reached into the shadow, and Mr Devereux
and his wife turned slowly, facing the galloping as it raced through
the darkness. We did not know what to expect.

Out into the moonlight, roped about his waist, raced a boy of our
own age, his arms thrashing the air, his unkempt pale hair bouncing
on his head. Round and round he went, his heavy boots thumping
and sparking on the cobbles, in and out of the revealing light. His
face as he raced towards us was empty, an idiot's face; froth was
forming around his mouth. Every time he raced into the dark, he
screamed his shaken cry.

After a while, Devereux pulled in the rope, taking the boy in his
arms. Now that he was still, we could see that the boy was unbelievably bent and frail. He could not walk properly, but that may
have been from exhaustion. They went, all three, into the house,
closing the door so softly that we could not hear it at all.

Del and Charlie were sitting on their beds, their faces turned
towards the window, appalled and horrified. I don't know what we
said to each other, or indeed if we said anything at all at that time.

That was thirty years ago. On holiday last year, driving aimlessly
in the region, I came across the valley once again. I didn't recognise
it at first. The road was wider and better surfaced, and there was an
air of prosperity about the place. But the abbey was the same. There
were many visitors there, and I walked along the grass, remembering

Charlie Bond who was killed in Africa in 1942 and Del Wellington who lives somewhere near Manchester and is a chemist.

I drove on, up the hill. The Youth Hostel is still there, still a hostel. It was a warm day, full of summer, but momentarily all I saw were the lucid moonlight and the faces of my two friends, as clear as my hand; all I heard was a ragged galloping over the cobbles.

Away Away in China

Early rising had always been a pleasure for him. Even when he had been in control of great industrial complexes, the prosperity of cities dependent on his judgement, able to order his life into whatever patterns he chose, he had still been at his office at eight every morning. Now, five years retired, the habit was part of him. He enjoyed the young day as much as he had when a boy.

He got up this morning very early. He had set his alarm clock the night before knowing he would not need it, and now, ten minutes before its stridency was ordered, smugly he turned it off. He shuffled his feet into decorous slippers, put on his robe, and went briskly to the bathroom. He shaved with small, precise movements and then took a shower. When he came out he was glowing. His table was prepared and he stood checking it, item by item, admiring his silver, his white tablecloth. Taking a can of orange juice from the refrigerator, he poured some into a tumbler and drank it slowly, waiting for the kettle to boil. The glass turned pearly in his hand and his teeth ached momentarily from the cold of the orange juice. He ate a piece of toast, unhurriedly, savouring it, and drank a cup of tea without milk. Afterwards he washed the dishes and put them away. It was by choice he lived alone. He walked into the bedroom and, as neatly as if he were packing a parcel, folded the sheets to the foot of the bed. Mrs Smethurst would come in and make all ready for his return. Really, he had no need to employ her. Orderly and careful, he made no untidiness, was meticulous in all he did, evidence of his good taste and unostentatious money was everywhere. Yes, he was wealthy and he lived comparatively simply; that's all there was to it. He was never lonely; a man of resource was not lonely.

Clothes were important to him and he chose them seriously. They were expensive, muted, very elegant. Today he would wear a cream shirt, silk, new, tactfully cut, with a Paisley bow tie. His suit, which he had put out the evening before, was Donegal tweed, least heavy of all tweeds, and he was tall and slim enough to carry it. He remembered how carefully he had chosen the material three years before and that he had paid enough for the suit to fit him perfectly. The cloth was subtly woven, in its mix was a hint of pink; never obtrusive, it was confident, somehow, and healthy. His shoes were hand-made and lovingly polished, but not new. When travelling he always saw to it his feet were comfortable. He stood in front of the mirror and recognised his vanity. He was as lean and straight as he had been long ago when he set out from his village, the newly qualified accountant, to that job in the Midlands. Puffing his lips in contempt, he thought of the ugly cheap suit he had worn then, thought of the dirty room in which he had been forced to work, in that gimcrack engineering firm. Well, it hadn't lasted long, he had soon moved to better things. He looked fine, his theatrical white hair brushed back, his face untroubled. As he straightened his shoulders more firmly he heard the newspaper fall through the letter-box.

He opened the door, the paper in his hand. It was dark, but little waking sounds of daylight came to him, the smell of the garden. Stars in the sky were bright as frost and it was going to be a clear day. Raincoat and case were ready for him in the front hall and he put his paper with them, on top of the case, near the neat label with his name, Alan Gwyther.

The taxi came at seven-thirty. He had never learned to drive and looked upon that ability as an accomplishment of unimportant people. He had been accustomed to travelling in pampered cars, Daimlers, Bentleys, for the last twenty of his working years a succession of immaculate limousines from Rolls-Royce. Uniformed chauffeurs, shut away from him by plate-glass shields, had driven him to hotel and conference. He could not remember any of these men clearly, although he recalled the name of the first of his drivers: Thwaite, a Yorkshireman. Dead now, thought Alan Gwyther, a long time dead. He had treated the men well, asked about their families, thanked them fully when a journey was over, gave generous tips. It had paid him to do so. Thwaite's face, long and pale, came unbidden to him, and he heard again his flat Yorkshire voice. The man had been ashamed of his accent; he had sent his daughter to elocution lessons despite Gwyther's sturdy opinion that an able child would learn how to speak properly once the need became obvious.

'Good morning, good morning,' he said heartily to the taxi driver. 'Good of you to come so promptly.'

They took thirty minutes to reach the station and Gwyther waited another ten before his train pulled in. He travelled first class, in a reserved seat, and a young porter, still slack with sleep, carried his case and saw him to his compartment. He was alone. He sat straight-backed in his corner seat, the folded newspaper on his knees, his competent hands relaxed. In Wales, he thought, they'll be having breakfast, my sister and her husband and her daughter. Soon they'll be bustling around in case some tiny aspect of my welcome has been overlooked. The whole village will know I'm about to visit them — I shall come to them like a missionary from another civilisation. People will call on flimsy pretexts just to catch a glimpse of me. He was amused by his fancy. Well, he was eager enough to see them.

The train gave a series of little coughs and barks and began without hurry to leave the station. On the road below the railway bridge he could see files of men cycling to work. It was bright daylight now, and a clear sun, too early for real heat, shone in the faces of the men, giving them unnaturally high colours. The slate roofs of the houses were more blue than the sky. Of course, he thought, these visits are good for me. They are necessary, they nourish me. They renew contact with my roots. He looked down at his impeccable suit and smiled.

Each time he made a visit to his sister's place he gave the suit he travelled in to his brother-in-law. Davy would accept the gift unwillingly, protesting, muttering. He could see Davy as he had been two years ago, holding the coat at arm's length, his eyes flickering doubtfully.

'Go on man, take it,' he said. 'Take it, Davy. You and I are of a size — I've too many suits. I can't wear them all.' And this was true. He knew that a powerful agent of his slightly malicious generosity was his wish to see Davy so discomfited, so unable to deal with the situation. He suspected that each of his given suits had been examined, assessed, admired, and put away in the wardrobe never to be worn. Poor Davy, he thought, and his stiff-backed, stumbling pride. He leaned back in contentment. He was cultured and assured, with the mellow confidence of long and recognised success. He had been in charge of great affairs and even now was not without power. The train, gathering momentum, hurled itself south through brightening England. It was going to be a hot day.

Urgent, obsessed by the demands of its time-table, the train sped through the bleak West Riding towns he knew so well. By lunch time they were running west through the Midlands; on his way to the dining car he spent five minutes looking with distaste at the bulbous chimneys of the potteries, imagining what his life would have been had he stayed there.

I'm well out of it, he thought, and then with a little sharp surprise, I've been very lucky.

Although the food was indifferent, the vegetables limp and yellow and the meat stringy, he lingered over his meal. The half bottle of claret was thin and metallic, but he enjoyed it, sensing the faint pink it brought to his cheeks. There would be no wine at his sister's house. He paid his bill and made his way along the swaying train to his compartment. They were passing through civilised Worcestershire countryside, heavy with harvest; heat haze trembled at the far edges of fields. Reaching his seat, he found a young woman sitting opposite. She must have got on at Kidderminster or Worcester. They smiled at each other, saying nothing, and he settled, picked up his newspaper, looked at her.

She was much the age of his niece, perhaps thirty. He liked her hair, dark as Mary's, and she looked like Mary, too. She was dressed in a summer-weight costume of pale fawn, the jacket of which was thrown over an empty seat. Her blouse was plain and expensive, her shoes excellent. She sat coolly groomed, her hands in her lap, relaxed and composed under his gaze. He approved of her. He thought again how much he looked forward to seeing Mary. A stubborn girl though, a mind of her own, that one. She should have left home years ago — with her ability he could have helped her to something worth while, she would have climbed. But she wouldn't leave. The hot afternoon entered the carriage and the old man sat deliberately upright against the heavy somnolence of the journey. Outside, the stubble glittered in the sun, the rich fields patched by shadows under the trees, the top-heavy elms and the wide oaks. He would have spoken if silence had not been so easy, if the warm steady rocking of the train had not lulled him into a state of paradoxically watchful sleep, if the golden and perfect fields had not come towards him one after the other, like an endless, beautiful country of his imagining.

In one of the fields, in a corner almost immediately below the raised embankment, a shot of colour held his eye. Two birds fed there in cautious harmony. One, its mail of feathers polished hard in the yellow light, a small, Oriental monarch strutting, like fine silk glittering, one was a pheasant. One leg uplifted and paused in a high step, thin claws stretched towards the ground, there it stood, neck stretched to peck at the stems. The other, humbler because of its shorter legs and small size, was a fantail pigeon, flown from a dovecote to glean in the cut fields. The spun metal of the pheasant and the blazing white of the dove burned against his gaze. As he leaned forward, not wanting to miss an instant of vision, the pigeon flapped puffily a yard into the air, landing again as untidily as a handkerchief. It was unimaginably white against the brown stalks of felled wheat and the deeper bronze of the pheasant. He gaped momentarily at the heraldic birds. Then they were gone and he was left, one hand against the glass of the window, half pointing, expressing both his own delight and loss and the hope that the girl too had seen the marvel.

She nodded at him. He could see she was amused, and his answering grin was shamefaced, recognising his comic transformation from drowsing old man.

'I've always been fascinated by birds,' he said. 'It's always astonished me that they should exist in the same world as us. There's a sense in which I understand animals, they are akin to us, have solid bones like us; but birds are so alien, so foreign . . . . When I was a boy in the country I would hold young birds from the hedgerow nests in my hands, and know absolutely that my palms did not understand what it was they held. Those extraordinary feathers — well, you saw the pheasant.'

She looked at him gravely.

'I've not thought about it,' she said. 'Birds fly across the sky and I see them, but I don't recognise them although I like the patterns they make. I am not concerned about them.'

This seemed to him astonishing. Everything that came to his eyes he classified, recognised, in a sense acquired.

'Are you travelling to Wales?' he asked.

'Yes,' she said. 'My parents have retired there, at Swansea, and I shall join them for a brief time.'

The girl talked easily. She was interesting and amusing and he enjoyed the journey enormously. They left the train at Swansea, she to meet her parents and he to travel in the single Pullman carriage that went on into Pembrokeshire. They shook hands like old friends.

'You may not see anything as dramatic as your two birds,' she said, 'but you'll like Wales. After a week you'll not want to leave.'

He shook his head, thinking of his books, his music, his house. Already they seemed too far away. But he was pleased that the girl had not recognised him as Welsh, that he had not been betrayed by his speech. Long ago he had tamed his accent until it was formidably neutral, restrained the modulations of his voice until it was cool and objective. The Pullman filled up with young soldiers returning noisily to Ireland. They piled their rough equipment where they could; unbearably red and moist in their coarse uniforms, they lounged awkwardly, their strong legs thrust before them. It was suddenly very hot in the carriage. Hunched in his seat, he was unreasonably irritated and uncomfortable. He was tired. The journey was far too long. He hoped Mary would have a car to meet him at Carmarthen.

Mary was waiting for him on the platform, waving like a child, yet she saddened him. He had not expected her to look so old, so visibly defeated. He climbed from the train quietened by her watchful eyes, the lines of tiredness and disappointment on her face. Her clothes were drab and ordinary, there was nothing left of her old vivacity. She held in one hand a bag of heavy groceries, and the knuckles stood out raw and bony as a man's. He saw to his distress that she was not like the fashionable girl in the train; she was clumsier, older, beaten.

'Uncle Alan,' she said. 'Lovely to see you. Did you have a good journey?'

'Fairly,' he said, 'fairly good. Perfect as far as Swansea, but after that . . .' He held up a hand in dismissal. 'How's your mother?' he asked.

'Waiting to see you, of course,' said Mary. 'This is Mansel, Mansel Edwards from the village. You don't know him. He had some business in town this afternoon and he's waited to drive us home.'

A serious young man stepped forward. He wore jeans and a faded blue shirt, the sleeves rolled. His arms and face were weathered and his supple boots covered with fine summer dust. He was inches shorter than Gwyther. He nodded, picked up the case without effort, and led the way to the car.

'Sit in front, Mr Gwyther,' said Mansel. 'It's cooler.'

Windows open for the buzzing heat, they moved through the town and into the hills. He knew every inch of this road. Twice a day he had travelled it when serving his articles with Phineas Griffiths; around the next bend would be The Rock and Fountain, the inn where he had met his friends on Saturday evenings; above the quarry was the farm where Charlie Phillips had lived. Blindfolded he could have recognised every bend and dip in the way, known the different sounds of the accompanying river, by the total familiarity of it, by instinct; he could describe stone by stone each of the plain old houses that stood, lonely and arbitrary, at the roadside. Some, he saw, were empty and abandoned; insidious weather was picking them loose.

'Elizabeth Winstone's house,' he said, pointing. 'Who lives there now?'

'Nobody,' said Mary. 'She's dead, dead these two years.'

'Elizabeth Winstone dead?' He was appalled. 'She can't be. Why, it's not long since I heard her sing at a concert in York. Beautiful, a beautiful singer, a lovely voice.'

He turned restlessly in his seat, shifting his hot old body to other comfortless positions. He was obscurely indignant at news of the singer's death, affronted and upset. He thought of her as he had seen her at York, vigorous, confident, her sturdy peasant's body controlled to the service of that gorgeous voice. Note after perfect note floated generously into his memory. Well, yes, it would have been six years ago.

'What happened to her?' he asked. His voice sounded querulous to him.

'Don't know,' said Mary. She was looking back at the singer's house. 'She returned from London, didn't like living there. And then one day we heard she was dead. It was in the papers; it's strange you didn't read it.'

'I didn't read it,' said the old man heavily.

'Not everyone can stand leaving home,' Mansel said, not taking his eyes off the road. 'Not everyone can take it, living far away.'

His voice was so slow and thoughtful and the old man searched for some deeper meaning.

'You have to go,' he said, 'where your gifts and your energies take you. One place is much like another. You make the place in which you live, it becomes your creation. And it doesn't matter where you die.'

'Not so.' Mansel shook his head in gentle dissent. 'Some people live more easily with their failure than others.'

'Failure?' said the old man wonderingly. 'But success was what Elizabeth Winstone had to live with. She had merely to organise her life about her achievement. She was brilliantly successful.'

'Doesn't one kind of success imply a balancing failure?' asked Mansel. 'Isn't it possible that her achievement was the result of a decision that was wrong for her, that it meant, for example, a life lived in places where she was unhappy?'

The old man grunted, but did not reply. He had taken his chances, followed his abilities where they led; but there was always an element of choice. Mansel would find out. He sat in silence until the car left the highway and turned down the narrower road to his sister's house. She stood outside her door waiting, wiping her hands on her apron, her dog at her side. Mansel drove away, his brown arm waving.

Gwyther was always surprised by his sister's frailness. In his mind she was the big girl on whom he had relied for almost everything. She had taken him to school on his first morning and on every reluctant morning until he was old enough to go alone; she it was who had so often bribed him from moods of stubborn temper with wild tales which set him laughing despite himself, his back still turned to her, had fed him ambitiously when their parents were out at market or sale, protected him equally from the assaults of older boys and the just punishments their father, that meek man, had sometimes threatened. He put his hands on her shoulders and they smiled at each other. The little shadows of his journey cleared away in the simple return of love.

'Margaret,' he said, 'you never change.'

Over tea he was excited and talkative, remembering events he had thought long dead. He was very happy, laughing, eating more than he should. When Davy came in from his few fields he stood there unnoticed, listening to them laugh.

'You're here then, Alan,' said Davy.

He was never easy with Gwyther. He thought of him as he had been as a boy, too quick of tongue and wit, thin, urgent, apart from the rest of them.

'Yes, I'm here,' sang the dapper old man gaily. 'Home is the sailor, Davy, home from the sea, and the hunter is home from the hills. Old times, old days — that's what we're talking about. Pull up your chair and tell me all your news.'

There was nothing Davy could tell Alan Gwyther, he could think of nothing to interest him. All he could speak of were the slow, important changes of the seasons and the rituals of life and death. He thought hard.

'Oh, no news,' he said. 'The place is changing slowly, I suppose, all the older people going one by one — there are few left who remember you now, Alan. That's about all. And Glanafon Farm has been sold. To a Pole; nice man, I met him yesterday. Name of Poniatowski, but he speaks good English. So he should — he's been living here fifteen years, he told me.'

'Language is a strange thing,' said Margaret. 'Look how well Alan speaks English, although he was brought up in the Welsh.'

'Uncle Alan has forgotten his Welsh,' Mary said. She had been quiet for so long that her voice, waspish and hard, startled them. She stared at her uncle. 'He's completely English now,' she said. 'He looks English, he sounds English, his attitudes are English. He hadn't heard of Elizabeth Winstone's death.'

He was dismayed by the unexpectedness and irrelevance of the attack, all his laughter collapsing about him. He got up quietly and took his bag up the stone stairs, each one worn thin and concave at the lip. He could remember his mother climbing these stairs, slowly, with such difficulty. That was long ago. He went into his room and put the case on the floor. Well, Mary must be a sad girl. All that

ability and no opportunity to use it, her life without interest or
variety, wasting her aimless time on trivial affairs. She had been such
a bright little thing. And not married of course. Perhaps that had
left her saddened and disappointed. He sat on the bed and looked
out of the window. The field sloped steeply down, interrupted by
an untidy summer hedge, the long whips of its brambles waving, to
the stream that ran alongside the village street. He could look right
on to the rooftops, identify the houses, people them with the families
who had lived there sixty years before. He had known them all, every
one of them. The short grass of the hills was a brilliant, moist green,
except for three or four fields where late hay stood uncut. Davy's
field was like a lawn, cropped tight by sheep and his short-tempered
Michaelmas geese. When he heard a car stop outside the door he
went downstairs. It could have been someone he knew, a friend from
the old days come to see him; but it was only Mansel and his wife.

Mansel's wife was a teacher. A fair, plump girl, she sat in a fireside
chair talking of the children in her class. She was so lively, so droll
a mimic that the old man's spirits rose.

'And do you teach them everything?' he asked. 'You must be
wonderfully busy.'

'They're only seven and eight years old,' she said, 'so there's
nothing brilliantly academic about it. I cope quite well with everything except music, and then I'm hopeless.'

Mansel was looking at her with amusement.

'No false modesty,' he said. 'You may not be the world's best
pianist, but you're not bad. In any case it's a lot easier than teaching
those little kids in Malaya.'

He turned to Alan.

'When we were out there,' he said, 'in the Far East, she used to
have a class under the trees in the centre of the village. She didn't
understand the language at first, but they got on very well, together,
she and the little brown kids.'

'How I envy you,' said the old man, 'going out to Malaya. Europe
I know well, of course, and I've made many business trips to
America and Canada, but never to the East. I could have gone, but
I was always too busy.'

'Alan is a great traveller,' said his sister. 'Where was it you were
last year, Alan? Salzburg, wasn't it?'

'Mansel is a forester,' said Mary, 'and he's been everywhere.'

'Hardly everywhere,' Mansel said, 'but we've tried to go wherever
the big forests are. We went out East the day after our wedding and
we were there three years. We've been to Africa too, and we spent

some time in Canada and in South America.'

'Now we're home,' said his wife, 'looking after Welsh forests and Welsh children. But we've been all over the world.'

Amused and attracted as he was by the girl's cheerful candour, her uncomplicated good humour, Gwyther was nevertheless piqued. He was a competitive man, a winner. Always in this house he had been the one to relate tales of travel and adventure, and now he was outfaced by a pair of youngsters.

'What about the songs?' he called. 'What songs did you teach the little Malaysians? What songs did we learn as children, Margaret?'

'The song you always sang, and you sang it until we were sick of the sound of it,' his sister said, 'was "Draw, Draw yn China".' I can remember Father threatening to send him to China if Alan sang it once more, just once more.'

'Of course,' said Gwyther, laughing. 'Of course.'

He began to sing quietly, the tune suddenly as familiar as his skin, and then stopped in consternation.

'You're right, Mary,' he said. 'I have forgotten a lot.'

But Mary sang alongside him, bringing the words back to him. He stumbled after her, his eyes on her mouth to catch the first syllables of words that he had lost.

> Draw draw yn China a thiroedd Japan,

they sang together.

> Plant bach melynion s'yn byw,
> Dim ond eilunod o'u gylch ym mhob man,
> Neb i ddweud am Dduw.

Confident now, he swung into the last lines.

> Iesu, cofia'r plant,
> Iesu, cofia'r plant,
> Anfon genhadon ymhell dros y môr,
> Iesu, cofia'r plant.

The laughter and clapping elated Gwyther. He caught Mary's hand.

'To the parlour,' he cried, 'all of us, we'll all sing it together.'

He sat down at the old American organ, pushing away at the pedals. It hadn't been used for years and he worked hard, the wooden treadles clacking and grumbling before the dry bellows held enough air to carry a tune. Only Mary had come with him, and along the passage he could see a shaft of electric light come from the kitchen. He could hear Mansel's voice talking quietly and Davy's deep monosyllabic answers. He began to play, his stiff fingers accurate on the naïve melody. He and Mary sang together. She stood beside his chair, singing seriously, her hands clasped in front of her like a little girl. Well, she was loyal, this one. When they had finished he closed the organ. It had been his father's. They left the room and went back to the lit kitchen. The quiet talking went on around them. It was as if nobody had heard him sing.

Later, in his room, the day's invisible humiliations came sourly to him. The night was cool; it was like the death of summer. His sister had turned back his sheets and the blanket carried near the top two wide bands of colour. It was new, a thick blanket of traditional design, woven locally. There had been one exactly like it on his bed when he had been a child. Many nights when he had been small he had lain in the dark, feeling the texture of the blanket as delicately as he could, with his fingertips. He had been convinced that he could tell the difference in the colour of the wool by feel, that when he reached the pink band, or the green one, he would know by the subtle difference of the wool. The moment he thought his hand had decided another colour he would use his torch, a flat torch with an imitation leather case and three glass lenses, one red, one white, one green. But this was a new blanket. He switched off his light and sat on the bed. It was incredible that he could have forgotten the words of that old hymn. How foolish he had been to imagine that they would all troop into the parlour to sing with him. He began to whisper the words of the song to himself and then, obstinately, turned them to English in his mouth.

> Away away in China and the lands of Japan
> Little yellow children live.
> Nothing but idols around them everywhere ...

He sat on his white bed and looked out into the night. He was away in China all right. Grimly he remembered the pheasant and flawless dove he had seen that afternoon, taking what comfort he could from the memory. He thought of his house, lonely and cold and deserted as he was, distant now as the idea of safety. He got stiffly into bed, sliding his thin legs along the sheets. He had forgotten to bring a glass of water. He would do without. A burst of men's voices came up from the village as the inn closed its doors after the evening's pleasure. He would not have been able to recognise one voice had he been there, not one voice. Perhaps he had been at the centre of things too long, perhaps his place was in the shadowy margins. The geese cackled briefly from the melancholy field below his window. He lay still and straight in the bed as a scatter of unexpected rain hit the pane, irregular, hard, stinging like tears.

A Roman Spring

I have this place in Wales, a small house set in four acres of pasture, facing north. It's simple country, slow-moving. I look down my fields and over a narrow valley, green even in winter. I go whenever I can, mainly for the fishing, which is splendid, but also because I like to walk over the grass, slowly, with nobody else about. The place is so silent that you discover small noises you thought had vanished from the world, the taffeta rustle of frail twigs in a breeze, curlews bubbling a long way up.

It's astonishing the old skills I find myself master of when I'm there, satisfying things like clearing out the well until its sand is unspotted by any trace of rotten leaf and its water comes freely through in minute, heavy fountains; or splitting hardwood with a short blow of the cleaver exactly to the point of breaking. I've bought all the traditional tools, the rasp, the band saw, the edged hook, the long-handled, heart-shaped spade for ditching. After a few days there I adopt an entirely different rhythm and routine from my normal way of living. Nothing seems without its purpose, somehow. I pick up sticks for kindling as I walk the lanes; I keep an eye cocked for changes of the weather.

We went down in April, my wife and I, for the opening of the salmon-fishing season. The weather had been so dry that the river was low, and few fish had come up from the estuary, ten miles away. I didn't care. We had a few days of very cold wind, and I spent my time cleaning the hedges of old wood, cutting out some wayward branches, storing the sawn pieces in the shed. After this I borrowed a chain saw from my neighbour Denzil Davies, and ripped through a couple of useless old apple trees that stood dry and barren in the garden. In no time they were reduced to a pile of neat, odorous logs.

They made marvellous burning. Every night for almost a week I banked my evening fires high with sweet wood, and we'd sit there in the leaping dark, in the low house, until it was time for supper. Then, one morning, the spring came.

I swear I felt it coming. I was out in front of the house when I felt a different air from the south, meek as milk, warm. It filled the fields from hedge to hedge as if they had been the waiting beds of dry ponds. Suddenly everything was newer; gold entered the morning colours. It was a Sunday morning. I walked through the fields noticing for the first time how much growth the grass had made.

From some neighbouring farm, perhaps Ty Gwyn on the hillside, perhaps Penwern lower down the valley, the sound of someone working with stone came floating through the air. I stood listening to the flawless sound as it moved without a tremor, visibly almost, toward me. 'Chink,' it came, and again, 'chink,' as the hammer chipped the flinty stone. I turned back to the house and told my wife. We had lunch in the garden, and afterward we found a clump of white violets as round and plump as a cushion, right at the side of the road. They grew beside a tumbledown cottage which is also mine, at the edge of my field where it meets the lane. The cottage is called Hebron. It wasn't so bad when I bought the place — I could have saved it then, had I the money — but the rain has got into it now, and every winter brings it closer to the ground. It had only two rooms, yet whole families were raised there, I've been told. We picked two violets, just as tokens, as emblems of the new spring, and walked on down the hill. Ruined and empty though it is, I like Hebron. I was pleased that the flowers grew outside its door.

As we walked along, a blue van passed us, and we stood in the hedge to let it through. Our lane is so narrow that very few people use it — the four families who live there, and a few tradesmen. But we didn't recognise the van. We heard the driver change down to second gear as he swung through the bend and into the steep of the hill, outside the broken cottage. We had a splendid day. In the afternoon we took the car out and climbed over the Preseli Hills to Amroth, in Pembrokeshire. The sands were empty; the pale sea was fastidiously calm. It was late when we got back.

The next day was every bit as perfect. I got up in the warm first light, made some tea, cleaned the ash from the grate, and went into the field. I took a small axe with me, so that I could break up a fallen branch of sycamore that lay beneath its parent in the bottom field. Beads of dew, each holding its brilliant particle of reflected sun, hung on the grass blades. I pottered about, smiling, feeling the comfortable heat between my shoulder blades. Over the sagging roof of Hebron I could see the purple hills of Cardiganshire rising fold on fold into the heart of Wales. I listened idly to my neighbour, whoever he was, begin his work again, the clink of his hammer on the stone sounding so near to me. It took me a little while to realise that it *was* close at hand. I was unwilling to believe that anyone could be away from his own house on so serene and beautiful an early morning. But someone was. Someone was chipping away inside the walls of Hebron.

I ran through the wet grass, reached the cottage, and looked through a gap where the stones had fallen out of the back wall. I could see right through to the lane. The blue van was parked there, and a thin, blonde girl stood beside it, her long face turned down a little, her hair over her shoulders. The wall was too high for me to see anyone in the house.

'What goes on?' I said. I couldn't believe that my ruin was being taken away piecemeal. The girl didn't move. It was as if she hadn't heard me.

'Who's there?' I called. 'What do you think you're doing?'

A young man stood up inside the house, his head appearing opposite mine through the hole in the wall. He was dark, round-faced, wore one of those fashionable Mexican moustaches. He had evidently been kneeling on the floor.

'Just getting a few bricks,' he said, his face at once alarmed and ingratiating. He waited, smiling at me.

'You can't.' I said. 'It's mine. The whole thing is mine — cottage, fields, the lot.'

The young man looked shocked.

'I'm sorry,' he said. 'I've had permission from the local Council to take stuff away . . . They say it doesn't belong to anyone . . . I'm sorry.'

'The Council are wrong,' I said. 'This cottage belongs to me.'

I felt stupid, standing there, talking through a ragged gap in a wall three feet thick, but there was no way of getting around to him, except by walking back up the field, through a gate, and down the lane to the front of the house, where the white violets were. The thin, silent girl was standing almost on top of the flowers, which made me obscurely angry. I turned around and hurried off, along-side the hedge. As I went I heard the van start up, and Hebron was deserted when I got back. I opened the door. They'd taken the frames out of the windows, the wooden partition which had divided the little house into two rooms, and an old cupboard I had been storing there. I was incredulous, then furious. I looked down at the floor. All my marvellous quarry tiles had been prized up and carried away. I could have wept. Nine inches square and an inch thick, the tiles had been locally made over a hundred years ago. They were a rich plum colour, darker when you washed them, and there were little frosted imperfections in them that caught the light. They were very beautiful.

I ran up the road, calling for my wife. She came out and listened to me, her obvious sympathy a little flawed because she was also

very amused. She had seen me stamping along, red-faced and
muttering, waving aloft the hatchet I had forgotten I was holding.

'No wonder they vanished so quickly,' said my wife. 'You must
have looked extraordinary, waving that tomahawk at them through
a hole in the wall. Poor young things, they must have wondered
what sort of people live here.'

I could see that it was funny. I began to caper about on the grass
in an impromptu war dance, and Denzil Davies came up in his new
car. As far as Denzil is concerned, I'm an Englishman, and therefore
eccentric. Unmoved, he watched me complete my dance.

But I was angry still. I could feel the unleashing of my temper as
I told my story to Denzil. 'They had a blue van,' I said.

'It was a good market in Carmarthen last week,' said Denzil
carefully, looking at some distant prospect. 'Milking cows fetched
a very good price, very good.'

'Took my window frames, my good tongue-and-groove partition'
I mourned. 'My lovely old cupboard.'

'I believe the Evanses are thinking of moving,' said Denzil. 'Of
course, that farm is getting too big for them, now that Fred has got
married. It's a problem, yes it is.'

'A young man with a moustache,' I said. 'And a girl with long,
fair hair. Do you know them, Denzil?'

'I might buy one or two fields from old Tom Evans.' Denzil
replied. 'He's got some nice fields near the top road.'

'They stole my quarry tiles,' I said. 'Every bloody one.'

Denzil looked at me with his guileless blue eyes. 'You've never
seen my Roman castle, have you?' he said. 'Come over and see it
now. It's not much of an old thing, but professors have come down
from London to look at it. And one from Scotland.' Kitty excused
herself, saying she had some reading to catch up on. I sat beside
Denzil in his new blue Ford, and we bumped along the half mile of
track that leads to his farmhouse. I'd been there before, of course.
Denzil's farmyard is full of cats. After evening milking he always
puts out an earthenware bowl holding gallons of warm milk. Cats
arrive elegantly from all directions and drink at their sleek leisure.

We left the car in the yard, and climbed through the steep fields
to a couple of poor acres at the top of the hill. Although high, the
soil was obviously sour and wet. Clumps of stiff reeds grew everywhere, the unformed flowers of the meadowsweet were already
recognisable, and little sinewy threads of vivid green marked the
paths of the hidden streams. Right in the middle of the field was a
circular rampart about four feet high, covered with grass and

thistles, the enclosed centre flat and raised rather higher than the surrounding land. I paced it right across, from wall to wall, and the diameter was nearly seventy feet. There was a gap of eight or nine feet in the west of the rampart, obviously a gateway. It was very impressive. Denzil stood watching me as I scrambled about. Everything I did amused him.

I took an old, rusty fencing stake to knock away the thistles growing on top of the bank and forced its pointed end into the thin soil. I didn't have to scratch down very deeply before I hit something hard, and soon I uncovered a smooth stone, almost spherical and perhaps two pounds in weight. I hauled it out and carried it down to Denzil. It was grey and dense, quite unlike the dark, flaky, local stone used for building my own cottage. And Hebron too, of course. I scored my thumbnail across it, but it didn't leave a scar. It was incredibly hard. Faint, slightly darker parallel lines ran closely through it, and a small irregular orange stain, like rust, marked its surface on one side. Denzil nodded. 'That's it,' he said. 'That's what they made the walls with. Hundreds and hundreds of those round stones.' My stone had been worn smooth and round in centuries of water, in the sea or in a great river. We were nine hundred feet high and miles from the sea or any river big enough to mould such stones in numbers, yet the Roman walls were made of them.

'They're under the road too,' said Denzil. 'The same stones.'

I looked down from the walls of Denzil's castle. It was easy to see the road, now that he'd said it. A discernible track, fainter green than the land around, marched straight and true, westward from the Roman circle, until it met the hedge. Even there it had defied nearly two thousand years of husbandry. Generations of farmers, finding that little would grow above the stones, had left its surface untilled so that the road, covered with a thin scrub of tenacious blackthorn, went stubbornly on. We saw it reach the road two hundred feet lower down, halt momentarily, and then continue undeterred until it was out of sight. I knew it well, on the other side of the narrow road. It was the boundary of my fields. I had often wondered why I should have had so regular a strip of difficult and worthless shrubs.

'Just wide enough for two chariots to pass,' said Denzil, 'That's what one of those London men told me. But I don't know if he was right.'

We looked with satisfaction at the straight path of the Romans.

'I've got new neighbours,' Denzil said. 'Down in Pengron. Funny people, come from Plymouth.' He looked gently toward Pengron, a small holding invisible in its little valley. 'They hadn't been here a week,' he went on, 'before they cut down one of my hedges. For firewood.' He let his eyes turn cautiously in my direction. 'Young fellow with a moustache,' he said, 'and a fair-haired girl.'

'How interesting,' I said, with heavy irony. 'And do they have a blue van?'

'Strange you should ask that,' said Denzil mildly. 'I believe they do.' We smiled at each other. 'Can you see,' Denzil said, 'that the Roman road must have passed right alongside Hebron? There must have been a house on that spot for hundreds and hundreds of years, I bet.' He was right. The old cottage sat firmly next to the dark accuracy of the traceable road, its position suddenly relevant. Carrying my stone, I walked back through the fields to have my lunch.

In the afternoon I drove over to Pengron. The house, its windows curtainless, seemed empty, but a caravan stood in the yard. The thin girl came to the door of the caravan, holding a blue plate in her hand. 'Good afternoon,' I said, but she didn't answer.

I've never seen anyone as embarrassed as the young man when he appeared behind her. He jumped out and hurried toward me. 'I know,' he said. 'You want me to take everything back. I will, I'll take it all back this afternoon. I certainly will.'

I felt very stiff and upright, listening to him. I could see all my tiles arranged in neat rows, six to a pile, on the ground. He must have taken over a hundred. He'd been at it for days, chipping away with his hammer while I wandered round in happy ignorance.

'I can understand,' I said in the most stilted and careful manner, 'that someone surprised in a situation as you were this morning is likely to say something, as an excuse, which may not be exactly true. But I have to know if you really have permission from the local Council to remove material from my cottage. If this is true, then I must go to their offices and get such permission withdrawn.'

He was in agony, his face crimson with shame. I felt sorry for him as I stood unbendingly before him.

'No,' he said. 'No, I don't have any permission. It's just that someone up the village told me that he didn't think the old place belonged to anyone. I'll take everything back this afternoon.'

I looked at my tongue-and-groove partition, my window frames. Unrecognisable almost, they formed a heap of firewood in one corner of the yard. Waving a hand at them in hopeless recognition of the situation, I said, 'It's not much use taking that back, but the tiles, yes, and my cupboard, and anything else you haven't broken up.' I walked back to the car, and he followed, nodding vehemently all the way. I was glad to leave him. When I looked in at Hebron later on, the tiles and the cupboard had been returned. I didn't enjoy myself much that day. It's stupid to be so possessive. The old cottage is an unprepossessing mess, not even picturesque. I ought to have been pleased that someone was finding it useful, but I wasn't. The lingering remnants of my anger pursued me through the night, and I was pretty tired next day. I took it easy.

I can't think why I went down to Hebron in the cool of the evening. I walked listlessly down the hill, becoming cheerful without energy when I found a wren's nest in the hedge. There never was such a place for wrens. They sing all day, shaking their absurd little bodies with urgent song. It was a good evening, cloudless and blue, a little cool air tempering the earlier warmth. I began to whistle. At quiet peace with myself, aimless and relaxed, I approached the cottage. When a man pushed his head and shoulders through the gaping window I was totally startled.

'How much for the house, then?' he said. He withdrew from the window, and stepping carefully, reappeared at the door, closing it slowly behind him. He was a very small man. Despite the mildness of the evening, he wore his reefer jacket wrapped well around him, and its collar high. He couldn't have been a couple of inches over five feet.

'It's not worth much,' I said. He pushed his tweed cap off his forehead and smiled at me, a sweet, wise smile, but incredibly remote.

'No,' he said, 'not now. Oh, but it was lovely sixty years ago.'

'Did you know it,' I asked, 'all that time ago?'

'Longer,' he said. 'More than sixty years ago. Since I first saw it, that is.'

He stood outside the house, his hands deep in his pockets. He stood very carefully, protectively, as if he carried something exceedingly fragile inside him. His breathing was gentle and deliberate, a conscious act. It gave him a curious dignity.

'Know it?' he said. 'For ten years I lived in this house. My brother, my mother, and me. We came here when I was five years old, after my father died, and I was fifteen when we left. I'm sixty-seven now.' We turned together to walk down the hill. He moved slowly, economically. We had gone but a few yards when he stopped, bent down, and picked up a thin ash-plant, newly cut from the hedge.

'I've been getting bean sticks,' he explained. 'I've left them along the lane where I cut them, so that I can pick them up as I go back.'

We talked for a long time, and I warmed toward him. He was a great old man. We stood there, the evening darkening around us, and he told me of people who had lived along the lane in the days of his boyhood, of his work as a young man in the farms about us, of the idyllic time when he lived in Hebron with his mother and brother.

'But there's no water there,' I said. 'How did you manage for water?'

'I used to go up to your place,' he said. 'To your well. Times without number I've run up this road, a bucket in each hand, to get water from your well. We thought it was the best water in the world.'

Slowly we moved a few yards on, and the old man lifted the last of his bean sticks from where it lay. Then he turned, faced resolutely forward, and prepared to make his way back to the village, perhaps a mile away over the fields.

'I've got to be careful,' he said. 'Take things very slowly, the doctor said. I'm very lucky to be alive.' He placed his hand delicately on the lapel of his navy coat. 'Big Ben has gone with me,' he said. 'Worn out. He doesn't tick as strongly as he used to.'

'Let me carry those sticks for you,' I said, understanding now his deliberate slowness, his sweet tolerance, his other-worldliness. He was a man who had faced his own death closely, for a long time, and he spoke to me from the other side of knowledge I had yet to learn.

'I'll manage,' he said. He bundled his sticks under one arm, opened the gate, and walked away. It was so dark that he had vanished against the black hedge while I could still hear his foot-steps.

In the morning I went into the field below Hebron. It's not my field; Denzil rents it from an absentee landlord, and keeps a pony or two in it. There's a steep bank below the hedge, below the old Roman road, that is, and Hebron's garden is immediately above the bank. As I had hoped, the ground there was spongy and wet, green with sopping mosses. I climbed back up and into the garden, hacking and pushing through invading bramble and blackthorn, through overgrown gooseberry bushes. In the corner of the garden which overhangs Denzil's field, everything seemed to grow particu-larly well; the hedge grass was lush and rampant, the hazel bushes unusually tall. I took my hook and my saw, and cleared a patch of ground about two yards square. It took me most of the morning. Afterward I began to dig.

It was easier than I had expected, and I hadn't gone two spits down before I was in moist soil, pulling shaped spadesful of earth away with a suck, leaving little fillings of water behind each stroke of the blade. By lunchtime I'd uncovered a good head of water, and in the afternoon I'd shaped it and boxed it with stones from the old cottage, and while it cleared I built three steps down to it. It was a marvellous spring. It held about a foot of the purest, coldest water. I drank from it, ceremonially, and then I held my hand in it up to the wrist, feeling the chill spread into my forearm. Afterward I cleaned my spade meticulously until it shone, until it rang like a faint cymbal as I scrubbed its metal with a handful of couch grass. I knew that I would find water. For hundreds of years, since Roman times, perhaps, a house had stood there: it had to have a spring.

I put my tools in the boot of the car and drove up to the village. If I meet my old friend, I thought, I'll tell him about my Roman spring. I saw him almost at once. He stood, upright and short, in front of the Harp Inn. There was nobody else in the whole village it seemed. I blew the horn, and he raised both arms in greeting. I waved to him, but I didn't stop. Let him keep his own Hebron, I thought. Let him keep the days when he could run up the hill with two buckets for the best water in the world, his perfect heart strong in his boy's ribs. I had drunk from the spring, and perhaps the Romans had, but only the birds of the air, and the small beasts, fox, polecat, badger, would drink from it now. I imagined it turning green and foul as the earth filled it in, its cottage crumbling each year perceptibly nearer the earth.

I drove slowly back. The next day we packed our bags and travelled home, across Wales, half across England.

Percy Colclough
and the Religious Girls

This is not my story at all. If not to Percy Colclough, then it belongs to my friend Tom Bevan, who told it to me in the taproom of an inn five miles out of Chichester on the A286, the road to Midhurst, in Sussex. The name of the inn is the Horse and Groom, and it is about a hundred and fifty miles and thirty years away from the scene of the story Tom Bevan told me.

Tom had left school in 1935, when he was fourteen years old, and gone to work in the mines. Anyone could tell he'd once been a miner. He has the high, heavy shoulders that years of hacking and shovelling give to a man, particularly to one working in the South Wales pits, where there was never enough room to swing a pick properly. He also carries on his face a few of the thin, indelible-blue scars all miners wear.

He told me this story in his emphatic voice, his fanatical pale eyes fixed over my shoulder on the resurrection of his memories. I had never known Percy Colclough, but as soon as Tom Bevan began to speak I could see him plainly. He had started work on the same day, at the same age, and in the same Aberdare pit as Tom Bevan.

For four years they had worked near each other, Tom Bevan with his father and Percy Colclough with an older brother. Tom paraded before me the two young men, hard, spare, muscular. I saw them clearly; I knew the way their cheekbones shone after the ferocity of their evening shaves, I could see the extravagant care with which they brushed their hair, docile with hair cream.

Work was brutal and hours were long in the mines in the late thirties. Together, Percy and Tom would walk over the mountain to the pithead, and they'd stumble home together after eight hours of backbreaking toil, too tired to speak, too tired almost to go to bed.

Their lives were extraordinarily narrow. From Monday morning until Friday night, they worked and ate and fell heavily to sleep, and all their pleasure would be packed into the brief weekend respite of Saturday and Sunday. Even this was an unadventurous leisure, almost ritualistic in its regularity: football, dancing, a visit to the cinema, drinking in the evening with one's friends. They never went farther from home than the dance hall at Pontypridd, eight miles down the valley. There they would gaze at young men from valleys four or five miles distant as if they came from the other end of the world.

Once a year, on a Saturday in August, they would go to Barry Island, or Porthcawl, or another South Wales coast town, in company with other miners, to a meeting of their trades union, the Miners' International Federation. I have a sepia image, as clear as if I myself had taken a photograph, of Tom and Percy, caught in midstep as they walk along the promenade, their white collars open, their jackets over their arms, the wide trousers then fashionable blown around their striding shins by a wind off the sea. That would have been a great journey for them — like a journey to Siberia, almost.

So it was enterprising of Tom, when, on a Saturday morning in the cold spring of 1939, he walked breezily along to the railway station, its one platform empty in the pale-yellow sun, and bought a return ticket to Cardiff. Cardiff, twenty-four miles away, was the big city; in the evening, its lights warmed the sky with orange promises of the exotic as far north as Tom's village.

Tom went down on the nine-fifteen, walked like a famous dandy around the two main streets, looked at the expensive shops and the girls newly blooming in the sun, had lunch at Woolworth's, went to a football match, and was home by seven-thirty. This was living. He told nobody of his escape from the valley, not even Percy Colclough. And the next Saturday he went to Swansea.

This was a longer journey and lacked the intoxicating, headlong directness of Tom's first venture. There was, for example, a change of trains at Neath, and he had to wait for ten minutes in a cold rain that drifted inexorably over the nearby hills and settled, as if for ever, on the whole of Wales. Then his carriage was full of comfortable families going shopping. On his trip to Cardiff, Tom had had a compartment to himself, so that he could take two steps from window to window and miss nothing of the scenery on either side. He had sung loudly, in his resonant baritone, the popular songs of the day — 'Begin the Beguine', 'Blue Moon', 'Stardust'. But now he was forced to sit, silent in his steaming raincoat, between two plump women, pinned in by their elbows. He lost, gradually and hopelessly, the bold spirit of exploration with which he had begun the day.

He was depressed, and a little awed, by the iron magnitude of Swansea Station. As grey and wet as the rain outside, it glowered down at Tom, its metal noises ringing ominously through his head as he gave half his ticket to the man at the gate.

Tom stepped cautiously out into the world. A huge square, as big
as a village, stretched in front of him, its raucous traffic checked by
an eloquent policeman on a dais. He was buffeted by people; the
wind ripped at his slapping coat. It was all too much for Tom. He
sidled along the pavement, his head down, searching for haven.

What he found was a small Italian café, squashed incongruously
between the splendid buildings of more prosperous concerns. It was
warmly shabby, its windows carried an array of advertisements for
concerts and boxing matches, maroon paint peeled in strips from
its door. With a long sigh of relief, Tom stepped into its odorous
darkness. A long counter stood along the far wall, the gleaming
coffee machine, hissing to itself, at one end. Plates of sausage rolls,
curling sandwiches, and doughnuts lay limply under glass covers.
Behind the counter, a muttering, fat old man was just visible. You
could order tea or coffee or Bovril or Horlick's. A little pot of crusted
mustard stood on each of the four marble-topped tables. It was
exactly like Carpanini's in Aberdare. Tom was at home. He sat
down in an upright and comfortless chair.

'I'll have a coffee,' he said firmly, 'if you don't mind.'

'One coffee,' said the fat old man. 'Yes, sir.'

The only customer in the safe dark of the café, Tom dozed away
the remaining morning, his eyes half closed, like a cat. At one o'clock
he took off his raincoat, hung it on a hook on the wall, and pondered
over the menu the old man handed him. He liked its restraint and
conversatism.

Pie and chips
Sausage and chips
Egg and bacon
Egg and chips
Sausage, egg, and chips
All with bread and butter and a cup of tea

He read with approval.

'Sausage, egg, and chips,' he said. 'I like a good meal in the middle
of the day.'

'Yes, sir,' said the old man. 'Sausage, egg, and chips.' He shuffled
off to do the cooking.

Tom ate slowly, with conscious enjoyment. From time to time he
glanced out the window, watching the rain stream down the glass
through the advertisement for Typhoo Tea, seeing the hurrying wet
figures of the passers-by. He was very happy. He wished only that
he had a daily paper, and when the old man, without a word,
brought him a grimy copy of the *Express*, he was pleased but not

surprised. Propping it against the sugar bowl, he read placidly, sipping his tea like a young man with time to spare.

When the two girls came in, Tom lifted his cup to them in gentle courtesy and wished them a good afternoon. They were pink from hurrying, they shook out their wet coats with exclamations of relief and surprise, they smiled at Tom Bevan. One of them was tall, fair, and elegant. She moved like a colt.

'What a day,' one of them said. 'The usual, please, Algy.'

'Egg and chips,' said the old man. 'Yes, Miss.'

The girls sat two tables away from Tom Bevan, examining the contents of their parcels, chattering away as briskly as starlings. Tom looked at them with pleasure. He pushed away his paper and spoke to them.

'How do you girls like living in Swansea?' he said.

They stopped talking and considered.

'I've never lived anywhere else,' said the tall, fair girl. 'It's all right though, living in Swansea. Very nice, really.'

'I don't live in Swansea,' the shorter, darker girl said. 'I live in Dunvant, just outside. It's a village.'

'We went to school together, didn't we, Elsie?' said the fair girl.

'And now we work together in an insurance office,' said Elsie.

The old man came in, two plates held in front of him.

'Ooh! Thank you, Algy,' said the girls together. 'It looks lovely.'

What nice girls, thought Tom Bevan, what pleasant manners. 'I had sausage, egg, and chips,' he said. 'I believe in a good meal in the middle of the day.'

'We've never had that,' said Elsie, 'although sometimes we have pie and chips. Mostly in the evening we have pie and chips, after the cinema. Don't we, Margaret?'

'That's right,' Margaret replied. 'In the evening.' She looked up at Tom Bevan. 'Where do you live?' she asked.

Tom Bevan told them. He told them about his journey to Cardiff; he told them of its glittering shops and its streets; he told them of the Taff River, black as oil, running through the heart of the town; he described the football match he'd seen. Then he told them of his work in the mine, and they listened carefully, interrupting him now and then with flattering little gasps of amazement.

'It's a world of its own, down there,' he said. 'I've seen things down there that would make you laugh, yes, and make you weep, too.'

'You must have,' said Margaret with admiration. 'We don't know how you colliers stick it as you do. Now, our work isn't exciting at all.'

'Not exciting,' agreed Elsie, 'but we have some fun, you know, in the office.'

The girls looked at each other, smiling, their eyes shining.

They took Tom Bevan into the small universe of their office, described the manager, the clerks, the other typists, told him of the little practical jokes that enriched the passing days.

'That Mr James can be a pig sometimes,' said Elsie, 'but he can't help it. He has asthma.'

'There's nothing worse,' confirmed Tom Bevan, 'than a bad chest.'

He held the palm of his hand for a moment on his own shirtfront.

'Do you know,' he began, 'that two winters ago, I had bronchitis so badly I couldn't breathe? I had to sleep all night sitting upright in an armchair, the blankets wrapped around me.'

The girls, full of sympathy, nodded softly to him.

The afternoon sped by. Tom, preserving what he hoped would be an interesting reserve, did not join the girls at their table, but he bought chocolate biscuits that they all three shared. He couldn't remember ever having met such attractive, sensible girls. He looked with satisfaction at their sophisticated clothes, their delicate shoes. There was no doubt that girls in the big towns knew how to behave.

When the girls got up to leave, Tom, springing to his feet to help them with their coats, felt keen disappointment. He handed them their parcels and moved to open the door for them.

'Good-bye,' said Elsie. 'It's been nice meeting you. I enjoyed our chat.'

'Thank you,' said Tom. 'So did I.'

'We might see you again,' Margaret said. 'We always have our lunch here on Saturdays.'

'I'm often here myself,' said Tom, with pardonable exaggeration. 'I might see you next Saturday.'

The girls stepped into the street, ducked their heads against the wind, and disappeared.

A glint of sun broke through the cluttered windows of the café. The rain had stopped. Tom took down his coat and shrugged himself into it. The world was warm and pleasurable. He said goodbye to the muttering old man, immobile behind the counter. 'Nice little place you have here, Algy,' said Tom. 'Very nice little place.'

The old man did not reply.

Outside, the streets had regained their normal proportions, the traffic was amiable and controlled. Tom strolled about for half an hour, returned to the station, caught a train, and departed for home. His carriage was empty, the late-afternoon light was golden, and Tom sang all the way to Aberdare.

On Sunday morning, Tom went to church, meeting, as he usually did, the tall and elegant figure of Percy Colclough. Percy was a deeply serious young man, and attended church three times every Sunday. He was astonished to learn that Tom had been to Swansea, but, keeping the Sabbath for solemn matters, asked no questions.

The next morning, however, on the way to the pithead, he spoke out boldly.

'What's it like in Swansea, Tom?' he asked.

'Lovely,' said Tom. 'Fine. They've got a huge station and a very nice café there.'

Percy Colclough laughed.

'It was raining,' said Tom defensively, 'and then I met these two charming girls.'

Percy Colclough stopped laughing. 'Two charming girls?' he said.

'Margaret and Elsie,' confirmed Tom. 'I'm meeting them again next Saturday. You can come along if you like.'

Percy whistled pensively. 'I might,' he said. 'I just might, at that.'

All week long Percy found opportunities for nudging Tom with an elbow, for winking slowly at him.

'Saturday,' he'd say. 'Still all right for Saturday, Tom?'

'I'll see you at the station about half past nine,' Tom would answer.

Tom was at the station early on Saturday. He had hurried through the holiday streets, bright with strengthening spring, but he knew that Percy Colclough would be there before him. He bought his ticket, moved through the barrier, and walked on to the platform. Tall, slim, his dark suit pressed and cleaned, Percy Colclough stood alone at the far end of the platform. He turned his head but gave no other sign of recognition. His black hat sat prim and straight on his head.

Tom hurried up to him, noting with approval the details of Percy's appearance — the glossy white shirt, the discreet small flower in his lapel, the shoes polished like mirrors. Under Percy's arm was a Bible.

'Good morning, Percy,' said Tom, 'and a lovely morning for our little escapade.'

'Good morning, Tom,' said Percy. 'I think we may enjoy ourselves today.'

Together the two young men stared down the track in the direction from which the train would come.

A heavy silence deepened until Tom could stand it no longer.

'For God's sake, Percy,' he said hoarsely. 'Why the Bible? Why the Bible, Percy?'

Percy Colclough stepped nearer. He looked with extreme care up and down the deserted platform. He lowered his voice, as if in fear that the heathen wind of April would lift his salacious words and scatter them broadcast over listening Aberdare.

'I was thinking,' he said, like a convict, out of the side of his mouth. 'Well, tomorrow being Sunday . . . and if these girls were any good . . . you know . . . we might stop over until tomorrow.'

When Tom Bevan told me that, in the Horse and Groom, I couldn't stop laughing.

'And did you,' I asked, 'did you stop over?'

'No,' said Tom Bevan. 'Of course we didn't. Those were two very nice respectable girls. Went to church every Sunday, the same as we did.'

Tom Bevan is a schoolteacher now. He lives in Hampshire, only a dozen miles from me. I rang him up to tell him I'd written this story, and he laughed.

'It's all true,' he said. 'Every word of it. And I'll tell you something else. Although he was so religious himself, when Percy Colclough found out that those two girls were also religious he was white with anger. He was angry for weeks, not speaking to me for over a month. And I never heard him say a good word about Swansea after that.'

The Girl from Cardigan

I was never exactly a cuckoo in the nest, since there was no chance of pushing anyone out of our house, large and demanding though I was. My grandmother and my mother were small and unyielding; their hardness was a prime fact of life: their elbows and hands were hard, their words were quiet and hard, hardest of all was the judgement of their eyes. I was, no doubt of it, idle, clumsy, without any promise at all. There were just the three of us. My father made his escape when I was a baby. I can't remember anything about him.

I went once to Francis Nolan's house, years ago, when I was about thirteen. 'Selwyn Howard? You're George Howard's boy,' Francis's dad said.

'How do you know?' I said. I hoped it was because I looked like my father, could claim resemblance to somebody. I certainly didn't look like the two dapper women in our house. But Francis's dad only laughed. I used to see him about. Years later he told me my father lived in Birmingham and was very happy.

Our house was filled with small, convoluted, and brittle objects. I only had to turn around and five or six of them lay broken on the carpet — fragile china baskets of china flowers, winsome, breakable dogs with tails that snapped at a glance. It didn't matter how many I broke. My grandmother replaced them at once from some inexhaustible store. She would take the dustpan and brush, remove the shards of my passage, sneer audibly at my great feet. As best I could, I would slink away. Slinking was difficult for me.

We lived in a small town in Monmouthshire, at the head of one of the coal valleys. Unemployment was endemic there, and enforced leisure gave rise to protracted bouts of philosophy and politics. Most men leaned toward politics, since it gave an appearance of energy and deceived some people into believing they possessed power and influence. It was, if you like, political theory, imaginative and vituperative. The hills about our town were full of men giving their views an airing; eloquence was commonplace.

True power lay in the hands of a small group — the aldermen and councillors of the town. To a man, they sold insurance and were prosperous. This was because they ran the municipal transport, the public parks and gardens, the collection of taxes, the whole organisation of local government in the town and its surrounding villages. They hired and fired, dispensed and took away. They were so corrupt that the Mafia never got a toe-hold among us. Those Italian boys would have starved.

In order to get anywhere in our town you had to buy insurance. When teachers, for example, got their salaries at the end of the month, most of them paid heavy insurance. The remainder of the teachers were the sons and daughters of councillors.

One day my mother and I were walking together down Wallhead Road. She was explaining to me that as I was eighteen it was time I found gainful employment and that no gentleman walked as I walked, his toes turned in, his knees bent, his arms hanging apelike at his sides, his expression vacant, his very being a shame and burden. No family, she continued, had been so vexed. 'And, talking of family, there's my cousin.'

Her cousin, Harvey Lockwood, was one of the councillors. His insurance business was reputed to be the richest in the county, his daughters, all three, taught in the best schools, his house was full of antiques and carpets. I had seen him smoking a cigar — symbol of incredible wealth. We had never been in his house. We were the poor relations. Seeing us, he thought to avoid us by crossing the street, but the traffic was not kind to him. My mother planted herself in front of him. For a moment, I thought he would knock her down, so steadfastly was he looking at something above her head.

'Good morning,' she said to Harvey. It was a nice morning, in fact, but winter was in her eye.

Harvey's start was a pleasant mixture of simulated surprise and delight. 'Elsie,' he said.

'You remember my name!' said my mother. 'That's amazing.' She said it cynically, and with reproof.

'Now, Else,' said Harvey. 'There's no need for sarcasm. After all, we're family. Our mothers were sisters, after all.'

I noticed that he had begun to wriggle and turn red. There was no cure for this, as I knew. My mother examined coldly the growing evidence of Harvey's embarrassment.

'And who is this?' he blustered. 'This young man can't be your Selwyn? What a size he's grown!'

'Hullo, Mr Lockwood,' I said nastily.

'Oh, Uncle Harvey,' he said. 'Call me Uncle Harvey.' He turned to my mother. 'Now that I look at him,' he said, 'he has a look of his grandfather about him. What a handsome fellow the old man was! What a big man! Pity he had such expensive habits.'

'That's a nice coat you're wearing, Harvey,' my mother said. 'And where's that lovely new car of yours?' Harvey winced. I could have told him he had no chance. 'When are you and Sylvia going to Paris again?' my mother said, turning the steel.

'What are you going to do with this young man of yours?' Harvey said. I had to admit he was game, but this was the opening my mother had been looking for.

'What indeed?' she said. 'That is something you might give a little thought to, Harvey. I see your daughters are all nicely settled, your brother Paul is an inspector of local transport. Selwyn must be the only member of the family who hasn't yet enjoyed your generous help.' Now that Harvey was on the run, she was almost happy. She smiled, she made small, graceful gestures with her hands. 'There's nothing available for him in the Town Hall, is there?' she said. 'He has a good brain, he's industrious. What's more, he can keep his mouth shut.' She offered this with a curious nod of the head.

Its effect on Harvey was instant and terrible. He gaped, he turned pale, and, grasping his briefcase firmly under his arm, he shot off into the traffic. 'I'll see what I can do,' he wailed, running.

'That's all right, then,' my mother said.

'Is that why we came out this morning?' I said.

'You're getting sharper, Selwyn,' my mother said. 'We might make something of you yet. Stand up straight.'

That is how I came to work in the Clerk's Department of the Town Hall. There all the legal work was handled, all the local by-laws interpreted, all the niceties of government at this level discussed. It was also the place where the aldermen and councillors came for their supplies of stationery.

Small amounts of paper and ink were appropriate, I suppose, for the men of power to conduct their legal council affairs. It was my responsibility to give them such supplies. I was astonished by the appetites shown by these men. Week after week they took away truckloads of paper, gallons of ink, relief nibs by the many gross, erasers, wooden rulers, loose-leaf binders, pencils, ruled foolscap and unruled foolscap, envelopes of every size and colour. It seemed I was in charge of an Aladdin's Cave of office supplies.

'Am I supposed to keep note of these withdrawals?' I asked Henry Morgan, an old man who had worked in the office for over thirty years.

'You are supposed to keep your eyes shut,' he said.

I took for my own use a notebook of impressive thickness with a hard blue cover. It gave every indication of weight and permanence. As our leaders took away their paper troves, I would enter, neatly and ostentatiously, a set of meaningless ciphers against their names.

After a while my colleagues noticed this habit and grew restive. Some of them, having cultivated powers of inattention and quietness over periods of long duration, were cautious of anything that might alter the smooth groove of custom. Others were suspicious that I was so far exceeding my duties that I might jump over their heads and achieve promotion — something that had not happened in the office for ten years. Wesley Graham was one of these. Wesley was a tall and personable young man who all day bustled about the Town Hall, his expression alert, his stride brisk. In his hand he carried a bundle of documents chosen at random from some file. His travels took him into every office in the building, and he was able to bring back to us innumerable items of news and interest. This was all he did.

'What are you writing in that notebook?' he asked me one day. He hovered like a hawk over the soft, expected prey of my answer.

'It's a wise man, Wesley,' I said, 'who knows his own father.'

I do not know why I said this, except that I had no better reply in mind. It threw Wesley Graham into wild confusion. He gasped, he hissed, he puffed his cheeks, he clutched his documents with both hands to his chest. 'You'd better be careful,' he bleated. I thought he was going to cry, but he went to his desk and buried his head in his arms. My colleagues, disturbed by this small drama, went back with unusual seriousness to their newspapers.

'What did you mean by that?' Henry Morgan asked me some days later — 'It's a wise man who knows his own father?'

'Nothing, Henry,' I said. 'I wouldn't like to say I meant anything profound or ominous.'

He looked at me uncertainly. 'I don't know,' he said. 'I don't know at all. You're a deep one.'

It was later that week that my Uncle Harvey came in. I went to meet him. 'Good morning, Councillor Lockwood,' I said. 'Let me take your coat.'

It was raining heavily outside, and my Uncle Harvey stood in his own small pool. Rain dripped from his hat, his nose, the hem of his coat. 'No, no,' he said. 'My business won't take long.'

This surprised me, for he was fond of making statements about his acumen, his probity, and his general superiority when compared to other men. And when he wanted supplies from my cave he needed at least twice as much as other customers. I awaited his pleasure.

'How are you getting on here, Selwyn?' he asked. 'Are you happy? I wouldn't like to think that I had put a young man of promise and ambition into a dead-end job like this.' He laid a hand like a flatfish on my shoulder, and a wet smile struggled onto his face.

'I'm fine here,' I said. 'Very happy.'

'No, no,' he said. 'I can see that you're out of place. A boy of your intellect and energy is lost here. I've had a word with the Town Clerk, and you'll be working with him from tomorrow, in his own office, where he can keep his eye on you and guide you.'

'Thank you,' I said.

My Uncle Harvey wrapped his wet coat about him and prepared to leave. 'Selwyn,' he said piteously, 'get rid of that blue notebook. The other councillors might object to it. It could be misunderstood.'

'Certainly, Uncle,' I said. 'It shall go at once.'

So it was that I entered the Clerk's Office, the centre of power, the heart of the web. The next morning I walked through the general office and those who had been my colleagues greeted me according to their temperaments.

'How did you do it?' said Henry Morgan, his expression composed equally of admiration and bewilderment. He sat at his desk, his copy of the *Guardian* folded so many times that only the crossword was visible. I would miss old Henry Morgan. On slack winter afternoons we had read together some of the novels of Thomas Hardy, and he had just introduced me to *The Turn of the Screw* and *The Aspern Papers*.

'Luck, Henry,' I said, 'and an inborn talent for the devious.'

'You're a dark horse,' he said. 'You'll take some watching.'

I flicked a wink at his amiable gaze, tapped the Clerk's door, and walked in.

Mr Felton was sitting in his chair behind a scrupulously neat desk, leather-topped. He had before him a sheet of paper. Mr Maynard Felton was short, trimly made, perhaps sixty years old. He could move quickly, with long, sharp strides. His suits were immaculate, his linen precise, his skin pink and clear. The most obvious thing about him was his baldness, or, more correctly, his elaborate coiffure. He let his silver hair grow very long at the back and sides of his head and then brought it to the crown, the strands meeting in a crest that ran the length of his dome. Beneath the plastered strands of hair, his naked skull gleamed. It was at this carefully disguised tonsure I stared while awaiting his questions. They were very general. He was interested in my family, in my ambitions and my curiosity. At length he seemed satisfied.

'You'll sit at that desk over there,' he said.

'Thank you, Mr Felton,' I said.

'Have you brought that blue notebook with you?' he said.

'What blue notebook?' I said.

We got on very well together. I can't say we were friends, but I
studied him closely. He was, for example, easily disturbed. His wife
gave him a new fountain pen and, since he was very clumsy in
practical matters, it became my responsibility to fill it when
necessary. Once, in a spirit of experiment, I used not ink but a
glutinous adhesive that came to us in bottles. Mr Felton could not
write with the pen, shook it venomously, swore, turned red, damned
all pens, and went home for the day. I learned that he was allergic
to the smell of oranges, and on one occasion when I wished him
gone for an hour or so I ostentatiously peeled an orange and sucked
it noisily. Mr Felton rose in nausea from his seat, clapped his
starched white handkerchief to his face, shouted, 'You dirty pig!',
and rushed, retching, from the room. In these and other ways, I
began to have some control over the affairs of the office. In particular,
I observed his clothes, which were beautiful and orthodox. I began
to feel in me the onset of dandyism.

One day Mr Felton came to work wearing his brown tweed, a
cream shirt with a paisley necktie, and the finest pair of brown shoes
I had ever seen. I admired them.

'I bought them at my brother's shop,' Mr Felton said. Mr Felton
had two brothers — Bennion, who kept the shoe shop, and Elwyn,
who was a butcher. All three had come to our town from Cardiganshire when they were young men, and had prospered.

'How much would a pair like that cost, Mr Felton?' I said.

I didn't want to know. I was giving him a chance to boast a little,
but the idiot overplayed it. He laughed. His laugh implied that I had
ambitions to purchase such shoes and that these ambitions were
ridiculous. His laughter was brief and dismissive. 'You can't afford
shoes like this, boy,' he said.

At lunch time, I told my mother of this remark. Since I had joined
the ranks of the comparatively wealthy, she had been notably more
congenial, had sometimes even asked my opinion on unimportant
matters. Her eyes gleamed. She was the most competitive woman I
have ever known; in her was the spirit of a great and cruel general.
'So that's what he thinks,' she said. 'Put clean socks on. I'll see you
outside the Town Hall at five o'clock.'

'We don't finish until five-thirty,' I said.

'Five o'clock,' she said. My mother was convinced that there was
no man-made law she could not countermand merely by ignoring
it.

First we went to John Montague's, a tailor shop whose doors were sumptuous and hushed — they closed behind us with the sound of paper money. There we bought a suit of such elegance that when I tried it on I could not find myself in the mirror. Of Irish thornproof, it was a closely woven heather mixture, subtle and distinguished. I was astonished to find that my wrists did not protrude several inches below the sleeves. We bought a shirt and tie of equal splendour. My mother engaged to pay for these luxuries over a period of twelve months.

'Now,' she said, 'for Bennion Felton.'

Bennion Felton did not look like his brother. He was round and comfortable, and years of bending at other people's feet had given him a stoop. He sent toward us one of his assistants, Alfie Edwards, a thin boy I had once to beat up for cheating at marbles. When we were small, of course.

My mother sent him reeling with an iron glance. 'I'll see Mr Felton,' she said.

Bennion Felton came forward, recognizing a customer of unusual mettle.

'I'll see some of your very best brown shoes,' my mother said. 'For my son.'

'For this young man?' said Bennion. 'Our best shoes are rather expensive, Madam.'

'We'll see them,' said my mother. Queen Victoria could have taken lessons from her when it came to dealing with lesser mortals.

'He has a very large foot,' said Bennion persuasively. We remained silent. He shrugged his shoulders. Soon the floor was littered with shoes. None of them looked like Mr Felton's admired footwear.

'I think we might like to try a pair like those you sold your brother recently,' my mother said. 'Rather a decent brogue.'

Bennion Felton brought them. They were beyond footwear — they were the shoes of gods. He named a price so far in excess of my monthly salary that inside I turned pale, though I did my best to look as if I bought such things by the dozen pairs.

My mother did not show any trepidation, whatsoever. 'We'll take them,' she said, 'since it seems unlikely there will be better in this shop.'

Crushed, little Bennion wrapped the shoes, took the money, bowed us out of his shop.

'I've been saving up,' my mother said as we walked home. 'It doesn't look as if you're going to grow anymore, so you might as well wear something decent.'

My grandmother examined my finery, approved the quality,

hoped that its purchase would coincide with a new, more graceful physical control on my part. Excessive size she felt to be a moral flaw and I must do my best to atone for it.

The next morning, dressed in my new finery, I breakfasted early and walked down to Anton's. Anton's was where men of fashion in our town had their hair cut. Until that day my grandmother had cut my hair. Anton's was empty.

'Good morning — uh, sir,' said Anton, puzzled. It was the garb and the assurance it brought me that puzzled Anton.

'Good morning, Bertie,' I said to Anton.

I had known Anton since we were six years old. Most of that time he'd been Bertie Turner.

'I thought it was you,' he said. 'You look really good. You really do.'

'See what you can do with the old top end, Bert,' I said. 'Something conservative and high class — what you might call a classic cut. Nothing foppish.'

He cut beautifully. My entry into the office that morning was sensational. Men reeled away. Wesley Graham turned ashen and sobbed openly.

Mr Felton was properly appreciative. He looked me up and down, he walked around me. I was suitably modest, merely lifting an interrogatory eyebrow.

'There's a committee meeting this afternoon,' he said. 'You'd better come, look after my papers, take a few notes, that sort of thing. You'll soon pick it up.'

After the meeting, Henry Morgan stopped me outside the Clerk's office. He told me he was worried about my welfare. 'You meet a funny class of person at those gatherings,' he said.

'What do you mean?' I said.

'All they think of is money,' he said. 'That's all Felton ever thought of.'

I told him I could handle the idea of money, but he was not consoled. 'You might think that uncle of yours — Harvey Lockwood — is a cunning one with silver,' he said. 'Let me tell you, Harvey Lockwood is a pygmy compared to old Felton — a feather, a hammer of air, a financial cripple, an infant mewling in the dark, an idiot counting pennies. I could go on.'

I invited him to continue.

'Who,' he said, 'built the Old People's Homes?'

'Patrick Parry & Sons, Ltd.,' I said.

'Right,' said Henry. 'And who built the two new schools down the valley, and the hospital extension, and the bus shelter? Who has the contract for the new Civic Centre, worth millions?'

'None other than that same Patrick Parry,' I said.

'Maynard Felton and Patrick Parry are as thick as thieves,' Henry said. 'Until Maynard became Town Clerk, Parry was just an ordinary carpenter. Work it out for yourself. You know what happens to men who worship money.'

I did. They grew rich. The next day I bought shares in Patrick Parry & Sons, Ltd. — my first investment.

'He won't take it with him,' Henry said on a later day, when we were again discussing Mr Felton's money. 'He won't even be able to keep it in this town. It will all go back to Cardigan.'

'Why Cardigan?' I asked.

'He married a girl from Cardigan,' Henry Morgan said. 'After his first wife died. She came up to keep house for him — years younger than he is. A distant cousin. Oh, they're clannish in Cardigan — they're close. They wanted someone right up next to him to keep an eye on his bank balance; they won't let any of that out of the family. It will go back to Cardigan. He has no children, you see.'

'You mean it was a plot?' I said. 'They meant him to marry this girl?'

'Of course,' Henry Morgan said. 'Imagine the farms they can buy with Felton's money. They certainly didn't want him to marry anyone else, some stranger who'd keep all that lovely clover for herself. What a clan! Mind, she looks after him, I'll say that. She's a good wife, the girl from Cardigan.'

That winter was long and stern. I remember it with some affection, because, walking to the office one morning, I slipped on a treacherous patch of ice beneath the snow and twisted my knee. I had to walk with the help of a stick, and when I recovered I kept the stick. It became recognisable, helped to define me. I still have it, although more expensive models have long since replaced it in the shops. Mr Felton caught influenza, struggled on, wheezing and coughing, and then took to his bed. At the end of the week, on Friday morning, I collected those papers that demanded his attention and took them up to Mr Felton's house.

'Watch out,' Henry Morgan said as I passed through the outer office, buttoning with care my new British warm, adjusting my scarf. 'Look out for that girl from Cardigan.'

Mr Felton's was a large, detached house, built of dressed blocks of the local grey stone. Quiet, rich, impressive. I rang the bell, and the girl from Cardigan answered. She was hardly a girl, but she was much younger than Mr Felton. She was dark, slender, rather severe. She let me in, and I went upstairs to Mr Felton's bedroom. He was in bed, his features sharper than usual and his skin the colour of rice. The furniture was heavy, gleaming. Mr Felton wore on his head a conical night-cap. I had seen such in illustrated copies of Dickens. We began to go through the papers.

'These,' I said, 'are all straightforward and require only your signature.'

He looked them through very carefully and signed them.

'These,' I said, 'require some decision from you. As far as possible, I've brought necessary supporting documents.'

He told me what his decisions were.

'This smaller group,' I said, 'is outside my understanding and is obviously for your consideration.'

He read them through with the greatest care, word by word. I had read them equally carefully.

'Are you sure, boy,' he said, 'that you don't understand these?'

I gave him a blank and blue-eyed stare. 'Certain,' I said.

Mr Felton got steadily worse. Each week I took him his papers. Mrs Felton would bring coffee to me, and chocolate biscuits. He would work his way laboriously through those documents that were concerned with his work at the office and then spend a very long time over the papers that detailed his more profitable activities.

One Friday he leaned back on his pillows and watched me sip my coffee. Mrs Felton had just brought it and had vanished silently down the wide stairs.

'My wife is much younger than I,' he said. 'My first wife died.'

'So I understand,' I said.

'She's my cousin's daughter,' he said, 'come up from the country to look after me.'

'Is that so?' I said.

'It isn't decent for a man and woman to live in the same house unmarried,' he said. 'I could see that.'

'Why not,' I said, 'and you related to her?'

He gave me a quick glance. 'There's more to it,' he said. 'You're a sharp boy and a big boy, but there's more to it.'

I thought he was going to tell me all about his money, but he didn't say another word. Mrs Felton let me out; the heavy door didn't make a sound behind me.

Maynard Felton's bronchitis turned into pneumonia and he died, just after Christmas. Henry Morgan and I, representing the office staff, went to his funeral.

'Did you see the two Felton brothers?' said Henry as we went back to the office. 'Looked pretty blue, and it wasn't just the cold. They were thinking of all that lovely money that they won't get.' Henry sounded very happy. We walked through the freezing dark, and he hummed and whistled all the way.

Mr Felton's house was sold. The girl from Cardigan returned demurely to that green country, her luggage full of money. Sometimes I've felt I can see the road to Cardigan, green as bank-notes, shining under the moon. Patrick Parry & Sons went bankrupt, but I'd sold my shares by then.

That was my early education in politics — sound, practical, informative. I've done well, I admit it. But I wouldn't say I am a self-made man. No, no, I was well taught. I was very well taught.

A Flight of Geese

My Uncle Wynford wasn't really my uncle; he was my great-uncle, my grandmother's brother. I used to visit him often on my way home from school. He lived in a small house at the edge of the village with his wife and two daughters. He also had two sons, but they lived in London and one of them was a famous footballer, an International. A colour photograph of him, wearing his International cap and shirt, his arms folded across his chest, stood on the sideboard. My uncle had given up regular work when he was a young man. He had come home unexpectedly early from the engine room at the steelworks and announced his philosophy of leisure. 'Anne,' he had said to his wife, 'I shall not be going to work again. There's too much talk about the dignity of labour. One life is all we have and I'm not spending mine in senseless toil.' And he never did.

Not that he was an idle man. His garden was neat and orderly; his work-bench, in the shed at the end of the garden, was swept free of dust and shavings; his tools, worn and polished with use, all had their proper place, and were sharp and clean. He could build a freestone wall, clear a chimney, repair plumbing. He was marvellously inventive with metal and stone, those old elements. But most of all he liked to work with wood. His hands held wood intimately, as if he knew all of its lost warmth and offered with his fingers and the flat of his palm a consolation for the tragic falling of trees. He made six crimson soup spoons for my grandmother, carved from the one piece of yew, polished hard and smooth. And he made her a little footstool for her use in chapel on Sundays. Many Sunday evenings I sat on that little stool, my head well below the top of the pew, noiselessly sucking a mint, reading a comic book while interminable sermons thundered above me.

Uncle Wynford made a stool for himself, too — a larger one. His was secular, not intended for Sunday use. It was painted in the most brilliant and glittering colours. The panel of the seat was decorated with an oval centre-piece, a landscape in which a lake of raucous blue lay beneath impossibly dramatic mountains. Water lilies grew close at hand, and birds — swallows, probably — performed their frozen arabesques above the water. Far away the little, leaning sails of yachts and skiffs stood white against the hills. Complex patterns, like those in the Book of Kells, covered the legs and the under-surface. My uncle normally carried this stool about with him. A short man, he found it useful to stand on in crowds, but mostly he just sat on it whenever he stopped to talk.

For his finest art was conversation. He loved above all else to be among a small circle of old friends, who made together a pattern of articulate life, each in his turn leading the discussion or telling a story, the others an essential, encouraging chorus. At all aspects of this activity my uncle was a master. Nobody could listen more intently to tales told many times before, nobody could time an urgent question more subtly, nobody else could invent such marvellous, rich detail. His voice was like an instrument. He could use it to entice, to chill, to bombard. On early autumn mornings he sat among his friends down at the square, he on his wooden throne, they squatting or sprawled at length on the warm stone.

It was my habit then to go to school very early. I used to run almost all the way, using an exaggerated stride and a very upright stance, arms bent high at the elbow, trying to look like Paavo Nurmi in a photograph I had seen in an old book about the Olympic Games. I was running across the square one morning, driving off the toes just like Nurmi, when my Uncle Wynford called me. 'Don't run, boy,' he said. 'You've no need to run. You have plenty of time.'

I tried to tell him that I liked getting to school early, that I liked being alone on the playground when it was silent and empty and the windows of the school were without life, but he just shook his head and held my hand, so that I had to stand by him. I wore a white shirt and grey trousers, and my shadow was very long and thin in the sun.

After a while Mr Carrington spoke. He was Frankie Carrington's grandfather. He had been a butcher, and kept snuff in a little silver box. He had a walking stick with a handle made of antler and was in every way precise and gentlemanly.

'Going up the street last evening,' he said, 'I saw Arthur Baker standing at his door with his dog — you know, that blue-roan cocker. It was sitting at Arthur's feet, near the front door. I hadn't seen the dog for some time.' Mr Carrington smiled as he looked back in his mind and saw himself talking to Arthur Baker. '"Well, Arthur," I said, "I haven't seen that dog of yours for some time, but there she is, safe and sound."'

'Quick-tempered fellow,' said Ginty Willis. 'Arthur Baker has a very quick temper. All the Bakers have. Like living in a box of matches in their house.'

'What did he say?' asked my Uncle Wynford. 'What did Arthur say to you?'

'That's just it,' said Mr Carrington, leaning forward, widening his eyes, tapping himself on the knee to impress us. 'He said nothing at first. He rushed down the path, and then, I swear, he almost shouted at me.'

'Angry, was he?' said Ginty Willis. 'Oh, a terrible quick temper.'

'Not so much angry as puzzled,' Mr Carrington said. 'And, yes, a bit frightened.'

'Frightened?' my uncle said. 'Why should he have been frightened?'

'Because the dog wasn't there!' Mr Carrington said. 'What do you think of that? Not there!'

'"What are you saying?" Arthur Baker shouted,' said Mr Carrington. '"My dog was killed a fortnight ago. Run over by a truck. What do you mean there she is, safe and sound?" And boys, when I looked again, there was no dog anywhere. Gave me quite a turn.' Mr Carrington pursed his lips and took out his snuffbox.

'Was it dark?' said Selby Davis belligerently. He wasn't really bullying; sometimes he stammered, so he pushed his words out quickly and roughly before he tripped over them.

Mr Carrington considered. 'Not dark,' he said, 'but certainly more than dusk. The house — the Bakers' house — was in deep shadow.'

'Could have been a shadow you saw,' said Selby Davis.

'It could have been,' agreed Mr Carrington, 'but it looked very much like Arthur Baker's dog.'

'Arthur was very fond of that dog,' said my uncle, 'and the dog adored him. There was a great bond between them. It could have been some form of manifestation you saw, Jimmy.' I hadn't known Mr Carrington's name was Jimmy, so I looked at him carefully, to see if it suited him.

Eddie D'Arcy progressed across the square, more a parade than a walk. His dark suit was superbly cut, his white shirt was dazzling, his silk tie was rich and sombre, his expensive black shoes utterly without flaw or spot. Despite the perfection of the morning, he carried an umbrella, rolled tight as a sword.

'Good morning, gentlemen,' said Eddie, his vowels without fault, his dignity unassailable.

'Good morning, Eddie,' the men said, smiling and nodding.

Eddie moved, full-sailed, out of sight, toward the office where he worked as a lawyer.

'Clever chap, Eddie,' said my uncle. He turned again to Mr Carrington. 'Jimmy,' he said, 'I'm prepared to believe that what you saw up at the Bakers' was a manifestation. Stands to reason that an animal's identity is bound up with its sense of place, and, in the case of a domestic animal like a dog, with its owner.' He warmed to his topic. 'Our lives — the lives of human beings — are astonishingly manipulated by animals. It is useless to ignore the fact that our lives are deeply influenced by those of animals. Take Eddie D'Arcy as an example.'

'What about Eddie D'Arcy?' asked Ginty Willis.

'Did I ever tell you about the D'Arcys' goose?' my uncle said.

Nobody answered.

'Old Mrs D'Arcy bought a gosling to fatten for Christmas,' said Uncle Wynford. 'Eddie was a little boy then. The bird had the run of the field at the back of the house. It grew and prospered — oh, it grew into a magnificent goose.' We could see that my uncle still admired the bird's every feather. 'Yes,' he said, 'it was a splendid bird.'

'I've done it myself, often,' said Selby Davis, in his angry voice. 'I prefer goose to any other bird. Properly cooked, a goose is lovely.'

'This was an unusual goose,' my uncle said. 'Called at the back door every morning for its food, answered to its name. An intelligent creature. Eddie's sisters tied a blue silk ribbon around its neck and made a pet of it. It displayed more personality and understanding than you'd believe possible in a bird. Came Christmas, of course, and they couldn't kill it.'

'Couldn't kill it?' Mr Carrington said, his professional sense outraged. 'It's not all that difficult. The best way — '

My uncle stopped him with a wave of his hand, as if conducting music. 'They knew how to kill it,' he said, 'but they were unable to do so. On moral grounds, if you like. They were fond of it. They loved it. The goose lived another twenty years; Eddie grew up with it. They all cried when, at last, it died. Except Eddie, of course.'

'Why not Eddie?' someone asked.

'You know how particular Eddie is?' Uncle Wynford said. 'Such clothes, such a dandy? How not a mote of dust shall settle on his linen, how his handkerchief must be pressed to a mathematical nicety. Imagine how it must have been for him, living in that house with an elderly, dictatorial goose. You ever tried to house-train a goose, Ginty?'

'I have not,' said Ginty. 'I imagine it can't be done.'

'It can't,' said my uncle, laughing.

'Geese are pretty bright,' I said. 'They're good guards. Some geese saved Rome from the invaders.'

'The boy's right,' said Mr Carrington. 'Well done, boy. I can see you're going to be a great scholar.'

'I had a cousin in Cardiganshire who was an expert with geese,' my uncle said after a silence. 'Kept all the varieties in his time. People used to come from all over the country to buy breeding stock from him. Oh, what a sight to see his flocks on the moors — great flocks of geese, marching like Prussians! He used to clip their wings at the elbow so they couldn't fly, and then, once they were old enough, out they'd go on the open moors, white geese, grey geese. They never strayed. At dusk they'd come high-stepping into his yard and the whole mountain would be full of their voices. I often stayed with him when I was young.

'He sent us a goose every year — two geese: one for Michaelmas and another for Christmas, always trussed and ready for cooking. He used to send them by bus — a bewildering journey, with many changes — but none of them ever failed to reach us. I used to wait here, on the square, for the bus to come in from Brecon toward late afternoon. The conductor would hand me a large hamper with our goose inside, and I'd stagger home with it. We used to cook it on a spit, rotating it in front of a blaze of a fire, a pan beneath to catch the melting fat. We took turns at basting as it spun slowly — first one way, then the other — so that it wouldn't burn. Every Michaelmas and every Christmas for years. What feasts we had then! Nor was that the end of the goose's usefulness. After the cooking we put the solidified goose grease in jars and kept it as a cure for sore throats and chest colds and bronchitis. I can remember my mother rubbing it on my bare chest and throat when I was a small boy. I can remember its gross smell, the thick feel of the grease on my skin. I hated that, although the old people swore by it as a curative.

'And even the bed I slept on owed its comfort to my cousin's geese, for the bed was stuffed with feathers from his birds. My mother made a huge envelope of blue and white striped ticking and filled it with goose feathers, making the whole thing plump and soft as a cloud. We all sleep well when we're young, but nobody could have slept softer and deeper than I did in my goose-feather bed.'

My uncle held out his hand in front of him. 'You see this hand?' he asked. 'The hand is a superb instrument. This hand of mine can do all manner of things: it can wield a hammer, pick up a pin, it can point a chisel to the exact splitting place of a stone, it can create, it can destroy. My cousin's hands were to do with geese. He had huge hands. Here, on the inside of his thumb and forefinger, he had long calluses, incredibly hard, from feathering geese. Every week he would kill and pluck some of his birds for market, and many more near Christmas and other busy times. He had slaughtered thousands over the years. And when he plucked them he did it swiftly, expertly, and the soft flesh would not be bruised or torn when he finished. I've seen him kill and dress hundreds of birds. He was an artist.'

'How old was he, Wynford?' Mr Carrington asked.

'Not a lot older than I,' said my uncle. 'Seven or eight years. But that's a lot when you're young. He was already at work on the farm when I was a young boy visiting there.'

'What's he doing now?' asked Selby Davis.

'He's dead,' my uncle said softly. 'Yes, he's dead these many years.' He shifted on his painted stool. He was far away, visiting an old sadness. 'He's been dead for years,' he repeated. 'One Christmas he had many geese, and he set to work early, day after day, killing and preparing them. The weather was intolerably cold. The mountains had a fall of snow, two feet deep and deeper in drifts. It never stopped freezing. Night and day not a gust of wind — only the deep stillness of frost. My cousin kept the dead birds in a long barn, where they hung in rows, heads down. The bitter cold worried my cousin. It was bringing in the wild things off the hills, the rats and foxes. He found himself staying more and more near his filling barn.

'One night he awoke from sleep, bright awake at once, certain that something was wrong. It was just after three in the morning. He hurried into his thick clothes and wrapped a blanket over his shoulders. There wasn't a sound in the yard; even the living birds were silent. The brilliant snow threw back every gleam of light, redoubled it, so the night was unnaturally lit. The barn door was locked and safe. Nothing was out of place. He opened the door and went in. The dead geese hung in their rows before him, untouched, pallid. The night was pitilessly still. My cousin moved along the stiff files, alert, waiting for something to happen.

'Then, in the cold barn, as if from high above him, he heard the call of geese, far away, the crying of wild geese out of the empty sky. He could hear them clearly, although he knew they were not there. He did not move. In an instant the barn was full of their loud honking; their flailing wings beat under the sturdy roof. He closed his eyes in terror, he wrapped his arms about his bent head, and through his barn flew the heavy skeins of great, invisible birds. Their crying filled his ears; the still air was buffeted by their plunging flight, on and on, until the last bodiless goose was flown and the long, wild voices were gone. He stood in the cold of his barn and opened his eyes. What he saw was this: he saw the hanging corpses of his own geese, every one swaying, every one swinging gently. And that was the most frightening of all.'

My uncle sighed. 'Poor old boy,' he said. 'Poor old lad. After a while they took him to Swansea, to the mental hospital, and he died there.'

'How do you know this?' asked Ginty Willis.

'He told me,' said Uncle Wynford. 'I went down to see him, and he told me. He was a young man, only thirty-two when he died. He had killed thousands of geese, thousands of them.'

'What was his name, Uncle?' I asked. I stood in the warm day as cold as if I were in the heart of that long-dead winter and were standing under the roof among the swaying corpses of Christmas geese.

'Good God!' my uncle said. 'Are you still here? Get to school, get to school! You'll be late.' I turned and ran.

All day my friends were indolent in the heat of the quiet classroom, moving sleepily through their work, but all I could see were the high arrows of the streaming geese, all I could hear was their faint and melancholy crying, and the imagined winter was all about me.

Sing it Again, Wordsworth

Last night I awoke with a troubled mind. It seemed to me that I had no roots, that there was no place, however distant, to which I could turn at so desolate a moment. Despite its familiarity, the years I've had of touching and using its furniture, its known sounds, I awoke lost in my own room. The house seemed to hang alone in space. I got out of bed and walked to the window, heavily, groaning a little, my feet turned out like those of an old man. The moon was high. There was light enough to show deep shadows under the bushes and to make sharp the angles of walls, but I recognised nothing. The world stopped at the boundaries of the garden. To imagine the solid lane which passes my gate, its hedges of elder and hawthorn, its green ditch, was an impossible act of the will. I tried in an agony of memory to recall the faces of the men who would soon be cycling in the dawn light along the lane to work. I could not remember one of them, though they are men I've known for years.

This house was built for me twenty years ago. I made its garden from the untouched meadow; the shrubs and trees grow where I planted them. I marked the new course of the little stream at the boundary, dug it out by hand, plank by plank bridged it. It is my home. Yet I went back to bed unable to imagine the feel of the spade in my hand, unable to think of the colour of the roses already abundant in the borders. I turned on my side knowing I would not sleep again.

The weathers and scenes of childhood remain long in a man's mind and I tried to remember them; but when I searched among the images of the past I found myself too far away. I have travelled away from those places for half a lifetime. Their summers are thin and cold, their voices inaudible. It was then that I realized there is no place mine without the asking for it, no place where I belong by clear right.

Sitting in the late afternoon sun, lounging, relaxed, I can smile at that fear in the night. I know that if I had to choose at this moment a place to be native to, I would be unable to decide. I think of the Dysynni Valley, the loveliest in Wales. I see the Dysynni River winding inland from its salt lagoon through the soft, coastal flats above Tywyn, past the village of Llanegryn where the squat little church, a holy place for over a thousand years, lies under a buffeting wind. Then the river cuts directly into the heart of Cader Idris, the

high, wild moorland. Round-shouldered cormorants fly in from the
sea until they reach Bird Rock and they sit there, on the harsh cliff
above the river, alert for migratory sea trout. I would travel farther,
the austerity of the mountains each side of me; I would climb to
Castell-y-Bere, aloof on its long rock, its great walls fallen. When I
was sixteen I stood one night near this castle, on the lip of a stone
ridge high above the Dysynni, and I saw another river, one invisible
by day, run straight and flat over the meadows and into the eye of
the moon. I could not believe what I saw. I climbed down the steep
face, leaped the fence, ran into the visionary water. It was quite dry.
I ran in the brittle stubble and dusty grass of a harvested field. What
I had thought a river was the light of the moon reflected in the webs
of millions of ground-covering spiders, each filament luminous with
borrowed moonlight. I stood in the middle of the glittering track
and looked the moon in the face.

  Or I could be a man of Dorset, that secretive, beautiful county.
We used to live there, near Sherborne. We rented a cottage in a lane
between Yetminister and Thornford. In a place of beautiful stone
houses ours was ugly.

  It was over a hundred years old but time had done nothing to
soften the raw brick of its walls. It had been a labourer's cottage,
built for a man who would spend all daylight in the fields. It was not
meant to be attractive; it was meant for poverty. Its rooms were
mean and damp, its windows narrow, fires burned reluctantly in its
niggardly grates. In summer a climbing rose, the good old noisette
Gloire de Dijon, ramped over the south wall and reached the roof,
filling the air with nostalgic perfume. Its buff flowers lasted through
June and occasional faded blooms hung on bravely into September.
It was as old as the cottage and its only decorative element. We had
no neighbours, but old Mr Ayling, who farmed nearby, sometimes
spoke to us. He let us walk in his pastures, showed us where the
horse mushrooms grew, enormous, flat, creamy, over an inch thick.
We'd put one in the pan and fry it as if it were a steak.

  One Saturday I walked away from the house, past Beer Hackett
church and up Knighton Hill. The year had begun to turn into
spring and fat buds were waiting on the trees. A cold sun shone,
windflowers were growing, frail and white, in sheltered places. I
marched through Lillington and up into hilly country near Bishop's
Caundle. Leaning on a field gate I looked down into the valley,
imagining it turned greener as I watched. Then, from the narrow
head of the top field, the hounds ran. Sixteen couple streaming in
freedom together, the full, beautiful pack, certain of their line,

unstoppable in their galloping. Behind them, riding hard, came the boldest members of the hunt. I could see old Mr Ayling. He had lost his hat and his long white hair was shining in the sun. Too far away to hear the sounds of the chase, I watched their brilliant, silent charge through the valley. It was exhilarating, heartwarming. I stood on a bar of the gate and almost cheered.

A movement among the fists of the new green ferns close by distracted me. It was a small dog fox, hardly more than a cub. I could see his wedge-shaped head. He came out of the hedge, grinning, measuring me with a quizzical little eye, and sat down, settling himself carefully on his thin hams. Vaguely embarrassed, I stepped off the gate and stood near him. He didn't move. Together we watched the disappearing hunt, together we watched the stragglers vanish awkwardly into the bottom wood. The little fox was panting lightly, but he was not distressed. He got up, gave me a sardonic glance, and trotted jauntily down the lane, his brush swinging. It was a revelation to me. I saw that I was on the side of the fox. Such experiences make a man native to a place; I could live in Dorset.

Or in Seattle, I could live there. To think of that Pacific city, ringed by conical hills and filled with the sounds of water, makes me homesick. I liked Seattle from the day I flew in. When I'd been there about a week I went into a tackle shop to buy a fishing licence.

'Are you an alien?' asked the sad, middle-aged lady as she opened her book of licences.

I was astonished and then ashamed. I had to admit I was an alien.

'It's more when you're an alien,' she said. 'That will be seven dollars seventy-five.'

I gave her the money.

'Don't be sore,' she said; 'I've been an alien fifty years. Ever since my parents brought me over from Huddersfield.'

I got in the Volkswagen and drove out to Quillayute, a little place on the Olympic Peninsula, and the next morning I took three jack salmon out of the Bogachiel before breakfast. The sun was not up, and I stood on a rock in midstream and threw my spinner into the margin of a fast current and the fish came to me. I went all over Washington State and I took steelhead from the Skagit River and the Stillaguamish River and cutthroat from Chopaka Lake and Jameson Lake and the Hood Canal. And later, sailing out of Aberdeen, I took big salmon from the ocean, but I was still an alien. Oh, I could live out there, just as I could live at Summer Cove, County Cork, a mile from Kinsale, on the north shore of Kinsale Harbour.

I'm deceiving myself, I know that. The little Dorset fox and the
lady in the tackle shop were right; I'm an outsider and an alien. I
have this insatiable thirst for other places. I cannot remain at peace
for long in one place. I've known this for some time, I see it plain.
I work alone, travelling haphazardly the length of the country, shake
hands with people I'll never see again, come home. Sometimes I
travel by train or plane, but mostly I drive.

Next week I shall drive to Birmingham, knowing every yard of the
way. Once I'd have got out my maps and guides, plotted the journey
with care, set off early so that I could see every ancient landmark,
fine church, old house on the way. For a happy morning I'd have
balanced the attractions of one route against those of another. But
that's all done now. Next week I'll drive to Birmingham taking the
fast roads and the journey will take just over two hours. I shan't stop
anywhere.

I went to college in Birmingham. I knew the place well when I was
young.

My homeward journeys, often late at night, are nearly always
unplanned and instinctive. Last year I was working on the North
Wales coast, near Prestatyn. I finished in the early evening and
decided not to stay for dinner. I paid my hotel bill and carried my
bags to the car. I wiped the midges from the windscreen, sat in the
car, fastened the safety belt, and went. I was going to make a fast
run. It had been raining earlier, but the evening was brilliantly dry
and sharp, the air washed clear. A few clouds moved out at sea, low
on the skyline. I sat upright and relaxed, utterly at peace, knowing
the extremities of the car as I knew my own skin, driving with the
fingertips. I came down the Ruthin road, the A525, neatly and
circumspectly, with an amused caution, knowing I could put the car
wherever I liked, sensitive even to the grain of the road.

At Ruthin I turned off for Corwen and Llangollen. It was dusk,
and a cold, erratic wind began to get up. Soon, before I reached
Oswestry, I switched on the headlights. The road was empty. I went
straight down the marches through Welshpool and Newtown before
hitting the A44 at Crossgates. It was raining hard when I got to
Kington. I stopped there and found a little coffee house still open,
spoke a while with the sleepy young Italian waiter, and drifted gently
out of town, the roads dark and wet. It was past midnight when I
drove through Hereford. The heavy rain stopped as I was leaving
the city. A policeman came out of a shop doorway, took off his wet
coat, and shook it.

I knew where I was in general terms, but the darkness and the rain

were making things difficult to recognize. I wanted to head for
Gloucester through Peterstow and Ross-on-Wye, a road I've driven
many times, but when I ran on to a long stretch of dual carriageway
I knew I was lost. I wasn't worried. I knew I'd meet familiar roads
soon enough. I pushed hard down the wide road, the car dipping
gently as it met small pools of water at the edge of the drying
surfaces. Two coaches passed, travelling in the opposite direction,
their interior lights bright. I saw people asleep in their seats, their
heads lolling against windows. The dual carriageway ended and
with it the sodium lights overhead. I began to swing down the bends
of a narrower road, the weight of sudden darkness oppressive. It was
raining again. The car rocked like a boat through the washing gutters
and I hunched my shoulders against the hills I felt were steep and
close on either side. One or two houses, unlit and blank, stood at
the sides of the road. Then I saw the river. I'm a sucker for rivers. I
stopped the car and got out. Wind lashed the ends of my coat, the
rain stung in its gusts. It was a lovely river; swollen by storms,
ominous, full to the lips of its grass banks, its loud, black thunder
rolled in the channels of my ears.

I got the big torch out of the car and walked down the road. The
one street of a village slept under the whipped rain and I walked
right through, to the far end. Then, on the left hand, a marvellous
abbey pushed its ruined walls into the darkness, very Gothic, very
romantic. I let the straight beam of the torch climb on its stones and
arches. I knew where I was. I was in Tintern, on the banks of the
Wye, looking at Tintern Abbey. A miracle of the night had brought
me there. A single light came from a distant hill farm, hanging in
the darkness a long way up. I watched it for a long time, wondering
what emergency had called its people awake at two in the morning.
It went out and I was left alone, listening to the loud river and the
swift noise of the rain. I danced a little soft-shoe shuffle at the side
of the road, in honour of William Wordsworth.

Laughing, I ran back to the car, took off my soaked coat, and drove
down to Chepstow. Soon I was sidling cautiously on to the M4,
heavy at that hour with groaning trucks out of Newport and Cardiff,
and two hours later I was in bed.

Next week I shall drive straight up to Birmingham and straight
back, unless I visit Arthur Marshalsea.

When I first went to college in Birmingham I lived in one of the
hostels and Arthur Marshalsea had the room next to mine. His
parents lived out at Sutton Coldfield, only a few miles away. Arthur

could have travelled each day, but he wanted to live in college. He came into my room the first morning of term; I was making my bed. He wanted to borrow a book, a dictionary. I could see that was an excuse. Arthur stood just inside the door, dressed in a dark track suit with red flashes. He was not tall, but very powerfully made, long-armed, deep-chested. He spoke slowly, using a deep, cultured voice. It wasn't the way he normally spoke, I could tell that. He was trying out one of the many personalities a young man adopts before he accepts the mask that best fits him, or, if he's lucky, presents his own face to the world. He didn't open the dictionary I gave him.

'Coming over to the dining hall?' he asked.

We walked over together and after that we did most things together. Arthur had more pure energy than any other person I've known. Most mornings I'd be the first to get up in our building. I'd potter about for half an hour, relishing the slow quiet of the early day, sit in my armchair and read, make a pot of tea for myself and perhaps for Billy Notley, who came from Worcester and took the same courses I did. I'd shave slowly, feeling the pleasure of a long day stretching out in front of me. I liked that morning silence, I liked my footsteps to echo through the empty halls and corridors.

But when Arthur got up it was like an electric storm. At once the place vibrated. Arthur would be singing, laughing out of his window at friends on their way to breakfast; he would be washing and shaving, surrounded by lather and steam, his towels spinning and flapping; he would be out and off at a run, springing over the ground. He ran everywhere. His knowledge of the city and the countryside around was immense. Most free afternoons we'd get out and Arthur would show me some strange area, streets of small factories, full of old men skilled in dying crafts; a long stretch of black canal, still, very quiet, only a few yards from the city centre; old markets where you could buy cheeses, lengths of cloth, brass candlesticks black with grime and age. I learned a lot about the city from Arthur. In return I talked to him about plays and novels, went to the theatre with him, wrote most of his essays. We played for the college soccer team, Arthur and I, he our one player of true quality and I a competent midfield player. We played other teams around the Midlands, sometimes on Saturdays, often on Thursday afternoons.

One Saturday morning we played at Dudley, a Black Country town near Wolverhampton. It was in early March, and a week of rain had made the ground heavy and difficult, but that day I was possessed by something like inspiration. I ran as if fatigue were a myth, I passed and tackled with a perfect stylish accuracy, I went around opponents as if they were insubstantial as mist. I scored two goals in the first twenty minutes, one with a precise lob from a long way out. It seemed to me that I knew every bounce of the ball. Near the end of the game Arthur took the ball in our opponents' half, turned inside the fullback, and ran, huge leaping strides carrying him over the mud. I ran inside him, a couple of yards behind. Reaching the penalty area, he checked the ball and pushed it delicately into my path. It was a perfect pass, perfect in weight and speed. I hit the ball with a full swing of the right foot and I saw, as I fell, how it flew into the top corner of the net. It was there, a complete goal, before the goalkeeper had begun to make his leap. I can still recapture every moment of that thirty-year-old game. Afterward I took a bus into the city centre and Arthur came with me.

The municipal art gallery was showing a visiting exhibition of paintings by Van Gogh. For the first time, all the great oils had been brought together, and suddenly I knew I wanted to see them, it was essential for me to see them. We climbed the steps and went in. I could see all the famous paintings I'd known only in reproductions and the sight of those intense and passionate statements set me eloquent. Moving from canvas to canvas I told Arthur of the splendour and individuality of Van Gogh's vision, of the unity of his composition, of the values he gave to the sun in this picture and that, of a thousand things I'd never thought of before but which were suddenly both simple and novel. It seemed to me then that I knew the purpose behind every stroke of the man's brush. In a few minutes I had collected a small, respectful audience. This didn't deter me. Aware of the farcical nature of the situation, I explored even wilder flights of invention and rhetoric, but while I was amused I thought that what I said was right and necessary, that there was little about art and life and Van Gogh which was unknown to me at that moment. It was an hour of serious and absurd play acting. At the end I was exhausted. Arthur stepped up to me and shook my hand warmly.

'Young man,' he said, 'that was a privilege and a pleasure. You have given us all a rare insight into the workings of a creative mind. I hope you will not be offended if I give you this as a sign of my appreciation.' He gave me a coin. I started to laugh, but Arthur held up his hand firmly, smiled at me as if he were some polite and well-intentioned stranger, and walked away. My other listeners pressed forward, murmured their gratitude, pushed their offerings into my hand. I held a solid fistful of currency there. When I got outside Arthur was waiting for me, leaning over the balustrade, laughing. We had enough money to visit the cinema and eat a generous dinner at a restaurant normally well out of our reach. Content and leisurely aristocrats, patrons and lovers of the arts, we arrived back late that night at our hostel.

Most evenings we sat in our rooms, working away with the thin plaster walls between us. Conversation was easy. Sometimes we sang. The singing was Arthur's idea. His voice was smooth and pleasant and he knew all the hits, but his great gift was for infallible harmony. However badly I carried the tune Arthur could so accept and modulate my errors that we always sounded good, a partnership of deliberate melodies. And as our time passed by, we got better. Arthur began to speak almost daily of his wild ambition for us to become a professional act, to stand in the dim and changing lights, dressed in tuxedos, singing 'How Deep is the Ocean', 'Blue Moon', 'My Funny Valentine', 'Stardust', and other standards from our long repertoire. I used to listen to him, but I knew it was fantasy.

He was my friend; we shared our money, our time, our work; we supported each other through the little communal storms which blew up occasionally. At the end we shook hands and parted. I went off to Taunton, Arthur stayed in Birmingham and became a teacher of physical education. He was a fine athlete, the fastest sprinter in the Midland counties.

A year later I went back up to Arthur's wedding. He married Sally, a slim elegant girl, taller than he. When it was time for Arthur to make his speech, he stood up, smiled, raised his glass to the guests, to his bridesmaids, and with a serious, touchingly humble gesture, to his wife. He didn't say a word; and then he sat down. Later, we watched them drive off to the airport. I haven't seen them since. We wrote to each other, Arthur and I, but the letters dribbled to a halt as time gave us other things. The Christmas cards came to an end. I never thought of Arthur Marshalsea.

Five weeks ago, when I knew I was to visit Birmingham, I asked the education people to put me in touch with him. It would be good, I thought, to see what the years had done for Arthur Marshalsea. Sometimes I remembered with a smile his escapades, could almost see him running, hunched, muscular, concentrating every yard of the way. Last night a girl who said she was Arthur's daughter telephoned me from Birmingham. I listened to the young voice, realizing that this was a girl I had not known existed. She had been born and grown into her responsibilities without my knowing she was in the world.

'Great,' I said. 'Nice of you to telephone. I'll be in Birmingham next week, and I'd like to see Arthur.'

She told me that Arthur had been very ill. I could call, but I must not be shocked when I saw him. Unusually strong and active, playing football regularly until he was nearly fifty, Arthur had set off last Easter to walk through the Lake District and come back the length of the Pennine Way. He had planned it for months, his journeys were marked, his climbs plotted, each piece of equipment tested. The girl and her mother had watched him leave the house with his backpack and his ashplant and tramp sturdily down the road. Ten minutes later he was carried home unconscious.

'It's his heart,' I said. 'He's had a heart attack.'

Not at all. An insidious virus, attacking his brain, had brought him down. For nine weeks he had lain in hospital, unconscious in his white bed. His return to the world was slow and painful. For a long time he had been deaf and blind. Even now, although improving, he cannot walk unaided, he cannot feed himself. Slowly he is learning to read again. His voice is often uncontrolled and often says the wrong words, which angers him. It was shocking to think of Arthur helpless. I wrote down the address as the girl gave it to me. They live just outside Knowle, on the way into Birmingham from Warwick. I know the place. I've walked along the canal bank at Knowle and watched the wild geese sit in the fields, spoken to the patient, laconic anglers waiting for small roach to bite. It won't be difficult to find Arthur's house.

After I spoke to the girl I took a glass of whisky and water and thought about Arthur. I went to bed, but sleep was not restful and afterward I awoke with a heavy mind.

I've been thinking of what I shall say to Arthur when I see him. I can hear already the falsely cheerful voice I shall use, the loud memories. Almost anything I say to him will remind him that he cannot walk, that his speech is guttural and false. How can I talk to him of the game at Dudley when he pushed the ball to me and I hit it sweetly even as I was falling? Or speak of the going-down dinner when we sang 'That Old Black Magic'? Frankie Smedley, too drunk to see the keys, had played for us, and the next morning he had had no memory of it at all.

The days are gone when nobody in the Midlands could run as fast as Arthur, when his voice was young and strong and he could hit any note he wanted with easy accuracy, and I'll not talk of them. I'll tell him about the Dysynni Valley, how the river begins up there in Cader Idris. I'll tell him of my time in Washington State, how the

waves hit the beaches at La Push and Grayland, rolling in behind
the cold fling of the Pacific spray. I'll invent Summer Cove for him,
describe the silken passage of the seals, tell him of my dark,
unintentional journey to Tintern.

But all the time I'm thinking of Arthur lying nine weeks in a coma,
his body in its clean linen being turned at the appointed times by
the brisk, compassionate nurses, being fed through sterile tubes.
Where was he then? He must have been away somewhere in some
solitary darkness, weightless, without senses. I imagine him moving
on some dark beach, so lightly he does not disturb a grain of the
sand. He can feel nothing. I should like to know where he was then;
I am consumed with a curious pity for Arthur Marshalsea, his
useless legs, his halting speech. I see in him a terrible general fate
about which we shall know very little. The still, sad music of
humanity . . . wasn't it? Sing it again, Wordsworth.

The Kingfisher

On the morning of his fourteenth birthday, James met his father in the kitchen. His father came to him and held him by the shoulders, at arm's length, and looked at him with such wry and compassionate warmth that the boy was at once convinced of the imminence of some great cataclysm. Almost the same height, they stared at each other for nearly half a minute.

'So you're fourteen,' James's father said. 'It seems no time since I first held you in my arms. With great trepidation and very gingerly, but I held you. And here you are, fourteen.'

'That's it,' James said.

'Fourteen,' his father said. 'Always a sad anniversary for men of our family. A sad day.'

He picked up his cup of coffee, walked to the window, and stared seriously over the garden. When he turned away from the window, he smiled almost shyly at James, as if they shared an enormous, obligatory knowledge — some ominous secret. 'Come into the dining room with me, James,' he said.

The dining room was cold and quiet. Its mahogany furniture sat solidly in place, heavy, smelling of polish. James remembered it arriving at the house when he was a small boy, sent south from his grandmother's home in Yorkshire. The room was rarely used.

'Sit down,' James's father said. 'It would be best if you sat down.'

James sat on a hard chair. Its seat had been broken long ago and repaired with some old craftsman's adhesive. James felt with his finger the small ridge of the mend. He could see a black streak of dry glue running the length of the wood.

'How do you feel?' his father said. 'We can postpone this if you don't feel up to it.'

'Get on with it,' James said. 'Whatever it is.'

'Admirably stoic,' his father said. 'I wish I had been as stoic when my father told me.'

'Told you what?' James said.

His father didn't answer. He moved quietly into a corner of the room, and then he spoke. 'James, when the men of our family reach the age of fourteen, they are thought old enough to bear a terrible knowledge. Generation after generation, from father to son, we have been told this secret, pledged to pass it on in our turn. Although what we learn has in many ways blighted our lives, made saddened men of us, we have all borne our sorrow bravely. I know you will do the same.'

Oh, God, thought James, rigid on his chair, we suffer from incurable hereditary madness. All over the country my cousins, tainted and cretinous, are shut away in stone towers. We are descended shamefully and illegitimately — incestuously, probably — from some nameless criminal family. He pushed away other terrors, too hideous to think of. 'Tell me,' he said, his voice a croak.

His father, upright and slim and still, stood in the shadows of the room. He was remote and impersonal. His face was dark. 'Remember, it is my duty to tell you this,' he said. 'I would willingly have spared you and kept this knowledge alone.'

'Hell's flames!' yelled James, his control at an end. 'Tell me!'

For a long moment, until the imagined echoes of his cry had left James's ears, his father waited. Then he spoke. 'There is no Father Christmas,' he said.

That had been almost two weeks ago, and James still laughed at the memory, although he had been wild with rage at first. He lay in bed listening to his father's voice through the open window, and little uncontrollable giggles made him shake. It was not yet seven o'clock, but this father was already in the garden. James knew what he was doing. He was standing among his rose-bushes, encouraging and cajoling. Every morning he spoke to them, full of praise if they were flowering well, like a general before battle if he felt they could do better. James got up and looked out at his father.

The lawn carried a heavy summer dew, and the marks of his father's footsteps were clear. He had wandered all over the garden, but he stood now near the rose bed, talking quietly and fondly. James could not hear what he was saying. His father's thin shanks stuck out below his silk robe. It was a glittering paisley robe in green and blue, tied at the waist with a sash of darker colour. Watching his father bend above the subservient shrubs, James thought he looked like an exotic bird, a peacock of some kind.

His father loved birds to come to his garden. He had widened the trickle of a stream that bordered this plot into two small pools, so that he could keep in comfort a pair of ancient mallards, Mr and Mrs Waddle. This morning, hearing the man's voice, they hopped out of the water and hurried loudly to him. Mrs Waddle, always the braver, marched to his feet and pecked at his brown slippers. She paused to look up, her head on one side, out of a round black eye. A yard away, Mr Waddle looked on benevolently. He was in his summer glory, his green head glossy, his speculum a trim bar of reflecting blue. James's father went off to the garage, where he kept a sack of poultry food.

It was then that a kingfisher flew in, paused above the stream, and dived. He was blue lightning, an arrow of light; his flight was electric and barbarous. He took instantly from the shallow water a small fish, stickleback or minnow, and perched on the wooden post that had held a clematis, killed by harsh frost two years back. James saw the brilliant turquoise of the bird's back, the warm chestnut breast, his sturdy beak. The kingfisher held the small fish struggling across his beak and whacked it savagely and expertly against the wood before he slid it down his throat. Then he flew, seeming to leave behind a visible echo of his flight, a streak of colour. James's father came out of the garage, holding a bowl of pellets. His ducks begged and skidded before him. He had missed the whole appearance of the kingfisher.

That afternoon, because his mother had gone to Birmingham to see her sister, James went with his father to the nursing home. His father would not go alone.

'Charles Emerson, to see his mother,' he said to the receptionist. 'And James Emerson, to see his grandmother.'

The nurse smiled at them and told them to go ahead.

The old lady lay inert in her white bed, her thin hair damp and yellowish against the pillow. James's father held her hand and spoke softly to her, but she didn't answer. Her eyes were closed. She didn't know anybody. Sometimes she had spoken, but her words were disjointed and incoherent. Now she neither spoke nor moved. James watched his father grow quiet and sad as the slow minutes passed. The small room was too hot. It smelled of sickness. The voices of boys playing tennis in the park came faintly to them. James was glad when it was time to leave.

His father drove furiously out of the car park, showering the neat red gravel behind the wheels of the car. He spun the big car roughly through Redmond Corner, his tyres protesting. It was always like this. He always left the nursing home in a rage of frustration, in an agony over his mother's decay.

James tapped his father's knee. 'Too fast, Dad,' he said. 'You'll get a ticket.'

His father braked, but said nothing. For several miles he drove carefully down the road, heavy now with afternoon traffic — the cars of businessmen, files of trucks taking their loads around Oxford to Southampton.

'You see what we come to,' he said at last, as if he were very tired. 'You see what time brings us to. We lie insensible in strange rooms, not knowing we are alive. The tyranny of the breath keeps us going. Your grandmother has committed the crime of growing too old.'

James had known these moods before. He sat at his father's side and waited for him to recover. He did not understand his father's anger and impotence. It was natural to grow old, natural for the body to wither and break; it was common mortality, the human condition. He wished very much for some comfort to bring back his usual ebullient, unpredictable father.

They stopped at the traffic lights near the Queen's Theatre. 'Tell me, Holmes,' James said to his father, 'what do you make of that old lady on the other side of the road, dressed in black?' It was an old game of theirs, although they had not played it for a long time.

His father's head jerked about, his long neck stiff — like an old heron stalking a frog. He was smiling. 'Ah' he said, 'you mean the retired Irish parlour maid, Watson? With a ne'er-do-well son in the Army and a pipe-smoking husband?'

'Holmes,' James said, 'you astound me! How on earth did you gather that information? Do you know the woman?'

'Never saw her before in my life,' his father said. 'But you know my methods, Watson. I knew she was a parlour maid because her right arm is six inches longer than her left — the result, Watson, of many years of carrying heavy buckets of coal to the upstairs parlours in which her employers sat.'

James laughed, turning in his seat to look at his father. 'Good gracious, Holmes,' he said. 'You do astound me. Go on.'

'A mere nothing,' his father said. 'I know she is retired because, apart from her evident maturity, she would not be about so early in the evening were she still employed. And as she is still wearing, although St. Patrick's Day is long past, a bunch of faded shamrock at her collar, she is undoubtedly Irish.'

'When you put it like that, Holmes, it's quite simple,' James said. 'But what about her son in the Army and her pipe-smoking husband? I have you there, I think.'

'Not at all,' said his father. He was well into the game now, his gloom forgotten. 'The shamrock is fastened to her coat by an old brooch, on which the word "Mother" is clearly to be discerned. The parcel she carries is addressed to a private in the infantry named McCarthy. It is safe to assume he is her son. That he is a ne'er-do-well is evident from the woman's dress. No decent son would allow his mother to go out so shabbily garbed.'

'Great,' James said. 'Pretty good. What about the husband?'

'That,' said his father with relish, 'is the easiest deduction of all. Did you not observe that the woman's clothes are spotted all over with tiny burns, small marks of scorching? They prove beyond all doubt that she has spent many years in the close vicinity of a man who is a careless pipe-smoker, undoubtedly her husband.'

'A full score,' said James. 'You haven't lost your skill.'

His father took the car past a row of parked vehicles outside the library. 'Your turn,' he said. 'Tell me, Holmes, what do you make of the sinister-looking man who stands outside the filling station?'

'You mean,' James said, 'the ex-sailor who subsequently became a policeman, was dismissed for taking bribes, and now earns a casual living as a gardener?'

'Holmes,' said his father, 'you astonish me.'

They ate supper together, silently, contentedly, and afterward James walked in the garden. The evening was still warm, and Mr and Mrs Waddle muttered from their stream. High up, the seagulls were trailing their irregular columns back to the beach. A little tatter of silk, Oriental in its brilliance, had blown from somewhere onto the lawn. James bent over it. It was the kingfisher. He picked it up, and it lay dead on his hand, light as dust. Its head rolled loosely of its own tiny weight, as if its neck were broken. James examined the short, blunt wings, touched the dry beak.

From the house his father began to sing. 'Questa o quella,' he sang, his voice breaking comically on the higher notes, 'per me pari sono.'

James held the dead bird on his open palm. He carried it to the long grass beneath the maple tree in the corner of the garden. He placed the bird in the dark grass behind the tree and stood above it, rubbing his hands together briskly. He would not tell his father about the kingfisher, not about its vivid morning flight across the garden, not about its small, irrevocable death. He would spare his father that knowledge.

My Uncle's Story

Sometimes my uncle drank too much. Ordinarily a morose man, silent, possessed altogether by a refined melancholy, his single gesture toward speech would normally be a sigh of the slightest possible audibility, an exhalation as soft as the air on which it floated. He was a still, downcast man, hunched in his corner, effaced by sadness.

But when he drank too much his eyes grew fierce, his speech blossomed and became oracular, the dark fancies of his usual gloom grew ripe and colourful. I saw this transfiguration only once, when I was ten years old. Returning late from a school concert where I and other boys had sung a number of roaring songs in which the brave Welsh had swung their swords around the musical battle-fields, I called on my way home at my grandmother's house. My uncle, a bachelor, lived with her. He was her oldest son. I went into the back room and there was my uncle, upright and luminous, enthroned on his wooden arm-chair. He looked marvellous.

I told my grandmother about the concert, how Jackie Colbert had dived through a hoop during the gymnastics display, tumbled awkwardly, and broken his collarbone, how Ronnie Protheroe had imitated a duck and a horse, and I sang for her the opening lines of the most patriotic of our songs. She was well pleased and gave me the crust of a new loaf, a piece of mild cheese, and a glass of milk.

Of all this my uncle seemed oblivious. He sat upright in his chair, his face fiery, smiling. He nodded occasionally as if he could hear conversations unheard by us. Serenely contemptuous of all around him, he dispensed favours to invisible favourites, dismissed invisible peasants with a wave of his hand. I looked at him with delight.

'What's the matter with him?' I asked my grandmother. 'Is he drunk?'

'He's merry,' my grandmother said. 'We might say he's merry.'

My uncle turned royally toward us and spoke.

'Do you think,' he said, in rich and jocular tones, 'that the world was made in jest?'

'Stop it, Wil,' said my grandmother comfortably. She was darning a grey woollen sock and had her steel-rimmed glasses on. My uncle didn't hear her.

'Read where you will,' my uncle said, indicating a long horizon of learning and study with the flat of his hand, 'read the Bible, the

Koran, read where you will. But the creatures of air and water have a separate wisdom.'

I thought about this. It seemed reasonable.

'That's enough, Wil,' my grandmother said, 'you'll frighten the boy.'

'I'm not frightened,' I said.

My uncle looked at me. His eyes were glittering and ecstatic.

'Don't be afraid, boy,' he said sharply.

'I'm not afraid,' I said.

'Remember,' cried my uncle in a great voice, 'tall gods walk the earth, but their feet are in the mud!'

He stood up and raised his arms above his head.

Great stuff, I thought, going home at a trot, leaping the wet ditch every fifth stride. Sometimes I missed and fell in.

'Where have you been until now; look at your boots!' said my mother, in a crescendo of disbelief.

I looked at my boots. The ditch had been pretty dirty. I had left a plain trail all down the hall.

'Remember,' I said sternly, 'great gods walk the earth, but their feet are in the mud.'

'What are you talking about?' my mother said. As I passed her she landed a grim slap to the back of my head and I staggered into the kitchen. She followed me. I could see she was intrigued.

'Where did you hear such rubbish?' she said.

'Uncle Wil told me,' I said, 'and also about the creatures of air and water. They have a different wisdom.'

'Oh, him,' she said. 'Been drinking, has he? I hope you don't take after him, that's all.'

I went to bed.

My uncle Wil hadn't always been melancholy. He was spry and sociable as a young man. Once, my father told me, my uncle had gone out with Elvet Parry and they had become famously drunk.

'Oh, they made a proper job of it,' my father said, slapping his knee with delight as he remembered my uncle's adventure.

My uncle and Elvet Parry had always been friends. As boys they had walked to Cardiff and, adding sufficient years to their ages, joined the army. This was during the Great War. They had been private soldiers in the fifth battalion of the Welsh Regiment, an infantry regiment, and fought in France until the last day of hostilities. When they finally returned home they were still only eighteen years old. They worked together in the local colliery. Most Friday evenings they met, pooled their money, and set off on a tour of the public houses in our village and in villages nearby. This is what they had done one winter Friday before I was born.

They began, as they always did, at the Wheatsheaf, a quiet, serious inn near my grandmother's house. Here my uncle and Elvet Parry spoke to some of their friends, talking slowly and gently, their voices hardly louder than the click of dominoes. The Wheatsheaf was a great place for dominoes. Relaxed, easy, the week's work in the past, the friends then began to visit, in reeling succession, The Dynevor Arms, The George, The Barley Mow, and The Greyhound. After this they left the village and made for The Blue Boar, a small tavern in the hills where the landlord was a friend of theirs, and where little regard was paid to the lawful hours of drinking. At midnight all the revellers were turned out. Sentimental fathers, wavering a little and very happy, went home to their wives and children. But my uncle and Elvet Parry, without such responsibilities, tottered into the night. Each carried two bottles of whisky, purchased as an after-thought from Dennis Montague, landlord of The Blue Boar.

'They could stand, then,' Mr Montague told my father. 'Oh, yes, they could stand all right. With help, of course.'

It had begun to snow, a fine dry snow with flakes small and pointed as needles. Hard particles of blown snow found the least crack between the slates of roofs and heaped themselves in frozen pyramids on the attic floors; they crept in drifts under the doors of houses, dying in leaking streams as the warm air hit them; they powdered the lanes and streets and fields with a glittering dust. It was very cold.

In the early hours of the morning the Griffiths boys, coming home from a dance in the town, saw my uncle and Elvet standing under the lamp that lit the village square. They stood close together and they were singing. They were singing, the Griffiths boys said, the songs of the dead war: 'Mademoiselle from Armentieres,' 'Tipperary,' 'Keep the Home Fires Burning,' 'Pack Up Your Troubles'. And as Desmond Griffiths cautiously unlocked his door, taking infinite care not to wake his father, Elvet Parry began a performance of rich nostalgia.

'Honest,' Desmond said, 'it was enough to make you cry.'

'There's a long, long trail a-winding,' sang Elvet Parry, 'into the land of my dreams.' And soft as a puff Desmond and Arnold Griffiths shut their heavy door and locked the singing out. That was the last anyone saw or heard of Elvet Parry and my uncle for two days.

The bitter weather kept everyone indoors. A few brave women

scurried to the shops, a few hardy children played in the light, unsatisfactory snow. It was an astonishment when, late that evening, my grandmother marched into my parents' house. She was wrapped in her thickest coat, a long scarf was wound about her head and fastened under her chin.

'Wil hasn't been home,' she said. 'He didn't come home last night. I don't know where he is.'

'Don't worry, Mum,' my mother said, 'he'll be holed up in some bar with Elvet Parry, not a leg between the two of them. Oh, a fine brother, he is. A fine name we'll have in the village with that pair.'

'I called at the Parry house as I came here,' my grandmother said. 'Elvet hasn't been home either. I spoke to his sister, Mavis. She's worried sick.'

'Men,' my mother said. 'They don't think.'

'They bought two loaves and a large tin of corned beef,' my grandmother said, 'knocked Mr Willis up until he came down to the shop and served them. One o'clock in the morning.'

'Did they, now,' said my father.

He took my grandmother home and then he went all round the village, speaking to his friends, mustering the young men. The next morning, at first light, the men met, grumbling and laughing, gloved to the elbows, muffled in clothes. They set out for the hills, moving quickly at first, and then, as they met the first steep, more slowly, calling to each other to keep in touch, poking their sticks into drifts, whistling their dogs. All day they climbed, finding nothing. By mid-afternoon it was almost dark. Snow began to fall, in heavy flakes. It was lovely, my father said, to see the line of torches strung along the hill, to hear the men call to each other through the falling dark. Subtly the snow altered familiar contours: the bleak slopes were swept and dark, the hollows filled and hidden by whipped drifts. At last they faced the erratic rim of granite which forms the summit of our mountain. Fissured and broken, it has been ground to its stubborn core by centuries of bitter weather. There they found Elvet Parry, at bay against a slab of rock. He stood on guard in the swirling fall, facing his friends as they climbed toward him.

'Halt!' he cried. 'Who goes there?'

'It's all right, Elvet,' my father said, 'we're the relief party. You can stand down now.'

'Thank God you've come, sergeant,' said Elvet. 'Private Thomas is in the dugout, badly wounded.'

'We'll look after him,' my father said. 'Take Private Parry down the line, men.'

My uncle was in a cave behind Elvet Parry's watchpost. He was
heavily asleep and wounded by whisky. Turn and turn about, the
befuddled comrades had been on guard in the confused hills,
thinking they were again at war. They were taken home and put to
bed, hot bottles at their feet, their curtains drawn against any
intrusion of curiosity. They were quite unharmed. The next day
they strode about the smiling village like returned warriors, like
heroes.

'They have no sense of shame,' said my mother, bitterly, as she
watched their triumphant progress.

But I delighted in this story and would ask my father to tell it at
least once a week.

'How did you know where to find them?' I asked my father.

'It was the bully beef and bread,' my father explained. 'They had
drawn their rations, exactly as they had when in the army, so I knew
they'd got confused and thought they were back in France. After
that it was just a matter of deciding where they'd hole up.'

'I don't know how you can be so tolerant,' my mother said, 'and
you a teetotaller. I'd have given them France.'

'They had a bad war,' my father said stoutly. 'You don't forget
the war. It's there, behind your life, every day. And your training is
always part of you. They were good infantrymen.' He was a soldier
by instinct as well as by training. His mind was filled with the great
battles of his life, Mons, Verdun, Salonika, the Dardanelles. He
wore always in the lapel of his jacket the miniature ribbons of his
medals, and every man who had fought in the Great War was his
comrade-in-arms and his friend; he would defend such a man to the
end.

When I could walk far enough my father took me to see the cave
in which they had found my sleeping uncle. In my imagination I
had seen an echoing vast of darkness, a vaulted black cathedral
where a pygmy uncle slept against a flat of basalt but it was no more
than a disappointing cleft in the stone, sheltered enough to turn a
wind, long enough for a man to stretch comfortably. When I saw it,
two sheep occupied it. They stared at me out of their skulls with
malevolent yellow eyes, and I hurried back to my father.

Oh, he was nimble and happy enough when he was young, was my
uncle. I can remember him as a young man, I can just remember
him. We were in my grandmother's garden and he was dancing and
grinning at me. His boots were brilliantly polished and I could see
the gleaming toe caps advancing toward me, prancing away. He

strutted on his toes, lifting his knees high, and he held a shilling between thumb and forefinger. His face was pink and mischievous; he wriggled his devils' eyebrows at me. I was terrified.

'Say it,' he wheedled. 'Say it, like a good boy, and you shall have this lovely shilling.'

But I stood mute in the bean rows and would not utter the blasphemous word he wanted me to repeat. My mother leaned scornfully against the wall of the house, confident of my perfect innocence. I was very small.

'He won't say it,' she said, 'not if you offer him a pound note.'

'Oh, Wil won't do that,' my grandmother said. 'I don't like admitting such a thing about my own son, but he won't put a pound note at risk. I'm surprised at him waving that shilling about. Wil isn't generous.'

My uncle laughed, stood up straight, and ran down the lane, in and out of the shadows. He was lithe enough then.

When the depression hit our valley and the collieries closed, my uncle lost his job. He took it hard. Each day, as I walked to school, I used to pass small groups of workless men on the village square. They spoke quietly to each other, seldom laughed, were united in strong bonds of friendship by a common hardship. But my uncle was never among them. He grew restless and bad-tempered; he walked the mountain paths for hours. One morning, calling at my grandmother's, I saw she had been crying.

'What's the matter, Gran?' I said. 'Where's Uncle Wil?' But she didn't answer. She gave me a bacon sandwich and hurried me off to school. That evening my mother said that my uncle had packed a few belongings and marched away. He had walked away to look for work in some other place and nobody knew where he was.

'He's just a tramp,' my mother said, 'a common tramp. I never thought he'd come to this.' But she sounded very sad.

I became accustomed to my grandmother living on her own in her scrubbed house. I grew accustomed to her long silences as she sat in her chair. When I told her about the drama and injustices of my life at school, she didn't laugh anymore, or ask questions.

'Jimmie Sullivan fell off the playground wall,' I said, 'and one of the big boys wheeled him home in a barrow.'

'That's nice,' my grandmother said, not listening at all.

I nearly forgot about my uncle. If I thought of him, I imagined him as a tramp, a man of great panache and cunning. I knew from my reading that tramps carried their food in red bandannas tied to the end of sticks and slung arrogantly over their shoulders. They had infinite freedom. They lit fires at the sides of roads and boiled their kettles; they drank from tin cups and slept, carefree, in barns. They shaved rarely, they wore huge boots with holes in the rough leather, they set snares for unsuspecting rabbits. I imagined my uncle such a man, but when I came to think of his face I couldn't remember it. I admired the romance of his life.

One day a letter came for my grandmother. In it my uncle said he was well and hoped all was well at home. There was no address. My grandmother and I pored over the postmark. The round impression was dark and indistinct, but together we decided the letter had been posted in Doncaster.

'Doncaster,' said my father, when I told him, and he unfolded his road map of Great Britain. It covered half the big kitchen table.

'Here it is,' my father said, putting the tip of his finger on Doncaster. 'It's on the Great North Road, he's walking the Great North Road.'

I looked with satisfaction at the bold, unswerving line of the Great North Road as it moved up the map from London, over the marks of folding, on and on. Nothing could stop it. The Great North Road! I thought of its unimaginable distances, I saw in my mind the great arc of its skies, I imagined my indomitable uncle, smaller than a fly, tramping on, day after day, up the face of England.

'Poor old Wil,' my mother said. 'I feel for him, sleeping in doss houses.'

Years later, when I was nine years old and rough and noisy and prepared to utter blasphemous words without any payment at all, my uncle came home. He returned during the two summer weeks when I was at Barry Island with my parents, and he was established, hunched and silent, in his corner when I saw him.

'That's your Uncle Wil,' my grandmother said. 'Say hullo to him.'

'Hullo,' I said. He sat unmoving in his chair, one thin leg crossed over the other, inert, long hands resting in his lap. I couldn't even see him breathe.

He looked at me quickly from under the white lids of his eyes and quickly away. I regarded him with the greatest thoroughness. He did not look like a tramp. He was neither jolly nor carefree and he was flawlessly clean. I had never seen such a clean man. It seemed as if he had used up all his allowable grime and squalor in his years on the road, and no speck of dust would ever settle on him again. His shirt, his black boots, the skin of his face and of his thin arms, for he wore his shirtsleeves rolled, were all gleaming. I did not recognize him. He was an old man. His hair was sparse and colourless, his narrow face deeply lined. He was very thin. I could see the bones of his face. His bold nose was cleanly and delicately formed and two deep lines ran down from the edges of his nostrils. His lips were pale and delicate, turned down in an expression at once resigned and infinitely sad. During the whole time I was there he seemed never to move. I had expected a great, beaming, winking man, a man who took what he wanted from society with a broad smile and a swaggering touch of the forelock. I found it hard to believe in this silent, hygienic man. Later, I heard him speak to my grandmother. His voice was harsh and brusque, and he kept his words to the minimum. It hurt me to hear him speak to her, it seemed as if he were giving orders to her, but she didn't mind. When he walked he found it difficult to straighten his shoulders, and his feet were hard as clubs. He hobbled along, bent and anxious, with short, painful steps. And after a while, since he never spoke to me, I ignored him altogether. Every Christmas I bought him a cigar. He would take my dutiful gift, unwrap it, roll it in his long fingers, pass it under his nose. Then he'd smile and nod. The memory of the one splendid moment when he told me about the great gods who walk the earth stayed with me, but I was never to have it repeated.

One Saturday, the day I played for the school first team, I called at my grandmother's on my way home from the match. I was tall now, had a man's voice, was an aristocrat in the school community. I carried my football jersey openly, a badge of my rank and fame.

'That's a pretty jersey,' my grandmother said. 'I always liked black and gold, a lovely combination.'

'The first-team colours,' I said, offhandedly.

'The first team!' she said, splendidly impressed. She waved a hand at my uncle. 'Wil,' she said, 'was never keen on football. Cricket was Wil's game. Wasn't it, Wil?'

The old man stirred, twisting his bent shoulders against the fabric of his shirt.

'Yes,' he said, 'it was. I liked cricket. I was a good player.' His voice was rough and challenging, as if we had been scornful of his ability.

'He used to play a lot of cricket,' my grandmother said. 'Oh, those white flannel trousers. The trouble I used to have getting the grass stains off.'

I couldn't believe he had ever played any game in his life.

'I was a batsman,' my uncle said. 'I've still got my bat. I keep it in the wardrobe in my room.'

'That's good,' I said. I wasn't too interested. When my grandmother took her basket to go down to the butcher's, I offered to go for her.

'No,' she said, 'I have to give old Millward a bit of my eloquence. The lamb he sent up last week must have been born several years ago. I've never known such meat. He needs keeping up to the mark.'

She went out through the front door, always a sign of seriousness in my grandmother. Normally we travelled through the back door and down the garden path. I picked up the paper and began to read. I was whistling.

'Do you want to see that cricket bat?' my uncle said. He startled me.

'I don't mind,' I said. His voice was still rough, but there was something in it that made me look up from my reading. I saw that he really wanted to show me his cricket bat. He sat on the edge of his chair, eager as a child.

'Go on, then,' I said, 'let's see this famous bat.'

He went upstairs and I could hear him open the door of his room. He came down with an old bat and a pair of white cricket boots. The boots were immaculate, without stain, the laces clean and fresh. My uncle put them down on the floor.

'They're good boots,' he said. 'I clean them up twice a year. I like to keep them nice.'

He must have had them for twenty years or more. They were laughable old boots; I'd never seen anything so old-fashioned.

'Yes, they're lovely boots,' my uncle said. 'So flexible. I couldn't get them on now. My feet are so stiff.'

He handed me the bat. It was very heavy and the handle was unusually long. Some of the whipping had come away from the handle and it snapped when I pulled it. All its strength had gone.

'It needs oiling,' my uncle said. 'It needs a drop of oil, a good rub of linseed oil, then put it away for a fortnight, then a good treatment of linseed again. It would be fine then, sweet as a nut.'

The blade was dark brown with age, and pocked on the surface where it had struck cricket balls in matches long before I was born. It was so dry that the skin of the wood was beginning to lift in little shields, in thin patches, away from the body of the blade.

'You can have it,' he said, 'if you want it.'

I knew he didn't want me to have it. He fussed about, reaching toward the bat as I turned it in my hands. The bat was finished, old and dry. It would break at the first stroke.

'I don't play cricket,' I said. 'It would be no use to me. But it's a good bat.' Be generous, I thought.

He took the old bat from me and held it with the greatest gentleness.

'The first time I used it,' he said, 'I scored fifty-seven with it. The first time I ever used it.'

I saw with surprise that he was very happy. He stroked the flaking wood with his hand and he was smiling.

'Uncle,' I said, 'what was it like when you were a tramp?'

For the life of me, I don't know why I said it. It wasn't in my head at all, and I was astonished when the words came out.

'It wasn't bad, sometimes,' my uncle answered.

'Why did you go?' I asked him. 'What made you just walk away?'

'You don't remember it,' he said. 'You don't remember what it was like. You're too young. But I remember day after day with nothing to do, no work, unused. Two years I was like that. I used to get up in the morning, wash and shave, get dressed, walk up to the library, read magazines six months old. Meaningless. In the afternoon I'd walk the hills, come home, sit here staring at the fire, go to bed. Every day without dignity or purpose.'

'I remember men standing about on the square,' I said.

'There were plenty like me in Wales,' my uncle said, 'young men, rotting away. But that isn't the real reason I left. There was something in me, oh, a wish to see what was over the horizon, I suppose. And it grew and grew until it was a great lump in my chest. There was no denying it. One morning I got up and I knew I had to go. I walked away, travelling light. I had nothing to carry. Your grandmother cried, but she didn't try to stop me. I marched up the valley and over Dowlais Top, and I'd never felt so free in all my life. It was as if the whole of my days had just been preparation for this, as if the air and the light and the short grass of the mountain were all mine, I owned them all.'

My uncle's voice had grown young and pliant. His blue eyes were shining. He watched himself, straight and youthful, step out of the past and walk for our inspection.

'I did well at first,' he said. 'Picked apples and hops in Hereford. It was good, working in the hop fields. Poor people came out of South Wales and Birmingham, whole families, grandmothers, parents, children, their dogs and cats. It was like a holiday for them. We lived in camps, and everywhere there was the rich smell of the hops, on your hands, on your clothes, in the air. I was very happy then, in Hereford.'

He was smiling, he held his head high.

'I worked with a boy from near Swansea,' my uncle said, 'about

twenty, two or three years younger than I was. Told me his name
was Terry. But names mean nothing, not on the road. You throw
your name away and somebody gives you another.'

'And what was your name, Uncle?' I asked him.

'It doesn't matter,' he said. 'Sometimes I had one name, sometimes another.'

I waited without moving for him to go on.

'We worked together,' my uncle said, 'Terry and I. We were casual
labourers in Gloucester and Wiltshire, digging ditches, breaking
stones, doing whatever came our way. We didn't earn very much,
but we were eating, living. Thin! You've never seen two such thin
boys. Well, I never seemed to have much muscle. Terry looked
worse because he was a tall boy. We worked together and we
tramped together, shared what we had. We were both boys from the
valleys. We travelled through Devizes toward the end of autumn,
and the nights were getting cold. We did what we could, helped on
market days, driving cattle. Some farmers gave us a copper or two,
but times were hard for them. We chopped wood. We had a week
planting young trees on a hillside, young fir trees. That was good.
We kept travelling east, bit by bit. We weren't making for anywhere
in particular. Some said that there was work in Slough. Perhaps we
were making for Slough.'

Imperceptibly, my uncle's voice had grown slow and sad. It was
as if he were speaking an elegy which he alone had preserved from
the wastes of time. There was something almost ceremonial about
his speech, as if what he had to say were long rehearsed, familiar to
him.

'We had a hard time of it,' he said, 'once the winter came. And
Terry worse than I did. He was such a tall thin lad. It was the rain
mostly, the rain that beat us. The dry cold was not so bad. We were
in Oxford on Christmas Day. We were singing in the streets by then,
begging. I was ashamed to sing, but Terry didn't mind. He'd stand
in the gutter and lift his head and sing, as naturally as if he were in
his own kitchen. I would hold my cap out to people passing by. We
didn't make much money. And the police were very difficult, they
moved us on pretty roughly. I think we were light-headed by then,
with cold and hunger.'

My uncle sat in his chair and held himself hunched against the
remembered cold.

'At the last,' he said, 'we were somewhere between Woodstock
and Bicester. I didn't rightly know what a state we were in. It was
January, early in January, and the wind was killing everything

before it. I could see the big fires we kept in the house, and smell beef roasting in the oven. I looked up at the stars in a sky without any help in it at all. I'd never seen anything so cold in all my days. There was no shelter anywhere. We came around a bend in that forsaken road and we saw a stack of big pipes, ready for laying new drains. They were about fourteen feet long. I put an old sack over the windy end of one, and we crawled in. I went to sleep at once, never stirred. Oh, I was tired. In the morning, when I woke up, I couldn't rouse Terry. I shouted at him, tugged him. He was dead. Thin, hard, frozen to the pipe. I couldn't move him. I didn't know what to do. Nobody passed. There weren't many cars about then. In the end, I walked away. I didn't look back. I didn't tell anybody. What could I do? I didn't know his name, I didn't know his address, where he came from, if he had a family.'

I saw in my uncle's eyes an old sadness. Troubled, grieving, he stared beyond me at the tragedy of his friend's death. He turned away, leaning back in his chair in his former defeated attitude, as if it were the shape into which his body, accustomed by long usage, naturally fell.

'What could I have done?' he said. His voice was resigned and exhausted, his speech a statement of his failure.

'I don't know, Uncle,' I said, but he didn't hear me. He sat limp in his chair, his face turned away, his hands flat on the blade of his old bat. He was so frail that I knew I couldn't have touched him, even to comfort him. I stood up. The pale skin of his scalp looked silver in the afternoon light.

I picked up my jersey and walked out into the garden. The last of the string beans hung on their sticks, together with the longest pods which my grandmother saved to form her next year's seeds. Very long now, heavy, they were brown and dry, swollen at intervals as the seeds grew within. I walked down the path and into the lane. And I began to run, I ran as if released, I ran with ferocity down the lane, in and out of the shadows, I ran faster than I had ever run before.

Blackberries

Mr Frensham opened his shop at eight-thirty, but it was past nine when the woman and the child went in. The shop was empty and there were no footmarks on the fresh sawdust shaken onto the floor. The child listened to the melancholy sound of the bell as the door closed behind him and he scuffed his feet in the yellow sawdust. Underneath, the boards were brown and worn, and dark knots stood up in them. He had never been in this shop before. He was going to have his hair cut for the first time in his life, except for the times when his mother had trimmed it gently behind his neck.

Mr Frensham was sitting in a large chair, reading a newspaper. He could make the chair turn around, and he spun twice about in it before he put down his paper, smiled, and said, 'Good morning'.

He was an old man, thin, with flat white hair. He wore a white coat.

'One gentleman,' he said, 'to have his locks shorn.'

He put a board across the two arms of his chair, lifted the child, and sat him on it.

'How are you, my dear? And your father, is he well?' he said to the child's mother.

He took a sheet from a cupboard on the wall and wrapped it about the child's neck, tucking it into his collar. The sheet covered the child completely and hung almost to the floor. Cautiously the boy moved his hidden feet. He could see the bumps they made in the cloth. He moved his finger against the inner surface of the sheet and made a six with it, and then an eight. He liked those shapes.

'Snip snip,' said Mr Frensham, 'and how much does the gentleman want off? All of it? All his lovely curls? I think not.'

'Just an ordinary cut, please, Mr Frensham,' said the child's mother. 'Not too much off. I, my husband and I, we thought it was time for him to look like a little boy. His hair grows so quickly.'

Mr Frensham's hands were very cold. His hard fingers turned the boy's head first to one side and then to the other and the boy could hear the long scissors snapping away behind him, and above his ears. He was quite frightened, but he liked watching the small tufts of his hair drop lightly on the sheet which covered him, and then roll an inch or two before they stopped. Some of the hair fell to the floor and by moving his hand surreptitiously he could make nearly all of it fall down. The hair fell without a sound. Tilting his head slightly, he could see the little bunches on the floor, not belonging to him any more.

'Easy to see who this boy is,' Mr Frensham said to the child's mother, 'I won't get redder hair in the shop today. Your father had hair like this when he was young, very much this colour. I've cut your father's hair for fifty years. He's keeping well, you say? There, I think that's enough. We don't want him to dislike coming to see me.'

He took the sheet off the child and flourished it hard before folding it and putting it on a shelf. He swept the back of the child's neck with a small brush. Nodding his own old head in admiration, he looked at the child's hair for flaws in the cutting.

'Very handsome,' he said.

The child saw his face in a mirror. It looked pale and large, but also much the same as always. When he felt the back of his neck, the new short hairs stood up sharp against his hand.

'We're off to do some shopping,' his mother said to Mr Frensham as she handed him the money.

They were going to buy the boy a cap, a round cap with a little button on top and a peak over his eyes, like his cousin Harry's cap. The boy wanted the cap very much. He walked seriously beside his mother and he was not impatient even when she met Mrs Lewis and talked to her, and then took a long time at the fruiterer's buying apples and potatoes.

'This is the smallest size we have,' the man in the clothes shop said, 'it may be too large for him.'

'He's just had his hair cut,' said his mother, 'that should make a difference.'

The man put the cap on the boy's head and stood back to look. It was a beautiful cap. The badge in front was shaped like a shield and it was red and blue. It was not too big, although the man could put two fingers under it, at the side of the boy's head.

'On the other hand, we don't want it too tight,' the man said. 'We want something he can grow into, something that will last him a long time.'

'Oh, I hope so,' his mother said. 'It's expensive enough.'

The boy carried the cap himself, in a brown paper bag that had 'Price, Clothiers, High Street' on it. He could read it all except 'Clothiers' and his mother told him that. They put his cap, still in its bag, in a drawer when they got home.

His father came home late in the afternoon. The boy heard the firm clap of the closing door and his father's long step down the hall.

He leaned against his father's knee while the man ate his dinner.
The meal had been keeping warm in the oven and the plate was very
hot. A small steam was rising from the potatoes, and the gravy had
dried to a thin crust where it was shallow at the side of the plate.
The man lifted the dry gravy with his knife and fed it to his son, very
carefully lifting it into the boy's mouth, as if he were feeding a small
bird. The boy loved this. He loved the hot savour of his father's
dinner, the way his father cut away small delicacies for him and fed
them to him slowly. He leaned drowsily against his father's leg.

Afterwards he put on his cap and stood before his father, certain
of the man's approval. The man put his hand on the boy's head and
looked at him without smiling.

'On Sunday,' he said, 'we'll go for a walk. Just you and I. We'll
be men together.'

Although it was late in September, the sun was warm and the paths
dry. The man and his boy walked beside the disused canal and
powdery white dust covered their shoes. The boy thought of the
days before he had been born, when the canal had been busy. He
thought of the long boats pulled by solid horses, gliding through the
water. In his head he listened to the hushed, wet noises they would
have made, the soft waves slapping the banks, and green tench
looking up as the barges moved above them, their water suddenly
darkened. His grandfather had told him about that. But now the
channel was filled with mud and tall reeds. Bullrush and watergrass
grew in the damp passages. He borrowed his father's ashplant and
knocked the heads off a company of seeding dandelions, watching
the tiny parachutes carry away their minute dark burdens.

'There they go,' he said to himself. 'There they go, sailing away
to China.'

'Come on,' said his father, 'or we'll never reach Fletcher's Woods.'

The boy hurried after his father. He had never been to Fletcher's
Woods. Once his father had heard a nightingale there. It had been
in the summer, long ago, and his father had gone with his friends,
to hear the singing bird. They had stood under a tree and listened.
Then the moon went down and his father, stumbling home, had
fallen into a blackberry bush.

'Will there be blackberries?' he asked.

'There should be,' his father said. 'I'll pick some for you.'

In Fletcher's Wood there was shade beneath the trees, and
sunlight, thrown in yellow patches on to the grass, seemed to grow
out of the ground rather than come from the sky. The boy stepped

from sunlight to sunlight, in and out of shadow. His father showed him a tangle of bramble, hard with thorns, its leaves just beginning to colour into autumn, its long runners dry and brittle on the grass. Clusters of purple fruit hung in the branches. His father reached up and chose a blackberry for him. Its skin was plump and shining, each of its purple globes held a point of reflected light.

'You can eat it,' his father said.

The boy put the blackberry in his mouth. He rolled it with his tongue, feeling its irregularity, and crushed it against the roof of his mouth. Released juice, sweet and warm as summer, ran down his throat, hard seeds cracked between his teeth. When he laughed his father saw that his mouth was deeply stained. Together they picked and ate the dark berries, until their lips were purple and their hands marked and scratched.

'We should take some for your mother,' the man said.

He reached with his stick and pulled down high canes where the choicest berries grew, picking them to take home. They had nothing to carry them in, so the boy put his new cap on the grass and they filled its hollow with berries. He held the cap by its edges and they went home.

'It was a stupid thing to do,' his mother said, 'utterly stupid. What were you thinking of?'

The young man did not answer.

'If we had the money, it would be different,' his mother said. 'Where do you think the money comes from?'

'I know where the money comes from,' his father said. 'I work hard enough for it.'

'His new cap,' his mother said. 'How am I to get him another?'

The cap lay on the table and by standing on tiptoe the boy could see it. Inside it was wet with the sticky juice of blackberries. Small pieces of blackberry skins were stuck to it. The stains were dark and irregular.

'It will probably dry out all right,' his father said.

His mother's face was red and distorted, her voice shrill.

'If you had anything like a job,' she shouted, 'and could buy caps by the dozen, then . . . .'

She stopped and shook her head. His father turned away, his mouth hard.

'I do what I can,' he said.

'That's not much!' his mother said. She was tight with scorn. 'You don't do much!'

Appalled, the child watched the quarrel mount and spread. He began to cry quietly, to himself, knowing that it was a different weeping to any he had experienced before, that he was crying for a different pain. And as his parents savagely and clumsily hurt themselves, the child began to understand that they were different people; his father, his mother, himself, and that he must learn sometimes to be alone.

The Wind, the Cold Wind

I was almost at the top of Victoria Road, under the big maroon hoarding advertising Camp Coffee, when I heard Jimmy James shouting.

'Hey Ginger!' he shouted. 'Hold on a minute, Ginger!'

He couldn't wait to reach me. He ran across the road in front of the Cardiff bus as if it didn't exist. There he was, large, redfaced, rolling urgently along like a boy with huge slow springs in his knees, like a boy heaving himself through heavy, invisible water. Jimmy couldn't read very well. Once I'd written a letter for him, to his sister who lived in Birmingham and worked in a chocolate factory; once he'd let me walk to school with him and other large, important boys. He stopped in front of me, weighty, impassable.

'I heard you were dead,' he said. 'The boys told me you were dead.'

His large brown eyes looked down at me accusingly.

'Not me, Jim,' I said. 'Never felt fitter, Jim.'

He thought that too sprightly by half. His fat cheeks reddened and he wagged a finger at me. It looked as thick as a club.

'Watch it, Ginge,' he said.

He was fifteen years old, five years older than I, and big. He was a boy to be feared. I slowed it.

'No, Jim,' I said smiling soberly. 'I'm not dead.'

'The boys told me you were,' he said.

He was looking at me with the utmost care, his whole attitude reproachful and disappointed. I was immediately guilty. I had let Jimmy James down, I could see that. And then, in an instant, I understood, for something very like this had happened to me before.

The previous winter, in January, a boy called Tony Plumley had drowned in a pond on the mountain. I'd spent a lot of time worrying about Tony Plumley. The unready ice had split beneath him and tumbled him into the darkness. For weeks afterwards, lying in my bed at night, I'd followed him down, hearing him choke, feeling the stiffening chill of the water. I had watched his skin turn blue as ice. I had felt his lungs fill to the throat with suffocating water, known the moment when at last his legs had gone limp and boneless. I had given Tony Plumley all the pity and fear I possessed. And later, in irresistible terror, I had gone with him into his very grave. Then, one day when I had forgotten all about him and was running carefree along a dappled path in the summer woods, there he was, in front of me, Tony Plumley, alive. I thought of all that sympathetic terror spent and wasted and I was wildly angry. I charged him with being drowned.

'It wasn't me,' Tony Plumley said, backing off fast.

'It was you,' I said. 'Put up your fists.'

But Tony Plumley stood still and cautious outside the range of my eager jabs. Taking the greatest care, speaking slowly, he explained that he was not drowned at all, that he had never been sliding on the pond, that his mother would not have let him. It was another boy, Tony Powell, who had dropped through the cheating ice and died. I had been confused by the similarity of their names. I stood there trying to reconcile myself to a world in which the firm certainty of death had proved unfaithful, a world in which Tony Powell, a boy unknown to me, was suddenly dead. Perplexed, I dropped my avenging hands.

'Get moving, Plumley,' I said.

He slid tactfully past me and thumped away down the path.

So I knew exactly how Jimmy James felt. I'd used a lot of emotion on Plumley and Jim must have been imagining my death with much the same intensity. I understood his disappointment, deserved his reproach, stood resignedly under his just anger. I knew, too, how the confusion had come about.

'It's not me, Jim,' I said. 'It's Maldwyn Farraday. It's because we've both got red hair.'

This completely baffled Jim. He looked at me in despair.

'What's red hair got to do with it?' he said loudly.

'We've both got red hair,' I explained. 'Maldwyn Farraday and I. And we live in the same street and we're friends. It's Maldwyn's dead. People mix us up.'

Jim didn't say anything.

'I'm going to the funeral tomorrow,' I said.

Jimmy James curled his lip in contempt and turned away, his heavy shoulders outraged, his scuffed shoes slapping the pavement. I waited until he had turned the corner by the delicatessen and then I ran. I ran past the shops still ablaze for the Christmas which was already gone, I ran past Davies's where unsold decorated cakes still held their blue and pink rosettes, their tiny edible skaters and Father Christmases, their stale, festive messages in scarlet piping; I ran past Mr Roberts's shop without looking once at his sumptuous boxes of confectionery, at the cottonwool snowflakes falling in ranks regular as guardsmen down the glass of his window; past the symmetrical pyramids of fruit and vegetables in Mr Leyshon's, the small, thin-

skinned tangerines wrapped in silver foil, the boxes of dates from
North Africa. I ran so that I did not have to think of Maldwyn.

Maldwyn had been my friend as long as I could remember. There
was not a time when Maldwyn had not been around. He had great
advantages as a friend. Not only could he laugh more loudly than
anyone else, he was so awkward that with him the simplest exercise,
just walking up the street, was hilarious chaos. And his house too,
his house was big and gloriously untidy. In the basement was the
workshop in which his father repaired all the machines in the
neighbourhood, all the lawn-mowers, the electric kettles and irons,
the clocks and watches. He also repaired them in the kitchen, in the
garden, in the hall, wherever he happened to be. Our fathers' ancient
cars were often in his yard, waiting for him to coax their tired pistons
to another paroxysm of irregular combustion. Mr Farraday's hands
held always a bundle of incomprehensible metal parts he was
patiently arranging into efficiency. He'd let us watch him tease into
place the cogs and rivets of some damaged artefact, telling us in his
quiet voice what he was doing. Sometimes, when we were watching
Mr Farraday, Maldwyn's two sisters, long, thin and malevolent,
would come round and enrage us. Then Mr Farraday would turn
us out of doors and the sisters would giggle away to play the piano
in another room. Maldwyn could roar like a bull. When he did this,
his sisters would put their hands to their ears and run screaming,
but Mr Farraday just smiled gently.

Maldwyn's parents had come from a village many miles away in
the west of Wales. Their house was often full of cousins from this
village, smiling, talking in their open country voices. They drank a
lot of tea, these cousins, and then they all went off to visit Enoch
Quinell. Everybody knew Enoch Quinell, because he was a policeman and enormously fat. My father said Enoch weighed more than
two hundred and eighty pounds. But Maldwyn's family knew Enoch
particularly well because he, too, had come from their village and
always went back there for his holidays.

We knew a lot of jokes about Enoch, about how he'd cracked the
weigh-bridge where the coal-trucks were weighed, how he was
supposed to have broken both ankles trying to stand on tip-toe. I
used to think they were pretty funny jokes, but Maldwyn would be
very angry if he heard one of them and offer to fight the boy who
said it. He was a hopeless fighter, anybody could have picked him
off with one hand, but we all liked him. On Saturday mornings he
went shopping for Enoch, for food, for shaving soap, cigarettes,
things like that. Sometimes I went with him.

Enoch lived in rooms above the police station, and we'd climb there, past the fire-engine on the ground floor, its brass glittering, its hoses white and spotless, past the billiard room, then up the stairs to Enoch's place. Once I saw Enoch eat. He cooked for himself a steak so huge that I could find no way to describe it to my mother. And then he covered it in fried onions. Maldwyn used to get sixpence for doing Enoch's shopping.

He had been working for Enoch on Christmas Eve. I hadn't known that. All afternoon I'd been searching for him, around the back of the garages where we had a den, in the market; I couldn't find him anywhere. Just as I thought of going home, I saw Maldwyn at the top of the street. He was singing, but when I called him he stopped and waved. The lights were coming on in the houses and shops. Some children were singing carols outside Benny Everson's door. I could have told them it was a waste of time.

'Look what Enoch gave me,' Maldwyn said. Enoch had given him ten shillings. We had never known such wealth.

'What are you going to do with it?' I asked, touching the silver with an envious finger.

'I'm going to buy Enoch a cigar,' he said, 'for Christmas. Coming over?'

We walked towards the High Street. Mr Turner, the tobacconist, was a tall, pale man, exquisitely dressed. He had a silver snuffbox and was immaculately polite to everyone who entered his shop. I knew that he and Maldwyn would be hours choosing a cigar for Enoch, I could already hear Mr Turner asking Maldwyn's opinion.

'Perhaps something Cuban?' Mr Turner would say. 'No? Something a little smaller, perhaps, a little milder?'

'Ugh?' Maldwyn would say, smiling, not understanding any of it, enjoying it all.

I couldn't stand it. When we got to the Market I told Maldwyn that I'd wait for him there. I told him I'd wait outside Marlow's where I could look at the brilliant windows of the sporting world, the rows of fishing rods and the racks of guns, the beautiful feathery hooks of salmon-flies in their perspex boxes, the soccer balls, the marvellous boxing shorts, glittering and coloured like the peacock, the blood-red boxing gloves. Each week I spent hours at these windows and I was a long time there on Christmas Eve. Maldwyn didn't come back. At last I went home. My mother was crying and everybody in our house was quiet. Then they told me that Maldwyn was dead. He had rushed out of Mr Turner's shop, carrying in his hand two cigars in a paper bag, and run straight under a truck.

'I've been watching for him,' I said. 'Outside Marlow's. He went to buy a cigar for Enoch.'

I went early to bed and slept well. It didn't feel as if Maldwyn was dead. I thought of him as if he were in his house a few doors down the street, but when I walked past on Christmas morning the blinds were drawn across all the Farraday's windows and in some of the other houses too. The whole street was silent. And all that day I was lost, alone. We didn't enjoy Christmas in our house. The next day Mr Farraday came over to say that they were going to bury Maldwyn in their village, taking him away to the little church where his grandparents were buried. He asked me to walk with the funeral to the edge of town, with five other boys.

'You were his best friend,' Mr Farraway said.

Mr Farraday looked exactly the same as he always did, his face pink and clean, his bony hands slow. I told him that I'd like to walk in Maldwyn's funeral. I had never been to a funeral.

The day they took Maldwyn away was cold. When I got up a hard frost covered the ground and the sky was grey. At ten o'clock I went down to Maldwyn's. The other boys were already there, standing around; Danny Simpson, Urias Ward, Reggie Evans, Georgie and Bobby Rowlands. We wore our best suits, our overcoats, our scarves, our gleaming shoes. The hearse and the black cars were waiting at the kerb and little knots of men stood along the pavement, talking quietly. In a little while Maldwyn's door opened and three tall men carried out the coffin. I was astonished by its length; it looked long enough to hold a man, yet Maldwyn was shorter than I. He was younger too. I hadn't expected that there would be any noise, but there was. Gentle though the bearers were, the coffin bumped softly, with blunt wooden sounds, and grated when they slid it along the chromium tracks inside the hearse. I knew that little Georgie Rowlands was scared. His eyes were pale and large and he couldn't look away. The wreaths were carried from the house and placed in a careful pile on the coffin and inside the hearse. I could see mine, made of early daffodils and other flowers I couldn't name. My card was wired to it. I had written on it, 'Goodbye Maldwyn, from all at number 24.'

'You boys will march at the side of the hearse,' said Mr Jewell, the undertaker. 'Three on each side, you understand?'

We nodded.

'And no playing about,' Mr Jewell said. 'Just walk firmly along. And when we get to the park gates we'll stop for a second so that you can all get safely to the side of the road. We don't want accidents. Be careful, remember that.'

'Yes,' Reggie Evans said.

Danny Simpson and Georgie Rowlands were on my side of the hearse. As we walked up the street I could see my mother and brother, but I didn't even nod to them. They were with a gathering of other neighbours, all looking cold and sad. We turned and marched towards the edge of town, perhaps a mile away. The wind, gusting and hard, blew at our legs and the edges of our coats. There were few people to see us go. At the park gates the whole procession stopped and we stood in a line at the side of the road. We saw the car in which Mr and Mrs Farraday sat, with their daughters. I didn't recognize them in their unaccustomed black, but Urias Ward did. I saw Enoch Quinell in one of the following cars, and he saw me. He looked me full in the face and he was completely unsmiling and serious. Picking up speed, the hearse and the other cars sped up the road, over the river bridge, out of sight. Left without a purpose, we waited until we knew they were far away.

'Let's go home through the park,' Danny Simpson said.

We walked in single file along the stone parapet of the lake, looking at the grey water. The wind, blowing without hindrance over its surface, had cut it into choppy waves, restless, without pattern. Everything was cold. Out in the middle, riding the water as indifferently as if it had been a smooth summer day, were the two mute swans which lived there all year round. They were indescribably sad and beautiful, like swans out of some cruel story from the far north, like birds in some cold elegy I had but dimly heard and understood only its sorrow. I remembered that these swans were said to sing only as they died, and I resented then their patient mastery of the water, their manifest living. And then there came unbidden into my mind the images of all the death I knew. I saw my grandfather in his bed, when I had been taken to see him, but that was all right because his nose was high and sharp and his teeth were too big and he hadn't looked like my grandfather. He hadn't looked like a person at all. I saw again the dead puppy I had found on the river bank, his skin peeling smoothly away from his poor flesh, and this was frightening, for he came often to terrify me in nightmares, and I also wept in pity for him when I was sick or tired. And I saw the dead butterfly I had found behind the bookshelves where it had hidden from the approach of winter. It had been a Red Admiral, my favourite butterfly, and it had died there, spread so that I could marvel at the red and white markings on its dusky wings, their powder still undisturbed. I held it on the palm of my hand and it was dry and light, so light that when I closed my eyes I could not tell that I held it, as light as dust. And thinking of the unbroken butterfly, I knew that I would never again see Maldwyn Farraday, nor hear his voice, nor wake in the morning to the certainty that we would spend the day together. He was gone forever. A great and painful emptiness was in my chest and my throat. I stopped walking and took from my overcoat pocket the last of my Christmas chocolate, a half-pound block. I called the boys around me and, breaking the chocolate into sections, I divided it among us. There were two sections over, and I gave them to little Georgie Rowlands because he was the youngest. Tears were pouring down Reggie Evans' cheeks and the wind blew them across his nose and onto the collar of his overcoat.

'It's the wind,' he said. 'The bloody wind makes your eyes water.'

He could scarcely speak and we stood near him, patting his shoulders, our mouths filled with chocolate, saying yes yes, the wind, the cold wind. But we were all crying, we were all bitterly weeping, our cheeks were wet and stinging with the harsh salt of our tears, we were overwhelmed by the recognition of our unique and common knowledge, and we had nowhere to turn for comfort but to ourselves.

Some Opposites of Good

When Mark opened the front door he could see Useless Lewis waiting for him at the corner of the street. Useless was poised in a tense crouch, his face tight and snarling. Without mercy he gunned down Mr Sweet's black cat, pumping bullets into its rich fur as it sat sunning itself in the doorway of the shop; then, straightening, he sprayed the street with bullets, smiling grimly at the patterned dust he raised.

'Goodbye Mark,' called Mark's mother from her kitchen.

Useless sweetly holstered the clenched fists of his imagined six-shooters, caught invisible reins in the tips of his fingers, and cantered down the road, slapping his haunches with the flat of his hand, whinnying. Useless was being the world's greatest cowboy.

'Hi,' he said to Mark.

On the way to school nothing escaped the vigilance of Useless's accurate fingers. He shot the tops from bottles of milk as they stood in doorways, he blasted cyclists as they sped innocently to work, he exploded the wheels of cars. At street corners he stood six feet tall, surveying the scene with his bleak, sardonic eye before calling Mark forward to walk in safety among the traps and ambushes laid in the shadows of the morning streets. Useless shot his way through them all. He was Mark's best friend, but he was an awful nuisance. Mark was glad when they got to school.

Although it was early, Jack Mathias would certainly be there before them. Jack Mathias lived a long way off, in a cottage on the mountain, and his mother was dead. When Mr Mathias went to work, very early, Jack would have to leave too, because his father would lock the house. Jack would have to wait alone in the school yard until someone came along to talk to him. He had dirty teeth and his shirts were always crumpled and dirty because of his mother, but everybody liked him. He was fifteen years old, a big boy and a great footballer, the best in school. He was teaching Mark to play.

They played in the open shed that ran down one side of the yard, where the boys sheltered when it was raining. It was paved with granite slabs, a yard square, made smooth and polished by the running boots of generations of boys. Jack Mathias was waiting there, in the shade of the roof. Between his feet he had the little flat stone they used instead of a ball and he was flicking it gently this way and that, absorbed in the performance of his faultless skill.

Useless was already stalking up the yard, stiff-legged and menacing, ready to shoot it out with any black evil, the thunder of his avenging guns held silent under his thumbs.

'Keck! Keck!' he said, bringing down two passing crows.

Mark ran into the shed.

'Right,' said Jack Mathias. 'You get five goals start, O.K?'

They ran until the shed was so full of boys they could no longer play without interruption, and then Jack Mathias showed Mark how to swerve and how to push the ball around one side of an opponent and run around the other.

'You'll have to learn to use your left foot,' said Jack Mathias. 'Watch this.'

He collected the stone with a cool sweep of his leg and, in the same movement, pushed it in front of him. But even as he jumped into his first stride, his right knee raised, the whole world stopped. Jack Mathias hung, arrested in mid flight, long arms aloft. The little stone went bobbling on, scuttling over the flagstones, making a tiny hollow noise, the only moving thing in the school yard. Everywhere groups of boys held their frozen attitudes, older boys like careless and lounging statues, small boys balancing precariously at the edges of energy. The first whistle had gone, and nobody must move. Mark, without the stir of a visible muscle, got ready for the second whistle. When it came, he shot into action, racing for the class lines in front of the school building. But he was a long way off and had to find a place near the end of the queue. Useless was four or five boys in front of him, and Mark waved to him. But Useless didn't see him. Useless had gone to live inside his head, he was galloping the wide and sunlit prairies of his imagination.

The teacher on duty was Witty Thomas, small, plump and beautifully dressed. This morning he wore a suit of silver-grey and his shirt was a rich cream colour. His tie was red with little silver flowers in it, and the fresh rose in his button-hole was as yellow as sunshine. He bounced about in front of the files of boys, his face pink, sending his thin voice shouting into the air, waving his arms at the sauntering impertinence of the older boys as they came slowly into a reluctant line.

'Come, come on!' screamed Mr Thomas. 'Do you think you've got all day?'

The big boys idled along, some smiling openly at histrionic Mr Thomas, some, their heads turned away, ignoring him.

Witty, in impotent fury, danced toward them on his little glittering shoes, and, as he came near, Useless, concentrating, steadying his

aim with the coldest deliberation, shot away, one after the other, the
pearl buttons on Mr Thomas's vest. He was narrowing his eyes to
focus on the last button when Mr Thomas saw him.

'What's this?' cried Witty Thomas, suddenly and terrifyingly
jovial. 'And what is this? Would you like to shoot me, Lewis?'

He grabbed Useless by the collar and pulled him out, shaking him
and jerking him. Mark could see the nailed soles of Useless's boots
as his legs swung in the air.

A small, delighted cheer came from the boys, but Mr Thomas
ignored it. He just smiled his frightening smile and began to cuff
Useless's head.

'So you'd like to shoot me, eh, Lewis?' Witty Thomas said. 'But
you wouldn't dare, would you, would you, would you!'

He punctuated his speech with quick slaps, but Useless cleverly
burrowed close to him, burying his head against Mr Thomas's
round little stomach so that the man couldn't swing at him.

'Leave him alone,' shouted Jack Mathias in his laughing, man's
voice. 'Pick someone your own size! Go it little 'un!'

Everybody knew that Mr Thomas was afraid to touch Jack
Mathias, because Jack's father was so big and rough.

Useless came back to his place and he was smiling all over. He
wasn't frightened, Mark could see that.

'Fifty years old,' said Damion Davies, who was tall and thin and
lazy. 'Fifty years old and still heavyweight champion. Just fancy!'

'Shut it, Davies,' said Mr Thomas, panting, 'or you'll get the
same.'

'Such a temper, too,' said Damion in his languid voice, and he
rolled his eyes in mock admiration.

'Lead on!' cried Mr Thomas, pointing, as if he were leading an
expedition into wildest Tibet. 'Lead on, the first row!'

Useless and Mark bent their knees and slid into the cold, stiff-
hinged desk they shared, being careful of the splinters, sharp as frost,
that would run into their thighs. They took out their books and
placed them neatly, ready for work. Mark looked at his friend. The
marks of Mr Thomas's grabbing fingers were plain on the back of
Useless's neck and his right ear was blazing red. You could almost
warm your hands against it.

'Does it hurt?' Mark whispered.

'Of course not,' said Useless. 'Witty couldn't hurt a fly.'

Useless couldn't read. Each morning Mark would have to help
him, listening to him mutter aloud the separate, clumsy words as
he stumbled from sentence to sentence. Mark worked hard with

Useless. He had stood for hours outside shops, making Useless read the price cards and the advertisements for chocolates, but it was no use. It was as if words had no meaning for Useless. He could not see that they added to each other as you said them, that the sum of the words was interesting and surprising. He listened to Useless drop the flat sounds one by one out of his mouth.

'Don't forget,' said Useless between sentences. 'It's Friday, pass it on.'

Most Friday mornings Mr Treharne, the Headmaster, came in to test the boys in spelling, in mental arithmetic and in the plurals and opposites of words. Mark enjoyed this. He would sit upright in his desk, his arms folded in front of him, hoping Mr Treharne would ask him some spectacularly difficult question. When this happened Mark's mind would become as clear as glass and he would see the answer right in the centre of his thinking. But very often Mr Treharne didn't ask him anything at all, preferring to spend his time being angry at those poor boys who couldn't answer anything. Useless was one of these.

It was strange about Useless. He was brave, he was loyal, he knew a lot of jokes. When he pretended, you could believe in the unseen world Useless would make around him. Mark just knew, just from watching Useless, that he had ridden a white horse to school that morning, you could see it. Although your real eyes would still see only a boy with short hair and freckles on his neck. Useless knew about real horses, too. His father had a pony and cart and one Sunday in the summer the boys had gone to a field near the river and caught the pony. Useless had held an apple in his hand and the pony had eaten it, very gently, with his crude brown teeth. Then Useless had leapt cleverly on the animal's back, wrapping the coarse hair of its mane in his fists. He'd hung on for a long while as the pony galloped clumsily around the field. A horse was unexpectedly heavy. Mark could remember the surprising weight of its hooves when they pounded the earth like an immense drum. In the end Useless had fallen off and lay on his back, puffing and laughing. He hoped Useless would be able to answer some of Mr Treharne's questions. He looked over at Useless and his ear was pretty nearly the normal colour.

Mr Pascoe, their own teacher, put his hand gently on Mark's shoulder, reminding him to get on with his work. The boy bent his head over his book and began to write. Mr Pascoe was young and kind and this was his very first job. All the boys liked him. As he wrote, Mark still thought of Useless, fallen and laughing in the grass by the river, remembering too the dark green of the clover patches, and their pink flowers. Mark began to write a story of two friends who had gone to a summer field and found there a horse so gentle, its breath so fragrant of sweet clover, so amenable and intelligent an animal that it was more companion than beast. It was thin, and seemed to have been cruelly treated, but there was about it a recognizable air of breeding, of a royal pride. For weeks, in the story, the two boys had coveted the horse, exulting in its increasing strength and beauty. Mark began to describe the glowing perfection of his coat, its docile manner, its unassuming pride. There was no doubt, Mark felt, that here he was making a prince among horses, a true Arabian. He was about to send all three of his heroes on some epic journey when the Headmaster walked in.

Mark slowly put away his story. He would have liked to have returned his lovely pony to its true owner, an eagle-profiled sheikh who lived in a camp high in the Atlas Mountains. After years of adventure, the boys would have handed over the superb horse. They would have been rewarded with jewels, made members of this most savage of Bedouin tribes. A great feast would have been made in their honour, with kebabs and raw sheep's eyes. They would have flown home famous and wealthy.

'Hurry up, boy,' said Mr Treharne, tapping Mark's desk with his cane.

Mr Treharne was not big, but he walked with compensating dignity and importance. He carried with him his own silence, hard and painful, and it was this sensation that filled the room now, as cold water might fill a bowl. Mr Treharne put his cane under his arm and drew back his lips in a grimace, revealing white teeth regular and artificial as a doll's.

Mr Pascoe stood nervously near his high desk.

'Sit down, Pascoe,' said Mr Treharne. 'Sit down, man. Where's your chalk?'

He took some chalk from the table before the boys. The air in the room was so still that Mark thought he could have plucked it like a guitar string. Then the testing began.

It was not too bad. First they did some multiplication tables and then questions about buying and selling things, buns, postage stamps, gallons of milk. Mr Treharne spoke very slowly and clearly, making sure every boy had heard; and then he'd pounce, his rigid cane pointed at arm's length, on some unready boy. He knew exactly which poor boys would find the questions impossible to answer. But most of them were prepared and alert, answering Mr Treharne confidently. It was going to be a happy morning. Even Mr Treharne was nearly smiling.

He turned about slowly, looking meditatively from one boy's face to another, but Mark wasn't fooled. He knew better than to relax.

'Galaxy,' Mr Treharne snapped, his stick under Mark's nose. 'You boy, spell galaxy.'

That was an easy one.

'You're a sharp lad,' said Mr Treharne. 'A bright lad.'

He leaned away as if to ask some other boy a word, and then whipped back.

'Idiosyncrasy,' he said.

Flawlessly and successfully Mark spelled idiosyncrasy, brontosaurus, yacht, zephyr, seraph, commission.

Mark was elated. It was like playing some vitally skilful and dangerous game, in which Mr Treharne was attacking him with something as sharp and violent as a sword, and only by the most agile and determined techniques could Mark beat him away. When the Headmaster asked him no more words Mark knew he had won. He felt hard and shining, as if every bit of him was clean and smooth, working with a silent perfection. He imagined all the world's words waiting for him to order them into formal and meticulous patterns. He sat upright on his bench, his back achingly straight, triumphant. It was a little time before he could listen to what was happening in the room.

Mr Treharne was no longer pleased. David Sheppard and Ronnie Howells were standing up, their hands behind their backs, unable to give the opposite of sour, and Mr Treharne was clicking his tongue in irritation. Two little red spots appeared on his cheekbones. Mark looked about; nobody appeared to know. He put up his hand.

'Put down your hand, Watkins,' snarled Mr Treharne, not looking at him. 'You've had your moment of splendour. Are you idiot enough to think that you alone know the opposite of sour?'

Mark pulled his hand down. Somebody tittered.

'The next boy to laugh,' said Mr Treharne, 'will find I have a painful cure for that condition. It is no matter for amusement to find we have two ignorant and lazy boys in a class.'

His face was sullen, the corners of his mouth drawn sternly down.

'The opposite of sour is sweet,' he said. 'Sweet. Do you hear me, Howells, Sheppard? Sit down. I have no patience with you.'

He watched the boys sit. There was not a sound in the room not even a breath. Little Frankie Rossi, the smallest boy in the class, stared terrified in front of him. Then he began, very slightly, to tremble.

Cautiously the boys waited, careful to do nothing that would disturb the man's dry temper, inflammable as straw.

'There will be others,' said Mr Treharne. 'Other boys, lazy fellows all of them, who will not be able to answer the simplest of questions!'

The boys shivered as he looked at them.

'Rossi, for example,' shouted Mr Treharne.

It was not fair to pick on Frankie Rossi. Although he was small, he was always cheerful and smiling. He and Useless were the worst readers in the class.

'Rossi,' said Mr Treharne. 'Give us the benefit of your erudition. Give us the opposites of long, dry, little, thin, good.'

He spat out each word, his face red and angry, cracking the face of the table with his cane, each stroke leaving a clean brown mark in the film of chalk dust on the surface.

Frankie Rossi began to cry, softly and quietly. Mr Pascoe was standing behind the Headmaster, his face pale, perfectly still except for his hands. His fingers were lifting and falling against the cloth of his jacket. There was no other movement.

Then Mr Treharne was striding between the desks, asking boy after boy for opposites to those simple words. It was as if a great storm, an unimaginable violence, had entered the familiar room and ripped away its safety. Mr Treharne moved and spoke with such fury that nobody had time to answer him.

At last he stopped, so close to Mark that the boy could feel his nearness. Mr Treharne was looking at Useless.

'And now we come to Lewis,' said Mr Treharne, almost whispering.

Useless stood in his desk, his legs bent where the bench pressed against the back of his knees. The whole desk was shaking slightly, as if it were alive.

'Lewis,' said Mr Treharne. 'I want you to tell me the opposite of good. Tell us all, Lewis, we shall await your answer.'

Mark let out his breath in relief. He had been praying as intensely as he knew how, willing for Mr Treharne to ask Useless something easy. Now everything would be all right.

But Useless did not answer.

'Think hard, Lewis,' said Mr Treharne. 'Think hard. It will be the cane if you do not give me the correct answer.'

Mark could see Useless's legs quivering, he could almost smell his fear. In an agony, Mark urged his friend to speak, sending the silent words across to him.

Useless lifted his head.

'Rotten, sir,' he blurted.

The brilliance and unexpectedness of Useless's word were like the sunshine, lighting up Mark's mind. He turned in astonishment to his friend, almost clapping aloud.

'Keep still, Watkins,' Mr Treharne said to him.

He whipped his cane through the air, making a pliant and cruel whistling.

'Come out, Lewis,' he said.

Mr Treharne could not have heard Useless. Mark put up his hand to explain.

'Put down your hand,' shouted Mr Treharne, in a sudden explosion of renewed temper. 'I shan't tell you again.'

But Mark knew there was a mistake. He smiled up at Mr Treharne.

'But sir,' he said. 'Useless's father, sir, he keeps a fruit shop, and he sells the good apples, sir, and he throws away the rotten . . . '

'Come out, Watkins,' said Mr Treharne.

Mark scrambled out of his desk and stood beside Useless.

'Hold out your hand,' Mr Treharne said to Useless.

Mark could not think that it was happening, that Mr Treharne could have failed to understand the wonderful accuracy of Useless's word. He was confused and indignant.

'Sir,' he said. 'You mustn't cane him. Rotten is a good opposite!'

And suddenly Mr Treharne was before him, grabbing Mark's wrist with terrifying ferocity, pulling the boy's arm out straight before him. He rapped Mark's knuckles sharply with the cane to open the hand. Then he raised the stick above his head and brought it cutting down on the small flesh in a full arc, across the base of the palm and the soft fingers. At first there was no pain at all, for a slight moment only, and then an agony so far beyond anything he had experienced before took away the boy's breath and left him gasping. He could not see anything, was only dimly aware that at his side Useless was being punished in his turn. Mr Treharne bundled the shocked boys into their seats. Mark held his burning hand between his knees and put his head on the hard wood of the desk so that nobody could see his weeping face.

After Mr Treharne had left the room, Mr Pascoe came over to Mark, talking quietly to him, trying to help him. The bell rang for morning break and Mr Pascoe let Mark stay in the room and Useless stayed with him.

'The pain'll go after a bit,' Useless said.

But all through the morning, long after he was able to look objectively at his beaten hand and touch the swollen skin of his fingers, the boy would shake with occasional sobs. He mourned not so much for his vanishing pain, nor the indignity of his beating, but because his safe world had collapsed about him. He wept because he had been shown a world without hope and without justice, a world in which the very words were without meaning.

In the West Country

When I was a young man, I taught at a school in Yeovil, a small town in Somerset. Nothing much happened in Yeovil. Each morning my children came dreamily to school, their fathers worked in shops or dairies or breweries, their mothers made the gloves for which the town had a reputation. Oh, I liked Yeovil very much. Its citizens spoke slowly, with a soft, creamy accent; its houses were built of golden, local stone — the gentle Ham stone; its life was slow and comfortable; I had many friends there. There was nothing wrong with the town, yet I never stayed there a day longer than was necessary. The last hours of every term would find me with my bags packed, waiting for the bell that would end school and set me striding away for Pen Mill station, a few hundred yards down the road, on the edge of town. I always went home to Wales and I always went by train.

Nothing would be moving at Pen Mill station. Only rarely would there be someone at the barrier to examine my ticket. Once inside, I could sometimes see, far away down the platform, a lone porter sitting on a trolley, looking steadfastly into the distance, not even reading. There would never be a train. But eventually one would arrive — a small, meandering train with an air of having strayed in from earlier, more rustic times; and when, at last, it set off again it did nothing to dispel this impression. There probably was a village in Somerset at which it did not stop but I cannot remember one. On we went, our roundabout, leisurely journey interrupted at such conurbations as Marston Magna, Queen Camel, Sparkford, Castle Cary, Bruton, Frome, Westbury.

It was at Westbury, on a day when we travelled more haltingly than usual, that I once left the train. It was Sunday, a day of clear summer, the air dry and cloudless, little motes of sun haze dancing in the yellow light. I walked out of the station and found, at the end of a green lane, a lake, like a mirage, fringed by reeds. There, on that lake, I saw for the first time the great crested grebe, a diving bird I had only read about. It swam low in the water, its dark body almost lost, its long neck holding aloft its ruffed and regal head; and it was joined by another grebe, and then one more, and yet another, until there were six of these remarkable birds swimming, or vanishing into the water. If it was water. It was an element so rare and fine, so unruffled by any passage of air or bird, that the very reflections of those grebes floated beneath their bodies complete in feather, in colour, in action. Waterdrops fell down from each flawless bird and up from each immaculate image, dissolving in each other as they met, in an equal harmony. I forgot the train, but when, hot, dusty, and amazed, I got back to the station, it was still there, somnolent and good-tempered, waiting for me.

On the other hand, if my friend Barney Eagleton was driving, we sometimes made very good time, rattling through those delicious fields as if there were in life a real purpose, a sense of urgent destiny. But this was a deception. Barney was also an enthusiastic bird-watcher, and a specialist at that — a heron specialist. I think Barney knew more about herons than any other man alive. Somewhere in north Somerset our train ran along a high embankment for a distance of several hundred yards. We could look down from our carriage windows on the tops of great elms in whose wide branches herons had for generations nested. In late spring, after the young birds had hatched, any engine driven by Barney Eagleton would rumble past these nests with infinite, heavy caution. And then it would stop. People would pull down their windows and lean out, watching the young birds wave their snakelike heads, nodding approval to Barney as he stood in his cab owning the whole flock. A few impatient souls — lovers, perhaps, or men from Bristol — would begin to mutter and look at their watches; and at last, bored beyond watching by the repetitive and unimaginative behaviour of young herons, we all would yell insults or instructions at Barney. He would sigh, turn to his levers, and, later than ever, we would roll ponderously away.

This was near Bradford-on-Avon, as we entered the valley of the Avon. Now a perceptible change would come over our progress, whether Barney drove us or not. We were nearing civilization; the great cities were coming toward us. Our speed became smarter, we were signalled away from the little stations with an urban confidence and panache. We left behind the huge tithe barn of Bradford-on-Avon and the weir below which the river holds great pike. Quite soon we would reach Bath.

Such cities are not best approached by train. They were there — expansive, prosperous, established — long before Trevithick drove his long-stacked old steam engine, the first in the world to roll on its own wheels under its own power, down the valley in Wales where I was born. The railway tends to enter old cities apologetically, running behind the backs of unimportant houses, hidden behind tall walls at the perimeter of things. And Bath is a great European city, important even before the Romans built it. Our train it is true, made the best of things outside of town, steaming along the valley with an impressive directness. But soon enough — as soon as we left Bathampton station — the very weight and presence of the city forced us in a wide curve to the south. Not much of the famous crescents and terraces could be seen from our windows. We would sidle into Bath Spa station, clamped in an elbow of the river between Dorchester Street and Claverton Street, and then we'd set off for Bristol — a brief run. And after that we'd rattle through the long tunnel beneath the Bristol Channel and come up among the hills and quick vowels of Wales. On the last possible day I would do the whole journey in reverse, ending in darkness among the little fields and lit farms of Somerset, leaving Pen Mill station still harmlessly deserted, walking the evening streets in the bland Somerset air. Bath was unimportant to me, a back cloth, an incident in a journey.

Yet years later I went to teach in Bath. It was something I never got used to. I lived in a flat in the city, and every evening I would go to sleep knowing that on the floors above my head other men were already sleeping, or preparing to sleep. We lived in layers, and this was foreign to me. Always I felt about me the whispers and rustling of other lives; I was aware of the great, serious eyes of people not known to me as they turned to their partners and began to speak of the little deaths of their hours. The tall house was full of nightlong sibilance. In hot weather I kept my windows open and listened to the one tree in the yard gasping. I cannot say I liked living there.

But there was much that was delightful. Each evening after work, and at weekends, I walked the streets of Bath — Broad Street and Green Street, Lilliput Lane and Orange Grove, Miller Street and Great Pulteney Street. Sometimes I went along the river-bank, with anglers stationed every yard of the way, up to Pulteney Bridge, and higher. I travelled to the villages which lie snugly about in the combes and hollows of the round hills: Monkton Farleigh and Monkton Combe, Limpley Stoke, Wellow, Englishcombe, Newton St Loe, Swainswick. Best of all I liked wet nights when the streets were empty. Once, on a night of appalling and splendid downpour, I alone saw a screech owl perched on the roof of the Guildhall, in the heart of the city. He cried aloud at the flattening rain, and I, sheltering momentarily in the post-office doorway to see him better, saluted him, knowing him to be, like me, an invader from simpler places. In the summer I sat on Beechen Cliff and watched the city below my feet. The city began to haunt me.

More and more, in the mists that hung, imperceptibly frail and shifting, at the corners of early-morning streets and above the hedges in the parks, I began to see Bath as it really was — made for people long dead. The parks and crescents presented themselves to me as if they were the calm watercolours of the eighteenth century. Autumn began to thin the streets. I would sniff the air outside the Assembly Rooms, certain I could detect the pungent ghost of a vanished snuff, blown away long ago by two centuries of weather, its lost, rich smell an aroma of the memory only. The world drove steadily into winter. In the evening, as I walked over Pulteney Bridge in the crisp dark, it seemed to me that we, the living, were the ghosts, we the haunting shadows, that the city existed in all its truth and formal grace for older lives than ours. A week before Christmas a muffling snow fell in the night and silenced everything.

That morning I went into Victoria Gardens. It was Saturday, normally the busiest of days, but only a few shopping women braved the streets, on necessary errands, and one or two children stamped knee-deep in the snow. It was bitterly cold, sly winds whipping from the curved surfaces of the snow a stinging powder, driving it against the wrists, against the cold cheeks and the neck. The park was deserted, apart from a black Labrador, thickset and sturdy against the whiteness, stumping along some way off. I walked under the chestnuts aimlessly, head down against the gusts.

'Hey, Doc,' cried a voice. 'Hey, Doctor!'

A big man was sitting on one of the park benches. He had cleared it of snow, and he sat there, expansive and relaxed, one arm extended along the back, as comfortable as if it were summer. He sat there unmoving in the grey light, his face under the shadow of a wide-brimmed hat, a scarf knotted at his throat.

'Doc,' he called. 'Hey, come on over!'

Even close up I could not see his face clearly, but he was a remarkable man; his size alone made him that. He sat on the park bench as I might a footstool. A thin raincoat was pulled across his great body, one hand, as large and white as a plate, rested calmly on his knee.

'How you keeping, Doc?' he said. 'This weather trouble you?'

'No,' I said. 'I seem to manage.'

'You always was one for keeping warm,' the man said, and chuckled. 'You always was,' he said again.

I looked about me. The lawns were hidden under snow blown by the inconstant wind, the trees at the edge of the park were insubstantial as smoke, the dog had disappeared. The big man and I were alone. I had never seen him before.

'Oh, you always could look after yourself,' he said. 'When you was in the Navy, I told your father: don't worry about him, I said, he'll not go short. He can look after himself.'

I had nothing to say. I stood in front of the huge man as he sat on his bench near the restless bushes. He was quite old, I thought. His feet, in worn black oxfords, were enormous. I had never been in the Navy.

Suddenly he took his arm from the back of the bench and bent forward. I could see the top of his worn hat. There was a black patch of grease at the crown.

'Here, Doc,' he said, 'have a look at this.'

He rolled up the right leg of his trousers. His leg was bandaged from ankle to knee, the bandage itself frayed and stained.

'Do you think this is right,' he said his voice indistinct as he bent down unwrapping the bandage, 'that my leg should be in this state? All these years, in a state like this?'

He lifted his great head and I could look full in his upturned face. He had been very handsome and was still impressive — a face clear-featured and aristocratic, sensitive, the nostrils high and beautifully formed, the mouth cleanlipped and firm. But his eyes were innocent and troubled, like a child's eyes, like the eyes of a child who suddenly does not understand the world.

'I was in the Navy, Doctor,' he said. 'Over twenty years, I was a matelot. You know I was; you saw me. Do you think I ought to have a leg like this?'

He rubbed his sleeve across his face. His mouth began to tremble.

'Let's see it,' I said.

He straightened the leg in front of me. The flesh was covered with running ulcers, some as big as a pinhead, some the size of a man's palm. The whole world seemed to have shrunk to a few square yards, a small, cold space just large enough to hold the old man and me. He was looking at me with an unnerving intensity of trust.

'It's bad,' I said. 'Quite bad.'

'What shall I do, Doc?' he said.

'Keep it warm and clean,' I said. 'Eat as well as you can, get up to the hospital and ask for treatment. Go there as soon as you can make it.'

'I will,' said the big man. 'I'll go today.'

'Wrap it up now,' I said. 'Don't let the cold get at it.'

'Somehow it's easier in the cold weather,' he said, bending down obediently and winding the narrow cotton around his shin. 'The hot weather plays havoc with it.'

There was no reason I should have said any of this to the old man. The unreality of the situation, the feeling that the park itself was taken from the known world and floating into limbo, the dim light and the misty edges of the trees, the bitter cold which made thinking slow and inaccurate — all contrived to make me accept a different identity, the one recognized by the old man. I turned away and walked down the path. After a few yards I stopped. I wanted to tell him to make sure to get to the hospital, that he must demand treatment. I turned around, but he wasn't there.

I ran back to the bench. It was still clear of snow, although a few large flakes settled on it as I stood there. I could see where I had stood in front of the old man, I could fit my shoes exactly into the deep, deep holes I had made, and I thought I could see the enormous hollows from the old man's feet.

I hurried into Royal Crescent and along Brock Street. I had never been so cold. Over the Circus the heavy sky held a few threads of ominous yellow light. Before I reached home the snow began in earnest again.

That afternoon I had a letter inviting me to accept a teaching job in Middlesex — a job I'd always wanted and never thought I'd have. It meant immediate preparation. I telephoned a reply and began at once to put my affairs in order, to leave the West Country. I saw my landlord, paid my rent, said goodbye to some people I knew. I didn't own much — a few books, some clothes, a packet of letters. On Thursday the snow had all gone, although the weather was still unfriendly. I walked over to Victoria Gardens and went right through, from one gate to the other, but there was no sign of the big man. The next day I walked down the hill toward the station, and bought a paper at the kiosk, and waited for my train. I was ready to go. I can remember now how eager I was to be gone. I walked up and down, tensely, lightly, like a sprinter before moving to his blocks. A fussy little engine came in on the opposite track, a few nondescript country coaches behind it. The driver leaned from his cab and shouted to me. He was redfaced, slow of speech, smiling. Barney Eagleton. He looked wonderful.

'How you been, then?' he called, his voice rich as cream.

His peaked cap, shining with oil, was perched comfortably on his head. He leaned his forearms on the edge of his cab.

'Barney, you old dog, it's good to see you.'

We grinned at each other across the width of the track.

'How's the herons?' I shouted.

He stopped smiling. 'They chopped down them elms up the line,' he called. 'A lovely heronry, that was — ever so old. Chaps as did it ought to be shot. Lovely birds, them was.'

'Ever see the purple heron, Barney?' I asked him. 'Lives in Spain and Greece and France and northern Italy?'

'No,' he said. 'It's just the plain old heron I see.'

'Or the great white heron or the squacco heron or the blue heron from North America?'

'Ah, don't,' said Barney. 'You'll drive me crazy.'

'Or the little egret or the buffbacked heron or the little bittern — great birds all?'

'What birds,' said Barney, 'what marvellous birds!'

I was so pleased to see old Barney that delight made me eloquent. 'The night heron, Barney,' I shouted, 'the beautiful night heron from the Mediterranean, with its red eyes and its long drooping white crest?'

'Splendid birds,' Barney raised his voice to the sky. 'All fine birds, and I wish they all lived in Somerset.'

I grinned across the lines at Barney.

'When you coming back to Yeovil?' he yelled.

A guard blew his whistle. Barney rolled his eyes, waved, and eased his engine out of the station.

I would never go back to Yeovil. Sooner or later all heronries fall. The train that was to take me from the West Country pulled in from Bristol — long, smooth, efficient as a bullet. 'Gwlad yr Haf' is what the Welsh call Somerset — the Land of Summer.

A Professional Man

I was not a willing soldier. At eighteen I had too many things of my own to do, too many places to go. I resented the idea — of having my days ordered for me, to wake to the bugle, to be known by a number, to wear a uniform which made me indistinguishable from many other young men. I had not long been aware of my individuality and found it exciting. Long avenues of time were open before me and I wanted to explore them as I pleased. I was, moreover, cynical about the great abstract concepts of patriotism and freedom. I was a surly conscript.

Yet the moment I walked inside the barracks that first afternoon I felt better. It was the sight of the coiled strands of spiked wire secured to the top of the already high perimeter wall that did it. They were so obviously mounted to keep soldiers inside the barracks, not enemies out. This paradox made me understand at once that armies are comic institutions. I brightened, I looked about with interest. With other young men I handed in my papers, was allotted a space in a dormitory, marched off to the dining hall.

Here we were given a meal of cold meat and bread and butter. We sat at the long scrubbed boards and prepared to eat. My neighbour, a heavy redfaced Yorkshireman, stared at his plate with suspicion. He turned it slowly around, bent forward to inspect it at close range, leaned thoughtfully away from it.

'What's the matter?' I said.

'It's this meat,' he said. He had a flat, cautious voice.

'What about it?' I said.

He turned upon me his brown, reproachful gaze.

'I can't recognise it,' he said. He was serious and puzzled. 'I'm a butcher. That's my trade, I know about meat. But I don't know what this stuff is. It's a bloody mystery.'

I looked with more interest at my mystery.

'Heart?' I guessed helpfully, but my companion was not impressed.

'Well, pemmican,' I said. But he did not listen.

We did not eat our meat, nor did the young men near us.

So began the mindless early days of our training. Our mornings were filled with repetitive drilling. We were very clumsy at first, but soon we marched and counter-marched in rhythmic complexities of accuracy across the barrack square. In the afternoons we performed some barren task or other, in the evenings we read, played cards, wrote letters. We weren't allowed into the little town. Life was boring.

Yet I enjoyed some of these physical things very much. I grew healthy and active. I ran long distances without distress, began to spend my free time in the gymnasium. The unvaried days passed without thought.

Occasionally we were given a job which had some purpose. When we had been soldiers for perhaps three weeks, I and seven of my fellows were set to wash down and clean three big transport trucks, large, square vehicles with canvas tops and sides, kept at the far end of the compound. The camp was not well defended there. Its boundary was no more than a fence of wire mesh five feet high, supported by concrete posts. A little grassy slope ran down to the fence and on the other side the visible free meadows stretched away, green and unhedged. Larks spun out of them, and, climbing perpendicularly, flung away their ecstatic notes. It was the first warm day of the year. The air was still and kind. We lolled on the grass, smoking, talking desultorily, drugged by sun. Our sergeant found us there. He was eloquent and angry. We stood at rigid attention while he blasted us, individually and as a group. He went on to point out that behaviour like ours would inevitably prolong the war, might even be the cause of eventual, unthinkable defeat. All over the world, he snarled, our comrades were fighting in the hot dust of deserts and the squalor of jungles, their sacrifices counting as nothing as a result of our irresponsibility.

'Now,' he said, 'you are all young. You get one more chance. I shall be gone an hour, and when I come back these vehicles will be shining. Do you understand, glittering! There will not be the suspicion of a speck of dust within ten yards of them. Move! Move!'

We moved. We shot to the hoses, the buckets and brushes. The sergeant called me back.

'You,' he said, 'I've been watching you. You've got a very nasty attitude, a very cynical attitude.'

'Yes, sergeant,' I said, stunned.

'You want to put your back in it,' he said, 'you'll never get on otherwise. So watch your step when I'm around.'

'Yes, sergeant,' I said.

The next morning a small, important corporal came into the dormitory and called my name.

'042 Graham?' he said. 'That you? Report to the adjutant at once. Jump to it.'

There was a sharp intake of breath from my contemporaries, who imagined me guilty of some enormous crime. The corporal, gratified, bustled off.

The adjutant was a heavy man, wearing a shy attempt at a military moustache. In civilian life he was a lawyer.

'Ah, Graham,' he said. 'At ease, Graham.'

He shuffled the papers on his desk.

'We've been looking through your records,' he said, 'the records of all you new men. To see where you might be best placed after your initial training, where you might best serve the army.'

He smiled, man to man.

'It seems, Graham,' he said, 'you're a well educated boy. Did well at school, destined for university.'

'Yes sir,' I said.

His breathing was so noisy I thought he must have asthma.

'Ah,' he said, 'well done. Why don't you try for a commission. Apply for entry to an Officers' Training Unit? We're always looking for keen, alert men, with the right background.'

'I've not thought of it, sir,' I said.

'Think of it now,' he said. 'Here you are at the start of what could be a splendid career, splendid.'

'I'd like that,' I said. I would have agreed to almost anything for a change of scene.

'Good man,' he said, 'good man, well done. We'll send your papers off as soon as we can.'

I went out of the office. My squad were drilling with others; perfectly, line by line, in faultless step, like metronomes they marched and wheeled and crossed, their loud heels falling as one on the tarmac, their arms swinging in unison, their faces so many white anonymous ovals. I did not want to be one of them. Walking away, I savoured my momentary freedom. The gym was empty. I changed and as I laced my shoes I sang, my voice echoing off the high glass roof. I dragged the vaulting horse into the middle of the floor, placed a springboard in front of it, walked away. I turned at the far wall, took a deep breath, and raced along the boards. I hit the springboard hard and soared in a leap of spectacular celebration over the horse. I landed wrongly and broke my ankle. I thought I heard it snap.

The break didn't knit, despite my youth and health. Eventually the doctors fastened a metal plate to the reluctant bone, re-set my lower leg in plaster and sent me to hospital to convalesce. I went in an ambulance, with a medical orderly as escort.

The hospital was on the outskirts of a Midland town which had been, when such places were fashionable, a popular spa. Victorian ladies and gentlemen had come to spend some time there, to drink the natural waters, redolent of sulphur, which were said to be specific cures for many illnesses. A whole service industry had sprung up about these visitors, and although the place was much less popular, remnants of the tradition remained. The town was rich in eating-houses and tea-rooms, had many boarding houses and hotels. The hospital to which I was sent was itself a hotel in peacetime, the largest of the hotels. It stood on a hill above the town, like a castle grown domestic and benevolent. We broken soldiers lived there in luxury, two to a room. We were there to allow our bones time to heal properly. There were men among us who had been injured in spectacular accidents, in bad landings by parachute, falls from cliffs while training as commandos, violent crashes on motor-cycles. They had long boards positioned to keep their spines and necks rigid, their arms were supported at shoulder height on curious platforms, they walked crab-like along the gracious corridors.

Lame and cheerful, we ate in the elegant dining-room, relaxed in lounges designed to comfort the excesses of an earlier generation. The weather was good, the hills open. Once the surgeons had paid us their morning calls the days were normally ours.

Those of us not able to leave the hospital grounds would play bowls on the green in front of the building, or a kind of cripples' tennis on the hard courts; but there were daring and lively men who would not be handicapped by their injuries, who were adventurous to the point of recklessness, and they went wider afield. I, with my small fracture, often joined them. We sometimes hired ponies from a nearby stables. Clambering into the worn saddles, we'd gallop through the streets of the little town, legs sticking out at grotesque angles, our stiff bodies jolting up and down. After an exploit like this I'd return to the hospital and tell my room-mate, Alastair Ball, what we had been doing. Alastair was one of the few injured still confined to bed. He lay there, his legs trapped in a web of ropes and pulleys, and he was unruffled, tolerant, amiable all day long. He was twenty years old.

I had never met anyone remotely like Alastair. He was rich, he had been to a famous school, he was enormously well informed. He spoke French and German. I had never left the country, but Alastair had lived in Europe — his father was a diplomat — had visited India. His speech, slow, calm, assured, was quite unlike my hurried and tentative sentences. He spoke to me in the evenings of politics,

finance, economics. His cold passion for mathematics almost convinced me of its clear beauty. I began to read the books Alastair
loaned me, to listen to the music he chose to hear on the radio. In
return I gave him full accounts of the events of the day as I saw them
outside our room. The war was distant and unreal. I never thought
of it.

At last Alastair was allowed out of bed. First on crutches and then
with the help of a stick, he walked to the bathroom, to change his
library books, to meals. The first time I saw him upright I was
astonished. He was a very tall man, easily six feet four inches. As he
grew stronger he began to walk the halls and corridors of our ornate
hospital, his stick sharp on the tiled floors. I spent a lot of time with
him then. On fine days we would be out on the terrace, moving
gravely on our incompetent legs, talking, always talking.

Our first journey outside the hospital grounds was to the town.
We sauntered to the bus stop in the August sunshine, happy in our
recovering strength, carefree. Alastair was explaining to me the
complexities of the Stock Exchange, but I wasn't listening too hard.
I knew I would go through life allowing the accidents and coinci-
dences of small days to take me with them. The Stock Exchange
was not for me. I had no idea of what I could do, what I wanted to
do. It was enough to sit in the bus in the summer heat, smiling as
the bus swung around corners, past the rough limestone walls which
hedged the fields, rolling downhill to the shops and houses. We got
off at the station and two blue butterflies, perhaps the Holly Blue,
danced in front of us all the way to the river bridge.

I loved the river bridge. I always stopped there, to lean on the
stone parapet. The river, an exquisite chalk stream, formed a deep
pool under the bridge, its flow so imperceptible it could be still, its
clarity unflawed so you saw every detail, the polished ledges which
formed the washed sides of the channel, the minute viridian ferns
lodged in crannies, the slate-coloured river bed. One bank was a
face of stone which reached the bridge itself, and the other was
lower, no more than a foot above the water. A grassy area led down
to it, bordered with wallflowers and marigolds. Small tables were
standing on the neat lawn and people sat there, drinking coffee.
Some rowing boats were tied up at the bank, substantial boats for
so small a river. Seven of our friends were attempting to climb into
the nearest of them.

It was a difficult business organising their limbs into so narrow a
space. Laughing, hauling and shoving, they dragged each other
about until they were all, somehow, seated and they began to move

into midstream. From above, the boat and its wild oars looked like an insect, a great beetle many-legged and bristling, which had fallen into the water and, having no idea where land was, paddled aimlessly on the surface. As I thought this, someone lost an oar, leaned precariously for it, and almost toppled out of the boat. At once the craft's uncertain balance was spoiled; it started to totter, to rock, it sent waves across the smoothness of the pool and then, as if it had a malevolent life of its own, it spilled its shouting crew into twelve feet of water. They sank with such grace it seemed the river might almost have supported them. Their lamed clumsiness, their plaster heaviness vanished from them. Turning slowly in the dreaming passages of the water, they were almost fragile as they drifted through the pure and silent element. We saw them reach the bed of the river and push again for the surface and then, with others, we moved to help them, holding to them long poles ready at the water's edge, throwing them life-belts, bringing them red-faced and dripping to the river bank. The whole action was so beautiful and so funny that none of us, rescued or rescuers, thought once of danger or possible tragedy. The squelching soldiers hired a taxi and drove in triumph to the hospital. Alastair and I had lunch in town, visited the bookshop, went back up the hill in the afternoon bus. When I got in my doctor told me that I would never have more than one-third movement in my ankle and I was to be discharged from the army.

That was a day early in the week, Monday or Tuesday. The following Friday, wearing a civilian suit, I walked down the hill to catch the London train. My career in the army was over. Alastair had given me one of his walking sticks, a Malacca, light brown in colour. It was too long for me, of course. I had to cut it down. I had said goodbye to men I had known for a few months, promised to write to them. I didn't write. That was forty years ago. I learned to manage my stiff ankle, it's not been difficult. I have some arthritis in it now.

It is an irony that I, who had no sense of direction as a young man and drifted with the wind, should have spent all my life since then in one profession, almost in one place. Directly from the army I went to the university. I was utterly at home. I took my degree and was appointed to teach at another university. I've been there ever since. It's been an uneventful life, but satisfying. My misgivings, my restlessness, have been small. I've specialized in Anglo-Saxon and Early English Literature and published a little work in the field. I have not been unsuccessful. In recent years I've become interested in Norwegian poetry of the Romantic period, the work of men like

Wergeland and Johan Sebastian Welhaven. I've translated some of
this work, but my resources are limited, my knowledge of the
language insufficient. Last month, when a chance opportunity arose
for me to visit the university at Bergen I accepted at once.

It didn't work too well. I had been loaned an apartment in a house
where all the tenants were professors and were away for the summer.
I was very solitary. The long daylight bothered me. I never grew
accustomed to the grey hours filling the streets long after I expected
darkness. It was colder, too, than I had anticipated. It took time to
get used to the place, to accept its northern face, to hear its voices.
Each day I walked down to the waterfront, past the fish market,
along the north wall of the harbour, back again. It was better when
I started going to the university.

I had there the use of a small office and a typewriter. The library
was open and the young librarian very helpful, although he couldn't
understand my interest in these 'small men', as he called them. I
worked there for a week, arriving each day about eight-thirty, leaving
at six in the afternoon, eating my lunch of bread and fruit in the
office. I made some headway. One lunch-time I decided to go down
to the harbour and buy some fish. Bergen is a great fish market and
I had seen the boats come in with staggering hauls, mainly cod, but
some hake and haddock. Mackerel too, and once a giant salmon,
well over sixty pounds, taken silver and glittering out of the green
sea.

I waited in the short queue, bought my cutlets, and turned sharply
into the man behind me. What happened was entirely involuntary,
much quicker than recognition, something instinctive.

'Alastair?' I said, 'Alastair Ball?'

The tall man bent his head down towards me and said something
in Norwegian. He was a man in late middle age, the hair below his
hat grey. He wore a light raincoat.

'I'm sorry,' I said, 'I don't speak Norwegian.'

'Ah, you English,' he said. 'Insular, insular English. You should
learn our language. It's not difficult. But *Britannia insula est* — that
was the first sentence in my Latin primer and it is a true sentence.'

He beamed down at me, a mild face, a solicitous face.

'I mistook you for someone I knew,' I said.

'A friend?' he said. 'You have friend who looks like me? Very likely.
I am a typical Norwegian, a Viking, you know? Well, just let me buy
my supper and I will see if I know your friend.'

His English was noticeably accented, if clear and fluent. He
turned to the fishmonger and afterwards we walked together past

the old building which had been the dwellings and offices of the merchants of the Hanseatic League. It is preserved now as a museum. I had been inside. I told the tall man my name and what I was doing in the city.

'So,' he said, 'very good. It is time someone took a little notice of us. Please let me introduce myself. I am Jens Edwardsen, a businessman of this place, but I have some culture, I am interested in painting, music, some literature. Welhaven, eh?'

He stopped in front of me and began to chant, marking the rhythm with his right hand, like a conductor.

> *Lydt gjennem Luften in Natten farer*
> *et Tog pas skammende sorte Heste.*
> *I Stormgang drage de vilde skarer;*
> *de have kun Skyer til Fodefaeste*

What do you make of that? That's Welhaven. What would you call that in English, The Wild Hunt perhaps? Isn't that very good?' He took off his glasses and laughed aloud. I began to like him very much.

'And now my friend,' he said, 'I must return to my office. We must work, you know, work will not wait for us. But perhaps you will be kind enough to have dinner with me this evening, shall we say at six o'clock, and afterwards we will go and hear some organ music. If you like organ music, that is.'

I was glad to have talked to him. The whole day seemed more cheerful. I walked through the centre of the city and for the first time thought it beautiful. I did not see the relative unattractiveness of the shops, did not object to the cold and choppy waters of the fiord. A fitful sun shone on the old fort of Fredriksburg.

We ate at an Indian restaurant and afterwards walked to Johannes Kirken, where a Dutch organist played a programme of music by Bach, Buxtehude, Couperin and Cesar Franck. The organ was superb and the performer excellent, but the church was no more than half full. We came out into the long summer twilight of Norway, walked through the parks and squares not saying much, at ease. About ten-thirty we sat on a bench near the Bergenhus, the palace of the Norwegian kings in the Middle Ages. Edwardsen lit his pipe and looked out over the roofs.

'I am interested to find out,' he said, 'who this friend can be, the man you thought was I.'

'Oh,' I said, 'it was a stupid mistake. It was someone I knew many years ago, when we were very young. It was just your height, I was startled by your height, your outline.'

Four or five magpies walked impertinently in front of us. I had
never seen so many magpies as there were in Bergen, in the parks,
in the streets, on the roofs of houses. In England they are country
birds, sleek and immaculate; but in Bergen they are everywhere,
raffish scavengers. Years ago, during the war, I thought they flew
like bombers, Dorniers maybe, with their long tails.

'So,' said Edwardsen, 'he was a tall man, your friend? You were
young together? Youth is a time of great friendships, I think. But
his face was not at all like mine, I would hope.'

He took off his hat and his glasses and stared at me earnestly.
There he sat, turned towards me, his hair grey, his face lined, his
long hands quiet on his knees.

'No,' I said, 'not at all like yours.'

He smiled, his eyes mischievous and teasing.

'Are you sure,' he said, 'Private Graham?'

And then I knew that my instinct had not been at fault, that behind
the face of the sixty-year-old man Alastair Ball was alive. I
recognised then the bones of his face, the shape of his hair, and in
a few moments I saw the young man appear.

'But why, Alastair?' I said.

He told me. He was a genuine merchant of the town of Bergen,
had been since 1945 when he had appeared there from Oslo with
all his documents perfect. He had a circle of old friends, he was
successful, comfortably off. I didn't understand.

'Can't you guess?' he said. 'I'm a collector of information. I sit
here and do business with men of many countries. I am near many
frontiers, Germany, Poland, Russia. I travel. People come to see me.'

'You're a spy,' I said.

'A professional man,' he said, speaking with his old, languid,
English voice, 'with a perfect cover until you came along, bawling
out a forgotten name to all and sundry.'

He grinned, and I with him.

'I shan't say anything,' I said.

'More than that,' he said. 'We won't meet again. And if we see
each other in the street we won't even say hello.'

'Was it chance,' I said, 'that I bumped into you in the fish market?'

'Pure chance,' he said, 'one of the hazards we can't guard against.'

He stood up and stretched. I saw then that he really was an elderly
man.

'How do you know I can be trusted?' I said.

He looked at me over his glasses.

'The wires have been busy,' he said, 'between here and London this afternoon. I've had your whole life in front of me since four o'clock. Blameless and trustworthy, that's you.'

'And if I hadn't been,' I said.

He gestured impatiently towards the waters of the sea.

'It's a rough game,' he said. 'Be glad you don't belong to it. Goodbye, I've always wanted to know what happened to you. I'm glad all has gone well.'

He turned away and walked down the slope, an erect figure, very tall, unswerving.

'Mr Edwardsen,' I called, 'I still have that walking stick.'

He flapped a hand, in acknowledgement or dismissal, but did not turn around. I let him go out of sight and waited fifteen minutes more. Walking alone through the empty streets I came upon a small memorial stone, to a boy who had been a messenger in the underground movement during the war. The Germans had shot him. Before I reached my apartment I found two more. I had not seen them before. I had not been looking for them.

Shaving

Earlier, when Barry had left the house to go to the game, an overnight frost had still been thick on the roads, but the brisk April sun had soon dispersed it, and now he could feel the spring warmth on his back through the thick tweed of his coat. His left arm was beginning to stiffen up where he'd jarred it in a tackle, but it was nothing serious. He flexed his shoulders against the tightness of his jacket and was surprised again by the unexpected weight of his muscles, the thickening strength of his body. A few years back, he thought, he had been a small, unimportant boy, one of a swarming gang laughing and jostling to school, hardly aware that he possessed an identity. But time had transformed him. He walked solidly now, and often alone. He was tall, strongly made, his hands and feet were adult and heavy, the rooms in which all his life he'd moved had grown too small for him. Sometimes a devouring restlessness drove him from the house to walk long distances in the dark. He hardly understood how it had happened. Amused and quiet, he walked the High Street among the morning shoppers.

He saw Jackie Bevan across the road and remembered how, when they were both six years old, Jackie had swallowed a pin. The flustered teachers had clucked about Jackie as he stood there, bawling, cheeks awash with tears, his nose wet. But now Jackie was tall and suave, his thick, pale hair sleekly tailored, his grey suit enviable. He was talking to a girl as golden as a daffodil. 'Hey, hey!' called Jackie. 'How's the athlete, how's Barry boy?'

He waved a graceful hand at Barry.

'Come and talk to Sue,' he said.

Barry shifted his bag to his left hand and walked over, forming in his mind the answers he'd make to Jackie's questions.

'Did we win?' Jackie asked. 'Was the old Barry Stanford magic in glittering evidence yet once more this morning? Were the invaders sent hunched and silent back to their hovels in the hills? What was the score? Give us an epic account, Barry, without modesty or delay. This is Sue, by the way.'

'I've seen you about,' the girl said.

'You could hardly miss him,' said Jackie. 'Four men, roped together, spent a week climbing him — they thought he was Everest. He ought to carry a warning beacon, he's a danger to aircraft.'

'Silly,' said the girl, smiling at Jackie. 'He's not much taller than you are.'

She had a nice voice too.

'We won,' Barry said. 'Seventeen points to three, and it was a good game. The ground was hard, though.'

He could think of nothing else to say.

'Let's all go for a frivolous cup of coffee,' Jackie said. 'Let's celebrate your safe return from the rough fields of victory. We could pour libations all over the floor for you.'

'I don't think so,' Barry said. 'Thanks. I'll go straight home.'

'Okay,' said Jackie, rocking on his heels so that the sun could shine on his smile. 'How's your father?'

'No better,' Barry said. 'He's not going to get better.'

'Yes, well,' said Jackie, serious and uncomfortable, 'tell him my mother and father ask about him.'

'I will,' Barry promised. 'He'll be pleased.'

Barry dropped the bag in the front hall and moved into the room which had been the dining room until his father's illness. His father lay in the white bed, his long body gaunt, his still head scarcely denting the pillow. He seemed asleep, thin blue lids covering his eyes, but when Barry turned away he spoke.

'Hello, son,' he said. 'Did you win?'

His voice was a dry rustling, hardly louder than the breath which carried it. Its sound moved Barry to a compassion that almost unmanned him, but he stepped close to the bed and looked down at the dying man.

'Yes,' he said. 'We won fairly easily. It was a good game.'

His father lay with his eyes closed, inert, his breath irregular and shallow.

'Did you score?' he asked.

'Twice,' Barry said. 'I had a try in each half.'

He thought of the easy certainty with which he'd caught the ball before his second try; casually, almost arrogantly he had taken it on the tips of his fingers, on his full burst for the line, breaking the fullback's tackle. Nobody could have stopped him. But watching his father's weakness he felt humble and ashamed, as if the morning's game, its urgency and effort, was not worth talking about. His father's face, fine-skinned and pallid, carried a dark stubble of beard, almost a week's growth, and his obstinate, strong hair stuck out over his brow.

'Good,' said his father, after a long pause. 'I'm glad it was a good game.'

Barry's mother bustled about the kitchen, a tempest of orderly energy.

'Your father's not well,' she said. 'He's down today, feels depressed. He's a particular man, your father. He feels dirty with all
that beard on him.'

She slammed shut the stove door.

'Mr Cleaver was supposed to come up and shave him,' she said,
'and that was three days ago. Little things have always worried your
father, every detail must be perfect for him.'

Barry filled a glass with milk from the refrigerator. He was very
thirsty.

'I'll shave him,' he said.

His mother stopped, her head on one side.

'Do you think you can?' she asked. 'He'd like it if you can.'

'I can do it,' Barry said.

He washed his hands as carefully as a surgeon. His father's razor
was in a blue leather case, hinged at the broad edge and with one
hinge broken. Barry unfastened the clasp and took out the razor. It
had not been properly cleaned after its last use and lather had
stiffened into hard yellow rectangles between the teeth of the guard.
There were water-shaped rust stains, brown as chocolate, on the
surface of the blade. Barry removed it, throwing it in the waste bin.
He washed the razor until it glistened, and dried it on a soft towel,
polishing the thin handle, rubbing its metal head to a glittering
shine. He took a new blade from its waxed envelope, the paper
clinging to the thin metal. The blade was smooth and flexible to the
touch, the little angles of its cutting clearly defined. Barry slotted it
into the grip of the razor, making it snug and tight in the head.

The shaving soap, hard, white, richly aromatic, was kept in a
wooden bowl. Its scent was immediately evocative and Barry could
almost see his father in the days of his health, standing before his
mirror, thick white lather on his face and neck. As a little boy Barry
had loved the generous perfume of the soap, had waited for his father
to lift the razor to his face, for one careful stroke to take away the
suds in a clean revelation of the skin. Then his father would renew
the lather with a few sweeps of his brush, one with an ivory handle
and the bristles worn, which he still used.

His father's shaving mug was a thick cup, plain and serviceable.
A gold line ran outside the rim of the cup, another inside, just below
the lip. Its handle was large and sturdy, and the face of the mug
carried a portrait of the young Queen Elizabeth II, circled by a
wreath of leaves, oak perhaps, or laurel. A lion and unicorn balanced
precariously on a scroll above her crowned head, and the Union
Jack, the Royal Standard, and other flags were furled on each side

of the portrait. And beneath it all, in small black letters, ran the legend: 'Coronation June 2nd 1953'. The cup was much older than Barry. A pattern of faint translucent cracks, fine as a web, had worked itself haphazardly, invisibly almost, through the white glaze. Inside, on the bottom, a few dark bristles were lying, loose and dry. Barry shook them out, then held the cup in his hand, feeling its solidness. Then he washed it ferociously, until it was clinically clean.

Methodically he set everything on a tray, razor, soap, brush, towels. Testing the hot water with a finger, he filled the mug and put that, too, on the tray. His care was absorbed, ritualistic. Satisfied that his preparations were complete, he went downstairs, carrying the tray with one hand.

His father was waiting for him. Barry set the tray on a bedside table and bent over his father, sliding an arm under the man's thin shoulders, lifting him without effort so that he sat against the high pillows.

'By God, you're strong,' his father said. He was as breathless as if he'd been running.

'So are you,' said Barry.

'I was,' his father said. 'I used to be strong once.'

He sat exhausted against the pillows.

'We'll wait a bit,' Barry said.

'You could have used your electric razor,' his father said. 'I expected that.'

'You wouldn't like it,' Barry said. 'You'll get a closer shave this way.'

He placed the large towel about his father's shoulders.

'Now,' he said, smiling down.

The water was hot in the thick cup. Barry wet the brush and worked up the lather. Gently he built up a covering of soft foam on the man's chin, on his cheeks and his stark cheekbones.

'You're using a lot of soap,' his father said.

'Not too much,' Barry said. 'You've got a lot of beard.'

His father lay there quietly, his wasted arms at his sides.

'It's comforting,' he said. 'You'd be surprised how comforting it is.'

Barry took up the razor, weighing it in his hand, rehearsing the angle at which he'd use it. He felt confident.

'If you have prayers to say . . .' he said.

'I've said a lot of prayers,' his father answered.

Barry leaned over and placed the razor delicately on the clean line near the ear where the long hair ended. He held the razor in the tips of his fingers and drew the blade sweetly through the lather. The new edge moved light as a touch over the hardness of the upper jaw and down to the angle of the chin, sliding away the bristles so easily that Barry could not feel their release. He sighed as he shook the razor in the hot water, washing away the soap.

'How's it going?' his father asked.

'No problem,' Barry said. 'You needn't worry.'

It was as if he had never known what his father really looked like. He was discovering under his hands the clear bones of the face and head, they became sharp and recognisable under his fingers. When he moved his father's face a gentle inch to one side, he touched with his fingers the frail temples, the blue veins of his father's life. With infinite and meticulous care he took away the hair from his father's face.

'Now for your neck,' he said. 'We might as well do the job properly.'

'You've got good hands,' his father said. 'You can trust those hands, they won't let you down.'

Barry cradled his father's head in the crook of his left arm, so that the man could tilt back his head, exposing the throat. He brushed fresh lather under the chin and into the hollows alongside the stretched tendons. His father's throat was fleshless and vulnerable, his head was a hard weight on the boy's arm. Barry was filled with unreasoning protective love. He lifted the razor and began to shave.

'You don't have to worry,' he said. 'Not at all. Not about anything.'

He held his father in the bend of his strong arm and they looked at each other. Their heads were very close.

'How old are you?' his father said.

'Seventeen,' Barry said. 'Near enough seventeen.'

'You're young,' his father said, 'to have this happen.'

'Not too young,' Barry said. 'I'm bigger than most men.'

'I think you are,' his father said.

He leaned his head tiredly against the boy's shoulder. He was without strength, his face was cold and smooth. He had let go all his authority, handed it over. He lay back on his pillow, knowing his weakness and his mortality, and looked at his son with wonder, with a curious humble pride.

'I won't worry then,' he said. 'About anything.'

'There's no need,' Barry said. 'Why should you worry?'

He wiped his father's face clean of all soap with a damp towel. The smell of illness was everywhere, overpowering even the perfumed lather. Barry settled his father down and took away the shaving tools, putting them by with the same ceremonial precision with which he'd prepared them: the cleaned and glittering razor in its broken case; the soap, its bowl wiped and dried, on the shelf between the brush and the coronation mug; all free of taint. He washed his hands and scrubbed his nails. His hands were firm and broad, pink after their scrubbing. The fingers were short and strong, the little fingers slightly crooked, and soft dark hair grew on the backs of his hands and his fingers just above the knuckles. Not long ago they had been small bare hands, not very long ago.

Barry opened wide the bathroom window. Already, although it was not yet two o'clock, the sun was retreating and people were moving briskly, wrapped in their heavy coats against the cold that was to come. But now the window was full in the beam of the dying sunlight, and Barry stood there, illuminated in its golden warmth for a whole minute, knowing it would soon be gone.

All You Who Come to Portland Bill

I made good time driving from Sussex down to Weymouth. It's a road I know well, around the back of Southampton, through Ringwood and Wimborne Minister on the A31 to Dorchester, then south through the protecting hills the last eight miles to Weymouth. I had done it before many times, and no longer looked out for the painted figures high on the church tower at Wimborne, nor the great mound of Maiden Castle, the prehistoric camp where, digging, they had found two skeletons clasped in each other's arms. It takes me just over three hours normally, three and a half if I stop at The World's End for a beer.

This was at the end of May two years ago. I drove along the front at Weymouth, looking for the hotel the education people had taken over for the series of teachers' courses I was to lecture at. It was eleven o'clock in the morning, the sun was out, and the place was deserted. I stopped the car and went into a restaurant for some coffee. I was the only customer. It was a nice place, very clean and attractive.

'Where's the Manor Hotel?' I asked the young waiter as he brought my coffee.

'About a hundred yards down,' he said. 'You can't miss it.'

The sun shone on the polished floor. I could see the marks of my shoes, the toes turning slightly out, leading directly to my table.

'Pretty quiet,' I said.

'Always,' he said. 'Except at weekends, and during the holiday season. In about a fortnight, then we'll be busy. We'll be at it up to the middle of September. Then we can go back to sleep again.'

I laughed. After the fast drive it was pleasant sitting there, talking to the young man.

'Are you from Dorset?' I asked.

'No, I'm a Devon man. Come up from Bideford,' he said. 'I've been here nearly six years though. I like it. The wife's mother owns this place. I can more or less do as I please.'

The door opened and a tall, untidy man came in. He was carrying a green suitcase. I don't think I've ever seen a man so loosely made.

'Excuse me,' he said, and his smile was remarkable, transforming his sad, lopsided face, 'could you tell me where the Manor Hotel is?'

'I'm going there,' I said, 'as soon as I've finished my coffee. Won't you join me?'

'Gratefully,' he said, 'very gratefully. The name's Talbot, John Talbot.'

He sat down and the young man brought him coffee. He drank it as though he needed it, smiling disarmingly at his own eagerness.

'It's a long walk from the bus station,' he said. 'I haven't a car, never learned to drive.'

I liked him very much. We walked out to the car, threw his suitcase on the back seat, and drove with dignity the hundred yards to the hotel. John had come down by bus from Cheltenham. He told me he was to be in charge of drama on this course, that he had been in the theatre all his working life. He'd produced plays in many parts of the world.

We were pretty busy for the first three or four days, but in the evenings John, Amos Thomas, the short dark man who lectured on art, and I went out and drank a little beer. We seemed, in the strange familiarity that such situations encourage, to know each other very well without knowing anything at all about the lives we led away from the Manor Hotel, our true, everyday lives in our own houses. I was, for example, surprised to learn that John lived in London, not in Cheltenham as I had assumed. He had been up there judging some amateur productions.

On Tuesday afternoon the students went off in sight-seeing buses to visit places of interest nearby, which left us free. We had lunch and walked down to the beach. It was hot and the sand was relatively empty, but I was too restless to sit there, my back against the wall. I was irritable after five days in the same small area, the same two hundred yards of a small seaside town.

'Let's go somewhere,' I said.

'Where?' stated Amos, his round body lying slackly on the sand.

'Anywhere,' I said. 'Anywhere at all. We can't waste an afternoon like this. Where can we go, John?'

'Ever been to Portland Bill?' he said.

He was sitting up alertly, his long back straight and his eyes interested.

'No,' I said. 'Let's have a look at it on the map.'

'It's no distance,' he said. 'I've been there often.'

I looked at it on the map. It was about seven miles, the road running out of the town and along the narrow causeway which joined the Isle of Portland to the mainland. The island was roughly triangular, and the farthest point was Portland Bill. There were three villages marked on the map, Easton, Weston and Southwell. They all looked fine to me.

'We'll go to Portland,' I said.

In the car the seats were unbearably hot. Amos tried to tell us that this wouldn't happen if real leather were used for car seats instead of the plastic substitutes we were forced to accept in these synthetic days. But I can remember real leather and it got just as hot. Amos wound the window down and smiled. The car climbed the steep to the west of town and we drove to Portland.

Dorset is a strange county. I lived there for a number of years when I was younger, in a remote house north of Blackmoor Vale. Often, in the afternoon of a smiling day, I would be surprised to see low, white mists, no more than a yard high, come softly over the water-meadows. More quickly than I could believe, the house would be marooned in these little mists, the sky would turn bleak, and we would be menaced by the weather. Perhaps menaced is the wrong word; it was indifferent to us. That was worse.

It was a bit like this at Portland. We parked the car outside a pub in one of the villages, Southwell it would have been, and walked down to the edge of the cliff. The sun was still bright and hot. We passed the lighthouse and looked down at the Race, that turbulent area where contrary tides meet, way down below us, chopping the sun's reflection into haphazard segments of glinting light as far as we could see. On our left was the Shambles light-boat, a clear black shape at the distant edge of the water.

But even as we looked the sea grew dull and grey, the sea-fret rolled in cold and damp over us, and the sun shrank to a small bronze weakness in the sky. We sat on a slab of grey stone on the grey grass and felt miserable.

'Let's go back to the village,' Amos said. 'It will be all right there.'

'I sat on this stone,' said John Talbot, 'on the afternoon of February 12th, 1944.'

He stared straight ahead as if he alone could see through the moistness of the sea-fret to the waves beneath. But he couldn't.

'I was in the Navy here,' he said. 'Stationed at Portland. I was on a destroyer. I came ashore that afternoon and walked out here, knowing I'd be alone. I'd had a letter from my wife with the morning's mail, and I'd kept it until I could be alone.'

I took a quick look at him. He was in agony.

'I sat on this rock,' he said, 'here, where I'm sitting now, and I opened her letter. She told me that she had left me, that she had, in fact, gone to live with someone else. I'd had no warning, I had no idea. I was twenty-three. I thought the end of the world had come.'

We sat together for a long time, saying nothing. I couldn't find anything to say. Amos was smoking his pipe as placidly as if he hadn't heard John Talbot speak.

'That was a long time ago,' said John. 'Let's go back and have a drink.'

'Have you seen her since?' I asked.

'No,' John said. 'But she's in South Africa now. I know that.'

We walked slowly back up the hill, got in the car, turned and drove away. We hit the sunshine less than a mile further on and it was so startling and delightful that I braked and stopped at the side of the road. We tumbled out of the car, grinning like idiots. We were right outside a cemetery and the suddenly harsh light made everything curiously unreal. The church was locked — not only locked, but obviously unused. There were strands of barbed wire across the windows and some of them were boarded up. We went into the graveyard itself. It was extraordinarily neat, the white curbs of Portland stone shining in the sun, the orderly rows of the grave-stones. Several people were walking decorously and quietly between the graves. A notice-board told us that this was a municipal ceme-tery. Eager to forget John Talbot's old grief, we found the whole place amusing, giggling silently to ourselves as we read some of the commemorative verses. At last we reached the north wall and looked over. There lay the older cemetery, the original graveyard belonging to the locked church.

It was completely untended. Just up the road some small-holder was boiling pigs' swill and the odour seemed to cling and stick to the ivy and convolvulus that ran unchecked over the toppling headstones, and the rank grass standing in ragged and stumbling tufts. We found a little iron gate set in the wall, and went in.

The graves weren't very old. Most of them dated from the end of the last century or a little earlier, but the Victorian masonry seemed absolutely right, and very comic. The sentimental angels leaning mildly through wreaths of climbing ivy made us laugh aloud. A tall marble column deliberately and artistically broken near the top seemed an absurd masterpiece to us.

John Talbot was in a fever of amusement. He ran from one old grave to another, leaving us long behind, reading the carved inscrip-tions, tearing away the rampant weeds from the more elaborate tombstones.

'Listen to this,' he called. 'Will you just listen to this!'

He stood knee-deep in the brambles near the far wall and began to chant in a solemn voice. His long, loose arms were high above his head.

'Wait a minute. We can't hear you,' said Amos.

We walked along, pushing and stumbling over the low mounds. John Talbot stood there, arms still aloft, smiling at us. He had begun to clear away the creepers from a small, square stone near the wall.

Amos and I placed ourselves alongside the life-size statue of a seaman, stone sou'wester on his head, stone arm heroically pointing out to sea. We stood underneath his arm.

'All you who come,' chanted John Talbot, smiling,

'My grave to see,
As I am now
So you must be.
So you must be
As I am now,
And in the grave
Lie here below.'

'Never,' Amos said. 'That's never what's there.'

'Look for yourselves,' said John.

We bent down. The headstone was obscured by heavy creeper, but John had cleared enough for us to read the verse.

'"All you who come, my grave to see",' said Amos. 'Whose grave is it, anyway?'

'We'll soon find out,' John said.

Some of the strands were as thick as a finger, but we ripped them away from their purchase on the soft stone. Soon we had cleared it almost completely. I saw the inscription first but the others must have read it at almost that moment, for when I turned to them, they were already amazed and shocked, as I was. What we read was:

Here lies
JOHN TALBOT
born 1853
died April 7th 1885

John looked grey and tired.

'There's the thing,' he said, and he laughed, with the corners of his mouth turned down. We all got into the car and we drove back to Weymouth. Nobody said anything. I think Amos was very frightened, but after the first shock I was all right. John and I stayed up very late that night and we finished a bottle of brandy.

The course ended next day. I was glad to leave. I drove almost as far as Portsmouth before I let myself think of John Talbot, and after that the damned rhyme ran in my head for days.

Lurchers

When my great-grandfather came out of the hills above Llandovery in 1864, his furniture on a flat cart, his pans in clanking bundles, his pots in wicker baskets, his two small boys kicking their legs over the backboard, you can be sure he brought his dogs with him. He was not migrating very far — not more than fifty miles — but he was leaving behind the green, Welsh-speaking county in which he had been born. He never went back. He walked with his wife at the mare's head through the hamlets of Halfway and Llywel, and his cousins the Gardners ran out to wish them luck and to give them parting gifts — small lustre jugs, packets of tea. Reaching Sennybridge, they turned south to climb the gaunt and sneering heights of the Brecon Beacons. Here the little boys climbed down to lighten the load as, dwarfed by height, silenced by darkness, the family crawled for hours under black Fan Frynach before they reached the top of the pass at the Storey Arms inn. Then they could see below them the spoiled valleys of Glamorgan, their sides already pocked with the heaped detritus of the Industrial Revolution, their skies lit by leaping flames from the furnaces or hidden by rolling smoke.

Yes, my great-grandfather brought the dogs. He needed them. He was not going to the foundries or the coal mines but to a farm on the clear hills above the newly smoking town. He would have a white house, thick-walled, four-square to the winds; he would have an enclosure of over forty acres and grazing rights on twelve long miles of open mountain. On those high, unhindered moors he would raise his sheep — not your demure symbols of meekness, all soft fleece and gentle bleating, but stubborn, short-tempered animals, malevolent and cunning, able to grow stout on the shortest grass, yellow-eyed as goats, fluent as goats on the rock faces. They could outrun the mountain fox, they could lie snug for days under a fall of snow in the hollow, fetid caves of their own warm breathing.

To contain such animals without dogs would have been impossible. They would have been among my great-grandfather's most valued possessions — more prized than the corner cupboard given to him by his mother, more valuable than the dresser and the six oak dining chairs made for him by Jonah Jenkins of Trecastle. He needed his dogs more than he needed the tough brown mare that pulled the cart. Without them he could not have commanded the long slab of the mountain, acres of sloping turf and bracken on which his sheep were to feed, he could not have stood alone and calm while the dogs worked above him, extensions of his will. Each obedient to its own set of signals, his sheepdogs ran, crouched, sidled, and slunk close, and faultlessly gathered in his butting and recalcitrant animals. Panting, they brought in the sheep for lambing and dipping and marking, they held and penned them for shearing, they cut out the sick and injured so that my great-grandfather could treat them with his home-made drenches and salves. And after his death, in my grandfather's day, the descendants of those dogs still ran the hills, hard, strong, heavy-coated, their names repeated generation after generation: Bob, Gyp, Mot, Fan, Meg, Dick, Carl — monosyllables easy to shout against the wind.

They were the strong aristocrats of the farm, moving stiff-legged and contemptuous through the yard, scattering the silly Buff Orpington and Light Sussex fowl my grandfather so admired, or sleeping thin-eyed in a patch of sun by the barn. They lived only for my grandfather, they had no existence without him. When he appeared around the dim back door and walked down the path, they swung in behind him, heads low, waiting only for the twitch of his hand to send them racing for the flocks. Wherever he went, two or three dogs padded silently behind him, as natural as his shadow. They were as close to him as his hands.

On warm afternoons we would sit together, old man and boy, talking. We spoke with wonder of the world outside the farm, for we shared an ignorance of that community which did not live directly, as we did, by what it produced. We believed completely that the rest of society was in some sense an immoral growth, a parasite like mistletoe, hanging without purpose from the great oak of our work. At such times we would look with pride at our dogs, seeing them as symbols of those puritan qualities we admired; they were staunch, loyal, infinitely hardworking, shy — like us — and sometimes sullen with strangers. And yet, although I loved my grandfather's sheepdogs and could work Bob myself, I did not want one of my own. I yearned for another kind of dog altogether — a long, silent hunter, a dog outside the law. I wanted a lurcher.

Sometimes a group of men — small men, dark, wary-eyed — would move through our big field on the way to the mountain. Beyond a nod in our direction, or a muttered good morning, they rarely greeted us. They were gypsies. They would have with them four or five lurchers, a kind of dog unchanged since the time of the pharaohs, with the lines of greyhounds but quieter, more secretive.

Most of them would have long hair. They were bred from working greyhounds, with an occasional cross of sheepdog or, sometimes, deerhound blood. They were beautiful. It was their sheepdog ancestry that enabled them to hunt silently, that made them hardy and resourceful, and instantly obedient, despite the raging instinct of the chase which came from the greyhound.

My grandfather would stand unspeaking, rigid with distaste, when such a little group crossed our ground. The gypsies would climb the stile and cross the railway line, the grey dogs would wind themselves sinuously through the wire or, effortlessly, without fuss, leap the fence. When the men had vanished, quietly with their quiet dogs, my grandfather would turn away, two sharp, unaccustomed spots of colour on his cheekbones, his mouth stern beneath his white moustache. He was a short, generally smiling man, extravagantly generous. He could whistle like a thrush. He knew where the early flowers grew, the windflower and the primrose, and where the mistle thrush, first of birds to nest, kept her spotted eggs. He never seemed to hurry. His speech was slow and quiet. But his rare anger was terrible. He hated lurchers — I could see that. I dared not ask him for one — though I wanted one of those lean outlaws far more than respectability — because I had no wish to set my grandfather's violence alight.

Still, once the old man had turned away, I would follow the gypsies at a timid distance. Standing in the shadow of a clump of stubby hawthorn, or almost hidden in bracken waist-high to a man, I would watch the hills for the lurchers — long, slim as stems, powerful, coursing and turning the blue hares of the mountain. I stood one morning in the red ferns, powder of winter frost unthawed on every brittle frond, when a tall lurcher stopped in front of me. I saw its eyes. They were large and gentle, curiously distant and impersonal. It opened its mouth in a kind of laugh, and I had a glimpse of the terrifying white teeth before it was whistled away and I ran downhill, frightened and elated, in the thin tracks made by the sheep. A lurcher can pull down a grown deer. According to record, in Cowdray Park, in Sussex, in the summer of 1591, Queen Elizabeth saw 'sixteen bucks, all having fair play, pulled down after dinner' by dogs very much like these lurchers.

Too soon, we had to leave the farm. We went to live at the edge of town, in a row of houses almost where the fields began, and every day my grandfather walked out into the country, smiling as best he could, and wrecked by age. Of our dogs we took only Bob with us. The big orange and white sheepdog, dignified and brilliantly handsome, was too old to work with a new master. He settled down well, sat mildly on our front lawn, was gentle with passing children. He lived a long time, dying when I was seventeen, a year or two older than he was. It was June, and we buried him in the garden and planted a cherry tree over him.

That summer I found a holiday job in a fruit-and-vegetable warehouse. I used to rise early and walk through the streets as the summer dawn gradually brought the town awake. I used to hump boxes of fruit onto the trucks for delivery to shops all down the valley. I liked it very much. On Saturdays I used to work right through to late afternoon, loading up, checking invoices and delivery notes, taking new deliveries from the growers, and then I'd get paid. I had never known such wealth. The whole world grew docile and manageable under the power of the three pound notes I carried away each Saturday. Whole perfumed empires opened up for my inspection — cafés, theatres, gentlemen's outfits with real silk ties. It was a heady time. On my last Saturday Mr Frimpton put three pounds into my hand, and then, with a light smile, two more. 'You've been a good lad,' he said. 'Buy yourself something special.'

That evening I went alone to swim in the river. September was already chilling the water, but it seemed warmer when the sun had gone down. It was my last freedom before school began again, and it was fine to be there, washing summer off my summer skin, lazing softly downstream. I got out in the dusk, as the bats were beginning to fly, and walked down the lane for home. A ghost of the moon was out in a sky still full of daylight. Long grass in the hedgerows was ripe and heavy, there was a faint odour of hay as the dew settled.

Three people were standing in the lane, and one of them was singing. The singer was Talbot Hamer, famous in our town as an outrageous firebrand, a drinker and a fighter. He sang with his head slightly raised and his arms at shoulder height in front of him, palms upward as if he held on his hands the airy weight of his lovely voice. He was singing 'The Last Rose of Summer', and he was not drunk. His two companions, men of his own age — thirty, perhaps — were listening seriously, and Talbot filled the lane with his perfect singing, as a river fills its bed.

'All her lovely companions,' sang Talbot Hamer, 'are faded and gone.' It was unbearably beautiful. We waited until the final note, sweet and poignant beyond our understanding, had died in the darkening lane. Talbot stood there smiling down at us, amused at our stillness.

'I didn't know you'd gone in for singing Talbot,' said one of the men.

'I have,' said Talbot, nodding dreamily, still aware of the song inside his head. 'I've been taking lessons for two years now.'

The music still held us, a sense quiet and more intense than silence. We stood there respectfully, not knowing what to do.

'Do you want to buy a dog?' said the other man at last, looking at me.

It was as if I were being asked to take part in a ceremony of gratitude. I looked at the long, pale dog standing at the man's knees.

'He's a good one,' said Talbot Hamer. The spell of his song was with him; he looked at the evening with an exalted eye.

'Yes,' I said. 'I'll buy him.'

'Two pounds,' the man said.

I took the two carefree pounds Mr Frimpton had given me and handed them over. The man put them in his pocket without a glance. 'He'll catch anything that moves,' the man said. 'Retrieve to hand. Gentle, obedient. I'd not sell him to anyone but you.'

'I believe you,' I said.

He handed over the dog's leash. The whole affair was so tenuous that I was startled by the weight and touch of the leash; it was heavy, smooth and heavy — real saddler's leather, and hand-stitched. It was pliable and slightly oily with use, about eighteen inches long, and fastened by a spring clip to the dog's wide collar.

'I'll take him, then,' I said.

The men stood aside and I walked past them, the dog going with me, unprotesting. He didn't look back.

'The name's Ben,' the man called. 'He's a good one, mind. You look after him and he'll look after you.'

I trotted away as Talbot Hamer sang again. '*Una furtiva lacrima,*' he sang. '*Negli occhi suoi spunto, quelle festose giovani . . .*'

I turned the corner and could hear him no more.

I took Ben into the house and had a look at him. He was bigger than I'd thought — all of twenty-nine inches at the shoulder — and rough coated. He was mostly white, but there were patches of orange on his body — on the ribs and right shoulder — and his ears were deep orange, almost red. He might have been two years old. I fed him in the kitchen — a bowl of crusts softened in milk. He ate thoroughly, carefully cleaning every particle of food from the dish, and then looked thoughtfully about him. His expression was both cynical and mournful, and he never looked any different all the years I had him. That's how I came to own my first lurcher.

Talbot Hamer was quite right; the dog was a good one. When he was with us, he was vastly obedient, without ever letting us believe that he was at all humble or subservient; he followed at our heels, alert for any order. But he was also independent, roaming the town at will. I often saw him swinging down the High Street with his loping, economical stride — deep-ribbed, solitary, detached from the scene, as if he were some thoughtful philosopher engrossed in a profoundly satisfying problem. On such occasions he did not seem to recognise me; he looked away tactfully, as if to let me know that he was his own man with his own concerns. He roamed very far afield. Men from outlying villages, seeing him with me, would often come up and tell me of his exploits in their parishes, for he was a famous lover, visiting for miles around.

He was also very fond of beer. He was at his best in small inns on winter evenings, when the talk was good. His method was a simple one, I was told. He would sidle in quietly, offering a token wag of the tail if anyone looked at him, sigh gently, and lie down out of the way in some corner. His eyes would grow soft as he looked beyond the walls at some distant and innocent memory. In a little while everybody would forget all about him. The old drinkers sat on their benches, laughed, pulled at their beer, wiped the foam from their mouths, and put their mugs on the floor, the better to illustrate a point in some hot debate. Casually, Ben would saunter over and join the group, stretching almost invisibly in the shadow of a bench or a chair. And then, dreamily and in complete silence, he would lap up the beer. Men who knew him would chase him out the moment his long head appeared around the inn door, and he often had to move very smartly. On the other hand, he also managed to drink a lot of beer.

He was wonderful in the country, an incomparable craftsman. He and I worked together. A little shift of his head would lead me unerringly to some animal — a hedgehog, maybe, curled up in his leaves and just about to stir, or a bird. I had never seen a snipe until Ben turned one out for me one heavy winter morning when the ground was hard and the only place for such shy creatures was on the softness at the edge of a stream. Ben held back, looking to make sure I was attending, and then moved noiselessly into the willows. At once, a snipe came rocketing out, breaking into erratic flight, uttering two stiff cries. Ben looked at me sardonically and then stretched his long body in a gallop over the frozen meadow. He was a hunter all his life, he could not be kept from hare or game bird. Well, that was long ago. Talbot Hamer is dead, the summer of his voice a memory.

The most beautiful lurcher I ever saw was Georgie Todd's Dagger

— a spectacular, golden dog Georgie owned when I first knew him, about fifteen years back. Oh, he was lovely, a great beauty, over seventy pounds in weight, and he moved like thistledown. His yellow coat was harsh to the touch, his eyes were dark and kind. He and Georgie were very like each other — large, quiet, diffident, and very gentle.

Georgie has a fruit farm the other side of the Downs, toward Pulborough. He grows apples mainly — Bramley's, Cox's, russets — but he has a few pear trees and a couple of acres of strawberries. The house is an old Georgian farmhouse, simply and beautifully preserved. The furniture is good, too, each piece shrewdly chosen. Georgie and his wife had taken great pains over it, bought carefully over the years, and have never been impulsive or haphazard. I always thought it strange that so neat and methodical a pair as Georgie and Phyllis Todd should have a dog at all, even one as striking as Dagger.

Their greatest enthusiasm is for the history of this part of Sussex — the Weald and the South Downs — and they are very serious about it, very knowledgeable. Between them, they've done some first-class research; Georgie does the field work, and Phyllis, a meticulous woman, looks after records and documents. Dagger was very much Georgie's dog. Without being in any way unkind, Phyllis seemed hardly aware that the animal was about. One day, in the Welldigger's Arms at lunch-time, looking at Dagger as he lay at our feet, I asked Georgie to sell me the dog.

'I shan't sell him,' George said. 'We get along very nicely; he's a sweet old dog.'

'Where did you buy him, Georgie?' I said.

'I didn't buy him,' George said.

He told me how, three years before, he had been walking down Bury Hill. It was a day of quite exceptional heat, after a succession of very hot days. Georgie had got up in the cool of the morning and tramped off to visit a church in one of the villages; he was tracing the ramifications of an old local family and had gone to look at the gravestones in the churchyard. Now, in the late morning, the heat was growing intense. Traffic wasn't as heavy in those days, and you could walk the roads with pleasure, but that day the dust was everywhere — chalk dust off the Downs, very thick, like powder. It rose in little puffs as Georgie plodded down the hill, getting into his nose and throat, making him think of the long, cool drink he'd have when he reached home. He sat on a stone at the side of the road to watch a gypsy caravan, pulled by a bay mare, climbing the hill toward him. It was a barrel caravan, its canvas stretched neatly over

its hooped ribs, and it was in good shape, but the mare was finding
the going hard; she was distressed and blowing as she dug into the
steep of the hill. A thin young man walked with her, a surly young
man, lean and dark in the face. They came slowly by, the caravan
heavily laden, well down on its two creaking springs.

'You've got a load on,' said Georgie, smiling.

The man didn't lift his head. George stood up. At the tail of the
caravan, tied to a spar by a rope heavy enough to hold a lion, was a
lurcher puppy. He tottered and swayed, yelping each time he was
dragged by the neck as the mare pulled gamely on. He was so dirty
that Georgie could not guess at his colour. He was far gone. Georgie,
surprised by his own anger, ran to the front of the van.

'Do something about the dog!' he shouted. 'You're killing him!'

Very quietly and deliberately the young gypsy led his mare to the
roadside grass and dropped the reins over her head. She stood there,
exhausted. The man said nothing at all. He took from his pocket a
black-handled clasp knife and opened it with his thumbnail. The
blade was long and glittering, thin with use and viciously sharp.
Georgie knew that his last moments had come and prepared to meet
his death as well as he could. All he could think of, he told me,
smiling, was to stand erect and die bravely. But the gypsy walked
slowly past him, down the side of the van, disappeared around the
tail. The puppy began to scream, and Georgie's quick relief turned
to indignation.

'My God,' he thought, starting to run after the man, 'he's going
to kill the dog.' But then the young man came back toward him, in
one hand the open knife and in the other the heavy rope, its fibres
freshly cut. The dog, unhurt, howled at the other end.

The young man bent down and lifted the animal, holding it to
Georgie. 'Take it,' he said. 'Take it away.' His voice was thick and
trembling, as if he held his violence in check only by the severest
effort.

'That was the first time I saw his face clearly,' said Georgie. 'The
man was desperate, and I became even more frightened. I still
believe that if I hadn't taken the dog — well, the fellow would have
knifed me. I grabbed the pup and ran downhill as fast as I could go.'

Georgie carried the dog home and, in time and with patience,
turned him into Dagger. He was a lovely dog, noble and unassuming. After his death Georgie never had another.

There's a parti-coloured dog that lives on the coast road with an
old gypsy couple. I saw this dog when it was a sapling, running loose
on Clymping beach, and I followed it home. The old man was sitting

on the step of his caravan, a wooden van, traditionally painted. The old people travel the road from Littlehampton to Portsmouth and back again. I often see them parked on some small plot of grass, their skewbald gelding hobbled close by.

'That's a nice dog,' I said to the old man.

'He'll come,' said the old man. 'In time, he'll come.'

'What's his name?' I said.

'Toro,' said the old man. 'It's a good name. You should always give a dog a name he can grow up to. I've had three dogs named Toro in my life, and they've all been good. Belle is a good name, too.'

The old man would not live well without Toro. There will not be many nights when the dog will not be silently quartering some rich man's fields, bringing almost apologetically to the pot the fresh spoils of the countryside — hare, rabbit, a pheasant so gently killed that the bronze feathers are not displaced.

The lurcher I have now, Jess, came to me from the dogs' home when she was twelve weeks old — a pathetic little waif, very ugly and awkward. But you could tell she'd be elegant; the length was already apparent in leg and back. At that time she couldn't manage herself at all well. Even her slight weight was sometimes too much for her, and she'd slowly collapse, spread-eagled, unable to rise and yelling with pain. At first we couldn't give her enough food — she ate all day long — and as she grew stronger she began to forage for herself. A poor sparrow once flew into the garden wall. It had hardly fallen to the ground when she'd swallowed it at a gulp. She began to catch wood pigeons. Slow to get up the birds would be, in their first clatter of flying, and she would grab one of them and, running on, take it to a corner of the field. Later I'd find two small pink feet — all that would be left of Jess's meal. But she's big now, a sturdy animal, full of grace and power.

I know quite a lot about her — where she was bred, her parentage, her precise age. When she was about twelve months and beginning to look as she should, I had her out on the lawn, chasing a ball. A young man came over and leaned on the gate, watching us. 'She's growing nicely,' he said. He was a pleasant young man — heavy shouldered, thick, tousled, fair hair above a round face. 'We've been keeping an eye on her,' he went on. 'We knew you'd got her.'

'Oh?' I said.

'I bred her,' the young man said. 'I had to leave her. And the rest of them — eight pups altogether. I put them in a box in the middle of the field and rang the dogs' home. Told them where to find the pups.'

'Why did you abandon them?' I said sternly.

'Had to. I was running,' he said, as if it were the most obvious explanation in the world.

I was mystified. 'Running?' I said.

'Yes,' he said. 'From the police. I had to leave everything — the van, wife, kids, everything. It's all blown over now.'

'What had you done?' I asked.

'Nothing,' he said, so virtuously I knew he was lying. 'I hadn't done a thing.'

We looked at Jess galloping about the garden, pouncing on invisible game behind the lilac trees.

'She's big,' the young man said. 'And fast. I'll buy her back. I'll give you a good profit, Mister.'

'No, thanks,' I said. 'I quite like her.' I started to walk toward the house when I remembered something. 'Tell me,' I asked. 'How was she bred?'

He took a small notebook out of his pocket and turned the pages. 'Here it is,' he said. 'I keep all the details in this book. Her father was a first-cross greyhound-deerhound. She favours him a lot — same grey colour, same little whiskers. And her mother was a little brindle greyhound, very fast. I gave her to my brother after these pups were born, but she got killed up on the Downs. Ran into a fence and broke her neck. Yes, it's all down here. Born April 12th, your dog was, one of eight pups.'

Gypsies call here pretty regularly, to offer me a profit. Jess would be a good dog for a travelling man. She's very fast, but it's not just her speed — she's a thinking runner. I've seen her catch seagulls on the beach, racing on the very last inch of sand next to the water so that the birds on land are unable to fly directly out to sea. They have to take off and turn back over Jess's head, and any gull that isn't above her astonishing leap is in real danger.

When I first had her, I kept her about the house for a week or two before taking her out. I put her in the back of the car one day, thinking to let her have a run near the river. When I reached the top of the village, I saw Alec Dougan come out of the post office. Alec owns a lot of land around here — a couple of thousand acres of arable land, enough pasture for a large and famous herd of Ayrshires, and a stretch of woodland it takes days to cover. I stopped to talk to him.

'How are you, old son?' said Alec, eyes alight, smiling. I could see he was going to tell me the latest racy tale of local high life. And then he turned the smile off. I watched the harsh resurrection of my grandfather's dislike of lurchers come into his face — the same downturn of the lips, the same stiffening of the neck.

'What's that you've got?' he said.

'Nice, isn't she?' I said.

'You've got trouble there,' he said.

'Come away, Alec,' I said. 'She's only a baby.'

'She'll hunt,' he said. 'You won't be able to stop her.' I could see him thinking of his pheasants. 'We're old friends,' he said. 'I won't ask you to keep her off my land, but watch her. And don't say I didn't warn you.' He went off shaking his head.

She hasn't been too hard to train, though, and she no longer hunts indiscriminately. But I have had moments of panic. Last spring, we walked on a holiday Sunday in the public woods. The paths were full of strolling groups come to see the renewed foliage of the beeches. Children ran through the grass. I had Jess on her lead, and she walked demurely at my side. Without breaking step, she dipped her long neck to a tussock, and, raising her head, gave me — put gently into my hand — a live cock pheasant. His gape wide with fright, he sat heavily on my hand. It had all been done so gracefully, so entirely without fuss, that nobody noticed at all. Completely unhurt, the bird sat there, and then, indignant, blundered off, his long tail feathers streaming.

Although I can safely whistle Jess off any chase at all now, she can still startle me. This morning the fields are covered with a light snow. It lies in the furrows and is blown in midget drifts in the lee of trees. The ground is so hard that it rings when you stamp on it. We went out early into the field behind Dr Medlicott's house, and I slipped Jess at once. Normally she bounds immediately into a frolic, running in circles, tossing twigs in the air, but this morning her moving was quite unlike play, and I should have recognized at once that she was on to something. There is a frightening directness and velocity about her serious running, a concentration of effort that involves the whole dog, bending everything to a single purpose, that of catching and killing. Before I could purse my cold lips to a single recall, she had picked up a rabbit in the shadow of a hedge. It was a run of at least two hundred yards and the poor creature hadn't time to turn away, hadn't time to squeal before its back was snapped and Jess was bringing it back, hanging loose from her killing jaws. It's easy to understand why landowners are wary of men who walk the fields with lurchers.

It wasn't always so. Such dogs were once owned only by princes. In ancient Wales, the gift of a rough-coated greyhound was a mark of the highest royal favour, and great poets, skilled in the strict measures, wrote complex odes to their lords begging such gifts. The young hero Culhwch, journeying to Arthur's court in search of initiation and adventure, went on horseback, dressed as a prince, miraculously accoutred. His horse was a light grey, four winters old, well ribbed and shellhoofed. His saddle was of gold, his tubular bridle bit was of gold, his battle-axe was keen enough to draw blood from the wind, his sword was hilted with gold, and his buckler was of gold and ivory. But his ultimate treasures were the two grey-hounds, white-breasted, brindled, that danced and cavorted in front of him as he rode. Sufficient evidence of his nobility in themselves, they each wore a wide collar of red gold, fitting from shoulder to ear. They would have been the old, rough-coated greyhounds, exactly the lurchers I've studied for so long, since the brindle colour did not exist in smooth-haired greyhounds until Lord Orford, in the eighteenth century, introduced a bulldog cross in order to improve the courage of his strain. What I am calling a lurcher is a dog that has come down unchanged through the ages; except that he was known until the seventeenth century as a greyhound, everything about him is the same. A strong, hardy dog, his lines the dominant graceful outline of the greyhound we know today, his coat longer and weather-resisting, from the occasional judicious crosses of sheepdog and deerhound, he is valued for his intelligence and ability in the field. His likeness can be seen in a thousand paintings and tapestries, because he was as necessary to the life of the court as he is now to the travelling man. Culhwch's dogs would have been true hunting dogs, bred for efficiency in all weathers, long-coated, tough. King Canute, a notably sensible man, laid down in his laws that none but a gentleman could own a greyhound, and I'm delighted by this evidence of the legitimacy of lurchers.

It wouldn't surprise me to find the lurcher becoming a fashionable dog in a year or two. It has many virtues: it is tactful, not quarrel-some; will curl up in the smallest space; is not noisy. Lurchers are big enough to be very efficient guards. I saw one walking along the Charles River in Boston two years ago, and it was evident to me that the girl who owned him was safe. It would be a desperate mugger who'd willingly face a lurcher; he'd very likely lose an arm. And they're gratifyingly good to look at; they'd cause a sensation in Greenwich Village. I saw, in a fashionable journal recently, a slim and disdainful lady, posed to display the perfection of her expensive clothes. She held on two leads two splendid lurchers. They're coming back. If I wear my country tweeds and carry an ashplant, my lurcher takes me into the most rarefied social circles; she becomes a sporting dog rather than the companion of gypsies, thieves, and tramps. Retired colonels write books about them, they are to be seen with rich racehorse owners and young men-about-town.

They are likely to be very useful very soon. As an experiment, a group of people in Wiltshire have been living for a year exactly as the ancient Celts did, raising scrubby animals, growing meagre wheat, sleeping in a thatched, circular hut. They have with them two dogs — lurchers — and are loud in their praise of these animals, which have proved essential to the success of their project. Come the destruction, when the last warhead has exploded and the world is an untechnical ruin and small groups of people live desperately on what they can catch, we lurcher owners will no doubt be the new aristocrats. Because of Jess I expect I'll have a grey horse of four winters, gold all over him. I shall be a prince.

A Seeing Eye

At bout ten thirty in the morning of the third Sunday in March, 1964, I was standing in a corner of the garage. I stood near the grimy skeleton of the old lawn mower and I was crying. Nothing loud and dramatic, just gentle, elegiac tears — anything stronger would have hurt my ribs. The previous day I had played my last game of soccer and I was mourning the passing of great times. The scene of my last encounter had been hard as ebony, the sky more colourful than bruises, the wind a flying iceberg. I knew that every muscle would be sore until Thursday. Moreover, turning awkwardly on the flinty surface, I had dislocated three toes on my left foot. Afterwards I had limped home like Lord Byron.

'That's it,' my wife had said when she saw me. 'You've played your last game of soccer. No more for you. A grown man coming home with his toes in plaster!'

I had no defence. I slept badly, and in the morning, coming downstairs on my butt, one step at a time, groaning, I felt she was right. I edged on my one sound foot towards my breakfast.

'You're too old,' my wife said, pouring the coffee. She was smiling, but we both knew she meant it. Breakfast was a sad meal.

Afterwards I took my soccer boots out of the bag and looked at them. They were good boots, very expensive. They would last another hundred games, but I would never wear them again. Meticulously I began to clean them. With the greatest care, with affection, I took away the grains of frozen mud from the seams of the leather, unwound the threads and flakes of grass that clung about the studs, polished the open surfaces, sole and upper, until they glistened. It was a serious ceremony. I was taking ritual farewell of skills I had learned and practised until they were habitual. From the age of ten I had played soccer almost every week of my life, and now it was over. I was finished. I was thirty-four years old.

Holding the boots by the laces, I took them into the garage and hung them on a nail hammered into the wood. That's when I shed those mild, necessary tears. I went back indoors and poured another cup of coffee. I felt better.

The papers had arrived, *The Observer* and *The Sunday Times*, their pages smelling comfortably of distant tragedy and momentary triumph. I opened one of them and turned to the book section. A long calm Sunday was opening out for me and I began to read three full columns of unblemished praise for *The End of August*, a first novel by Tom Bridge. I'd never heard of Tom Bridge. His photograph was in the middle of the page, a confident young face, narrow, careful, his thick hair prim and orderly.

His novel was about a few days in the lives of three old ladies, long-time friends and neighbours, in a small American town in the Midwest. It wasn't much of a scene to be ecstatic about. But when I read a long quotation from the book, a solid passage about a field in which some country show was to take place, I have to say I saw the field in front of me. I saw the flags and bunting flutter against the dark of the trees, I saw the roped-off square of the car park, the arenas in which the mountainous gentle shires and expensive ponies would on the next day wheel and trot, their tails plaited with ribbon, red and blue and white, their brasses jingling. The trim white tents were up, small ones for judges and the members of the committee, wide marquees for displays of craft and poultry, for eating lunch and drinking beer and cold fruit punch. The boards were on their trestles ready to support the prize collections of heavy vegetables, jars of translucent honey, pears and apples too big to hold in one hand, the ripe and flawless roses. The tradesmen's stands were pitched about the field, the saddlers', the seedmen's, stands for farm machinery, for veterinary products. It was the late evening before the show, and the whole wide meadow, empty of men, waited. The smell of trampled grass, that green scent, was in the air. A thin mist, promise of hot weather, hung a foot above the river. I could have tossed a stone into the water, rubbed my hand across the dry bark of an oak.

How he must have looked at things, Tom Bridge. How well he understood the surfaces and textures of the world.

He was twenty-three years old and he had written his novel while still a student. He had set his old ladies alive and talking into a palpable, beating world of his own making, with real weathers, with its apt forms and patterns. All over England that morning men were opening their newspapers and a twilight American showground unfolded before them. Twenty-three years old. I closed my paper quietly and placed it on the floor, near my swollen foot in its loose slipper.

'And now,' I said to myself, without any hope at all, 'you're even too old to be a writer.'

The railway line between Chichester and Arundel, in Sussex, crosses the river Arun near its estuary, not a mile from the sea. In the right season, if the train is slow enough, you can look from the rumbling weight of the bridge and watch the massed sea trout, those wavering shadows, facing upstream, waiting for fresh water, ready to run. The river is always good to look at. Downstream, small boats, hauled up on the bank or scudding about on the water, furl their coloured nylon sails in the wind that comes off the sea. Looking north, you can follow the river's course until you face with a start the high, romantic front of Arundel Castle a few miles away, closing against you any further sight of the Arun Gap. If this is what happens, if you are seduced by the river, you miss seeing the small pond that lies almost hidden a few yards from the river bank. Small, meek, crescent-shaped, it has no relationship with the river, although so close a neighbour. The first time I saw it was on a cold morning four years ago, a January morning, early, a hard frost everywhere.

I had been waiting too long for the train, standing on the platform, the silver fur of frost blurring the edges of the wooden planks, the backs of benches open to the weather, the wrought iron rails. My hands and feet were without feeling. When the train came in I jumped for a seat and huddled into my coat, my hands deep in my pockets. The carriage was almost empty; a few business men, dark-suited, slumped in open-eyed sleep or absorbed in the *Financial Times* were my only companions.

After a few minutes I cleared a few square inches of the misted window and looked out. I knew by the noise that we were crossing the Arun Bridge. And then, framed by the opaque surface around my cleared space, I saw this marvellous little pond, white, utterly still.

Dry sedges fringed the water, and frost had turned them all to brittle silver. There was no movement. A small bare tree, a hawthorn, stood on the higher bank. Some water birds sat on the surfaces of the pool, two white swans, some mallard, three small black and white diving ducks. They were unmoving. The water, taking the dull colour of the sky, did not reflect them. It was still as glass. I might have been looking at a marvellous crystal toy made for a child of the great czars. I was enchanted. Later, when I had finished my day in London and come home through the dark, I looked on my large-scale map for the pond. It wasn't marked, nor have I found it marked anywhere, although I see it every time I make the journey. I've seen it on summer evenings, with slow Friesians standing in it under the hum of flies, I've seen it in the clear light of morning, I've seen it many times.

There must be a way, through the low-lying fields, along some lane, through a churchyard maybe, there must be a way to that small water, but I've never found it.

Chinner Mason knows the path, as he knows all small paths for miles around. I see Chinner most days. I saw him this morning, as I was shaving. He was moving through the copse behind my house, sturdy, upright, his round head high. I watched him for a while, letting the lather on my face grow flat, full of admiration for the easy, silent way he moves among the trees, but I didn't call to him. Chinner has his own quiet occupations, his journey through my trees would not be without purpose.

When I went to 'The White Horse' after lunch, Chinner was there, in his usual place, his back to the window, playing draughts against himself. I called him a pint of beer and put it at his side. Chinner is a big man, not tall, but very strongly made. His jackets always look too small for him, so tightly is he buttoned into them, so completely does he fill his clothes. He is perhaps sixty years old. He looks like an old athlete who has fallen on soft times.

'Fancy a game, then?' he said.

'Drink your pint, Chinner,' I said.

I wouldn't play Chinner at any game, knowing I wouldn't leave until my wallet was empty. He smiled and went on with his complex moves.

'Still got your little dog,' he said.

I just stood at the bar, didn't reply.

'Heard him barking as I went past your place this morning,' said Chinner tranquilly. 'Nice little dog. How old is he, six or seven?'

'Six,' I said.

Chinner wears glasses, the pebbles so round and thick they make his face expressionless. The frames are repaired with twists of wire and pieces of adhesive tape. His sight is supposed to be very bad.

'You've wasted that little dog,' he said. 'You should have worked him. Game little dog. I'd have had him through every hedge and thicket in the parish. What a pity. He's too old now.'

'Maybe,' I said.

'I had one like him,' he said, 'oh, twenty-five years ago. Little Norfolk terrier, came off Tim Howell's bitch. Hard as stone, he was. I lost him once in a fox earth up Petworth way, and he was there three days before we dug him out. My brother was alive then, and we went up three days in a row, digging. Ground was hard, too. We could hear the little devil, barking and snarling away, so we knew he was alive and had something in there. He wouldn't come out until everything was finished, we knew that.'

'Why did it take you so long?' I asked.

Chinner Mason grinned.

'We shouldn't have been there at all,' he said. 'We were were on somebody's land, never mind whose. We dug in the dark, really, before dawn. Five o'clock one morning we came on him. The earth was down below a big oak in the hedge, down in the root. More like a cave, but the entry was narrow. Well, the fox is a very narrow animal, get through the eye of a needle. The terrier had killed the dog fox and he'd died in the entrance, right between two stones, and my little fellow was trying to get past him to kill the vixen. Oh, he was game, that little chap. My brother put his arm down to grab him by the tail. Little bitty tail he had, just a stump. He turned in a flash and bit my brother. Almost took his thumb off.'

Chinner laughed merrily.

'My brother began to hop about, swearing, blood all over his hand. We couldn't make too much noise or the keeper would have heard us. I pushed my spade down and forced him off with the back of it, and then I grabbed him. We made off pretty sharp, I can tell you.'

He tells a good story. That's why we call him Chinner.

'What happened to him?' I said.

'The little dog?' said Chinner. 'Oh, he was a disappointment in the end. Cousin of the wife's came down from London, for a holiday. Well, cousin of the wife's mother really, woman of forty or so. Took one look at the dog, called him a dear little thing, all that rubbish, tickled his stomach. Made a proper fool of him. Dog wouldn't look at me after. She took him back to London with her.'

He looked with sorrow down the years at his lost dog.

'Proper little worker, he was,' said Chinner. 'Hard as stone.'

'Chinner,' I said, 'do you know that little pond the other side of the railway bridge?'

'What of it?' said Chinner softly, his face blank as the moon.

'You ever been there?' I said.

'I might have,' said Chinner cautiously.

'How do you get to it?' I said.

Chinner looked down at his draughts board and moved a piece with great care.

'What's it to you?' he said.

'I've seen it from the train,' I said. 'I thought.I might go there.'

'There's no carp in it,' said Chinner quickly, 'nor tench neither, if that's what you're after.'

'I don't want to fish it,' I said. 'I just want to stand by it.'

Chinner stared at me. 'You're mad,' he said.

I knew I'd get nothing out of Chinner except tall tales. I finished my beer and walked to the door.

'So long, Chinner,' I said.

'My advice,' said Chinner, 'is to find your own way to places. Then you don't ever forget. You know every leaf of the way, every stone, every blade of grass. Find the way for yourself and keep your eyes open.'

Three times in a week I'd made my way up from Sussex to a little place on the Avon and Kennet Canal, outside Newbury. I'd bought a small cabin cruiser very cheaply, from an advertisement in a Southampton newspaper, and I was looking for somewhere to moor it. It was a shabby craft, dull in colour, scuffed, in need of a lot of work. I was ashamed of it. But I'm not a sailor, I need a humble boat, something gentle. I imagined myself floating through the fields of England on the calm and ordered waters of the Avon and Kennet, never more than four feet in depth; but first I had to get a mooring. I went up to Newbury and someone told me of this little place a few miles outside the town. It took me some time to find it. I had to drive through a coal-merchant's yard, then down a rough track through several fields until I came, surprisingly, to a wharf. It was lovely there, a beautiful stretch of water. I loved it the moment I saw it. Quite a lot of boats were moored there, tied to pilings on the bank; smart fibreglass cruisers large enough to live in, three long traditional barges painted with roses and windmills, smaller boats like mine, if not as dingy. There was nobody about. A small shed carried a sign saying 'Office', but when I knocked nobody answered. I tried the door and it was locked. That was a Monday afternoon, last May.

I went up again on the Thursday, and saw nobody. I took my lunch with me, salad and a bottle of white wine, and I sat at the water's edge to eat it. Afterwards, feeling a little chill, I walked about. The owner's name, I saw from a plate outside his office, was Benjamin Mitchell. I wanted very much to meet Benjamin Mitchell. I was going back to the car when I saw coming towards me a small jaunty man, quick-stepping, sharp and serious of face, his hands deep in the pockets of an overcoat too long for him. I waited for him, smiling.

'Mr Mitchell?' I said. 'Mr Benjamin Mitchell?'

'No,' he said without breaking his stride, walking past me.

I hurried after him.

'Do you know where I can find Mr Mitchell?' I said.

'Never heard of him,' he said.

He walked to the end of the wharf, crossed a stile into the next field, and walked on. For a moment his brisk little figure stood against the sky. He didn't look back.

The following Saturday I went again. I drove through the coal merchant's yard, past the piles of shining fuel, past the dusty trucks. I saw nobody. I went through the fields and on to the wharf. Standing alone outside the office was my little, jaunty friend. He looked like a jockey, wrapped in his coat against the cold.

'Mr Mitchell not about?' I said.

'I don't know any Mr Mitchell,' he said.

I shrugged and walked away. The little man called me back.

'What do you want this Mr Mitchell for?' he said.

'I have a small cabin cruiser,' I said, 'and I'd like to moor it here.'

He took a large key out of his pocket and unlocked the shed door.

'In that case,' he said, 'I could be Mr Mitchell. Come into my office.'

I went inside. It was very clean. Two hard chairs stood against the wall and a bare table was placed under the window. A calendar, still showing January, hung on the wall.

'So you want to tie up your boat here, do you?' said Mr Mitchell. 'That can be arranged.'

We agreed the fees and I arranged to bring my boat. It was over in a few minutes.

'Thank you,' I said. 'I had begun to think I'd never get this done. I never saw anyone, even in the coal-yard.'

'Mine,' said Mr Mitchell. 'The coal-yard's mine.'

He seemed to think this was an explanation.

'Why didn't you let me have the mooring when we met last Thursday?' I said.

'I was watching you,' he said. 'Decided on Thursday to come and have a closer look at you. I'd seen you Monday, when you was here Monday. I'm a careful man. I like to have a good look at people, I like to know who I'm taking on. I could see you was nothing to do with the police, for example.'

He leaned back in his chair, looking at me sternly.

'Last thing we want is the police,' he said. 'Reasonable men don't need the police. I decided you and me could do business, and so we have. You pay me when you see me, I keep an eye on the boat for you. No harm to anybody, all very simple. Whatever I do, I take a good look at it first, a good long look.'

'It seems a good policy,' I said.

I've had the boat there ever since. I don't use it a lot, but I know it's safe.

Sometimes the sea off the South Coast is so calm you'd swear it has no life. It lies there, iridescent under the sun. There's no evidence of a tide, and you can wait too long for the splash of a lazy wave to flatten itself without energy on the beach. The world is still, dream-like, quiescent. On such days I walk the shore. You can see a long way out, but at the horizon you cannot see which is sky and which water. Dotted about on the brilliant flatness of the ocean are the black, unmoving shapes of the fishing boats, the sturdy one man craft that fish the inshore waters and set their lines of lobster pots. John Digby has one of these boats, and he's certain to be out there. I've known John Digby since he was a small boy.

I had an old car then, an Austin Devon that had done far too many miles. Most weekends I'd be under the car performing my amateur miracles. One day I crawled out and John Digby stood there, waiting for me to emerge. John and I often had long talks. He was a serious boy, about nine or ten at the time.

'Got time to come down the back fields, have you?' he said.

'Is it important?' I said. He nodded.

I wiped my hands on a rag and we set off, through my land, down the lane by Eddie Welland's house, into the fields. Three narrow fields, one following the other. A stream runs all the way through them.

'You'll like this,' John Digby said. 'You won't have seen anything like this.'

Just into the last thin field, close to the edge of stream, he showed me a mallard's nest, very simply made, built against a tuft of longer grass. It held ten or eleven pale eggs.

'Is that it?' I said.

'It's a start,' he said.

Turning away, he walked a dozen yards and showed me another nest, with fewer eggs. He was smiling, he had more to show me. In a small area he pointed out four nests, hidden in the grass.

'You don't often see so many nests so close together,' he said. 'Mallards usually pair up and their nests are pretty lonely.'

Then with triumphant modesty, like a great conjurer who destroys his previous miracles by performing an even greater illusion, he showed me yet another. Clinging tightly to the stream's bank, hard against a briar, the nest was covered with leaves and soft dry moss. With his hand the boy uncovered the eggs. I had never seen so many.

'Forty-two,' he said. 'I counted them. Four or five ducks are using this nest, young ones. These eggs won't be fertile. I bet you've never seen a nest like this before.'

'Never,' I said.

'I've been watching them,' John said. 'I come up every day. The ducks using this nest were late hatches last year. I keep an eye on them.'

'It's kind of you to let me see them,' I said. 'Thank you.'

'Nobody else knows,' he said. 'I haven't shown them to anybody else. I knew you wouldn't find them on your own.'

We walked back through the fields. As we left, a small flight of mallard feathered in behind us.

'I'm going into town this afternoon,' I said, 'if I can get the steering right. Would you like to come along?'

'Into town?' he said. He was a courteous boy, but his scorn was visible. 'What would I do in town? What is there to see?'

I've watched him grow up. He's a slow, tall man, long in the chin, not unlike his father. I used to go fishing with him and he was infinitely tolerant with me, making sure I got the best places, that my line was right, my bait properly set; but I don't go any more. I don't have the immense, casual, unbroken concentration that keeps him offshore through the night. I begin to watch the flakes and showers of phosphorescent light break off the black waves, I get restless.

'Do you know where we are, John?' I asked him, last time we were out.

'Of course,' he said, surprised.

'How can you tell?' I said.

He didn't answer for a while.

'I know the sea's paths,' he said. 'I know where the surface grows choppy and the colour of the water changes, I've done this so often I might as well have signposts out here, pointing out the way. I know where the rocks are, the sunk wrecks where the conger sits. I know where the sea bass and the cod run. It's just looking. All you need to be a fisherman is an eye. It's just like when you walk the streets, you know them. You've watched them.'

Sometimes John Digby brings back bass or a lobster to the back door. He'll stand talking for ten minutes. When he leaves he'll know that I've moved the onion bed, that I have a larger light fixture in the garage. He'll know that I have a new sweater, that I've put on seven pounds, that a tile on my roof needs fixing.

All you need is an eye.

When I came out of Bell Hall it was still raining, the insidious West Coast rain so persistent that people ignore it, don't talk about it. I walked up the road with Al Norman, my worried student. Al didn't know whether to go to Boulder or Aspen when the quarter ended. I know nothing of either place, but they have great names, like Samarkand, or Tashkent. I liked being a visiting writer, I enjoyed reading the work the students handed in each week with such proud trepidation. When classes changed, Al usually walked with me to the car park. He was a little older than most students, a truck driver who had come back to school.

'What do you want to do there, Al' I said, 'in Aspen or Boulder?'

'I'll find something,' he said. 'I have friends in both cities. It won't take long.'

I shook my head at the footloose American young, taking off at a touch for distant places. I imagined them, roaming all over the world, their back-packs neat and proficiently balanced. The rain began to trickle down my neck.

'What about your writing?' I said. 'Do you intend to continue?'

'Oh, I hope so,' said Al, so earnestly I knew he wasn't sure.

We stopped outside the library. Hundreds of students were milling about, rushing to classes. Among them, removed from them, remote, tall and exquisitely dressed, perfectly dry under his wide umbrella, walked Stanley Carter, on his way to take a graduate class in modern fiction. He was very distinguished and looked it. Every day, as we passed, we exchanged greetings, a few words, a wave of the hand. But now he stopped, looked at me with amusement, and said, 'Arthur, you look totally foreign'.

In an instant I was aware of my navy raincoat made in Sweden and bought at Marks and Spencers, Oxford Street. I felt the strangeness of the plain brown shoes I had worn all over England, the uniqueness, in that place, of the woollen shirt woven at a small mill in Dyfed, in Wales. In an instant I could see the thousands of miles that stretched between me and what I knew most about.

'Dammit, Stanley,' I said, 'I am foreign.'

He laughed, gave a little bow, and walked serenely to his class. Al, ducking into the library, had been amused at this confrontation. I saw him grinning to himself as he disappeared through the door. But I, walking to my car, was elated. I strode forward through the blown threads of the rain, under the constant drip from the trees, and I felt fine. What instinct had suggested to Stanley Carter so unerringly accurate a word?

'Foreign,' I said, rolling it around my tongue, 'foreign.'

It had a marvellous feel to it, it was exotic and mysterious, it was a match for Boulder, or Colorado. Or, for that matter, Tashkent.

Katherine and I were staying at a little place not far from Bristol, in Vermont. We had been there three weeks when Paul O'Brien telephoned.

'Stay with us in Boston,' he said, 'before you leave for England.'

Paul is a writer and a good one. We've known him for years and he and Margaret have often stayed with us. He's relaxed and cosy, a great wit and a great friend.

'Tom Bridge is in town,' he said, 'and wants to meet you. Can't think why. We'll have a party.'

I put the telephone down and thought about Tom Bridge. Through the years I'd seen his books appear, watched his fame grow; but after that first astounding paragraph from *The End of August* I had read nothing of his. I looked through the shelves of our borrowed house and came up with a book of verse I hadn't known Bridge had written, a paperback copy of that first amazing novel, a collection of short stories called *Relics*, and two late novels. I sat down and read them all through, at a sitting. It took me far into the night. Afterwards I went to bed and didn't sleep. My mind was full of Tom Bridge's people, the cars they drove, the houses they lived in, the theatres and galleries they visited. I knew the sort of meals they ate. Out there, in the states I had never seen, their old parents waited, I knew, for letters and telephone calls. He could make even the unconsidered blades of his grass as real and solid as those in the perceived world.

We had a fine party at Paul's. He knows a lot of interesting people and the house was full of good laughter. Bridge came late, very cool, alone. He was a tall man, his fair hair turning grey, the skin on his high cheekbones smooth and pink. He didn't talk much, but his listening was both courteous and intense. He stood, it seemed, at the edge of action, within earshot, never involved. We spoke so little to each other that I was surprised to receive, a few days later, a letter in which he praised something I'd written, said he'd been pleased to meet me. It was a very formal letter.

Tom Bridge is a very formal man. I've never seen him dressed other than in a dark suit, his shirt immaculate, his tie decorous. We meet every time I visit Boston. We may even be friends, but it's hard to know. Last time we met we all went to see the Red Sox play. I've developed a passion for that aggravating team. Paul and I were partisan and noisy, but Tom Bridge sat erect and silent, missing nothing. I know that he was storing away every flicker of light, every sound, every manifestation of human action so that he could transfer whatever he wanted into the little perfect worlds he made for his stories. It's a strange, an admirable talent. Afterwards, that evening, we went as guests of George Stanwell, an enviably rich man from New York, to a restaurant.

It was a fine restaurant, the service tactful, the light perfect, neither too brilliant for conversation nor too dim for us to see each other. The prices, though, were comically high. Katherine signalled her amusement to me. Nothing escapes Tom Bridge. He leaned gently towards her and said very quietly, 'Order what you like. The Stanwells are very rich indeed.' That was nearly all he said during the evening.

We came out after midnight and stood in Commonwealth Avenue, looking for a cab. The Stanwells had taken their car and gone. Tom Bridge was saying his goodbyes.

'Good evening,' he said gravely, 'Mr and Mrs Metcalfe. Good evening Mr and Mrs O'Brien.'

His face was a white blur in the night, with nothing, not even the flare of a match, to bring it out of the darkness. He turned and, in one step, he couldn't be seen at all.

The Holm Oak

They left Southampton through Eastleigh and Chandler's Ford. The traffic was heavier than he had anticipated. A new layout, badly signposted, machines like sleeping animals at the roadside, let them bypass Winchester. Most of the trucks went north on the London road and driving was quieter on the A34. It had rained after dawn and surfaces were steaming in the early sun. Just before Newbury, near Beacon Hill, they stopped for a flask of coffee. Humps of small tumuli, round and smooth, stood nearby in the ancient fields. They disturbed Rhodri. He was not of their time, nor of their place. The bones in those old graves were alien to him. The gentle country, almost treeless, brought him no warmth. Elizabeth sat in the car, relaxed, smiling so faintly that he alone could know it. He drove on towards the M4.

He took the slope to the motorway and his wife, turning to the rear window, told him all was clear.

'Not a thing in sight,' Elizabeth said. 'Not a thing.'

She was suddenly alert, consciously enjoying the journey. He sidled the car across the empty road into the fast lane, slick as oil through the gears, accelerating.

'Not bad,' Elizabeth said, 'that's the best bit of driving you've done today.'

'I know,' he said. 'I did it from memory. I used to climb that ramp every Friday night when my father was ill, so my hands just took over.'

Ahead of them, appearing and reappearing among the undulations of the road, files of small cars, five or six at a time, keeping together as if for protection, scurried westwards.

'Every Friday I did it,' Rhodri said, 'for over three years. One summer I drove the Alfa Romeo. What a car. Sammy told me when I bought it I should have bought a mechanic to go with it. It never let me down on this journey, otherwise it was utterly hopeless. British racing green, it was. I used to come down this road, ninety, ninety-five, roaring like a lion.'

'What happened to it?' said Elizabeth. She'd heard it before. She liked him to talk when he was driving.

'I gave it to a fellow in the math department,' Rhodri said, 'Gary Lewis, bright lad, good with cars. I'd had enough. It blew up in Portland Terrace and I pushed it into a side street. I never saw it

again. This car's a bit different, though. This is luxury. Good of
Sara to lend it.'

'She'd lend you her arms and legs,' Elizabeth said, 'she thinks
you're perfect.'

Rhodri saw his sister, nine years old again, her long, thin legs, her
hair rioting, her angular, frightening energy. Every day she had taken
him to school, fierce and protective, his hand grasped in her hard
hand. The day he had fallen out of an apple tree in Thomas's
orchard, she had lifted him into the old man's wheelbarrow and
pushed him all the way home, both of them bawling. Once she had
stood between Rhodri and the headmaster, when the man had
threatened punishment. She had stood there tensely, not moving,
full of quiet fury. Griffiths, the man's name had been, Mr Griffiths,
a tall, fair man. He had turned away, helpless against her, amused
and chagrined. Sara had been thirteen then.

Fine rain began to fall as they crossed the Severn Bridge, but the
roads were drying and the washed fields green and fresh when they
left the motorway near Chepstow and travelled quiet ways to Usk.
The northern slopes of the Beacons were already shadowed with
purple, the river, silver under a reflected sky, ran on benignly.

'It looks lovely, doesn't it?' Rhodri said. 'The great, comfortable
flanks of Mother Earth, the green valley below them. But in winter
those hills are killers. Remember Margaret Harris?'

'No,' said Elizabeth. 'Before my time probably.'

'I didn't know her,' Rhodri said. 'Her brother Aled was at the
university with me. She was a district nurse in these parts, visited
the sick in their homes, mothers with new babies, that sort of thing.
She went out one winter morning to one of the hill farms, the snow
came, blotted everything out. They found her a few yards from her
car, frozen to death. It's not only the cold, it's the wind that goes
with it.'

Below them, at the river's edge, two anglers, unmoving as heron,
watched their lines float down the lazy stream.

A neighbour had lit a fire in the grate when they reached the old
house, but it had done nothing to disperse the heavy smell of damp
which filled the rooms. An uncomfortable chill soon depressed
Rhodri. But for a few weeks in August, the house was rarely used.
Elizabeth threw open the doors, pulled down the windows. A thin
blue film of neglect covered the floors, the sills, the arms and backs
of chairs. After their father's death Sara had taken the best of the
furniture, the round dining table and its eight chairs, the Georgian
corner cupboard, good Swansea china which had belonged to their

great-grandmother, the long-case clock which showed not only the time, but the phases of the moon. Sara had all these. They shone in her immaculate house in Southampton, under her guardian eye. What was left was workaday stuff, familiar to Rhodri as the skin of his hands. The big pine table, its top scrubbed white in his mother's day, was grey now. Inexplicable stains were sunk deep in the soft wood. They had eaten at this table. He had run home from school knowing that it would be covered with the great meals of his mother's kitchen, loaves straight from the oven, salt bacon, pies and cakes. Afterwards, all cleared away, it was there he sat doing his homework, the house quiet and warm, an oil lamp hanging in a shaped metal bracket from the ceiling, another, the liquid visible in the ruby glass of its bowl, behind his books. Electricity had been late arriving at the farm. His father would have been reading in his wooden armchair, awkwardly at one side so that his dog Cymro, one-eyed, testy and much loved, could sit with him. Now the chair stood in its dust against the wall. It was a dead house.

Outside the air was warm and very still. Several farms away a dog barked, without anger. The brown remains of February snowdrops lay withered in the grass opposite the front door. Rhodri leaned on the gate into the top field. The land fell away in a gentle slope and the far hedge was hidden, but for the big oak.

His father had loved the one tree. It was an evergreen oak, a holm oak, the only one, they had believed, in the county. The last of the sunlight was falling on its glossy leaves.

Once, a small boy, he had found his father standing under the tree. He had climbed through the fields from the river and his father was standing in the deep shade of the tree. He was completely still, his head bowed, his outstretched hand just touching the tree's bark. His eyes, Rhodri had seen, were open. There was about the man's stillness an absence which had frightened the little boy. Rhodri had gone home troubled, and now the memory, coming to him unasked, made him fretful and anxious. He lifted the cases from the car and carried them indoors.

'The beds are fine,' Elizabeth said. 'Mrs Evans has kept them beautifully aired. We shan't catch pneumonia.'

She looked about her, assessing what was to be done before she would think the house warm and comfortable. A little elbow-grease, she thought, a little paint. It could be worse.

'Come and have your supper,' she said.

The morning, perfect as memory, brought its peace to Rhodri.

Together, he and Elizabeth restored the house to order, swept the floors, began to clean the windows. The late spring air, mild and clear, invaded the rooms and passages, refreshed them. When, after lunch, Phil Rees stopped his Land Rover in the yard, Rhodri went cheerfully to meet him. Phil had been in the same class in the village school. They had known each other for over thirty years. Once, when they were eight or nine, they had been two of a group of children wildly excited because school had just ended for the summer holidays. They had marched, singing and laughing and waving sticks pulled from the hedge, along the road, down the lane past the farm, down the hill and up the other side, exulting, not stopping until they returned to the village. For Rhodri, a shy boy, almost without friends, it had been a vision. It had seemed to him then that he had never seen such colours, heard such voices, known such excitement. Phil Rees had worn a jersey of so clear a blue that Rhodri knew he would never see its like again. But now Phil was a heavy man, round-shouldered, shrewd. He climbed out of the Land Rover.

'Welcome home, Rhodri,' he said. 'How long are you down for?' He walked to the field gate and leaned his arms on the top spar, his movements slow, deliberate.

'Your grass looks good,' he said. 'Young Mervyn keeps the grass very well for you.'

Together they looked across the grass, vivid and weedless.

'There used to be wild orchids in this field in my father's day,' Rhodri said.

'Selective weedkillers nowadays,' Phil said. 'They keep the grass wonderfully clean. And let's face it, your Dad didn't mind a few odd weeds on his land.'

Rhodri smiled. It was true. His father had kept his pastures untouched, but for a little fertilizer. He had loved the purple orchises, old inhabitants of the fields.

'Not the best of farmers,' said Phil, 'but we miss him. He's been dead — seven years, is it? — and we all miss him.'

'Remember the time he tried to start a herd of Jerseys?' said Phil. 'Jerseys, up here? He had no chance.'

'He liked quality,' Rhodri said. 'He couldn't stand an animal without a touch of class.'

'Well, we miss him,' Phil said. 'He was the brightest man for miles around, always reading. He knew about music and medicine. When I was a kid he taught me the names of the stars. He was the man we went to when there was trouble.'

'He was a fine man,' Rhodri said.

'Like a lawyer,' Phil said. 'We need him now, with all these EEC rules for milk farmers. He would have filled the forms in for us, gone down to Carmarthen to represent us. We've been sadly helpless since he's gone.'

Rhodri nodded at his old friend. He knew how involved his father had been in the small community.

'Oh, we all depended on him,' Phil said. 'He could talk to anyone. He would just put his old hat on his head, and he was as good as any man. He was an aristocrat.'

'There must be someone else,' Rhodri said.

'Not like your father,' Phil said quickly. 'Your Sara could have done it, but she had to go off to be a doctor. And you, you look like your father, you're tall and slow-moving and like him in the face, but you never cared for the place. You were always going to be a stranger.'

'That's not true, Phil,' Rhodri said. He was more deeply hurt than he had imagined possible.

'Look at you,' said Phil, 'in your expensive clothes, your shirt, your soft pullover, your American shoes. You don't begin to look as if you belong here.'

'You resent me,' said Rhodri. 'By God, Phil, you resent me coming back.'

'I'm sorry,' said Phil. 'I shouldn't have said that. You have to go where your work is, I suppose. But I pass this house four times every day and I see its blind windows and I think of the cobwebs building up inside. There aren't any voices, not of people or animals. It isn't right. There you are in America and the house is falling down. The rain only has to get in under the slates and it's finished. Why don't you sell it?'

'It's been our house for more than three hundred years,' Rhodri said, 'I couldn't.'

'It's useless as it is,' said Phil. 'A young man could make a good living in it. Think of a strong youngster now, with his wife and a child or two, what he could do with this place. The land's in good heart, let it go.'

Rhodri, conscious of anger, did not answer.

'Seven years ago,' Phil said, 'I saw your father by that old oak of his. I'd have had it down years ago, if it had been mine. He was looking very rough, yellow in the face, moving slow and painful. What's up, Mr Llewellyn, I said. He told me then he was dying, that he had cancer. He knew all about it. We stood there in the field and we talked, man to man.'

'I know that,' Rhodri said. 'I've always been jealous of that. To talk to him as you did and under those circumstances was my right. I am his son.'

'That day I was his son,' Phil said. 'A man can be another man's son, and in his turn he can be another man's father, when the need is there. You were in New York, and I was here.'

Elizabeth sat in her clean house. She could do no more until they decided what was to be redecorated. The floors gleamed, the cupboards were neat, everything was in its place.

'I see Phil's in good voice,' she said.

'You didn't come out,' Rhodri said. 'He would have liked to speak to you.'

'I thought you were involved in some serious talking,' Elizabeth said. 'Your face was black as thunder.'

'He wants me to sell the farm,' Rhodri said.

'What did he say?' Elizabeth said. Her voice was tranquil, very neutral.

'This has always been our place,' Rhodri said. 'He knows that.'

He sat in his father's chair, his legs stretched before him, trying consciously to relax, to appear as if he were not upset.

'He seemed to think that I have a duty to the community to make sure someone lived here,' he said querulously.

'He has a point,' Elizabeth said. 'We can't use the place, we don't need it. Once we get back to New York we never think of it.'

'I don't have to think of it,' Rhodri said, 'I know it's here, always.'

'Oh, come away,' Elizabeth said. 'I've seen you. You can't wait to get back to your laboratory.'

The fire was burning freely and generously, the last of the old apple wood, cut years ago and stored in the shed. When evening came it would dance away the shadows in the corners of the room, it would easily keep away the cold which would come as the sun went down.

'Phil had a good word for my father,' said Rhodri, 'blamed me for not being as good a man.'

'He was remarkable,' Elizabeth said. 'So handsome, so tolerant. I found some of his old diaries in the dresser drawer and I've been reading them. He was brilliantly able. He was wasted here.'

'That's not what Phil thinks,' Rhodri said. 'He thinks they need someone like him, they still miss him.'

'I don't doubt it,' Elizabeth said, 'but if you've read those year-books of his. Oh, how tragic, that evidence of an intelligence searching without guidance, his vast chaotic reading, his amazing information. His insights were often splendid, and often hopelessly wrong. Imagine what he could have done, given an education.'

'I know,' Rhodri said. 'For years he was convinced that the world was six thousand years old, then he discovered archaeology. And there he was, into carbon dating and all the rest of it. He used to stay up into the early hours reading my math books.'

'He wasn't going to have you like that,' Elizabeth said.

'No,' said Rhodri. 'He pointed me at a university the day I started school, and Sara before me.'

'He was wise as well as clever,' Elizabeth said. 'He was locked into this place. He was going to make sure you were free. How delighted he would be to know of the concerts and plays you go to, that you've heard all the great tenors, seen Olivier and Guinness.'

'Olivier was his idol,' Rhodri said. 'When I saw him in *Othello* years ago I sent my father a full account, theatre programme, everything. He kept all my letters. I suppose they're still here, somewhere.'

'Sara has them,' Elizabeth said. 'She has this foolish idea that one day you'll be a great man and she can edit a collection of your letters.'

Rhodri smiled, leaned back, looked thoughtfully at his long hands as they lay idle on the arms of the chair.

'I'd have to offer it to Mervyn first,' he said. 'If ever I sold this place. He might not want the house though, he's not married.'

'He's only twenty-four, give him time,' Elizabeth said. 'It's not a bad idea. He's kept the fields well for so young a man. And he is your cousin, it isn't as if it were going right away.'

'His mother was my mother's cousin,' Rhodri said. 'He's not a Llewellyn.'

'What's it matter?' Elizabeth said, with sudden passion. 'Can't you see your father wanted away from this place, made sure his children got away? What is there for you here? Sell it, rent it, give it away, we don't need the money. Forty-six acres of thin topsoil on a hill. If someone needs it, can live on it, can start three centuries of a family on it, let them have it. We, you and I are at the end of the line, transient. The land will always be here, but we shan't.'

Rhodri stood abruptly, grinning down at his wife, her flushed and ardent face.

'What are you going to do?' she asked.

He shrugged his shoulders, pulled down the corners of his rueful mouth. 'I don't know,' he said.

He went out into the field and looked west. The holm oak was dark against the end of the sun. He walked towards it and looked at it carefully. He knew it from its topmost leaf to the grass about its base. There, he said, is the snag on which I used to climb into its branches, there the limb to which Sara climbed to tie a rope. She had fastened an old tyre to the rope and it had been their swing for years. He walked about the tree, noting it. It was an act of something more than mere recognition; he knew the tree. He knew every inch of its bark, the shape and substance of its regenerating head, the quality of its dead leaves as they fell to the grass, the sturdy thrust of its trunk, the noise it made in storms. He knew that it grew within him with the same accuracy and certainty and stubborn reality, that he was aware of the great claws of its roots, grasping the land he had always thought his own.

He closed his eyes. The tree was still with him. He could not imagine any power strong enough to uproot it.

Reverse for Dennis

Once a year, on the first day of March, on St David's Day, we held in our school an eisteddfod, a celebration and performance of those arts and that culture for which the Welsh are held to be pre-eminent. It was quite popular with the boys. Preparations for the event disrupted the orderly procedure of the school throughout the dark month of February, and a clever boy, entering a shrewd selection of events, could wander at will about the damp corridors for weeks on end, pretending here that he was on his way to recite Kipling's 'If' to an eager committee of listeners in the library, and claiming there that he was going to collect his sheaf of water colours, a late entry for the fine art section. Above all, the ebullient competitive spirit which lay uneasily dormant within us was stimulated into constructive action. Serious boys could be heard muttering aloud the sculptured periods of their speeches, learned boys searched the pages of *The Shorter Oxford English Dictionary* for words absurd and recondite enough to cause gasps of amazement on the day. Some of us gave up, temporarily, our more normal activities, fighting, football, the cunning evasion of all serious and responsible behaviour.

I was quite good at the eisteddfod business, if for an unlikely reason. Unwilling to expose myself to the good-humoured public banter of my fellows, I did not enter the singing competitions, or the verse speaking, or even the impromptu speech, the real motivation of which was the subtle introduction of as many double-entendres as possible. The best speakers never reached the finals of this event. My friend Arthur Purcell, whose grandfather was a local politician noted for polysyllabic eloquence, was marvellous at the impromptu speech. Only Michael Cleary could equal him. Their wild, irreverent humour, their wayward scorn, their biting awareness of every weakness of the ruling dynasty of our establishment, ensured their regular abrupt dismissal from the competition. Michael Cleary left school early, running away to work in a racing stable where he soon became a steeplechase jockey. Occasionally he would send us photographs of himself being spectacularly separated from a horse as it collapsed in mid-air above some disastrous fence or other. He was a great loss to us all. But Arthur Purcell remained, the sharp barbs of his wit growing more bitter and outrageous. Nobody was immune from his sudden, puncturing sallies.

It was the written competitions I made my territory. These were entered anonymously, our identities hidden by noms-de-plumes. I excelled in the manufacture of such aliases, loved the discovery of the many masks I used. It is true that my enthusiasm meant that I had to write essay upon essay, poem after poem, in order to employ the names I invented, but I would not abandon them. So the Tutankhamun Kid would provide a hurried ode on the mutability of the seasons, Boudoir of Splendid Petals a superficial defence of belligerence as an art, K. Ataturk III some wry platitudes about the necessity of civilization. Once, by error, I won the essay prize for fifteen-year-olds. The judge, a retired man of letters, unsmiling, dry in every joint, announced the negative qualities which had induced him — in an admittedly bad year — to award me first place. 'First then,' he had said, holding my pages at arm's length, between thumb and finger, 'First is *Oblomov Rides Again*. Whoever he may be.' I stood up with a casual modesty designed to deceive nobody and acknowledged my identity. 'A great thing, but mine own,' said Arthur Purcell, kicking me on the ankle with just enough force to enable me to hold back a cry of pain. And all about me my friends mimed horrified and exaggerated surprise. The next year, as Felis Concolor Couguar, a character I had discovered in a life of John James Audubon, I won the poetry competition with some energetic lines about a cat. This was my greatest triumph. In fact, Couguar's poem was not bad at all. He had modified it with some skill from a poem by D.H. Lawrence.

The literary events were always decided in the morning of St David's Day; musical competitions took place during the afternoon and evening. We sat, the afternoon of Couguar's victory, listening to choir upon choir, to solo violins, to oboes, flutes and harps, to the smirking vocalists. I remember none of them. Late in the day, when we could see only the darkness of evening through the high windows, and dim lights hung from the beams above us, a young man got up to announce the results of the musical composition. Our composers had been asked to set, for voice and piano accompaniment, 'To Daffodils', by Robert Herrick. Arthur Purcell and I had read this poem and we preferred not to think about it. In our opinion, to set it to music was an occupation for idiots. But one competitor, said the young man, had done it brilliantly. His nom-de-plume, he announced was *Sinned*. A connoisseur of such disguises, I was stunned by the implications of this one, by its brevity, by the force and subtlety of its attack. I sat up. Who could it be? 'I think,' said the Headmaster briskly, 'we can guess who this is. It's

Dennis Williams, isn't it. He's written his name backwards.' I recognised this as an act of genius. He had transformed his mild, placatory, given name, the name of a saint, into a monosyllable of unseemly power.

I had seen Dennis Williams many times before, but had never really looked at him. He stood, tall and slender, perhaps a year older than I was. His smooth pale face was closed and tranquil, he was smiling very gently to himself. He wore a coat of speckled Irish tweed and grey worsted trousers, beautifully cut, very expensive. His hair, thick and wavy and parted on the left, was a vivid and truculent red. 'A contemporary sensibility,' said the judge, 'an exciting talent, a gift for the unexpected phrase.' Dennis Williams gazed thoughtfully at some spot on the far wall. Asked to go to the piano to play the accompaniment, he shrugged slightly and walked through the rows of seated boys as if he did not see them. He carried always with him his own agreeable solitude.

His soloist was Idwal Rowlands, a hulking boy whose voice remained, despite his fifteen years, a pure and flawless soprano. He was six feet tall, and solid. His face was a choirboy's face, round, pink and sincere, and comically irrelevant above his brawny frame. Beside me Arthur Purcell, struck afresh by the incongruity of that ill-matched voice and body, shook with stifled laughing. I looked at Dennis Williams as he began to play. He struck from the keys a handful of jeering chords and a tinkle of dissonance. Idwal Rowlands wrinkled his clear brow and prepared to sing. 'Fair daffodils,' he piped, 'we weep to see You haste away so soon; As yet the early-rising sun Has not attain'd his noon.' All about me, affected by Arthur's snorted giggles, boys were staring glassy-eyed and rosy in their efforts not to laugh. Spike Hughes had stuffed his handkerchief into his mouth. 'Stay, stay until the hasting day,' carolled enormous Idwal, oblivious of us all. Then suddenly we became aware, nearly all of us, of the piano. Alongside the dulcet melody, almost a parody of the sweet noise of the words, Dennis Williams was playing a sharp and mocking accompaniment, pointed, jagged, telling us something of a sturdy despair at once profound and full of energy. It was an astonishing experience. Our applause was puzzled, respectful. Afterwards I went up to Dennis and told him how much I had liked the song. He gave the faintest indication of a smile, said nothing. I would like to claim that Dennis Williams had been my friend, but it would not be true. Quiet, amiable, impregnably self-sufficient, he seemed alone even when with other boys. He moved, tall and relaxed, on the edges of my life, where we nodded to each other. Once I saw him rowing, alone, on the lake at the edge of the school grounds, and I waved to him. He brought in his heavy boat, spinning the oars expertly, and invited me to join him. As I stepped into the boat I saw his large, nimble hands, the thickness of his long wrists. We didn't say much, just moved without effort over the simple water, above the weeds, above the still trout. That was a perfect afternoon, one preserved against time. And once, walking through the small park behind Wesley Street, I came upon Dennis sitting on a bench, his long legs stretched before him, his eyes almost shut against his cool knowledge. He was eighteen then. I thought him cultivated and experienced far beyond my achievement.

That evening my cousin Sara met me in High Street. 'I didn't know,' she said, 'that you were a friend of Dennis Williams.' It was almost an accusation. 'I'm not,' I said. 'Don't be silly,' she said, 'I saw you in the park this afternoon. Talking together, the pair of you, thick as thieves.' The world to her was uncomplicated and direct, she sparkled with energy. 'Maybe,' I said, 'but we aren't friends. We just talk to each other sometimes.' I looked at her doubtfully. It was the sort of inane statement she would not accept. But she was gazing past me with a look of ethereal greed. 'He's lovely,' she said, 'dreamy.' I was appalled. Such behaviour was frighteningly untypical of Sara. 'You're mad,' I said. She didn't answer. 'Dreamy!' I sneered. 'So handsome,' Sara said. I thought about it for a while and could not agree. I objected. 'His hair is red,' I said. 'What's that got to do with it, fool,' said Sara, and she turned away to walk up the road with bustling, confident steps.

Well, Dennis Williams had a lot of class, I recognised that. His father was a doctor, rich and popular. Dennis always dressed beautifully, he took long holidays abroad, he was generous and softspoken. I could see what Sara meant. In September he was going to medical school. I saw him, late in August, walking over the golf course with his Airedale, Max. He had an old walking-stick which he threw for the dog to retrieve. I've always liked Airedales and Max was a good one. No longer young, grey was beginning to fleck the black of his saddle, but he still ran like a puppy after that stick. Dennis took it from the dog and waited at the edge of a bunker for me to come up to them. He told me then he was going to Edinburgh to study medicine. 'My father went there,' he said. 'I've always wanted to be a doctor.' It was a hot evening. The course was deserted but for three figures on a distant green. We could hear them laughing. 'That's great, Dennis,' I said. I bent down to pat the old dog. 'What about your music?' I said. 'I thought you were keen on music.' Dennis was scratching his initials into the sandy turf with the ferrule of his stick. Faintly, patiently, with infinite care, so that I could scarcely see the letters. 'Music?' he said. 'That's just playing about, isn't it!' And then, with a sudden irritation he ripped through the impeccable D and W until the scored grass held no trace of them.

I don't know what went wrong at Edinburgh. I was busy with my own affairs, growing older, learning to be cool and fashionable, to be amused at everything. But in the spring and early summer of the next year I began to see Dennis about, and someone told me that he was no longer going to be a doctor, that he had given up medical school and was working in a lawyer's office. I knew the place. My friend, Willie John Edwards, was a junior clerk there. Whenever I saw him, Dennis looked all right; I mean he looked happy, in control. We didn't say much to each other. I asked Willie John about Dennis. 'He's strange,' Willie John said. 'He's so quiet. He'll be in the office an hour before you know he's there. Doesn't talk, doesn't whistle. If you make a joke, he just smiles. He's a nice, strange fellow.' 'He's always been like that,' I said. 'He's bright,' Willie John told me. 'He's very bright. He'll make a good lawyer, everybody says so.' It was just a casual conversation I had with Willie John one day when we were playing tennis. Frankly, I didn't think about Dennis very often.

But it was a shock when I learned he was dead. That August, in the year I was eighteen, I went to London for a fortnight, to stay with my aunt in Dulwich Village. I was going to the university that next term. I took to London, had a great time, saw all the galleries, most of the theatres, two famous athletics meetings at The White City. I was reluctant to go home. The day I travelled back was wickedly hot. I hung about in Cardiff waiting for a train to carry me through the narrowing valleys and everything was dry, powdered with dust. Children sat in whatever little pools of shade they could find, and the city drowsed. I reached the last station in late afternoon and humped my bag into the yard. There was no taxi and I walked two miles to the house, uphill all the way. I think of that walk with surprise now, but it was nothing to me then. I could have walked twenty miles without fatigue. There was no one at home. I made myself a meal, took a shower, went out into the lengthening evening. Down town I saw Harry Pritchard, a boy I'd known for years. Harry was very surprising; in less than twelve months he'd grown from one of the smallest boys around into a thin giant of six feet three inches. He'd not long joined the police force. 'Coming to the cinema?' he said. 'It's cool, and there's a smashing double feature — "The Mummy" and "The Return of Frankenstein".' 'Oh Harry,' I said, 'your appetite for the Gothic is voracious and unsubtle.' 'Sticks and stones,' he said contentedly. 'Come on, I'll buy you an ice-cream.'

The cinema was almost empty. It was pleasant there in the cool gloom.

'What about your friend, then?' Harry said. 'What about poor Dennis Williams?'

'What about him?' I said. I was thinking of the colossal technique of an American hurdler I'd seen at The White City. He'd risen like a bird to every obstacle, his stride unchecked, his rhythm smooth and effortless. He had won by a distance.

'Come on,' Harry said, 'don't pretend you haven't heard.'

'I've been up in London,' I said. 'Didn't get back until six o'clock. Tell me all.'

'He's dead,' Harry said. 'Dead and buried. He gassed himself over a week ago, nearly a fortnight ago. Silly little fool, no need for it.'

I sat there, looking at the frivolous horror on the screen. 'Why did he do it?' I said.

'Absolutely no need,' said Harry roughly. I could hear the indignation in his voice.

'Some girl,' he said, 'told him she was pregnant and he was responsible. You'd think he'd have gone along to somebody, for help, for advice. We don't live in the Dark Ages, for God's sake.'

'Dennis wouldn't go to anybody,' I said. 'He was always his own man, he'd come to his own decisions. He always seemed to me to be sufficient to himself.'

'He was a fool, then,' said Harry. 'How did he know the girl was telling the truth? She could have been mistaken. Why didn't he go to his father? His father's a doctor, he'd know what to do.'

I didn't answer. I was helpless in the dark of the cinema, unable to understand. 'He had a lot of style,' I said at last. 'Dennis would have done it with style. It would have been a superb gesture.' I didn't mean anything. It was an attempt to claim for Dennis his individuality, his singular quality, a defence in my mind against the tragedy of his action.

But it made Harry angry. He leaned over and began to mutter vehemently to me. 'Style, is it!' he said, very quietly and quickly. 'Style? — it was a hideous and ugly suicide, that's what it was. Do you know who found him? Willie John Edwards found him. Willie John, without an ounce of harm in him. There's not much style about that.' He sat back, outraged.

'Oh,' I said, surprised. 'It happened in the office.'

'Yes,' said Harry. 'He went in on the Sunday evening, late, and he wasn't found until Willie John opened the doors on Monday morning.'

'Poor old boy,' I said, pitying both of them.

'He was in a terrible mess,' Harry Pritchard said, 'terrible. They go an inhuman colour, did you know that?'

'No,' I said. I could see Dennis Williams playing "To Daffodils", hear Idwal Rowlands's sad, high voice. It seemed a long time ago. 'And his hair,' Harry Pritchard said, 'that lovely red hair of his. It had turned quite dark. When they carried him out I saw his hair had turned dark.'

Then I knew that Dennis Williams was indeed dead, that he had gone from the world for ever. It was the detail of the hair that got me. We sat in the electronic darkness for a long time, silent, unmoving. 'Oh hell,' Harry said, 'this is a miserable old world. Why don't we go out into the daylight and look at it?' We walked out and the sun still shone. Two little boys, perhaps ten or eleven years old, passed us, laughing, their arms brown as summer.

Gamblers

On the hills outside the town, near the river and, further out, on the bleak moor, lie bundles of enormous masonry. The gaunt towers, the unlit, vaulting arches, the great walls of cut stone, are ruined and empty, their heavy margins flawed and irregular where parts have tumbled away. When I was a kid I used often to stand near a single fallen block, looking at it. It was a frowning grey, grass grew about its edges, a golden lichen furred its tiny crevices. Sometimes I'd climb on top of it, lie back, stare to the tops of the dark walls around, ominous, heavy, without purpose. I could not imagine any use for them at all. They were all that remained of the iron works which had been the reason for the town. I had never seen them working. Perhaps there were old men who had known this, perhaps they had worked there.

I used to wander often about the works, particularly on gloomy days when the sky had the colour and something of the weight of those dull stone ruins and the rain beat without ceasing on those streaming walls. I knew the galleries, their floors covered with a soft dust of powdered limestone mortar, I had examined the cogwheels, taller than I was, rust-covered, much too heavy to think of shifting, that lay abandoned and broken against the walls of mills and cooling-towers. It was in the works that I learned to fix a night line. One of the streams coming off the mountain had been channelled underground beneath a maze of ovens and engine rooms. It emerged just below the works, through a low tunnel. You could follow it, walking along a ledge of stone deep into the mountain, your hand on the exquisite, damp curve of the arched roof, until your nerve failed. I never went in far. Some people said there were rats in there. One warm day, sitting on the grass at the tunnel's mouth, I saw three trout swim out of the darkness. Easy and sinuous, they lay facing the current. The water was so clear that I could see their freckled colours, their red and black spots. An uncle of mine showed me how to set a night line. Every evening I'd get a few yards inside the tunnel, my baited hook ready, tie the line to a nail I'd hammered into the wall, lower the line gently into the water. A couple of lead shot about eighteen inches up from the hook kept the worm in an enticingly natural position. I've caught many a breakfast that way. But that was years later. The only other people to use the old works as much as I did were the gamblers.

There is a sense in which life itself was a gamble in our town. Hardly a man had work. In the whole length of our street, only two men could say they were employed, yet there was an air of urgency about the place, and a reckless, bitter gaiety. People kept busy. Many of them were serious gamblers; undeterred by lack of money, they could speak with authority of blood-lines and handicaps, were walking libraries of form, knew the idiosyncrasies of all the race tracks in England, not one of which they had ever seen. They used to lay complex and intricate bets, trebles, accumulators, little side bets on the way, their ramifications causing hours of study and demanding a mastery of reckoning that accountants could envy, and all for an outlay of sixpence. Using matches for stakes, or perhaps cigarettes cut in halves, they would play card games of desperate intensity and skill. They searched for evidence of good fortune wherever they thought it could be found, in racing, in decks of cards, in the spin of a coin. The first gambler I knew was Owen Doherty.

The Dohertys lived near us, and Owen was the oldest of nine boys. He was shabby and elegant, walking slowly and straight-backed through the world, his thin, Irish face with its high cheekbones expressionless. I never saw Owen Doherty laugh at anything that was funny, although occasionally he'd give a high sharp bark of contempt at any opinion he thought particularly futile. He was much older than I, over twenty years older. I admired him because he was the best pitch-and-toss player in the district.

The young men used to play pitch-and-toss with pennies, or more probably half-pence, in a narrow lane behind the houses. I used to go down and watch them. From time to time, when I was very small, they'd send me away, since the game was illegal, liable to be interrupted by a patrolling policeman, and I at five or six would be a handicap to them and a source of information to the police. But I'd not gone far, continuing to watch from a tactful place higher up the lane.

The game was very simple. The boys used to take their coins between finger and thumb and aim them, with an underhand swing of the arm, at a mark about fifteen feet away. They used a small stone or a peg in the ground at which to aim. The player whose coin landed nearest the mark would collect the coins, place them on the flat of his hand, and toss them, glittering and spinning, into the air. A complicated system of heads and tails, which I never completely understood, decided the winner. Oh, to see Owen Doherty step up to the line, glare about him to demand the silence necessary for his total concentration, take the edge of his jacket in his left hand so

that its drape should not impede his throw, lean forward, and
sweetly aim! And later, as he placed the coins fastidiously along his
palm and thin fingers, examining them so that their positions were
absolutely right, holding them, waiting for the wind to die away
before he threw them up, then we'd watch, knowing such artistry
rare and sacred.

Only once did the police ever raid this game, as far as I know, and
I was older then. I was at the head of the lane, bouncing a tennis
ball on my right foot and counting aloud to see how many times I
could manage it, when I heard yelps and shouts at the other end
and the coin-tossers raced past me, going flat out. I looked down
the lane and there was Sergeant Wilson, red-faced, pounding
towards me at a frightening speed. I took off at once, despite my
innocence, and had overtaken all the fleeing criminals long before
they'd had time to scatter. I turned right at the top of the lane, sped
along Victoria Street and doubled back through Albert Road. Then
I sat on our window sill, looking virtuous and innocent, as I had
every right to. I wasn't even breathing hard. I was about fourteen
then. This race was the cause of my graduating to the card games,
hard, serious, for real money, that were held most nights in the old
works.

Every boy in our town would have known the difference between
a three of spades and a cup of tea at a very early age. I certainly did,
but my knowledge stopped right there. For some reason I could
never understand even the simplest card games. I would have been
hard put to it to give a blind man reasonable exercise in a game of
Snap and the satisfaction of Brag, Pontoon and Bridge have never
been known to me. I was teaching Muirhead, our cat, to jump
through a hoop. She was refusing consistently, and mewing in a
conciliatory manner. Pretty soon, I knew, she would bite and
scratch. I was glad when the boys came up. They told me that I was
just the fellow they wanted for their card school. Flattered but
realistic, I told them that I couldn't play cards and that I had no
money.

'No, no,' said Owen. 'We don't want you to play. We want you
as look-out. The way you went past us this morning, why there can't
be a policeman in the force to live with you. What do you say? A
shilling a week, for three evenings work. Up at the old works.'

We worked out a neat ploy. A disused railway track, its metal and
sleepers long ago lifted to leave only the cinder ballast, led through
the works, and I was to use it as a running track, supposedly training
there while keeping a sharp lookout for policemen. Gareth Stephens

had an old pair of shorts he'd grown too big for and he gave them
to me. I liked them. They were of white silk, with blue lines round
the waist and down the outside of the legs. Wearing these, a white
vest and a pair of gym shoes, I began my employment, jogging along,
practising my starts, occasionally stopping for deep breathing and
bending and stretching. I grew to like it very much. I trained
sincerely, revelling in the increasing strength and stamina I began
to recognise. I trained every night and on Saturday morning,
forgotten were the card players, forgotten the plan by which, if the
police ever came, I was to trot gently and inconspicuously towards
the gamblers where they sat on stone benches under one of the great
arches, warning them by whistling 'The Last Round-up'. Even so,
it should have been easy. Down before me, below the slope of the
mountain, I could see the roofs of the town small and far away.
There was no cover on the mountain, not a tree, not a bush. The
scattered remnants of a few low stone walls, which had once
contained the fields, the moor had long taken back and could
certainly not have hidden a policeman. But nothing had happened
for so long; I had been nearly two summers training in front of the
works, and I had become unwary. I had become engrossed in my
running, the running had taken over. So that one Friday evening,
cloudless, in late July, I was suddenly astonished to see five stout
blue bodies a couple of hundred yards away.

I turned and trotted back towards the works, prancing, knees high,
shaking my arms as they hung limply at my side, as if to loosen the
muscles. Behind my neck I thought I could feel the policemen
mustering for a brief charge, and I could stand it no longer. I
exploded into a frenzied sprint, all thought of 'The Last Round-up'
forgotten.

'Police! Police!' I hissed, whipping past the cavern like a short,
white Jesse Owens. 'Move, for Christ's sake!'

I kept on running until I was two hundred yards down the track,
and then slowed gently to a walk, hands on hips, getting my breath.
Then I turned and trotted back, breaking into fast sprints of twenty
yards or so, straight out of the trot. I'd read about this in an old
book by Jack Donaldson, who had been World Professional Champion in the days when shorts were worn below the knee. That book
was a mine of information. It also had details of a high protein diet
which was guaranteed to take a yard off your time, but I knew I'd
never have the money for it. I raced past the empty arch. A
policeman was bending down, collecting a scatter of cards that had
fallen to the ground. The other four were looking up at the hillside.

I could see the dark figures of the gamblers bucking like stags up the steep. Decorously, I slowed.

'Do you know them, boy?' said the policeman. 'Do you know any of them?'

'Who do you mean?' I answered.

I shaded my eyes with my hand so that I could look more easily up the hill into the sunset. My friends were satisfactorily away.

The policeman sighed gently.

'Never mind,' he said.

He stood looking at the cards in his hands.

'At least we gave them a fright,' he said.

It was then that Mr Everson appeared, stepping delicately over a bundle of stones at the fallen edge of a wall. Mr Everson was a middle-aged gambler who sometimes sat in with my friends. He held in one hand a small bundle of plants and leaves and under his arm was a thick book with a respectable black cover.

'Good evening, gentlemen,' he said. 'And a very lovely evening too.'

The policemen watched him as he came mildly down the track. They didn't answer.

'Look at these,' said Mr Everson, detaching a few dark green leaves from his miscellaneous bouquet. 'The leaves of the wild violet, gentlemen, and here, a little late and therefore faded, the flower itself. A marvel, gentlemen, a marvel.'

Mr Everson chuckled with satisfaction over the fistful of flowers.

'It's astonishing', he said. 'Don't you find it astonishing, to think that a mere fifty years ago the glare from these furnaces lit up the sky for miles around and nothing would grow on these hills because of the stench and fume of burning sulphur? And now, see, the violets are growing. Quite astonishing.'

Mr Everson held out his violets. Every time he said 'astonishing', he opened wide his guileless eyes. It was quite a performance. A pair of ravens which lived high in the walls came out and croaked derisively, but the policemen said nothing. Mr Everson walked through their silent suspicion.

'Come along, boy,' he said. 'You've done enough for one night. We don't want you to get stale.'

I picked up my sweater and, side by side, we walked away. All the time I expected the policemen to call us back, but they didn't. Mr Everson was perfectly calm, treating me with courtesy, as an equal. He was not only old, he was lame. He couldn't have run away with the others. When he was young he had injured his right knee playing football and the leg was permanently bent. Yet he walked strongly, taking a very short step off the right foot and gliding down in an immense long stride on his good leg. More excitingly, while he walked he grew tall and short in turn. On his injured leg his face was level with mine, but his left leg turned him into a tall man, a foot above me. So his voice soared and fell, too, as we walked into the town. He spoke to me about the wild flowers mainly. He knew all about them. He could outwit the police. He was a very clever man.

As I grew older my admiration for Laurence Everson grew too. We became friends, in spite of the difference in our ages. He was both intelligent and amusing and in another place and at another time he could have done great things. But in the waste and wilderness of our town he was able to cultivate only his individuality. He was well-read, scholarly even, and he belonged to several libraries. His interest in politics was informed and cynical, but he loved all kinds of sport. Whenever I'd call on him, I'd find him reading, his head resting on one hand, bent over his book. He always read at a table, sitting on a hard chair, the book fairly close to his face because he refused to wear glasses. It was a big face, large-featured, and he had flat lemon hair on top of his head, shading to grey around his ears. I didn't know he wore a wig until after his death, when one of his brothers told me.

Laurence was a fine snooker player and twice a week for years we played together. He taught me everything, from the basic grasp of the cue up. He taught me how to let the weight, the lead in the heavy base of the graduated wood, do the work, to bend low over the table so that the forward stroke would brush the knot of my tie, to use side and stop. From him I learned the correct bridge for every shot and to recognise a situation so clearly that I could carry in my mind not only the shot in hand but the next five or six shots. And we bet on every game we played during all that time, sometimes straightforward wagers based on a handicap which decreased as I improved, sometimes on some wild, surrealistic series of events which he improvised as he went along. Laurence Everson would bet on anything.

'Beautiful day,' he'd say. 'Bet you it will rain before two thirty-three.'

And we'd sit there, watching the second hands of our watches. Once we spent a whole afternoon betting in even pennies on his canary, a cinnamon-yellow Border that lived in the kitchen. First we bet on the precise second when it would sing and when that palled, we bet on the pitch of its first note, checking the result on

Laurence's piano. This was the time he'd been ill and I'd gone into
see him. Mrs Everson looked pale and anxious, but Laurence looked
fine. He sat in an arm-chair, a rug about his knees, remarkably
strong and imposing. He was sixty then.

After he recovered we went to Cardiff to see Glamorgan play Essex
in the county Cricket Championship. We went by train and I won
a few coppers on the journey, betting on the colour of the shirt worn
by the next man to enter our carriage. We were in plenty of time,
found good seats and prepared to have a day of it. We couldn't have
chosen better weather, hot enough to give the whole game a
dream-like clarity and yet comfortable enough for those of us who
sat in our shirt-sleeves. In those days Glamorgan had an opening
batsman named Smart, and he was very good. He played that day
as if inspired and he'd scored fifty before lunch. Laurence and I ate
our sandwiches and opened our bottles of beer. A couple of white
pigeons fluttered on the grass in front of us, strutting for crumbs.
We were perfectly contented. After the interval, Smart continued
where he left off, playing shots of perfect timing and invention. Soon
he was punching the ball all over the field. The Essex fast bowler, a
youngster who never made the grade, suddenly dug one in so fiercely
that it bounced head high and viciously, but Smart, leaning elegantly
back, hooked it off his eyebrows. It was perfect. The ball came right
at us and Laurence, holding up a nonchalant hand, held it easily
and tossed it back, laughing. A few people near us called and clapped
and he turned around to say something. I could see his face, his
amused eyes, and then it seemed to go to pieces, as if every muscle
had suddenly snapped. He keeled right over and I held him as he
was falling. God, he was a weight. People were helpful and competent. A doctor arrived within minutes and we got Laurence away to
the hospital. He was quite unconscious and I stood around help-
lessly as they worked on him. It was his heart.

After a while he came to. He looked appalling. His skin, always
sallow, was blue, and it seemed he could open only one eye.

'Did Smart get his hundred?' he whispered.

I could scarcely hear him.

'Yes,' I said. I had no idea if it were true.

There was a long pause. I thought he'd lost consciousness again.

'Thank God for that,' he said.

The doctor looked at me. He was a young man, perhaps a year or
two older than I was. His white coat seemed a size too large for him
and he looked cautious and sad.

'Your father?' he said.

'No,' I said. 'A friend. I've known him a long time, though.'

'He's not good,' said the doctor. 'He's not at all well. I don't think he'll make it.'

We were talking very quietly away from the bed, near the door. Laurence said something and I moved back to him.

'What time is it?' he asked.

I looked at my watch. It was four-thirty.

'Bet you,' he said. 'I'm still going at five o'clock.'

He could barely speak.

'Done,' I said. 'Ten shillings.'

That was an impossibly large bet for us.

'He's game,' said the doctor. 'By God, he's game.'

We sat there for a long time listening to Laurence breathing. It seemed fainter and shallower. At last he spoke. He had no voice at all, but there was expression, somehow, in his terrible halting whisper. You could hear his amusement.

'Pay the wife,' he said, 'if I win.'

He opened his eyes for the last time and I think he would have grinned had it been possible.

'Think of it,' he said. 'At last. At last one of us is on a dead cert.'

I told all the boys that, and they all liked it, all those truthful and gallant gamblers. It was difficult to get Mrs Everson to take the money, until I explained that it was a debt of honour, Laurence's last wager. She was a small, hard woman, very proud of Laurence.

'Gambling,' she said tremulously. 'It was his life.'

Johnny Trevecca and the Devil

At eight-thirty on that first golden morning of the new term I stepped with optimism into the lambent air. My satchel was under my arm, my pencils were sharp as skewers, my pen brimful of purple ink. I was prepared. I turned into High Street and looked about for company. About a hundred yards ahead, opposite Maylott's newspaper shop, Joey Smith was pushing his bike along. He was laughing at Wayne Somers and Billy Giardelli. They waited for me, smiling, glad to see me. Billy Giardelli was carrying an old briefcase of his father's, black, with a brass zipper and lock, very impressive. Billy's father was a lawyer. We walked together up the hill and along Gloucester Crescent into the park. Already, although it was early, the comfortable warmth had brought out a few old men to sit on the benches, their newspapers folded beside them, their mild unseeing eyes turned into the sunlight. Wayne began to tell us how his brother had smashed up his father's car.

'He's mad,' Wayne said. 'He hadn't told the old fellow he was taking the car, and then he got frightened because they were out so late. Two in the morning it was. He went to a disco with his friends. they all piled in, six or seven of them, and my brother took it down Billings Hill, flat out. When he got to the bottom he couldn't make the bend and he scraped the off-side all along that high wall. Knocked a big dent in the front wing, took the paint work off the side, grooves in the metal you could lay your fingers in. Pulled the door handles clean out. Nobody was hurt, though.'

I imagined with pleasure the door handles popping like corks from their hard locks, and then I saw an unknown boy walking along at the edge of our group.

He was an extraordinarily neat boy, even for the first day of the new school year. He walked with long regular strides, dipping slightly as his front foot hit the ground. His suit, obviously new, was of some smooth cloth, flannel perhaps, soft and well-fitting, the colour of caramel. His brown shoes were polished to a spotless radiance. I knew that if he were to come a yard nearer I would be able to smell the unmarked leather of the new satchel he carried, but he didn't come any nearer. I looked openly at this silent heavy-shouldered boy walking apart from us. His pale hair, parted on the right side of his head, was thick and sleek, cut close at the nape of his neck and over his ears. The skin of his face was clear and

his complexion very fair. But the face itself was surprising. Although
I could see he was young, a boy of our age, it was as if a man looked
out of his eyes. I had never seen him before, but Billy Giardelli knew
him.

'Hi, David,' he said. 'I didn't know you were coming to our
school.'

'Transferred,' the boy said, 'transferred at the end of last term.
This will be my first day here.'

'Good for you,' Billy said, 'well done. You'll like it. Boys, this is
David James. He lives down at the other end of town, in Nelson
Street.'

We looked with respect at David James. It was rough down there
in Nelson Street, a narrow brutal area near the river. No boys came
to our privileged school from those bitter houses. David James
moved coldly among us as we made room for him, his man's mouth
almost sneering. He walked at the heart of our curiosity, a disturbing
and suddenly dangerous figure.

'Whew!' said Joey Smith. 'It's pretty tough, isn't it, Nelson Street?
I wouldn't like to live there.'

Poor harmless Joey: it was what we all wanted to say. But David
James turned on him like a destroyer and punched him terribly over
the heart. Joey's bike fell to the ground as David hit him again, and
again, heavily, deliberately. We were appalled — we had never seen
such punching. He swung his blunt fists into Joey's body with
massive weight, every blow struck to hurt, driving the air from Joey's
open mouth in dry grunts. Joey held his fat little arms outstretched
in front of him, pushing with his open palms in helpless gestures,
trying to smile through his pain and fear as if he couldn't believe
what was happening. Billy Giardelli jumped between them, covering the ferocity of the blows with his briefcase. It looked for a
moment as if David James would hit Billy, attack us all. We were
horrified. Ours was a soft middle-class school. We had not know
such close violence existed. David James confronted us, his great
hands clenched, his arms hanging loose, and we were soft as pigeons
before him. Then he saw our astonishment and dismay, and he
stepped back, suddenly ashamed. His whole powerful body relaxed,
and he stepped quietly back, not looking at us. I understood then.
He was a boy from another tribe come suspiciously among us,
unaware of our rules, prepared to defend himself against anything
he felt to be hostile.

'Joey didn't mean anything,' I said. 'There was no need to hit him
like that. Everybody knows what it's like in Nelson Street.'

'What do you know about Nelson Street?' David James said. 'It's all right there. We can do without your lot.'

His voice was quiet, his anger spent. He walked across to Joey. Joey was bent over, shivering. He looked as if he were going to be sick.

'Sorry, Joey,' David James said, roughly.

Joey's face was white and his mouth trembling.

'It's OK,' he said. 'A misunderstanding.'

Wayne Somers picked up the bike and wheeled it forward. We all went up the drive, and nobody said a word. I don't know why David James made me his friend. We had little in common; we weren't even in the same class. Because he knew no French or Latin, David was in a lower year than the rest of us. Yet that first afternoon he waited for me after school, and we walked away together. When we reached the tennis courts, he took a pack of cigarettes from his pocket and held it towards me.

'Want one?' he asked.

I shook my head. I had smoked experimentally from time to time, but I knew this was different. David lit a cigarette casually, with automatic skill, cupping his hands around the flame of his lighter. The fingers of his right hand were heavily stained. He drew the deep smoke into his lungs, gratefully held it, and then breathed it easily through his nostrils into the air. He told me that he had smoked regularly for more than five years, since he was ten years old. We walked through the park, talking. A pair of swans floated on the lake, the cob bad-tempered and bullying. Everything David said astonished me. Our lives were so different that I began to imagine that the very words we used were only remotely connected, that identical sounds meant different things to us. I caught bewildering glimpses of boundaries of knowledge and experience I had not known existed. Every afternoon that week we went together as far as High Street before going our different ways home. On Friday evening David asked me to call at his house after lunch the next day.

Saturday was flawless. The sun, benign and generous, shone with brilliant intensity, as if it meant to burn away the whole of the dying summer during that one September day. Its spendthrift warmth beat on my head and my back as, pretending a confidence I didn't possess, I swaggered in the early afternoon through the poor streets that led to David's house. I was alert for unimaginable dangers, for sudden terror against which I had no defence, but everything was quiet. The houses drowsed in the sun, doors open to the heat. Dirty children played on the pavements. A sickly smell, compounded of careless house-keeping and too many people, hung over the place.

David's house was almost at the end of Nelson Street, one of a pair considerably larger than the other houses. It was three-storied, with two wide stone steps leading up to the door. I lifted the brass knocker, and let it fall on the square metal anvil beneath. The knocker was shaped like a hand, as large as my own. Its fingers held a sphere of brass, and it shone so perfectly that the brief print of my warm hand had marked its surface. I could see my image in the dazzling brass, a waiting figure in a green shirt. David's mother opened the door. She stood in the dark hall, a little anxious woman with sharp eyes. She seemed very old to me, much older than my mother.

'You'd better come in,' she said. 'David won't be long. He's gone up the road to see his uncle.'

The door closed behind me, and Nelson Street was shut out. Not a sound entered this cool house from the outside world. It was frighteningly clean and silent, the cleanest house I had ever seen. The tiles on the hall floor, alternately red and blue in a diagonal pattern, shone with polish, the mahogany furniture in the room to which I was led carried an opulent lustre, the pembroke table like a mirror, the sideboard ornately carved. A tall grandfather clock, very old, with the maker's name painted on the face of it and a man in a blue coat firing a fowling-piece, ticked away in the quiet. There were bowls of flowers on the tables and the window sill, roses, brilliant orange calendula, asters, tall gladioli. Little Mrs James stood in front of me.

'You are David's new friend at school,' she said. 'He's told me about you.'

I agreed that I was.

'I hope,' she said, 'for all our sakes, that you're a nice boy. It isn't easy for a boy from these parts to win a scholarship to a school like yours. This is David's big chance. He didn't want to take it, did you know that? It's important that he does well.'

I sat on the hard edge of a chair, listening.

'You must set him an example,' Mrs James said, leaning forward, her eyes already accusing me of failing in my duty. 'You're a boy from a good family, with many advantages. You must see to it that David works hard, is happy at school. You'll do that, won't you.'

'I'll try,' I said.

But these were responsibilities out of my keeping. I knew I'd never be able to influence David James: I was no leader of men. When David came in he bustled me at once into the hot street, and that

was the only time I was ever inside David's house. He seemed to
have no father, and he spoke rarely of his mother. He had a sister
who had gone to London and was a secretary. Why did they live in
that shabby street in the richly furnished house? Where did Mrs
James get the money to keep David so well-dressed, so supplied with
plentiful pocket money? These were extraordinarily worrying questions. I never found any answers.

We walked along the road until we were joined by other boys —
Arthur Thompson, Bevan Burrows, the two Sullivan boys, little
Cecil Everson, David's friends. We lounged past old ladies sitting
on kitchen chairs outside their houses, past little children grown
sticky and fractious in the heat, past the dark shops which sold dry
small oranges, patent medicines, shoelaces, tins of beans. We were
making for the hills. Johnny Trevecca was sitting on the parapet of
the river bridge with his whippet, Betsy, and he jumped off and
tagged along.

I'd seen Johnny before, often. I'd watched him as he shuffled
down High Street, his rapid comical feet turned out, his plump little
body, dressed in hand-me-downs, jerking urgently as he hurried
along. He would rush from shop to shop, begging what he could,
an apple or a stale bun, shouting scattered thanks if he were given
anything, reviling the shopkeeper if he were sent empty away.
Johnny was a character, a harmless natural, his round cheerful face
twisted out of the true, his short hair black and straight. He marched
with us, telling us over and over that it was a fine day, occasionally
bursting into a brief snatch of singing.

Climbing the hill with those boys, I felt like someone from another
world. Their clothes, frayed and patched, in rough materials, baggy
at the knees, their shapeless limp collars, their worn shoes, all set
them apart from me. I didn't understand them when they spoke to
me. They argued incessantly among themselves, jeering and threatening, their only purpose, it seemed, to establish some sort of
superiority over one another, however temporary. They wrestled
savagely, threw one another to the ground, punched, promised even
greater violence. After a while I saw what was happening. They were
demonstrating their order in that small society, parading their
strengths for my inspection. Arthur Thompson and David took no
part in these rituals. David's superiority was so evident that it was
taken for granted. He was the sole judge in any argument, his
decision unquestioned. Arthur Thompson's position was his by
right of size and strength. The other boys, David apart, were afraid
of Arthur. He walked, huge and unthreatened, in their midst. The

boys hurried to agree with his flat statements, laughed at his jokes, accepted without resentment his offhand blows. Below him the social order was more confused. I was being invited to show what I could do, to challenge wherever I felt I could win, so that they could define me, allot me a place. But I could take no part in their pointless arguing, did not understand the haphazard ceremonies of their fighting. David was watching me closely, enjoying my discomfiture. At last, puzzled by my lack of response, the boys dismissed me and began to bait Johnny Trevecca. We sat in the warm afternoon grass above the town, and they began to taunt Johnny. Lazily and tolerantly they mocked him, imitating his odd gait, sneering at his clothes, making obscene remarks about his sisters, his mother. He sat defenceless, sullen, impotently warning them of vengeance. Then Kevin Sullivan threw a stone at Johnny's dog. It was a little stone, inaccurately flicked. He hadn't even tried to hit the dog, but the little animal ran cringing to Johnny's side, and a rougher sport began. Johnny held the dog under his jacket as the stones began to patter about them, light pebbles at first, and thrown without malice. But a kind of lust entered the game, and soon the two innocents were showered with hurled stones, hard, accurate, stinging and cutting. Johnny Trevecca struggled to his feet and ran, crouching and ducking, out of range. Blood crept from a small wound in his scalp. He was crying desperately.

'You idiots!' he was shouting. 'You bloody idiots! You want locking up, the lot of you!'

His round little face was intense and red as he clutched his whippet to him. It was the first time I had ever thought of Johnny Trevecca as human, with an ability to feel sadness and love. But Arthur Thompson rose ponderously to his feet, brushing the dry grass from his arms. He was slow and deliberate; there was about him a stupid affronted dignity. He strode with his rolling heavy step to Johnny and quietly took the little dog from him. Johnny did not resist. He turned his head away and wailed like an animal.

'Oh, give me my dog,' he sobbed. 'Oh, make him give me my dog.'

'You must not call us idiots. You are an idiot, and you must be taught a lesson,' Arthur Thompson said.

We sat on the ground about twenty yards away and watched the two boys. Dermot Sullivan was whistling, almost silently, between his teeth; but the other boys were absorbed, tight with anticipation. Johnny Trevecca began to howl aloud, running a few steps this way and that in front of Arthur Thompson. I had never seen such terror.

'A lesson, Johnny,' Arthur said. 'I am going to kill your dog.'

His great hands closed about the dog's throat, and the creature began to thrash and kick, its shrill whimpering cut short. Johnny was crying in an agony of helplessness.

'Put the dog down, Arthur,' David said. It was the first time he had spoken in a long while. 'Put it down, or I'll twist your head away from your shoulders.'

Arthur Thompson might not have heard him. The dog's struggles were desperate.

'Put it down, Arthur,' David said, just as quietly, 'or the boys will have to carry you home.'

'You can make me put it down,' Arthur Thompson said, almost singing the words. His face was red and smiling; sweat shone on his cheeks. 'But can your friend there?' Still holding the dog, he released his strangling grip. He looked at us, sly and stupid. 'Can your friend make me drop the dog?' he said.

'He doesn't have to,' David said. 'I tell you to put the dog down, and you'd better do it.'

The huge boy laughed softly, bent down, and laid the little dog on the grass with something like tenderness. It sat there panting, very distressed, and then it ran to Johnny. Without a word Arthur came back to us, nodding his head in a kind of triumph, pleased. He smiled at me as he thumped down beside me, looking hard at me, waiting for my reaction. The other boys watched me cautiously. I chewed unconcernedly on a grass blade as if the whole affair was no concern of mine, as if irrational cruelty happened about me every day and left me untouched. Johnny Trevecca was running to safety down the hill and along the dirt road. Then, far off, made small by distance, he turned and waved his fists at us. The little black dog pranced around his feet. Johnny danced and waved, his tiny gesticulating figure comical and remote. He might have been shouting at us, but we were too far away to hear him. We laughed at him, the tension broken, the challenge luckily dissipated.

'He's fortunate,' David said. 'He never remembers anything; in ten minutes he'll have forgotten all about us. He's always happy.'

We looked down at the dazzling river, aflame in the sun.

'Look at the tempting water,' Cecil Everson said. 'Let's go for a swim.'

And we all got up and walked down the hill.

I had never swum in the river below the town. Compressed between the two arches of the bridge into a strong and buckling current, the river broadened almost at once into a slow pool. Two factories discharged their daily waste into it; the rubbish of the town

seemed to have collected in it. Sandstone pebbles at is edge, brown
and spotted as eggs, were covered by a thin crust of dirt; but I had
to swim there — I could not avoid it. I undressed slowly on the bank.

'Get in as quickly as you can,' David said. 'All the old women in
the town will be complaining to the police if we stand about naked.'

Cecil Everson was already in the water, puffing about in the
shallows, grinning, water-beads shining on his pallid skin. Arthur
Thompson was stepping clumsily in. The water was already up to
his knees, and his obese and powerful body, round and hairless,
made him look like a giant baby. Timidly he went in, step by step,
and then, gasping, he dived clumsily into the deeper water. They
swam badly, these boys. They were self-taught, without style,
wasteful of energy. David was swimming cautiously on the far side
of the pool, out in the weight of the current. Bevan Burrows was
making no headway at all. Ahead of him Arthur Thompson was
grimly bludgeoning the water, blowing hard. I shook off my clothes
and dived in, fast and shallow.

It was lovely. I went up the full current in a fast crawl, passing
Arthur's unbelieving red face, turned under the bridge, and shot
down again. I was playing their game, and I knew it. Not one of
them could swim as I could. Arthur Thompson's stubborn strength
had taken him to the bridge. Time after time he reached his
stretching arm to grab a length of thick rope dangling from an iron
ring set in the wall, but each attempt died as the swift current carried
him downstream. Easily I swam in the teeth of the river, lifted an
arm, swung myself out of the water, gripping the wall with my toes;
then I turned away, flicking off the stone and straightening down,
deep into the heavy water. Above me I saw Arthur's kicking legs as
he struggled against the current, and then I had sped past and
popped up at the tail of the pool. About me the boys laughed in
admiration and surprise.

'He's like a comet,' Arthur Thompson said, wading ashore pink
as a rose. 'He's some swimmer, your friend. I see him come off that
rope and the next thing he's flashed under me, like a comet.'

I dried in my shirt, refreshed and happy. I had not known I wanted
to be accepted by these strange boys, but now I was. I had shown
them my strength, and I had been given my place: I could outswim
them all.

'Come on, swimmer,' said David, with irony, as I put on my shoes.
'Time you went home for your meal.'

And then began a time of happy and reckless freedom for me. My
normal life began to seem unreal and artificial. At school I did no

more work than was necessary to keep out of trouble, was not co-operative nor unco-operative; I was absorbing David's values, his attitude of suspicion and antagonism toward authority. I came alive only during the evenings when I ranged the wild streets with my new friends. When the year turned into winter and the nights darkened, in the worst of the weather David and I would go to his uncle's place. David's uncle was an undertaker, and his premises formed a square about an old cobbled yard backing on to the river near David's house. The shiny black Daimler hearse and the limousines which carried the mourners were garaged in converted stables at the back of the yard. The workshops were housed in a long low building to one side. There too were stored the lengths of elm and oak that would be shaped into coffins, in an airy shed so that they would season well.

We were there often, David and I. I grew to know a lot about that trade. I knew where the fittings were kept, the metal handles and nameplates, and could be trusted to get the correct sets at busy times. I often took telephone messages and was helpful in general ways. I learned how to plane a length of wood as smooth as satin, to measure it with my eye so that I could detect an irregularity easily. I grew to like the smell of the hot pitch with which the cabinets were sealed. Often I held for old Christy Lewis, who had worked there for more than forty years, the length of plank which would form one side of a coffin, while he used his saw to cut the parallel grooves an exact inch apart and all the same depth in the thick of the wood so that the plank would bend symmetrically to form the shape of a shoulder. I made myself useful often. But David was invaluable, the equal of any of the carpenters and better than most. What I liked best were the evenings when work was light and we could sit near the fire which always burned in the open grate. Many stormy evenings, when the other boys were huddled in the doorways of locked shops, or sitting together under the arches of the railway bridge, David and I were warm and helpful in the carpenter's shop. Sometimes Johnny Trevecca would be there too. His innocence opened many doors for him. He was often the butt of many practical jokes; more than once he was made to lie in a making coffin, his eye rolling in fright as the men pretended to nail the lid over him. But all was kindly meant in that place. Released, he would race into the night, shouting at us from the safety of the dark yard; but he would return within fifteen minutes, smiling, childlike, without malice. For a whole week of rainy evenings we taught Johnny to write his name. He was wholly illiterate, and we had to invent reasons which seemed

to him acceptable for the use of the symbols we taught him. So J
was a hook, O a ring, H goalposts, and N — the most difficult —
the cemetery gates. It was good that rainy week when nobody died,
and we sat every night teaching Johnny his four letters. He gripped
a carpenter's pencil in his stubby fist and laboriously traced his name
over and over. At last he could write it without fault, and his delight
was boundless. I began to see his name all over town, chalked on
walls and hoardings, pencilled on the station timetables; wherever
he could he printed his bold plain statement, the most innocent and
triumphant graffiti I have ever seen.

One Friday evening in the middle of December David and I
entered his uncle's yard. It was very cold, and a miserable heavy
wind drove the rain in wet gusts into our faces. We picked our way
over the cobbles, avoiding the awkward pools that had gathered in
areas where the stones were missing. One light was on, a single bulb
at the back of the carpenters' shop, but when we went in there was
a big fire in the grate and Christy Lewis and Benny Trelawney were
sitting there, tossing offcuts of planking on the blaze. Benny was
smoking his pipe. It was warm and comfortable in the dimness. We
took off our coats and sat down. Johnny Trevecca stood in the
shadows, singing to himself and making a pile of wood-shavings on
one of the workbenches.

'Soon be Christmas,' said Benny Trelawney.

'Roll on,' I said. 'Only another week of school left.'

'Can't think why great boys like you would want to go to school,'
Christy Lewis said. 'What are you, fifteen, sixteen? I'd been working
years at your age. David could start here tomorrow; his uncle is
waiting for him. Lovely little business he could have, in due time.'

We sat in the hot light of the fire, and Christy fed it pieces of wood
one after the other, watching the tendrils of flame grip and cling.

'Did you finish that piece of French polishing, Christy?' David
asked.

Christy nodded. 'On the bench,' he said. 'A nice piece of wood
too, came up well.'

David got up and looked at a plaque of polished oak which lay on
Christy's bench.

'Still wet,' he said.

'Will be for sometime,' Benny Trelawny said. 'But he makes a
nice polish, does Christy. Just the right amount of resin in the
alcohol. Too much makes for a sticky polish, too little — well, the
polish has no depth.'

David came back to his chair. The heat was making us all drowsy.

'A funny time, Christmas,' Christy said.

'A good time,' Benny said, 'a good time for everyone.'

'Not always,' Christy said. 'Funny things happen. Ten or eleven years ago I was sitting here, in front of a fire like this, three days before Christmas. It was a Saturday. There was me, Bobby Lewis — he was my cousin, you ought to remember him, Benny, you had his job here after he died — Paul Marshall who used to work for the Water Board, he's dead now, poor soul, and the boss, David's uncle. Oh, it was a terrible night, cold and wet and a high wind, as bad as tonight. We didn't want to go home, it was that bad. We stayed here, playing cards for pennies. About eleven o'clock the door opened and a gentleman came in. Tall and dark, oh, very tall, taller than Sergeant Coker, the policeman they used to call Longshanks. In he came, this gentleman, and he stood in the doorway, bending down, very pleasant and smiling. Asked us if he could shelter from the rain. A really nicely-spoken man. He was soaking wet, so we put him to sit next to the fire. After a bit he sat in with us, took his hand with the cards. Very pleasant, tall, smiling gentleman, but something funny about him. Bobby and I both noticed it — we lifted our eyebrows at each other. Something uneasy.'

We listened comfortably to the old man's gentle story. Johnny Trevecca crept close and squatted down. The wind blew harder, and a few spots of rain hissed down the short chimney and spat in the flames.

'What do you mean, uneasy?' said Ben Trelawney.

'Hard to say,' Christy said. 'Just a feeling we had, but we were proved right. Well, there was the fire, for a start. We had a bigger fire than this. A huge fire seems right just before Christmas. We were burning old elm offcuts and some green branches from the old apple that used to stand in the corner near where we keep the hearse. Crabby old apple that was, too, but it burned lovely. Well, this gentleman, he took his place by the fire, and as he sat down, up leaped the flames toward him. And every time he stretched his hand to the flames, they came forward to meet him, as if they were alive — you'd swear the fire was a living thing. That was a strange thing. Once we got playing cards I forgot all about it. To see that man deal cards! He was an artist. The hour grew later and we played on. In those days we got paid on a Saturday night, and we'd had a good pay, overtime, Christmas bonus; it added up. Almost one in the morning and our pockets were empty. We'd lost it all. David's uncle had lost more than twenty-five pounds, a lot of money in those days. We were finished — our kind gentleman had all our pound notes in his pocket.'

'What did you do?' I asked.

'Nothing,' Christy Lewis said. 'Nothing we could do. We'd been beaten fair and square. That man could make the cards talk — he could make them sit up and beg. He got up smiling, nice as you please. Oh, the storm was at its peak then, thunder rolling around as if somebody was banging a bass drum inside your head.'

'I don't like thunder,' Johnny Trevecca said. 'I'm afraid of that.'

'He got to the door,' said Christy Lewis, 'stood there and thanked us. Hoped he'd see us again some time for another game. He walked very awkwardly, you know. Did I tell you that? He wasn't graceful in his walk. As he turned to go out, ducking through the doorway, a flash of lightning lit the whole place up — oh, a brilliant flash. And for a second we all saw it clearly. We couldn't move for shock; we were knocked speechless.'

'What was it?' Benny asked. He was leaning forward, his mouth open. I think I was too. We all waited for the answer.

'We saw it, just for that instant,' Christy said mildly. 'It was his foot. He had a cloven hoof. We saw it in the lightning, and then, whisk, he was gone.'

'Good God!' Benny said. 'It was the devil!'

At this Johnny Trevecca jumped to his feet, his eyes wild and frightened, trembling.

'I'm going home,' he said, hoarsely. 'I don't want to see the devil.'

I grabbed him as he ran for the door. I think now that I had been affected by the story, half frightened perhaps, and I wanted to show that I didn't believe any of it, that I knew it to be a skilful game played in the half-light by the old man. But Johnny was wild with fright and far stronger than I had imagined. He sent me reeling and spinning away from him. I would have fallen if I hadn't pushed out my arms to save myself. The heel of my left hand pressed squarely on the polished oak plaque. I felt its tacky surface saw the sudden imprint of my skin, the long fine whorls of my palm, the mark below my thumb where I'd scarred it on barbed wire when I was small. Everybody stopped laughing. We could hear Johnny Trevecca run yelling through the yard as he raced for home.

'I've spoiled that piece,' I said, 'that French polishing.'

'I saw you,' David said, his voice expressionless and remote. They gathered around the workbench, looking at the print of my hand.

'It's not so bad,' Christy Lewis said, putting on his glasses. 'We might be able to do something about it. What do you think, David?'

David looked down at it, judging, measuring.

'We might,' he said. 'It will take time, Christy.'

I was at the back of the group, looking at the three heads bent over the marred work.

'I'm sorry,' I said. Nobody paid any attention to me. David and Christy talked together, and then Christy went off to the storeroom for his oils and polishes, his bottles and pads.

'I'm sorry, David,' I said.

He nodded absently. He wasn't angry — it was merely that I had no part in what he was doing.

'It's late,' he said. 'You'd better go home.'

I walked over and took my raincoat off the nail on which it hung. It was still wet, and I put it on with difficulty.

'I'll see you next week,' I said.

'I shan't be in school next week,' David said. 'Don't wait around.' Surprised, I looked at him, and saw once again the man's face he wore on the first day I'd seen him. We were again strangers, and I was a boy to him, not worth his odd maturity. I was being dismissed; somehow I had failed him. I went out into the night. The rain had stopped, and racing clouds, full of menace, blew overhead. I knew something terribly important had happened, but I wasn't sure what it was. I was at once elated and ashamed. The house was in darkness when I got home, and I remembered that my parents had gone out to dinner at the Jamiesons's house. I had a bath, got into my dressing-gown, and went into my room. It was warm and familiar. I took down my album of British empire stamps and examined each page minutely. Every postmark, every adhesive hinge was known to me. I had never been more awake. I went to my desk and got out my schoolbooks. Opening my geography book, I began an outline map of Africa, my hand immensely sure and skilful. I worked on for more than two hours, until I was tired, and then I went to bed. There, before sleep, I went over again the events of the night. I was very happy. I began to see that there had been a decision taken which was as much mine as David's, that for too long I had been moving on the wrong road. Part of me had wanted very much to run with the wild boys, but at the end I would have had to come home. I had not helped David at all. He had seen that he would move naturally into his uncle's place, his easy skills recognised and valued, that I had no place in that world. I was filled with relief, and I was grateful to David James for having released me, for sending me back.

The following week I asked Michael Jefferies, a boy in David's year, if David was in school.

'No,' he said. 'David has left school. Gone to work as an under-taker, or something. Just as well, really. He never seemed at home here.'

'That's true,' I said.

'Hurry up,' called Joey Smith, waiting down the drive for me. 'I have to call at the library on my way home, then we can have tea at my house.'

I ran downhill to join him.

A Piece of Archangel

Oscar came over on Saturday morning and we measured the room for the bookshelves I wanted. I made a rough drawing of the sort of thing I imagined, we decided on the lengths of cut timber we'd need, and Oscar made a list of them. I got ready to go down to the sawmills.

'What shall I get, Oscar?' I asked. 'Deal or pine?'

'Get what you can as long as it's straight,' Oscar said. 'Wood is like gold these days.'

We've done a lot of jobs together in this house, so many that I'm accepted at the sawmills as a genuine self-employed carpenter, able to buy my timber at trade rates; but I always dress the part, wear overalls, push a steel rule in my pocket. I saunter into the office with bravado. Oscar, the genuine tradesman, laughs at my act.

'You'd better get parana pine,' he said. 'It's reliable, and cheaper than deal. Some of it is pretty.'

I took the wagon through the town and stopped on the river bridge before I reached the wharves. The tide was on the turn and the river was momentarily without turbulence, holding a brief calm between the weight of the incoming sea and its own heavy direction down the valley. The sea trout were in. I could see them lying in irregular columns, heads upstream, unmoving. They'd run with the tide, though, once it turned. Thinking of fishing, I drove on toward the river wharf, to the sawmills. Two old men were hauling planks from a rack of hardwood close by. I stopped near the office and walked in through the trade entrance. Gus wasn't there. There was a brass bell on the counter, an old one with a plunger on top. When you smack the plunger with the flat of your hand some kind of striking mechanism is activated. I gave it a try, knowing that all I'd hear would be an unmetallic thud. It never worked. It was probably the oldest bell of its kind in the south of England. The whole office was a museum. On its walls were advertisements for products which had been unobtainable for thirty years or more, samples of ancient and outmoded remedies for damp walls and leaking roofs stood on the shelves. Gus wouldn't have a thing changed in his office. I settled down to wait.

I'd been there about five minutes, leaning on the counter, dreaming, when the door opened and a young man came in. His name is Hardisty and he's a jobbing builder in the neighbourhood, can turn his hand to anything. We're on nodding terms. He's thin and fair and perhaps twenty-five years old.

'Gus not in then?' he said.

'When is Gus ever in,' I answered.

'Lazy old basket,' he said. 'Gone off to have a cup of tea, I shouldn't wonder.'

He took out a cigarette and began to sing softly to himself. We waited in amiable patience until Gus arrived, bustling.

'Right, sirs and gents,' he said. 'Who's first?'

Gus is a little, wiry man, with a crest of white hair. He looks and moves like a terrier, all eagerness and swift little legs. I pushed my list towards him. He read it slowly, pursing his lips, shaking his head doubtfully.

'Oh, come on, Gus,' I said. 'There's nothing difficult there.'

'I don't know, I don't know,' said Gus. 'There's this six by one, we might not have this six by one. Want it prepared, do you?'

He looked up as the old man came in, closing the door slowly behind him.

'Here they come,' Gus said. 'We've got all the rogues in this morning. Hullo Ted.'

'Prepared, Gus,' I said. 'Prepared and cut to those sizes.'

'Oh dear, oh dear,' he said, 'and Saturday morning too. You know the boys will want to leave early. It's half-day, you know that.'

'Stop moaning, Gus,' said the old man. 'Get on with it and give the man his wood.'

'You want it in parana pine?' Gus said. 'What's it for, shelves?'

'Yes,' I said. 'I'll want it nice and square.'

Gus shot through the door.

'You'll be lucky,' the old man said. 'There's no square timber these days. They don't season it, they send it out green. Damned if it wouldn't grow if you stuck it in the ground.'

Hardisty and I nodded. The old man slid down and squatted against the wall, prepared for a long wait.

'I know where there is some good stuff,' the old man said. 'Marvellous stuff. Down in Marlborough Square. They're breaking up those big old houses, what material! The floor boards are eighteen inches wide and never a shake in them. I can't think why they're pulling those houses down, marvellous boards, they are. You'd have to get all the old polish off, all the varnish, sand them down to the clean wood. But you'd have something when you finished. All oak it is. You'd have the heart of England there.'

'They got any doors there?' Hardisty asked. 'I could just do with a couple of good doors.'

'Doors?' said the old man. 'I should think they have. Why, those doors are the real thing, beautiful solid panels, made true all those years ago by fine craftsmen out of honest wood, not this stuff they send out today. And lovely fanlights over them, not Georgian, no, Victorian. Of course, it just depends on how they were taken out. If they've been ripped out by the monkeys they employ today, well, you'll have to look at the hinges. Solid brass, those hinges, solid brass hinges, big, smooth. Swing like a Rolls-Royce they do. It makes me boil to think of those hinges being ripped out, those lovely screws driven into the wood, straight and true, countersunk perfectly, all those years ago. My old man worked in Marlborough Square, when they were building. Before I was born, that was. Have they got doors? It would take the three of us to carry one of them!'

'Thanks, Ted,' said Hardisty. 'I could just do with a couple of good doors. I might go down and have a look at them later on.'

He looked out of the window across the river. The wind was whipping the surface of the river and a few hunched gulls sat on the mooring-posts.

'It doesn't get any warmer, does it?' he said. 'Here it is, nearly September and we've had no summer.'

'I'm retired,' said the old man, 'I been retired seven years. Seventy-two I am. I can pick and choose my jobs. I only do what I fancy, a bit of cabinet-making, a bit of quality repairing.'

'You're lucky, then,' said Hardisty.

'I am, that,' old Ted said. 'I wouldn't like to work with the muck they sell you today, especially on the building. I don't have anything to do with the building now. Carpentry? They don't know what it is. Anybody with a hammer and a couple of six-inch nails is a carpenter these days.'

We said nothing for a long minute.

'Here,' said the old man. 'This will surprise you. Do you know what I found in my shed the other day? I went down for a bit of timber — I always keep a tidy little stock, keep it nice and dry, stack it properly with air circulating all round it — I went down there for a bit of timber and, right at the back, what do you think I found? I found a piece of Archangel.'

I looked at Hardisty for help, but he turned up his palms and lifted his eyebrows in mimic ignorance.

'Forgotten I had it there,' said Ted, immensely satisfied. 'I put it away again. That'll come for something special, I said to myself. Nice little piece of ten by one it is, about nine foot long.'

'I can't think,' I said cautiously, 'when I last saw a piece of Archangel.'

'I haven't seen any since the war,' Ted said. 'Oh, I saw plenty during the war. I don't suppose this boy has ever seen any.'

'I haven't,' said Hardisty. 'I don't know what you're talking about. What is Archangel, anyway?'

'There,' said Ted. 'I knew he hadn't seen any. Timber, that's what Archangel was. Long planks of beautiful white timber. Softwood, it was. Came out of Russia, from a forest near Archangel. That's how it got its name. It used to come into Littlehampton and Shoreham on Russian boats, great lengths of it, with the grain running on and on, straight as a ruler. Never a knot in sight. It was lovely.'

'Expensive, was it?' Hardisty asked.

'No, it was cheap,' Ted said, 'it was quite cheap. And what wood to work! It would cut like cheese and wear for ever. You could polish it with your handkerchief. I used to love working with it. We used it everywhere. I'd put in a floor of Archangel, every plank snug and tight, all running smooth from wall to wall and I'd look at it. It was so white I didn't like to walk on it, I didn't like to leave the marks of my boots on it. White as snow. Or silver, more like. That's it, silver.'

'Where is it now, Ted?' I asked.

'Gone,' he said, 'all of it gone. The Russians used it all up in the war, most like.'

'They've got other forests, I bet,' Hardisty said. 'They just don't want us to have the stuff.'

'No,' said Ted, 'it's all gone. Once you start to cut down trees it doesn't take long. When I was young you could buy English oak, beech, what you liked. Not now. All over the world the great forests are going. You'd think they would never end, but they do. And we're so spendthrift, so extravagant. We use the best wood first. The best always goes first.'

Gus rushed into the office and drew his order book towards him, tucking the thin blue carbon paper under the top sheet.

'You're lucky,' he said. 'We found you some nice stuff, some really pretty pine. It'll work up nicely. Shelves, you said?'

'Bookshelves,' I said. 'Thanks, Gus.'

He wrote out my ticket laboriously. He's short of two fingers on his right hand, lost them in the sawmills when he was a boy, and since then he's worked in the trade office, over thirty years. He still finds writing hard. He's nice enough, is Gus. I paid him, and went outside to load my timber into the wagon. Hardisty was busy explaining his needs to Gus and I said goodbye to old Ted. The wood was ready in a neat pile right by my wagon. I loaded it and drove away.

Oscar was sitting in the sun when I got back. He'd set up his portable bench and all his tools were ready, his chisels and screwdrivers, his electric saw, his sander. We took the sawn wood out of the wagon and looked at it carefully, piece by piece.

'It's not bad,' Oscar said. 'The long pieces are all slightly out of true, but by the time we screw them into place they'll be all right.'

We worked quietly together, measuring, sanding, setting the frame square. The shelves began to take on the tall, spare shape I'd hoped for. At lunch time we sat together on the patio, eating sandwiches. I ran my hand along the smooth length of one of the planks. The grain was lovely, a faint pink running through it.

'It looks good,' I said to Oscar.

'It'll make up pretty well,' Oscar said, looking calmly down at the shelves. 'We'll put a couple of right-angle brackets on the corners, at the back where you won't see them. It'll be firm enough then.'

'You ever see any Archangel, Oscar?' I said.

He looked at me, grinning.

'Wherever did you hear of that?' he said. It isn't often I surprise Oscar. I told him about the old man at the sawmills.

'That'll be old Ted Armitage,' Oscar said. 'I know old Ted. He used to work with my grandfather from time to time. Ted would know about Archangel, all right.'

'You ever see any?' I said.

'Of course,' he said. 'I used to follow my grandfather all over the place when I was a kid. I lived in his workshop, worked harder there than I ever did at school. He kept all sorts of timber in his little yard. He had a lot of rosewood one time — he loved hardwood, did my grandfather. He taught me pretty well everything I know. He told me all about Archangel.'

'I didn't know about your grandfather,' I said.

'How could you?' Oscar said, 'you've not lived here above ten years. My grandfather was dead when you came to this house. Well known and respected he was in these parts. He left me all his tools, his lovely chisels, thin and glittering, his saws, his huge square old planes, smoothing planes and jack planes. Over a hundred years old they are, beautiful. I've still got them. Nobody will ever use them again, not with the power tools we have nowadays. My old lad would have spurned this job we're doing today.'

He looked mildly down at our making bookshelves. I'd known

Oscar since I first came to this house and called him in to put up a flight of stairs into the loft. He was young then, in his late twenties, quick moving and impulsive. He's settled a lot, but he still has his easy confidence, the assurance brought to him by his precise skills.

'What's wrong with it?' I said. 'What's wrong with making bookshelves?'

'Nothing at all,' Oscar said, 'but grandfather wouldn't have brought this wood into the house. It would have been oak for him, properly seasoned, perhaps from a tree he'd felled himself. Then he'd have looked at it for a bit, deciding which surfaces he'd show, for the look of the grain, for the appearance of the finished piece. Oh, he would have taken his time over that. And he wouldn't have screwed it together, as we shall, and braced it. No, he'd have used his sharp little saw and the whole thing would have been fitted together with mortice and tenon joints, every one of them identical, perfect. Then glued and clamped. And every corner would have been true. The shelves would last longer than the house.'

'Would you like to do that sort of work?' I said. I had the idea of commissioning some piece of furniture, a chest maybe, or a tallboy, and allowing Oscar to work with love and pride, like his grandfather.

'Not me,' he said. 'We haven't time for such things. Your shelves will hold books as well as any my grandfather made. And we'll finish them today. They'll be standing in your room tonight. My old lad would have taken a week.'

He stood up and brushed the crumbs from the front of his red shirt.

'We are different people,' he said, 'living in a different world. What's the point of using skills no longer necessary? What's the point of dreaming of a world full of Archangel? There isn't any. We have to use what's left. When there isn't any timber left, we'll find something else.'

We picked up one of the long side panels and began to measure it for the fitting which would enable me to adapt the widths between the shelves.

'How long has the old man been dead?' I asked. I was interested in him.

'Fifteen years,' Oscar said. 'He died fifteen years last February.'

I held the wood while he drilled the small holes for the bronze screws we were going to use.

'I was working at Horsham at the time,' he said, 'on that estate the other side of the railway station. Nice houses, good quality. I was living there then, in Horsham, not long married, about eighteen months.'

We put down the plank and picked up the next.

'My mother telephoned the site office and asked the foreman to let me know the old chap was dead. I came down that afternoon. He'd left me his house, tools, furniture, everything. Well, I was always with him, and I was the only grandson. I'd looked after his garden for years, since I was big enough. His chickens, rabbits. I just stepped right back as if I'd never been away.'

'I didn't know you'd ever left here,' I said. 'I always think of you as part of this place, like the trees and houses.'

'I've been about,' Oscar said. 'I served my apprenticeship with a big firm, worked in Bristol for a few weeks once, was in Leeds, Birmingham. I was quite a while in Birmingham. It was a good firm. They wanted me to stay when I'd worked my time, but I'd rather work on my own. I came back, worked here and there, never far away. I was married when I was twenty.'

'You surprise me, Oscar,' I said. 'Why haven't you told me this before?'

'We never got round to it,' he said. 'It was talking about old Ted Armitage that brought it on now, I suppose. And I didn't think you'd be interested. I think of your mind full of bookshelves as far as the eye can see, with the files of books waiting for you to use.'

He grinned at me.

'I've lived here ever since the old man died,' he said. 'It was as if he knew something was wanted, something needed doing. We were up there in Horsham and we'd just lost our first baby, Enid and I. A little girl, lovely little thing. I was astonished when I first saw her, such small hands. She was holding them up to her mouth, and waving them now and then.'

'What happened?' I said.

'When she was four months old,' Oscar said, 'she died in her cot. She hadn't been ill. Nobody could explain it. It happens sometimes, everybody told us.'

He stopped drilling and lifted the wood to his eye, judging its accuracy.

'But it was obviously time for a new start,' he said. 'We had to put things behind us. After we buried my grandfather we moved straight into his house and we've lived there ever since.'

'I'm sorry,' I said, 'about your baby.'

'Over and done with,' he said. 'It's not often I think of it. Enid does, I know; but what is gone, is gone. There's no sense in wishing for things past. There's no sense in hoping for things to come back.'

We'd finished the shelves by the end of the afternoon. I wasn't going to have them stained or polished in any way, just the plain smooth wood. Oscar approved of this.

'They look a bit raw and new,' he said, 'but they'll darken. As you use them they'll acquire a few marks here and there, become yours, get a bit of character.'

We piled his folding workbench and the tools into his truck, and I paid him.

'Want some plums?' he said, tucking the money into his pocket. 'We've a huge crop of Victorias, far too many for us.'

It's sensible to accept what Oscar offers. He gives generously and proudly, a proud man, fiercely independent.

'I'd like that,' I said, 'I'm fond of plums.'

'Follow me down, then,' he said, 'and bring a basket.'

Oscar's two little boys were in the garden when we arrived and they helped me to fill my shallow basket with purple Victoria plums, an old sort from an old tree, lush and full, the flawless bloom on them. I got in the car to drive away and all three stood to watch me go, their attitudes identical, the same smiles, their feet turned out in the same way. Oscar put his arms around his sons.

'Who needs Archangel?' he said.

That night I filled my new bookshelves, sorting the books and arranging them carefully, watching them bring the room to life. It was a splendid thing to be doing. I enjoyed doing it.

Keening

Her name had been Mary Flood. She had kept that name for twenty-three years, until she got married. She had been born a long time ago in a small place in the valley of the Lee, well beyond the town of Cork. She could not remember the name of the village. Sometimes that happened. But she could see in her mind the white houses and the green hill behind them whenever she wanted, she could smell the fresh cold trout her father brought home from the river. She could not remember her father very well. Last night, though, when she was at the falling edge of sleep, she had seen vividly herself as a small dark girl standing with her mother beside the door of their house. She had been lying in her good bed, but what she had felt at her shoulder blades and down her back was the rough stone of the cottage wall. She knew that what she remembered then was right, her old body remembered it, her skin remembered.

She could not recall her father, just sometimes she thought she heard his voice. He had been a violent and drinking man. Her Aunt Bridie had said so when she came up from Cork for the wake, and Aunt Bridie was her father's own sister. Her father lay dead and stretched within the house and Mary was in the garden behind, sitting among the blackcurrant bushes. She loved the smell of blackcurrants, the pungent leaves, the dark wood. Her mother said they smelled like cats. That day the sun was out and bees were active among the pink flowers. Mary sat entranced in the middle of their murmuring.

Inside the house, the women began to mourn. Softly at first, they tried their diffident voices, self-consciously, unwilling to give easy way to the richness of their sorrow. It was not until their raised, melancholy cries reached her clearly that Mary understood what was happening. She lifted her head, listening.

In a while she joined the soaring ululation of the women with her child's voice. She was happy in the warm evening, among the bushes. She sobbed aloud in thoughtless imitation, for happiness.

Her sister Eileen came out of the house and gave her a good shaking. Eileen was fourteen and working up the hill at Dr Price's house, where there were four bedrooms although Dr Price had no children at all. Mrs Price took the village girls as they became old enough and trained them to be housemaids in England, if that was what they wanted. Otherwise girls worked on the farms, or went off

to Cork, or just stayed gossiping at home. Quite soon Eileen would
be going away to England. She warned Mary with a lifted finger and
went back indoors. Mary hung her head. All her life she had lived
with the guilt of that discovery.

Mary went gladly to Mrs Price when it was her time. She had
grown tall and large-boned. Her hair, short and straight, was a thick
mop about her head, but Mrs Price taught her how best to brush it
from her forehead. It was a pleasure, Mrs Price said, to have at last
a girl both eager and intelligent. Despite her seeming awkwardness,
her impulsive heavy limbs, Mary was deft and clever. The heavy
work, the laundry and the outside cleaning was easy for her, but she
was good at delicate things too. She could serve afternoon tea,
covering the tray with a lace cloth, arranging the elegant thin china
with confidence, the plate with its light burden of sandwiches, the
bread thin as paper.

Best of all Mary liked ironing the doctor's shirts. On Monday she
did the laundry, the great white sheets without a mark on them, all
the linen of that spotless household, and on Tuesday she ironed.
She worked in the big kitchen, heating her irons on the range, testing
their warmth near her face. Everything was starched in those days.
When it came to the doctor's shirts, Mary really set to. Such
beautiful garments they were. She would tease the hot nose of her
iron into the folds of the cloth until she was satisfied. There never
had been a girl, the doctor said, to put such a gloss on his cotton.
She used to brush his suits too. He had tweed suits from a fine tailor
in Dublin, six of them, one for each day of the week. On Sundays
he wore a suit of dark worsted. Mary often watched him leave the
house, clean and shining from top to toe. He was a tall man, his face
round and pink as a doll's, his thin, white hair parted high on his
skull. He would step down the drive to his carriage, brisk as a boy,
and Mary would be proud that the shirt on his back was perfect, not
a faint of a wrinkle in it, not an inch but had felt the skill of her hot
iron. Mrs Price wanted to find Mary a position in London. She said
that Mary would be a treasure in the best of houses, but then Eileen
wrote to say that she wanted Mary near her in Bristol. So that was
settled. She was fourteen years and five months. The doctor felt
deep in his pocket and gave her a silver half-crown. He told her to
be careful in the world and never to forget the good home she came
from. Mrs Price gave her a kiss.

The next day she went down to Cork with the carter, leaving in
the thin dawn. She had with her the best dress newly made, her
clean changes, her prayer book and her beads, all folded away in a

small case. There was a thin frost on the top of the garden wall when she left, and on the grass. The stars were still out, high and pale in the sky. She had never been back to the village. Her ship slid between the kind green arms of the land and that was the last Mary saw of Ireland. That was the way of it. But she had been a good daughter, writing to her mother each Sunday and sending money when she could. She had been a better daughter than Eileen, if the truth be told. Eileen met her at Temple Meads Station in the middle of Bristol. The train had run for hours through the little towns of Wales, and then Cardiff and Newport. It had stopped in the Severn Tunnel, beneath the river. The carriage windows were blacker than night and Mary was sure she could feel the chill of the river waves coming down from well above her head, she thought the air she was breathing grew damper by the second. At last the engine had given a few little shrugs and slowly and heavily begun to move away, dragging its trailing coaches into the English daylight. So Mary had been glad to see Eileen standing unsmiling and solid at the ticket barrier. She remembers to this day the coat of navy wool that Eileen had been wearing.

Eileen worked for an old lady and gentleman who treated her like their own. She lived there like a princess with her own room and bathroom, and a free afternoon every week. The next day she took Mary to the house, two streets away, where Mr and Mrs Arbuthnot lived. Who would have thought that day, with all her advantages and her life in front of her, that Eileen would have taken the veil?

By that event Mary was already past eighteen and long settled with Mr and Mrs Arbuthnot. From the start she had loved the tall house with its high ceilings, she loved the way the stairs curved up from the wide hall. Twice a week she polished the mahogany stair rail, from top to bottom, all four floors. There wasn't a morning in all the time she lived with the Arbuthnots that she didn't rise without giving thanks for her fortune, without looking out of her window under the eaves at the gleaming angles of the slate roofs stretching away down the hill and into the city, where Mr Arbuthnot worked. He had his own offices, with men working for him, and was to do with shipping. Sometimes he brought with him for dinner great sea captains who sailed over the world, and then Mary would serve special meals. Mrs Arbuthnot would plan such a dinner for several days, always discussing the details with Mary, and then she would send Mary out to buy the materials. On the day itself Mary would have the dining room gleaming and would spend the afternoon checking the best silver, laying the white cloth of heavy damask,

placing the china, under Mrs Arbuthnot's supervision. In time she
could do all this herself, right down to choosing the flowers for the
table. She knew the grain on every piece of furniture, the patterns
in the carpets. More and more she took on herself the managing of
the house.

What she liked best of all were the summer evenings when Mrs
Arbuthnot took her into the long walled garden and told her the
names of the plants and shrubs. Espalier pear trees, Conference and
Belle Etoile, grew on the sunny west wall, a great russet apple, tall
as an oak, in the corner, an old vine, still bearing a heavy crop of
grapes, twined under the long glass of the greenhouse. In the nine
years she lived there Mary grew to think of the house as her home.
Sometimes she felt that it was her own house. Although it is nearly
sixty years since she last walked out of its door, the routine of her
days there is with her still. If God were to plant that house in front
of her she could go right in and take over.

'You're a competent girl, Mary,' Mrs Arbuthnot often said.
'You'll make someone a good wife.'

She had got married from the house. It was Walter Bloomfield
had taken her away, and that's who she is now, Mary Bloomfield.
She had first seen Walter Bloomfield at a church dance the summer
she was eighteen. She hadn't wanted to go, but the priest had made
such a show of it that she agreed in the end.

'I want to see you at the dance, Mary,' he'd said, 'so mind you
come now.'

He was only a boy from Rosslare after all, not all that older than
herself, and trying his best. Dwyer, his name was, Father Dwyer. It
was a lovely evening. She wore a white linen dress with a red belt
on it and she walked through the long warm shadows stretching on
the pavements. She'd seen Walter Bloomfield at once. He wasn't
tall, but he was a well-knit man, very graceful. He stood up and
made the most of himself. His hair was close and dark and he bore
a neat moustache on his lip. She could see he was a proud man. His
navy blazer was a good one, his white shirt, the collar up as young
men wore them those days, was spotless. She was surprised when
he walked over and asked her to dance. They'd spoken scarcely a
word the first time they danced.

The Bloomfields lived in a big old house in Clifton. There were
three stone steps up to the front door, which was the glossiest black
door Mary had ever seen. Right in the middle was a large brass knob.
Walter had three brothers and four sisters and they never stopped
talking and teasing. In that house everybody smiled, they rarely grew

angry or emotional. The garden was full of the boys' motorcycles, hutches for the rabbits and pigeons they'd kept when they were younger, vegetables and flowers growing haphazardly in what seemed the wrong places. Mary, silent and happy among them, loved them all. She would watch the girls go out, Ethel and Alice, dressed in their brave colours, laughing, and she thought there never had been such gallant girls in the world. Alice and Ethel worked in the city, Ernestine kept house and Maud, the oldest sister, was married and lived in Swindon. Their mother was long dead, but old Mr Bloomfield sat in the heart of his family. He had his chair near the range in the big kitchen, a wooden chair, high-backed. He was a short, plump man. He seemed to be looking far distances with his pale eyes, but he was sharp enough. When he spoke they all listened. He had been a lawyer's clerk, coming down from the country near Stroud when he was a young man, and he still sometimes went into the office. Walter worked for the same firm, and he would be a lawyer himself when he passed his exams. Mary loved the way the children looked after their father, warmly, almost without having to think. The girls got up from time to time to plump the cushions behind him, the young men brought him matches for his cigarettes, watched him tactfully. The old man had an accordion, a small instrument with leather straps to put one's hands through, its ivory stops yellow with age. He would take it into his hands from time to time and play glancing little melodies.

'Before he and Mother were married,' Walter told her, 'he would walk over the fields to Mother's house and she could hear him as he came, playing his accordion all the way.'

After that Mary could see Mr Bloomfield as a slim boy who lived long ago in some rural perfection, fair-haired and blue-eyed and playing his dancing melodies under the trees. She had been very sad when the old man died the year before she and Walter got married.

Their first house was a small, semi-detached house in Hotwells, near enough to his office for Walter to cycle to work. There was a tiny garden in front and a larger one at the back, and they kept both immaculate. They furnished very carefully, buying nice old pieces as they could afford them. It was Mary's pride to keep her husband and her house without flaw. She still had some of that furniture, shining from her care as if it had some inner light.

Walter was a good lawyer, careful and forthright. People trusted him and he began to prosper. When the children came along, they looked for another house, finally buying one in a Georgian terrace. Mary knew she would never want anything again in her whole life.

She had Patrick, and then Philip and then Kathleen, named for her mother. She had her house. Most of all she had Walter, around whom everything revolved. She was proud of him, of his distinct quiet voice, of his stillness. When he came home tired from his office, she saw to it the children did not annoy him unduly. She watched him through the windows as he walked through his garden, his hands behind his back. He was a good, serious, quiet man. She looked after him.

Then, when she thought they would have no more children, Dominic was born. She was delighted with him. He had her large, strong build, he was happy and generous. His great brown eyes looked at her with complete trust and innocence. It seemed to Mary that she knew what perfection was. When the child caught diphtheria she was outraged and desperate. She nursed him with a ferocious devotion that excluded everything else. She knew the other children crept quietly about the house, she was aware that Walter came to her from time to time, whispering, listening to her absorbed answers. When the little boy died Walter took her away and the doctor sedated her.

But she could not be comforted. In the days following Dominic's death she could see his face still before her, flushed with the fever. Time and again, as she stood awake and desolate in the house, she heard the child call for her. When her children came timidly to her, she clothed them and fed them by instinct, without knowing.

The year turned into autumn and the nights grew early dark. She took to leaving the house at dusk and walking abroad, pushing her heavy body along without grace, her lips stuck forward in a scowl, her eyes on the ground. She spoke to nobody. She would walk until she was exhausted, returning to fall into a heavy sleep. When in time the face of the little boy began to fade from her mind she was in agony. She began to see him as if he were a long way off, at the end of a tunnel, smiling at her, and at last he went. But she never lost his voice. Even now she can call it up by an act of will, Dominic's voice, calling her. At night, or in her light sleep just before dawn, she will start up at the child's call and answer him. If he were alive he would be a man of fifty.

She came home one night from her stubborn plodding of the roads. Walter was not in his chair, waiting for her as he always did. He stood against the window in the dark room and she saw his outline. He was so thin and bent she scarcely recognised him. She switched on the light and looked at him. His face was grey and lined. He told Mary of his unhappiness, that he could no longer live as

they had through the months of her mourning. She could see that
something vital had gone from the man.

In the morning she cleaned her house in a fury of action. All day
she scoured and polished. When her children came home from
school she welcomed them. They sat together and ate supper, but
the children were wary of her. From that day on she sent them
lovingly away each morning and met them at the door when they
returned, yet it was not the same as it had been.

That year, the week before Christmas, they packed their furniture
and moved to Shrewsbury. Walter had taken a partnership in a
country firm owned by a friend. He had remained silent and
withdrawn, he had grown to hate Bristol. Mary stood in the empty
house and felt nothing. The years of her care were as nothing. They
drove north in the cold evening, flurries of snow taking them along
the roads. Dominic was left in a small grave miles from Mary's life.

The house they bought was outside the town, to the west. It had
been a farmhouse, but all the land had been sold separately except
for the garden, walled on three sides, and an orchard of four acres.
Cider apples grew there, Beauty of Bath and Tom Putt. Hard, red
apples, old varieties. They lay under the untended trees all winter.

Walter bought ten goslings in the spring. They grew quickly and
lived in the orchard, foraging in the long grass. They were immensely knowing, raising their strident voices as Walter came up
the drive in his car. He loved them. Most evenings he spent some
time with them; they knew his voice, came to him when he called.
Often he would lean on the fence, looking towards the hills of Wales,
the pied birds about him. Some of the geese lived for twenty years,
still there when the children persuaded Mary to sell the house after
Walter's death. Well, the children had grown and gone, the house
was too big. She had got a good price for it, she was well provided
for.

She is a square old woman living in a small house the children
chose for her, with everything to hand. Not all the children, for
Patrick was lost at sea during the war. A dark, handsome boy, with
too much charm for his own good. She smiles at the thought of
Patrick. She has photographs in her parlour of all her children;
Philip, mayor of his town, so good to her, so proper, Kathleen, living
in Cambridge and mostly a voice on the telephone, dead Patrick,
dead Dominic. She has lived here for over two years and does not
like the house. It has no style, it is too new, generations of lives have
not used it and polished it and given it the idiosyncrasies of use and
love.

She is in her garden now, burning away the detritus of years. She is eighty-two years old and it is time to do this. She has made a bonfire in a corner of her garden and is burning the photographs of people she has forgotten, the letters which came at Christmas as regularly as the seasons, and faltered, and stopped. All she has left to destroy are the tidy bundles of Walter's papers, taken from his desk. They are in order, dated, meticulous, old bank accounts, copies of business letters, the children's school reports. She is suddenly fiercely angry with Walter. He had no right to die, to go so quietly out of life. She was not ready for that. She is a sturdy fighter.

What she has in her hand now is her father-in-law's birth certificate. It is brown with age, the paper thin and very delicate, but the words still clear. The print is red and elegant, the handwriting that leisurely script people used at the end of the last century. The certificate records the birth of Daniel Bloomfield in Stroud, in February of 1874. She had never thought of that plump little man, Walter's father, as a baby, as somebody's son. Lemuel and Hannah Bloomfield's son. She almost hears again the tunes he played on his accordion, she can see again his daughters, those bright and gallant girls long dead. Her own sister Eileen is dead. She had been to see Eileen towards the end, she had been an old nun among others. There had been two or three long grey hairs on Eileen's chin.

'Make your peace,' Eileen had told her.

But she would never make her peace, she would struggle on.

She drops the flimsy paper and sees the last of Daniel Bloomfield hang above the embers of her burning, curl, and flame. It is now she hears her own voice rise in lamentation over the smoke of her fire. She is not keening for any death, not for her father's distant end, not for Dominic's death still bitter with her. Her mourning is not for Walter, her faith in him is strong and the sense of his care is still about her. She is crying aloud for the burden of her body and its solitariness. She laments because her life is to be one of memories, and she weeps for the sorrow and pleasure which had been hers. Her voice is clear and powerful, she does not halt its rising, its desolate falling.

The Brighton Midgets

There was nobody in The Victoria when I entered and I wasn't surprised. All night a storm had lunged in off the sea, carrying the weight of winter with it. Loads of gravel had been lifted off the beach and blown irregularly along the sea-front. It lay in wet drifts in gutters and doorways. Toby Williams was out with a gang from the public works trying to get the road cleaned up, but the wind still blew in rough gusts.

'Might as well be in Siberia,' an old man said to me, his eyes watering. He scuttled into Smith's to get his morning paper.

There was a good fire in The Victoria. The brass and gilt and red glass, much of it genuine period, shone in the warmth. It was quiet. The two young men who owned the place, failed artists both of them, had made it look nice. I sat down and waited for Big Sam Bailey who was already late. I did a lot of business in The Victoria, you could call it my office. I am not a qualified accountant, I just took over after my father died. I was seventeen. I left high school and carried on, making up the books and computing the tax for a number of small firms.

Big Sam Bailey looked really bad when he came in. His face was blue and he was bent into his top-coat. He's an old man, he was a friend of my father's.

'What are you having, Mr Bailey?' I said.

He leaned, gasping, against the bar.

'Let me catch my breath, boy,' he said.

After a while he stood up, smiled, wiped his eyes, and thumped the bell that waited for him on the counter. Vernon Tethers minced in from the back of the building, his earring agleam.

'Give me a brandy, Vernon,' Big Sam said. He looked at Vernon with an objective distaste. 'If you've got that Spanish brandy, make it a double.'

He rubbed his enormous hands together. He really is a big man. 'The cold gets into your bones,' he said.

I had never seen him like this. I've known him since I was a small boy. A loud, laughing brash man, he used to slip me a secretive pound note so awkwardly that everybody saw his generosity. He'd helped me when my father died, knowing that I had done the real work for two years or so. He's a lovely old man.

'I've been up the crematorium,' he said. 'By gum, it makes you think. And it's cold. Freeze a brass monkey.'

'Friend of yours?' I said.

'Fellow my own age,' he said, 'known him years.'

Vernon came up with the drinks. Sam sneered as the young man turned away.

'I'm too old to change,' he said. 'I remember when this house was a nice pub. Very busy, lovely trade. All sorts and conditions coming in and out. And I remember it before that, when it was very rough, this was a very rough area. All the nobs went further up the beach in those days. We used to come down here every Saturday night, closing time, watch the fights outside. Oh, it was rough.' He shivered, took a sip of his brandy.

'That overcoat of yours,' I said, 'that ought to keep you warm.' I leaned forward and tapped him on the chest.

Big Sam looked down complacently, smug in his splendid coat.

'Remember Tommy Farr?' he said, 'Perhaps you wouldn't, before your time. Fought Joe Louis, fifteen round decision, robbed is my opinion. Welshman, though with a name like that he ought to have been an Irishman, or perhaps a gipsy. I've known gipsies called Farr. After he left the ring he retired down here, had a nice little house along the coast.'

Sam was feeling better. He began to smile, his colour was much more jovial.

'I've heard him singing,' he said, 'in this very room.'

He stared about contemptuously. 'Course it wasn't tarted up like this then, this was in Joe Livesey's day, old Joe, your father knew him. I've heard Tommy Farr sing in this room, tink-atonk on the piano, sing a few songs. Very soft voice he had, very smooth.'

'I've heard of him,' I said.

'You would have.' Big Sam said, 'Very famous in his day, very gallant fighter.'

We took our drinks to a table near the fire and removed our coats. Sam hung his tenderly on a coat-hook.

'I was in London,' he said, 'not so many years ago. I was in a taxi going for Victoria Station, late for the last train. We swung into the station yard, over those cobbles, you know where, and there was Tommy Farr running for it. He must have been seventy then, if a day. My taxi-driver sat up as if I'd stabbed him. "It's Farr, it's Tommy Farr!" he shouted. Couldn't have been more excited if the Queen herself had walked across and given him a medal. "Tommy!" he was yelling, "Hi, Tommy Farr!".'

'What did he do?' I said, 'Tommy Farr, I mean?'

'Well, that's it,' he said, 'he was marvellous in a way. He turned and waved without missing a step. And just see him running! It was a sight to see.'

'Fast?' I said.

'Oh, fast enough,' Sam said, 'but it was more than that. It was the freedom of it, the elegance. He ran with long flat strides. He didn't run like a young man, but like a marvellous old man. With certainty, somehow, and dignified. You could feel the weight and size of him, above his long legs. He had a big hat, a bit like a Stetson, and a coat like this, very like this. The front of it swung open with every stride, you could see the silk lining. I knew then that one day I'd have a coat like that, and I have.'

We smiled at each other with shared pride.

'Real camel-hair,' he said, 'the real stuff.' He was very contented.

'Could be,' he said, 'could just be this is the same coat.' He widened his little eyes at me. 'You know where I got it?'

I knew where he'd got it, but I shook my head. I couldn't stop him telling me anyway. He always went on like a force of nature, like the storm wind off the sea.

'Where I buy all my togs,' he said, 'and have for years. From old Erasmus Merriweather, up in the Lanes. What stuff he has in that old ruin of his — he has the best of everything. And do you know why?'

'Tell me,' I said.

'Because he buys up the clothes of all the wealthy dead. He buys gentlemen's wardrobes.' In Sam's voice I could hear the genteel echo of Erasmus Merriweather's speech. I'd bought a suit from Erasmus once, grey flannel chalk-stripe. I always felt cold in it.

'Buys them from the relatives, the rich relatives,' said Big Sam, 'gets them cleaned and pressed, sells them to the discerning poor like me. Only he hardly ever buys anything big enough for me. That's why I've wondered if this could be Tommy Farr's coat.'

'It could be,' I said. I could see that it meant a lot to Sam. 'I didn't know you were keen on boxing.'

'Not keen on boxing!' said Big Sam, astonished, 'Come on down to the office and I'll show you something.'

'All right,' I said. I knew I had to go there anyway. He hadn't brought any of his documents along, his accounts and receipts, the old check-stubs, the stuff I needed to make out his tax returns. He was getting old. He forgot a lot of things. We muffled up and went out into the wind.

It was dramatic to see Sam change. His face fell away, his full cheeks shrank against his teeth, he shrivelled within his opulent coat.

I couldn't believe it. Sam was a man who had spent his life out of doors. He sold the used cars which were his stock in trade off the streets, his office was a wooden shed on a small plot of ground he owned. I had thought he was invulnerable. He shuffled along as if the stones under his feet were snares and traps, were made of sheets of implacable ice.

'Don't worry, boy,' he said, 'had a bit of a shock this morning up at the crematorium. I'll be all right.'

The dead couldn't have been colder than Sam's office. He switched on an old two-bar electric heater and sat at his desk. He didn't take off his coat. He was a long time searching in the back of a drawer, but finally he took out a vanilla envelope, shaking from it a bundle of photographs. He shuffled them about, muttering and humming until he found what he wanted. Two black and white photographs, post card size. Gently he flattened their bent corners, passed one to me. It was the likeness of a young man, a boxer, fair-haired, sturdy, his arms flexed. About his waist he wore an enormous gilt belt, elaborate and garish.

'That's Freddie Miller.' Sam said, 'Champion of the world, featherweight. Came over to England and beat everybody. This was before the war, in the twenties. Very strong, very competent. Punched very hard to the body. Punched as if he wanted to break you in two.'

I looked at Freddie Miller. His face was quizzical and intelligent.

'He looks quite pleasant.' I said, 'He looks a decent young man.'

'Why not?' Sam said. He was looking at the second photograph, seriously, intently.

'That's me,' he said, 'the kid on the right.'

In the second photograph Freddie Miller, still in his boxing trunks and wearing his championship belt, stared smiling out at me. He held, one on each arm, two small boys, both in trunks, ridiculously large boxing gloves on their hands. I looked at the young Sam. I recognised him easily. He held his head rather low and he was grinning as if he was very well aware of the absurdity of the whole situation, as if he alone understood that this was all acting. The other small boy sat up proudly on Freddie Miller's arm, straight-backed, serious. His hair was slicked back and lay flat on his skull. His narrow face was unsmiling, his whole expression composed and stern.

'How old were you then, Sam,' I said. It was the first time I'd ever called him Sam. It was seeing him as a little boy, I think.

'Eight,' he said, grinning, 'I was a veteran of eight years old. And Barty was nine.'

'Barty?' I said.

'Barty Sullivan, my partner,' Sam said. 'Bartholomew. We were the Brighton Midgets. Fought all over the place, Colston Hall in Bristol, the Crystal Palace, Ninian Park in Cardiff. When those photos were taken we were fighting at the Albert Hall. I could show you fight bills with our names on, Liverpool, Reading, oh everywhere. We were a novelty. We looked very small, of course. We were only young lads.'

He took the photographs from me.

'Barty's dad,' he said, 'was an Irishman, came from Ireland. He was a waiter here in town. First time I ever came to Brighton was to go to Barty's house — his dad married my mother's sister. I lived out Lewes way, my dad worked on farms all his life, very respectable family we were. I was the only child.'

He stared at the photographs as if he had never seen them before, with a sort of hunger.

'All those years ago.' he said, 'Who'd have thought it!'

'So Barty was your cousin,' I said.

'First cousin,' said Sam. 'His father put us up to it, boxing I mean. I think he always wanted to go in the ring himself, but he never had the physique for it. Thin man, he was, very thin. Dressed well, had bad feet. Barty looked a lot like him. Of course it was all a bit of a joke.'

'What do you mean?' I said.

'It was like this wrestling.' Sam said, 'On the television. Barty was the good one, I was the evil one. Barty stood up straight and played the game while I rushed about hitting low, punching on the break, all that stuff. Then in the third round Barty would catch me one and down I'd go. Little Thespians we were, the pair of us. Only Barty really believed it.'

He put the photographs in his long envelope, pushed the drawer shut.

'Until I got tired of it,' he said.

He was grinning.

'I used to have old Billy Dando in my corner.' he said. 'Bill used to flap the towel at me between rounds. He had a head like a potato, hardly any teeth, but he was very sharp just the same. He could see I was getting restless, told my uncle so. One night, in the The Ring, Blackheath, it was, not a very important bill. Well I was getting quite big then, for my age. I was much bigger than Barty.'

He told me how the two boys had entered the ring under the blue smoke, bowed and waved at their introductions, turned to touch gloves as they had many times before at the sound of the bell.

'And then I stepped in,' Sam said, 'and walloped Barty. I hit him right between the eyes. We couldn't hurt each other really, the gloves were like pillows. He fell down and sat on the floor, looking at his father. It was as much as I could do to stop laughing. When he got up I hit him down again. That was the end of the Brighton Midgets.'

He leaned across his desk, laughing, remembering.

'I haven't thought of that for years,' he said, 'Barty never forgave me.'

'What happened to him?' I said.

'In time the war came along,' Sam said. 'Barty joined up at once, couldn't wait for his short back and sides. Looked lovely, he did, in khaki. He was a handsome boy. Married a little girl from out Shoreham way, very nice. Her father was a fruiterer.'

'You weren't in the Army, Sam,' I said.

'No,' he said. 'That was a lucky accident, you might say. I left home to work down here in the market, self-employed, doing a bit of this, a bit of that. My call-up papers went to my father's house up in the country, and we had the same name, Samuel Lewis Bailey. My old man had no imagination. And slow, I can't say how slow. I'd tell him a joke Monday and he'd start laughing Friday. My mother was dead by this time and my father was living alone. Big man he was, as big as I am. Red face, the skin stretched tight across the bones. You'd think working in the fields he'd have a nice tan, a nice colour, but no. Every time the sun came out, he turned red.'

He looked down the years at his father and sighed gently.

'Nice man,' he said, 'Gentle, quiet. The only thing he cared about were his cows and his dog.'

'What did he do about your call-up papers?' I said.

'Ah,' said Sam, 'He thought they were for him. He walked into Lewes and told them that there was a mistake, that he was too old to join the army. Fellow asked him if there was anyone else of that name living at that address. There wasn't. Last anyone heard about it. By the time the war was over I had a little bit of money, had made a start in business.'

'Let's have that stuff,' I said, 'All your bills and receipts for last tax year.'

I could see I wasn't going to have any lunch that day.

'It was about that time I met your dad,' Sam said. 'What a head for figures, what a memory.'

'He was pretty good,' I said. He wasn't at all extraordinary, in truth, but he was persevering, industrious, absolutely honest.

'What happened to Barty?' I asked.

'He couldn't settle at all.' Sam said. 'He came back from the army full of himself. He'd been a sergeant, fought in the desert, El Alamein, all that stuff. Couldn't find a job good enough for him. He even left town for a couple of years, tried his luck in the Midlands, Coventry, Birmingham.'

'What a pity,' I said.

'I gave him a job,' Sam said. 'You could see he hated it. Hated me. He was hopeless at it, he couldn't sell ice in the Sahara. One day I thought I'd talk to him, see if I could get him to see sense. We had two drinks in the Embassy and I had to drive him home. He couldn't take any alcohol at all. I hadn't known that. I got him inside his house. I could see his wife was frightened, and Barty was very difficult. Truculent you could say. Asked for his dinner. She took it out of the stove, Betty her name was. Without a word he threw it into the grate, food, plate everything.'

'What did you do?' I said.

'Put him to bed,' said Sam. 'When I got him in the bedroom I gave him a few digs to teach him a lesson. No way to treat his wife. Next day he didn't come to work. I never saw him again.'

Sam started to look for his papers. Normally he put them all in a cardboard box and handed the whole lot over. It took me a week sometimes just to put them in some sort of coherent order.

'Didn't go far, Barty didn't,' Sam said. He held a sheaf of bank statements in his hand. I could see they belonged to the previous year. 'But I never saw him. His wife left him and I used to see her about. Good thing they had no children.'

'They might have saved him,' I said, 'if he'd had children.'

Sam shook his head. He was rummaging in the top drawer of his old wooden filing cabinet. 'I had them all in here together for you,' he said. 'No, Barty was finished. He lived over in East Sussex, on his own. Ah, here's some of them.'

Pleased, he gave me a fistful of miscellaneous papers.

'That's where I've been today,' he said, 'Up the crematorium, seeing Barty off. His wife phoned me last night to tell me that Barty was dead and the service was this morning. The police had got in touch with her. Upset me, I can tell you. He was almost a year younger than I am and, oh, he was a handsome boy when he was young. It makes you think when something like that comes along.'

He had found the whole of his accounts, much more neatly and sensibly arranged than usual. I put them in my case and prepared to leave.

'It's cold in here, Frank,' he said, 'Don't you think it's cold? These old heaters don't give much warmth.'

'You'll be all right,' I said.

I shut the door behind me.

Frank was my father's name.

Fire Fire

The fields had been holding their faces up to the sun since dawn. Already the developing heat had burned away a thin mist from the land. It was going to be another hot day. For nearly seven weeks there had been no true rain, only a heavy dew that dried in an hour under the first warmth. Yellow evidence of ripeness was creeping up the stalks of wheat and barley; the hay was rich and somnolent, waiting for sharp blades. All over the county farmers were at work, their hot tractors smelling of oil, their big-uddered cows swinging weightily to the meadows after the relief of milk. But in Danycastell, Mervyn Pritchard slept on.

He slept deeply and innocently, as he had always slept. When at last he was disturbed by the bawling of his restless cows, he awoke like a child, at once, abruptly. He leaped out of bed, took the bundle of his clothes in one hand, his boots in the other, and danced down the wooden stairs. His small, plump body was as agile as a boy's. From the cobbled yard his twelve cows lowed their protests.

'You can wait, damn you,' he said mildly, 'Another five minutes won't hurt you.'

He filled the kettle and put it on the stove to boil. Then he dressed. He folded back the neck of his shirt and began to wash at the kitchen sink. He washed deliberately, with pleasure, rubbing a thick lather into the crevices of his skin, feeling the bristles of his beard scrape against his hard palms. He swilled away the soap, pouring silver water again and again over his face and neck until the skin squeaked under his hands. He dried on the towel that hung on a peg behind the door. When the kettle boiled he took a large stoneware tea-pot from a shelf and made tea. It was his favourite tea-pot, one with a plain brown glaze, heavy and full in the bowl. He carried it to the table. Only then did he call up the stairs to his wife. He heard her turn in the bed.

'We're late,' he shouted, 'And that boy hasn't done the milking. Bring my tea out to the dairy, there's a good girl.'

Her reply was muffled and incoherent.

'Bloody boy does as he likes,' Pritchard said quietly, to himself.

He trotted across the yard in a quick, unreasonable temper. He wouldn't be in time now to get his full churns to the top of the lane, where they should have been collected by the truck. It would mean loading them on his pick-up and hauling them up to the main road, hoping he'd catch the truck on its way to the processing factory. Otherwise he would have to pour the lot down the drain. He set his cows in their stalls, working deftly, none of his irritation showing as he adjusted the suction cups that would take away the tight milk. He spoke to each animal, his voice soft and low, as he bent to them. When he was a boy he had worked as his father told him, the two of them in harmony. But things were different now. The young knew everything. He looked along the placid line of his cows and the last of his anger left him. He delighted in them, admiring and assessing their straight backs, the line of haunch and shoulder, the deep strong bodies. He had bred them all, had known each one as a tottering calf drinking from a bucket, watched them as fresh heifers, skittish and unpredictable. He admired the haphazard patching of their black and white hides as other men look at paintings. When his wife came into the dairy with his tea, Mervyn Pritchard was whistling.

'It's our own fault,' she said, 'Bryn told us he was going to work for Mr Carruthers today. He's helping with the hay.'

'What's he doing there?' Mervyn said, 'Isn't there plenty to do here?'

'Not really,' said his wife, 'Not enough for two men. And we don't pay him a proper wage.'

'Wage, is it,' said Pritchard, suddenly roaring, 'Did I get wages from my father? It was enough for me to know that the farm would come to me in my turn, and it will go to Bryn in his turn. By looking after this place he's looking after himself.'

He turned away. Two swallows came and went to their nest in the beams above his head. Their young were almost ready to fly. They would soon be gone.

'Bryn is seventeen,' said Mary Pritchard, 'He needs money. And he needs more than one small place, a few fields he's walked in all his life. He wants other people.'

'It's Carruthers,' said Pritchard, 'I know what the trouble is. Carruthers with his new machines and his pedigree herd and his pockets full of money God knows where from. I know only too well what the trouble is.'

His face had turned brutish and sullen, his small bright eyes angry. He hated Carruthers, the Englishman who had come in and bought a number of farms, running them as a single unit. He hated Carruthers's efficiency and confidence, his sunny assumption that the world was a simple and happy place. He sneered at the man's expensive clothes, imitated his accent.

'There's nothing wrong with Carruthers,' his wife said, 'He'd be friendly if you gave him a chance.'

Pritchard did not answer. He could see in his mind's eye the little farms as they had been before Carruthers came, each with its old house, each with a family he had known all his life. Their fields had been hedged with hazel and hawthorn, with holly and rowan here and there, untidy, straggling hedges. Some of them had sizeable oaks, so they were very old. But they weren't good enough for Carruthers. He had ripped them out, thrown four or five fields into one, built fancy white fences about them, as if they were city gardens.

'No good will come of talking to Carruthers,' he said.

'I don't know what's come over you,' said his wife. 'What has Carruthers ever done to you? You're so moody these days, I don't know when to speak or when to keep quiet. Everybody thinks you're so light-hearted and pleasant and it used to be like that. But how can I deal with you now? One minute you're sunshine and the next you're thunder.'

It was true. Pritchard knew it was true. Not long ago he would never have been late for milking, not long ago his yard would have been as orderly as a barracks. Mary was right. He put his hand gently on the woman's shoulder and grinned.

'To hell with Carruthers then,' he said, 'Let's forget him, and let me get this milk up to the top road or it will never reach the factory. We can't afford that.'

They stood close together, listening to the rhythmical sucking of the pump, watching the small convulsions of the hoses as they carried the milk to the tank.

Heat haze obscured the distance as Pritchard stood at the roadside, waiting for the truck to come down from the hill farms. In the fields around, the cut hay lay in swathes, or waited, pressed in bales, to be carted away. It was a good year for hay. The air was perfumed with its heady drying. From Dan-yr-Allt, from Ty Gwyn, from Carruther's land which almost surrounded his own, Pritchard could hear the dry shuttling of machines as they circled the fields, harvesting the hay. He closed his eyes against the light, imagining his own fields. He saw the deep colour of his grass, the stems sea-green and the heads tawny, yellow, lime-green, changing when a little wind ran through. Like water, like a sea. When he was young they had cut the hay by hand, he and his father, with help from neighbours. They had used the old scythes, beautiful tools curved in blade and handle, each one subtly different, grown to fit its owner. They had reaped the fields, moving as one man, forward and back, gracefully, swinging. An old skill, not many could do it nowadays. Although they still cut like that on the high farms, cropping the thin, pale hay by hand on slopes too steep for machines. The trick was to take the grass back with the thick of the blade, flat, level to the ground and very close to it. Then the stems stood up for cutting as the edge came sweetly forward, the scythe so balanced that it swung of its own volition, on the hinges of your arms, on the fulcrum of your waist. The stems fell crisply in the forward sweep of the scythe so that its working music was a dry, swinging whisper, swing . . . and back, swing . . . and back. It took a long time. Pritchard opened his eyes as the truck came along the road.

The driver was a stuttering boy from the town. Together they heaved the churns over the dropped tailboard. Pritchard chained the board in place and slapped the truck's side, sending the milk on its way. He had been worried about it, but now he was free. The sun shone on him, promising him a day of infinite leisure. He climbed into his old pick-up and drove into the village.

Coming from the brilliant light into the gloom of Evans's shop, Pritchard could sense someone standing at the counter.

'Hello, Mervyn,' said Maggie Jenkins, her voice full and sly. 'We don't see you very often these days, do we. Quite a stranger.'

Maggie Jenkins. He'd gone to school with Maggie Jenkins, and a proper trouble-maker she'd been, reporting every misdeed to the flogging headmaster. The beatings she'd caused for him and Dickie Davies were beyond number. She hadn't changed, she still had a mischievous tongue.

'You don't see much of Dickie Davies, do you?' she said.

She might have been reading his mind, the witch.

'No,' he said shortly, 'Let's have some cigarettes, Evans.'

Evans, in his white coat reached up to a high shelf for the cigarettes.

'Mervyn is very busy,' he said, 'he has no time now for those tricks.'

He winked at Mervyn as he handed over the packet.

'Remember the time,' said Maggie Jenkins, 'when you locked the headmaster's lavatory door and he couldn't use it for three days? In the end he asked Dickie to do something about it and Dickie brought him a bucket.'

Evans snorted behind his counter.

'He caned you both,' Maggie Jenkins said thoughtfully, 'Not that it did either of you any good. Still, it's strange you don't see anything of Dickie, you and he were such friends.'

'A ne'er-do well,' said Evans, 'A loser. Mervyn is better away from him.'

'Mary keeps you on a tight lead, I expect,' Maggie Jenkins said, 'I know I would. The number of times I've seen you and Dickie staggering home! Before you were married, of course.'

'I'll have some matches, Evans,' Mervyn said, 'Keep Maggie Jenkins out of your shop or you'll have no trade left.'

The woman laughed easily, in her deep, slow voice.

'You're a tamed tiger, Mervyn,' she said, 'You're a pussy-cat.'

Standing outside, in the heat, Pritchard thought of Dickie Davies, the tall, thin boy who had been his friend. Dickie had been perfect, inventive in his fun, reckless in his escapades, loyal in his friendship. Together they had roared through the Saturday summer towns, had sung in winter against the weather.

Dickie had never married. Now that his mother was dead, he lived alone in a small, profitless holding in the hills, a dozen miles away. Pritchard looked up at the sky. The hot spell would surely hold a few more days. He would cut his hay tomorrow. He climbed into his truck and set off.

Dickie Davies stood at the door of his falling house, shading his eyes, watching Mervyn bump down the rough lane.

'I thought it was you,' he said, 'I've been thinking of you all the week. Come in.'

The ash and spoil of unraked fires stood in Dickie's grate. The house smelled of poverty. It didn't matter. They began to speak as if they had met only a day before, their friendship continuous and unflawed.

'Let's go outside,' Dickie said. 'I've got a bottle of whisky. Come outside and sit on the bench.'

He moved slowly, his shoulders bent. His clothes were sour, his boots unlaced, his face lined and unhealthy. It was difficult to see the lively young man he'd been.

'Look rough, don't I?' Dickie said, 'Well, I am rough. I'm old and broken, Mervyn, that's what I am.'

'We're neither of us old,' Pritchard said, 'Some real food and a bit of care and you'd be as good as ever you were. Come down to us for a couple of weeks and let Mary fatten you up. Do you a power of good.'

Davies shook his head.

'You've been lucky,' he said, 'Things have worked out for you, and I'm glad. But nobody's immune, boy, nobody.'

A few skinny hens scratched in the barren corners of the yard, a goat stared from the rampant nettles.

'The years,' Dickie Davies said, 'They're like a bloody fire, boy. They burn and burn, and when they're gone — we're just cinders.'

Pritchard looked on in silence. The day seemed suddenly cold.

Davies reached down for the bottle.

'Not a cure,' he said, 'but a real comfort. Drink up. There's more where that came from.'

It was dark when Pritchard left the broken house. He drove through the lanes with exaggerated caution, singing the songs he and Dickie had sung together long ago, feeling a maudlin compassion for the soft moths he swept to death in his headlights. His home was unlit and unforgiving, and he stumbled to bed. Before dawn he dreamed that a malicious wind arose, with hail and hammering rain. It was so palpable a storm that he awoke with a start into a windless night, recognising his dream as the image of his guilt. A white owl, its talons ready, drifted past his window as he turned again to sleep.

The morning kitchen, swept and shining, reproached him as he ate his breakfast alone. His cows were already milked. He could hear the tractor at work in the top field. Bryn was cutting the hay. Pritchard leaned on the gate, watching his son as he turned his machine about the field. The boy was good, the tractor might have been part of him. Pritchard felt a sudden pride, in the plentiful hay as it fell, in his land, in his son.

'We'll do this together,' he said, 'I'll give you a hand. Go down and get something to eat. I'll carry on here.'

The boy looked at him with scorn.

'Do you think you can?' he jeered, 'Do you feel up to it?'

Pritchard put a hand to his head, comically mocking his pulsing hangover, confessing his fault, smiling at his boy.

'Yes,' he said, 'I can do it.'

All day he worked under the sun, sick and sweating. Dust from the dry earth covered him, pointed stalks of hay worked under his shirt and stabbed and worried his skin. And in the evening, calm and spent after his shower, out of the comradeship of their shared labour and for the love of his son, he agreed that they should visit Carruthers. The boy was eager.

'You'll love it, Dad,' Bryn said. 'He's got a great place there.'

Pritchard sat in Carruther's huge room, gazing out of the French windows on to the lawn. He had walked Carruther's fields, stood in his new dairy, admired his herd. The man had sixty milkers, and some young stock coming along. His cows were Ayrshires, a sturdy, temperamental breed; they'd take some managing. Mervyn sipped at his sherry. He wouldn't want to change places with Carruthers.

Bryn and Carruthers were looking at a map of the area, so large it almost covered a wall. The man was talking vividly, outlining his plans. He showed them where he was going to build his grain drier, where the Dutch barns would replace the stone building, with walls a yard thick, in which the old Thomases for generations had carried out most of the tasks of the farm.

Pritchard sat up.

'You're not going to pull down the big barn?' he said. He could not believe anyone would do such a thing.

'We have to move with the times, Pritchard,' Carruthers said, 'We must be efficient, make the best use of what we have.'

He was a tall man, a smiling man, brisk and assured.

'But the land doesn't change,' Mervyn said. 'It was here before us and it will be here after us. We are its servants, not its masters. God won't make any more land.'

Relaxed after heavy labour, tolerant in the golden evening, he spoke pleasantly to Carruthers. The man would learn in time.

'Those of us who have lived here all our lives,' he said, 'and our fathers too, before us, we know the old careful ways of using the land, ways which have grown up gradually and quietly. We don't deal in fashions. We change only when we see the need.'

'But you don't,' said Carruthers, 'You don't change when there's need.'

'He's right, Dad,' Bryn said. He stood by the man's side, his eyes bright. 'We could do much more with Danycastell.'

Carruthers stabbed a finger at his map.

'Look at this little field of yours,' he said. 'How big is it? Four acres, five? It's no use to anyone. Scrub and bramble and cotton-grass. You couldn't even keep geese on such a place. But drained and cleaned, ploughed a few times, d'you see how it could be added to your big pasture, to your great advantage?'

Mervyn looked down at his shoes. He loved his rough field. It was there he had gone as a boy, when he was troubled, for his necessary solitude. Three springs surfaced there, losing themselves in viridian moss, making a sodden bog of the ground. Everywhere there were tufts of reed, and brambles grew in enormous banks over the blackthorn hedges. Once, on his thirteenth birthday, chastened by feelings he could not understand, Mervyn had gone to his small

wilderness and stood there, unaware of time. A fox, red as autumn
bracken, had stepped delicately quite close to him, and stopped,
alert, head raised, its forefoot lifted in the act of stepping. It had
looked at him with its green eyes. For the first time, Mervyn knew
of another world alongside his own, a remote and inhuman world.

'I'd not like to see the field changed,' he said gently, knowing that
Carruthers would never understand.

Carruthers laughed.

'You're a hopeless case,' he said, 'but I must admit you're a great
stockman. I wish I had your eye for an animal. I can plan and
manage, I'm a good businessman, but I can't see an animal as you
do. I've watched you at the market. You look at creature after
creature as they enter the ring, weighing them up, dismissing them.
Suddenly one fills your eye and you're a different man. It's a great
gift. You should capitalise on it.'

He waved his pipe at Mervyn.

'That's one reason why I'm glad you've called this evening,' he
said, 'I'd like you to look over my young rams — you know I have
a lot of Suffolks. These youngsters are early born, and I've kept back
about thirty of them. I need two or three for next season's breeding
and I'd like your opinion.'

The young rams were beautiful, their saffron backs broad, their
black legs clean and well-boned, the pale lemon eyes gleamed in
their fastidious heads. Mervyn had never seen better. He set to work,
rejecting one after another until there were five sheep penned in a
corner of the field.

'I can't separate those,' he said, 'you should keep them all.'

'Too many for me,' Carruthers said, 'you've got a few sheep,
Pritchard. I'd be obliged if you took one of them, if you think he'd
be of use to you. After all, you've been kind enough to sort them
out for me.'

Mervyn turned away.

'It was a neighbour's act,' he said, 'I don't want a fee.'

He was embarrassed. The man had no idea of how to behave.

'Take it, Dad,' Bryn said. 'We could use one of them, we really
could. Mr Carruthers would like to give you one.'

The boy was eager, excited. Mervyn looked at him. The farm
would belong to Bryn. It was time he had some place in its affairs.
Pritchard turned and held out his hand to Carruthers.

He put the new ram into the field next to the house, where he could
see it through the kitchen window. Sometimes he opened the gate

from the lane and went into the field and stood, admiring the animal. Its fleece was crisp and yellow, it was upright and masculine. Pritchard began to dream of next spring's lambs, when his flock would be revivified. The ram made him consider his whole farm afresh. He could start again, he would make Danycastell a model for the countryside.

The summer died away slowly and magnificently, the morning air carried in it a little chill. Mervyn went down to his unused field, pushing his way through thorn and bramble. Everything was dry, the small rills of the springs were dry, the ground dusty. If he burned off the rubbish now, when everything was ready for the flames, then he could drain the cleared field. He could deepen the silted ditches, cut and order the hedges. Plough it, sow it with grass seed. It would grow fine grass, enough to keep a dozen prime sheep, the best of his crop of lambs.

He made a pile of old sacks, splashed on some fuel. The heap lit at the touch of a match, but burned slowly, under a pillar of smoke. Pritchard threw on an old tyre. Now the fire began to roar, although the sunshine was bright enough to make the light, clear flames almost invisible. The noise was suddenly huge, cracking and plundering, flames scurrying everywhere, leaping from tuft to tuft of the dead reeds. Pritchard stood back, exultant and aghast. The whole field was alight. Fragments of soot floated high in the hot air, out over the other fields, over the house. Flames puffed up at his feet and he stamped at them, savagely, in alarm. The fire was out of control. Pritchard raced for the yard. His clothes were hot against his body, his eyes weeping and smoke-filled. He grabbed a spade and began to dig furiously at the edge of the fire, beating and slapping as the flames approached. He did not know how long he laboured. His lungs were filled with smoke, his boots and clothes scorched. But the fire was dying. He could see that it was dying. It had been a surface fire only, furious and terrifying, but the old stubborn hedges had restricted it to the dry growth of the field. Charred skeletons of hazel stood black in the burned field. At the edges of destruction tiny ghosts of flames revived as they caught at unburned flakes, and died again. Pritchard leaned on his spade. He was tired.

He did not hear Mary at first, did not understand her urgent haste. He looked about, thinking that some of the fire had escaped, that somewhere it was running through his farm. Then he heard clearly. He had not closed the field gate near the house when he had raced in fear for the spade. His ram was out, and Mary could not find it. Pritchard began to run towards the high road. His face was masked with soot and ash, his red mouth gasped as he dragged for air, there was white skin around his wet eyes. His ram might already be dead on the road. He imagined his lovely creature, beautiful, stupid, stepping on its arrogant velvet legs, black as charcoal, under the wheels of great trucks, crushed and dead on the concrete. His lungs were burning. He toiled on grimly, not aware that he was groaning.

A Sacrifice

When I heard that Jonathan was in the Cottage Hospital I rang the Matron.

'Yes, you can certainly visit Mr Elder,' Miss McPhail said, 'Remember that visiting hours are from two-thirty until four-thirty and not a moment later.'

It's a cosy little hospital and McPhail not as starchy as she sounds.

'Hand on heart, Matron,' I said, 'I won't stay late. I'll bring the old boy some cigarettes.'

'That you will not,' said Miss McPhail, very stern. 'I've a heart case in the ward, poor man, and I'll not have *him* burned in his bed.'

I thought that a bit hard but Matron was adamant.

There are six beds in the men's ward, but only two were occupied. Jon's bed was on the right hand, next to the window. He looked, as usual, immaculate, his white hair trim, brushed flat against his skull, he wore his grey hospital pyjamas as if they came from Saville Row. From the hall his face, curiously unlined, looked attractively pink and healthy, but I knew that his colour was a network of thin red veins which spread on to his cheeks from the wings of his nose. A drinker's face, of course. When he saw me, he lifted an elegant, thin hand.

'My dear boy,' he called, 'How splendid of you to visit me. Do come and sit down.'

I sat on the plastic chair at the side of the bed, shaking Jon's locker as I did so. The heart patient was fast asleep, his breathing scarcely audible.

'How are you?' I said to Jonathan.

'Perfectly well,' he said, 'remarkably well. Really, they look after one excellently here. I told my doctor this morning that the service is quite equal to that of my London club.'

It's a good little hospital. We're lucky to have it. They repair our accidental cuts and bruises, settle us down when we need to recuperate. I've been in for treatment several times myself, for asthma mostly, and once when I scraped a knee after a fall from my cycle. Of course we have to go to Reading or Oxford for anything serious, real surgery, or a significant illness.

'I can't tell you how sorry I was to hear about Paul,' I said. 'As you know I was away last week, didn't hear about him until I got back.'

He said nothing, pursed his fastidious lips and let his gaze drift to the opposite window.

Fair enough, I thought. He doesn't want to speak of it.

'Doesn't your day pass slowly?' I said. 'How do you spend the time?'

'In conversation, you know,' Jonathan said. 'And life here is so orderly, so arranged. I have the greatest affection for true organisation, for a meaningful framework within which a man can live. It makes for security and happiness. I am very content here. Then there is a humane arrangement with the library by which a patient is allowed to borrow as many as six books at a time.'

He pointed to a neat pile on top of his locker.

'Do examine them, dear boy,' he said, 'every one is a volume I have long wished to read, but life's tedious details somehow prevented this. You are looking at that superb Life of the Duke of Wellington — you are aware that Wellington conducted his campaigns while rigidly enforcing the strictest moral behaviour among his troops? So sensible of him. Encouraged the loyalty and friendship of the countries he occupied, invaluable to his success. Napoleon, of course, allowed his soldiers complete license — brutality, rapine, that sort of thing. Not that I've read the book yet. Unfortunately they couldn't find my glasses.'

He laughed with brisk amusement. I thought he looked wonderfully vigorous and happy and I said so to Murchison, the house doctor, on my way out.

'Oh, Jonathan's all right,' said Murchison. 'We brought him in for observation, a safeguard against shock. He's not as strong as he looks.'

'What's he like generally, though?' I asked. I'm fond of Jonathan.

'In wonderful condition, when you consider the way he's lived,' said Murchison. 'He's got a liver like an old saddle, naturally. Otherwise there's not too much wrong with him. He's pickled in gin, I suppose.'

Jonathan was drinking gin the first time I saw him. That was in the bar of The Feathers three years ago, a few weeks after I'd come to live in the village. Driving past, I'd always coveted Stanley Burchall's house, and when he left to go and live with his daughter, I stepped in and bought it. A seventeenth century house, calm and sound. Needed some work, though. Stanley had let it go rather.

September was warm that year. I'd spent the morning hacking away in my garden, which had been badly neglected. I felt as dry as a sponge in the Sahara and walked down to The Feathers to put things right. Jonathan was there, at the bar, sitting on a high stool. He was dressed in a tweed suit that would never wear out. A silk paisley scarf was tucked into the neck of his shirt. We didn't speak, except to wish each other good-morning, but I listened, fascinated, to him as he spoke to the landlord. I've never heard anyone speak with Jonathan's unhurried precision and accuracy, although his brother Paul was almost his equal. That morning he picked his way delicately, on tip-toe almost, so unerringly and casually through the thickets of his enormous vocabulary that I followed his conversation as though he were the Pied Piper. I'm accustomed to it now, but it's still a delight. I drank three glasses of lager and stayed in The Feathers far too long. I had stiffened up too much to work in the garden that afternoon.

I got into the habit of calling into The Feathers about noon. I'm a methodical man, and once I had things running smoothly in the house I seemed to have plenty of time. One does, I suppose, when one's on one's own. I have my lunch at The Feathers most days, just a salad or a plate of sandwiches. Jonathan was always there. He'd walk in from the cottage he shared with Paul, and he'd drink gin and tonic, talking all the while, until Sammy Price called for him at two-fifteen. Sammy keeps the garage and owns the local taxi.

'Ah, Mr Price is here,' Jon would say, 'Have you time, Mr Price, to join me?'

'Thank you, sir,' Sam would answer, 'A pint of bitter would go down very nicely.'

And Jonathan would finish his drink, Sam would carry a crate of beer, a bottle of sherry and one of gin out to the car. Jonathan would climb in. They'd rattle off to the cottage. Paul drank sherry, Jonathan drank gin; the beer was shared in the intervals between their more serious drinking. In the evening it was Paul's turn to visit the inn, drink his sherry, be driven home at closing time. I didn't visit the place at evening. The brothers were rarely out together, although at Christmas time they called punctiliously on their neighbours, bringing small gifts. They had a cat, Jonathan explained, of which they were very fond, and made sure the animal was never left alone if they could avoid it. They were local men, Paul and Jonathan, of that class in which men did not have to work, but took up some dignified profession almost as a hobby. Paul had been an architect, Jonathan apparently looked after family money which had come down to them. Jonathan and I met most mornings, got on well together. I like words, I like to listen to Jonathan. I'm a silent man myself, heavy-voiced, but I read a lot.

I didn't meet Paul, to speak to that is, until the day Sammy Price failed to turn up to drive Jonathan home. A cold day, a bitterly cold, March day. We weren't surprised when Sammy didn't make it. He has trouble with his chest and hadn't looked well for a week or more. Jonathan was concerned about Sammy.

'Most inclement weather,' he said, 'and a cutting wind. So dangerous for someone with a bronchial weakness, like Sammy.'

Unusually, his speech was a little slurred, and he looked shaky on his legs. I saw him for the first time as a man up in his sixties. It occurred to me then that any serious deviation from his daily ceremony might easily disconcert him.

'Sam will be all right,' I said. 'Sit here a moment, Jonathan. I'll get my car and drive you home.'

Ned Fewell, our landlord, looked up from the tankard he was polishing.

'A good offer, Mr Elder,' he said. He held the glass up to the light. 'A very generous offer.'

'Very generous,' said Jonathan, 'and it would be ungracious to refuse. Thank you, dear boy. I should not wish Paul to be alarmed because of my lateness.'

I brought the car around, put the bottles in the back, saw Jonathan was comfortable. The village streets were deserted, swept clean by the brutal wind. It was about five miles to Jon's house, a long way for the alcoholic brothers to walk, every day, in all weathers. The few trees at the side of the road were completely leafless, the fields without a thread of the new grass we were all waiting for. I had to brake to avoid a little group of pheasants, four females and a male. He was handsome, his burnished feathers brilliant in the drab light, the one touch of colour in our journey.

'The Romans brought them, you know,' said Jonathan. He looked benignly at the strutting bird. 'And of all their legacies to us I sometimes think the pheasant is the most to be admired. There are other reminders of Roman occupation here not nearly as attractive. Not least this stretch of road upon which we are travelling. So boring, running on and on, straight as a line, paying no attention to the spirit of the country. Really, your car is infinitely superior to Sam's taxi.'

He was slumped in his seat, his overcoat collar around his ears.

'Take the next on the left, dear boy,' he said. 'It's marked No Through Road.'

I would have missed the lane but for Jonathan's warning. Just wide

enough for one vehicle, it cut through an untidy wood much in need
of attention. There are a number of such pockets of timber in this
part of the country, degenerate remnants of the great forest which
covered most of southern England for centuries after the eclipse of
the Romans. There's a small copse behind my house. It has nothing
special in the way of trees now. They're mostly birch and sycamore,
and a lot of scrub. The great oaks are all gone. I've seen fallow deer
there, and a badger one early morning, when I couldn't sleep.

We couldn't have driven more than half a mile along the track
when the wood opened out. On the left of the road the trees and
thick undergrowth gave way to rolling common, covered with gorse,
coarse yellow grass and bracken; on the right, behind an irregular
green, stood three sizeable cottages, each in its large garden, with
apple orchards between. Beyond, a landscape of sleeping pasture
stretched all the way to the Wiltshire hills.

'What a wonderful place,' I said.

He sat up and looked about.

'I suppose it is,' he said, 'Paul and I are accustomed to it. We've
always lived here, were born here. So was my father and his father
and, I sometimes feel, all of us back to Adam. The first house is
ours.'

I stopped the car at the gate and helped Jon out. I've never seen
a neater garden. A man from the neighbouring farm did the work,
Jon said, and also mowed the green in front of all three houses. We
walked down the path and Paul opened the door to greet us.

He was very like Jon, very recognisably his brother, but smaller
and somehow less clear-cut. He hovered by the door, diffident and
uncertain, surprised perhaps to see me there. He was older by two
years than Jonathan. I didn't go into the house. I carried the bottles
from the car and left them by the door. There were some Staffordshire pottery figures in their windows, I saw them as I turned to
leave. I know something of Staffordshire ware, and these were
superb.

After that I always ferried Jonathan home if Sammy Price was
unable to do it. Sometimes Sammy would be booked for a wedding,
or to take someone to the railway station. Once Mrs Smethurst used
him to drive her down to Bath to stay with her daughter. Sammy
would let me know when such a thing was to happen and I'd make
sure I was there, at The Feathers, in time to collect Jonathan and
take him home. I did so every day for nearly two weeks when Sammy
sprained his ankle picking apples. I suppose I know Jonathan as well
as most people in the village.

After I left the hospital I sat in the car park for a while. For some
unknown reason I was a little restless, in need of something to do.
I went home, parked the car in the drive, and decided to walk out
to Jon's cottage and search for his glasses.

He needed them, I persuaded myself. He was eager to know
everything about the Duke of Wellington. Swallows, not long
arrived, were hawking fairly high up, summer was already in the air.
I went at a good pace, enjoying the exercise. I couldn't live in a city.
There was nobody about when I got to the house. I walked up to
the front door and knocked, although I knew there couldn't be
anyone inside. Habit, I suppose. The door was unlocked, a large,
solid door, with a latch. I walked straight in. There was a wide,
square hall, lovely stone flags on the floor, worn thin by the feet of
generations of Elders. I could smell smoke, but not a strong sensation. Then I opened the door into what must have been the living
room. I'm not a delicate man, but I was appalled. I had never seen
such filth. The carpets were so dirty that there was no visible trace
of any pattern. Dust was everywhere, thick and solid, on the surfaces
of the furniture, on the window-sills, in the folds of the the curtains.
Empty bottles were arranged in untidy ranks against the walls, some
fallen and lying where they had rolled. On the floor were three
buckets, half full of some unimaginable liquid. Gagging in my
throat, I looked for Jon's glasses. They were not to be seen. They
were not in the kitchen either, not among the scraps of rotting food
on the table, not near the stove, covered with congealed grease.
Cursing, I went upstairs. Oddly, the bathroom was respectable, the
bath itself quite acceptable. I searched among jars of expensive
hair-dressing and after-shave. I began to feel better, more hopeful.

I crossed the landing and went into the first bedroom, a large
room, low and plain. The smell of smoke was strong there. The
walls and curtains were black with soot and thick cobwebs of soot
hung from the ceiling. The room was almost bare, a small table
under the window, a chair, a wardrobe against one wall, all black-
ened. And in the middle of the floor the bed on which Paul had
choked to death. In one corner it had burned down to the springs,
the wooden frame charred to a black fur. I stood inside the door and
let myself look at everything, and when I had seen all I stepped away
and went into Jonathan's room. This quite defeated me. It was
squalid beyond my comprehension. The sheets on the bed were
thrown back. Stained heavily with irregular brown patches, they had
not been changed for months. I made myself look around for the

glasses, and when I could not see them I ran downstairs and into the open air.

Outside, recovering, trying to understand, I walked about on the green for some time. Jonathan's cat came out of the bushes. She's a good looking cat, a long-haired tabby, mild and talkative. She was thin, of course. She came to me, mewing, so I picked her up and took her home with me. I carried her all the way. After a couple of hundred yards she lay comfortably in my arms, a warm little thing. She's settled down perfectly. I've never had a cat.

I went to see Jonathan the next day, but I didn't tell him I'd visited his house. He was in great form. Talking away, his voice strong and round, he made me believe that he sat right at the centre of everything that happened in the hospital. It was clear that he revelled in small worlds, small domestic communities. I understood why The Feathers was so important to him. But I was uncomfortable when he spoke of his house. I should have mentioned that I had been there.

'I wish you'd call at my place, should you ever go out that way,' he said. 'I've decided to set in hand a great deal of reconstruction and eventual redecorating there. I've already spoken to the builders about it.'

I wriggled a bit and said I'd be glad to do what I could.

'Merely a watchful eye,' he said, 'I shall arrange to be away while the work is done, and if you exhibit a friendly concern I should be obliged.'

Jon is remarkably practical in many ways, shrewd, too, and observant. I could see that he was already making detailed plans for his future. I asked him what he intended to do in the house.

'Oh,' he said, 'you'll like my ideas, I'm sure you will. Among other and less drastic alterations I am making the two large bedrooms into one room. So much more convenient now that Paul won't be there. And the whole of the interior is to be painted white, every room in the house. Such purity and cleanliness you understand. The white walls here at the hospital have impressed me greatly.'

It was the first time he had mentioned Paul to me since his brother's death.

'The woodwork,' he said, 'will be in a soft pale gray. With a tiny hint of pink, quite like a wood-pigeon's breast. Not as strong a colour, perhaps. Sumptuous, but delicate.'

He leaned back on his pillows and smiled gently, seeing in anticipation his cleansed and innocent house.

I was encouraged to ask him something which had been worrying me.

'About the inquest,' I said. 'May I take you along? I might be of some help during what will certainly be a stressful time.'

He detached himself deliberately from the conversation, his lips set, his head turned away.

'I shall have completely new furniture,' he said, 'Scandinavian probably, but not teak. Those clean, spare lines you know.'

I didn't say anything.

Jonathan waved his arm. He was clearly irritated.

'My doctors,' he said, 'are attending to all that. The doctors and the police. I've given a statement of my evidence to the police. I am not to be called.'

I was not surprised. In villages we tend to arrange things in civilised ways. The authorities had obviously decided it would be unkind to ask Jonathan to describe in public exactly how he had found his brother. Not that it would have been an ordeal. Jon loves an audience, and I was fairly certain that he was now quite well. Dr Murchison must have been very helpful in organising matters so quietly.

The inquest was held in the county town, fifteen miles away. I went along. I love ritual, the ritual of the law, the ritual of the church, the continuing energy of rural customs long grown meaningless. They hold so much of our history in their repetitive patterns, add assurance and order to our everyday chaos. There were not many of us in the court room, it was not a notable death.

There was evidence of identification — Jon's sworn statement and corroboration from the old doctor who attended the brothers. Ned Fewell, surprisingly at ease in the witness box, gave a guarded account of how much Paul and Jon normally drank, and of their regular visits to The Feathers. Even in Ned's tactful and conservative narrative, it seemed a frightening amount of alcohol.

'Did Mr Paul Elder visit your hotel on the day of his death?' asked the coroner.

'No. But Mr Jonathan did,' Ned answered.

He said that Jon had drunk his gins, spoken to everyone as he usually did, and settled down to wait for Sammy Price. Sammy had not arrived.

'How did Mr Elder react to this?' asked the coroner. He seemed amused by this vignette of life at The Feathers.

'He was a bit upset, like,' Ned replied.

'Do you mean he was angry?' the coroner suggested.

'No,' Ned smiled. 'I've never seen Mr Jonathan angry all the years I've known him. He was just a bit upset. It's a long old haul out to the common, carrying those bottles. I tried to get him to leave them, one of sherry and one of gin as usual, but he would take them. He did leave the beer. He must have been all in when he reached his house.'

A police sergeant read Jonathan's account of finding his brother. It was strange to hear that precise and mannered voice somewhere behind the policeman's flat delivery. I found myself waiting for the emphasis of Jon's eloquent hesitation before some particularly felicitous phrase, but of course the sergeant flattened them all out.

Jonathan had left The Feathers at two-forty and walked home. I was away for the week, as he had known. Otherwise, he said, he would have asked me to take him. I was quite touched by this. He had found the walk more than tiring and when he reached his door he was exhausted. He had no idea of how long he had taken, but felt that he could not have arrived before five o'clock. He had opened the door, taken his bottles into the kitchen, and called Paul. Paul had not answered. Jonathan was not perturbed, knowing that Paul frequently went to bed after his lunch. He had gone upstairs, noting as he did so a strong smell of smoke. He had hurried into his brother's room and found Paul lying on the bed. Paul was fully dressed but had removed his shoes. Smoke was rising thickly from the covers and Jonathan had found breathing difficult.

He must have been very confused. Recalling that one should close all doors and windows to prevent a fire from spreading, he had moved over to the window. 'It took me a considerable time,' read the sergeant on Jon's behalf, 'before I eventually closed it.' He had left the room, shutting the door carefully behind him, and gone into the garden. Here he had searched for a large watering can, filled it with water, and carried it upstairs. He had poured the water carefully over the smouldering covers, over his brother's body, 'making sure,' he had dictated, 'that there wasn't the slightest possibility of a further blaze developing.' A great deal of smoke resulted from all this, and Jonathan had been almost overcome. Completely exhausted, heavily affected by the smoke, virtually unable to see, Jonathan had managed to reach his own room. He had fallen on to his bed and remembered nothing until he had awakened, or perhaps regained consciousness, some time later. It was dark. He had gone back to Paul's room and, finding his brother unmoving on the bed, had gone for help to his neighbour. It was a very factual, clear statement.

After that it was straightforward. Paul was dead in a room so filled with smoke that it was perilous to enter it. He lay on a bed which had quietly burned down to its springs, and was still hot when his body was lifted from it. The medical evidence was clear that the cause of death was asphyxiation; Paul had died from the fumes. The coroner brought in a verdict of Death by Misadventure, adding a warning about the dangers of smoking in bed. We stood, a small group of saddened people, and filed out.

I met our vicar on the street, a young man, Tony Henebry. I'm not a regular churchgoer, but I like him and I like our old church. It's a Norman foundation, not big enough to have been spoiled by the fashion for modernisation which ruined so many lovely places around the turn of the century. It has some fine Elizabethan family tombs, unrestored, showing the marks of slow time. Tony and I walked down the High Street and decided to have lunch together. He told me a rather remarkable thing. He had often met Paul in the early evening, he said. Tony would go into the church, expecting to find it empty, and there would be Paul. He would be sitting quietly, always in the same place, near the east window, underneath a memorial plaque for a cousin of his grandfather, a young officer killed in the Great War.

'It's all right, vicar,' Paul would say, 'I'm merely waiting until opening time, you know.' And he'd smile his dim smile.

'I think he took some comfort from being there,' Tony said. 'I certainly hope so.'

I don't know. But Tony's little story made Paul much more real to me, more complex and defined than he had been in life. I wondered if he had been a good architect.

In the afternoon I went out to Jon's house. The garden was full of rubble. There was a heap of sand on the path and the old, sorry furniture was piled in the garage. Already the dividing wall between the bedrooms had been removed and two men were making good the plaster.

When next I visited Jonathan I told him that things were moving. By then he had left the hospital and was staying at The Marlborough, in town.

'I'm immensely grateful to you,' he said. 'You have no idea how eagerly I'm looking forward to my return home. It is altogether a new start for me. All my clothes, you know, were completely spoiled, my whole wardrobe, acrid smoke through them all. And much as I lament the loss of some of my shirts in particular, it has been a most invigorating experience to purchase entirely new outfits . . . in my youth I was a dandy, you must understand. Yet I'm even more excited at the thought of my house, revivified one might say, awaiting me.'

Jonathan has family in Warwickshire, cousins, his only living relatives, and he stayed with them until his house was ready. He telephoned me every Friday evening, punctiliously describing the events of his week. Yet I was always aware of his need to know just what was happening at his house, and I was careful to make notes of any visible progress. As it all came together, I sent photographs up to Jon and this pleased him. At last all was ready, his new furniture in, the curtains hung, the house and its accoutrements glistening. I drove to the railway station to meet him. I'd bought a new Landrover while Jon had been away, and this drew his admiration. Sitting beside me, smiling, recognising with delight familiar landmarks, he spoke of his cousins.

'They're delightful,' he said, 'quite delightful. Not young any longer, we're none of us young, not even you my dear fellow, but they're still extraordinarily pleasant girls. They made my stay so enjoyable.'

He was in the highest spirits, animated and alert.

'Tell me, Jonathan,' I said. 'Your statement at the inquest. Did you really pour water out of a garden can over Paul?'

'Of course,' he said. 'What else was one to do?'

I can't excuse this. I should not have persisted with this.

'When you poured water on him,' I said, 'was he alive? Didn't he move or anything?'

'Naturally he was alive,' Jonathan said, his voice sharp. 'Do remember that he spoke to me.'

There had been no mention of this at the inquest.

'What did he say?' I asked.

'He said, "You're very late, Jonathan. I thought you weren't coming." Something like that.' Jonathan said, 'And then I poured water over him. By that time I was overwhelmed by fumes, you know.'

We turned into Jon's lane and under the branches of the roadside trees. They were so heavy with autumn leaves that they almost scraped the roof of the car.

'I've got your cat,' I said. 'Shall I bring her back?'

I had to make myself ask him that. I've got used to her. She's a most winning animal, it's good to have her around the house. Since she's there I don't go out quite as often, rarely to The Feathers even.

'Is she happy?' Jon asked, tranquilly. He was relieved I had changed the subject. 'If so, she might as well stay with you. She was Paul's cat, she might not approve the changes in her environment.' And he laughed quietly.

I drew up outside the house. It stood behind its green and garden front, shining. We got out of the car and I lifted Jon's luggage over the backboard. The builder was there, with the keys, ready to show Jon around. Jon danced down the path, crowing with happiness. I followed along with the cases and put them down in the hall. I might as well not have been there. Jon was already up in the new bedroom and I could hear his excited voice as he admired his white walls. I shouted my farewells up the stairs.

He called me, and I stood in the stairwell while he looked down from above.

'If Paul were to come back,' he said, 'he wouldn't recognise the place.' And he waved.

I got into the Landrover, turned it, drove home.

I've been sitting in this chair all evening, thinking things over.

I don't know that I'll go to The Feathers tomorrow. I don't think I can do that.

Acknowledgements

Acknowledgements are due to *The Sewanee Review* where 'Brighton Midgets' first appeared.

Sliding was first published in 1978, and *The Girl from Cardigan* in 1988.

The Author

Leslie Norris was born in Merthyr Tydfil in 1921. Formerly a teacher and headmaster, he has for many years taught literature and creative writing in American universities, most recently at Brigham Young, Utah, where he was Christiansen Professor of Poetry.

Although he is not as prolific a fiction writer as poet, his volumes of stories have been widely acclaimed; indeed *Sliding* won the David Higham Prize. This *Collected Stories* celebrates Leslie Norris's seventy-fifth year and his return to Wales, and is the companion volume to his *Collected Poems*